ROAD
TO
SHANDARA

Ken Lozito

ROAD TO SHANDARA

ISBN: 978-0-9899319-1-5

Published by Acoustical Books, LLC
KenLozito.com

Cover Design: Alexandre Rito

3rd Edition

Discover other books by Ken Lozito

Safanarion Order Series:
Road to Shandara (Book 1)
Echoes of a Gloried Past (Book 2)
Amidst the Rising Shadows (Book 3)
Heir of Shandara (Book 4)
The Warden's Oath (Short Fiction)

For my wife, Michelle.

CHAPTER 1
THE AWAKENING

The university campus was a buzz of bleary-eyed students going to and from class. Some exited the buildings with a slight spring in their step having finished another semester, while others were in such a haggard state that each step was carefully placed as if they walked on a path of eggshells and the slightest misstep would reveal just how unprepared they really were.

Having finished for the day, Aaron left Robertson Hall, home to the college of engineering sciences. Only one final exam separated him from a summer internship before starting graduate school, and he couldn't wait. He headed to the parking lot and quickly located his old-style Jeep CJ7. Aaron had rescued the old CJ from a farm about a hundred miles from his house. His father thought he was crazy, but under the dirt and rust, a beast slept. "Beast" was the Jeep's nickname and was a running joke between him and his father. He'd spent a year restoring it. The black paint shined and the chrome circling the traditional round headlights gleamed. The soft top was down, of course. Unless it was raining, the top to his Jeep always stayed down.

There was nothing like driving with the top down and the wind blowing through his hair...freedom.

His mother had sent him a message asking that he cover for one of the horse trainers at his grandfather's stables. He didn't mind helping out and knew that his days working with the horses at the stables were numbered.

The drive out to the stables never took long, and a half hour later he came within sight of the tall hedges that ran the length of the property. He turned onto the long driveway lined with red maples. As he closed in on the main house, Aaron's brows drew forward and he clutched the steering wheel. Bright, flashing red lights from police cars parked outside his grandfather's colonial farmhouse lit up the area. Aaron steered to a stone wall, threw the shifter into park, and climbed out of the Jeep. A knot of police officers and paramedics gathered near the stairway that led to the house. At the top of the stairs, Zeus, his grandfather's wolf half-breed, stood with his head lowered and teeth bared. A deep growl rumbled from Zeus's chest and his ears were pinned back.

Aaron spotted his mother speaking with the police officers. "What's going on? Is Grandpa okay?"

His mother turned to him. "I don't know. We can't get in. Zeus won't let anyone pass."

"Ma'am," a police officer interrupted, "if we can't get the dog out of there, we're going to have to put him down. We can't wait for Animal Control if someone inside needs our help."

"No," Aaron said, stepping up to the stairs. "Let me try."

Aaron heard his mother ask the police officer to give Aaron a chance.

There was no way Aaron was going to let them shoot Zeus. He had been in the family for years. The screen door to the house was propped open. Aaron craned his neck and tried to peer inside, but didn't see anyone. He placed a foot on the first step and stopped. Zeus narrowed his eyes at him and shifted his gaze to the people behind him.

"Easy, boy," he said slowly. "It's me."

Zeus's hackles were raised and his whole body quivered. Aaron took another step forward, and Zeus bared all his teeth, unveiling the peaks of the Rocky Mountains inside his mouth.

Aaron never took his eyes from him, his stare neither challenging nor yielding. "Zeus," he said evenly, trying to get Zeus to calm down with the sound of his voice.

"I need to get in there, boy. Come on," Aaron said.

Zeus's ears perked up, and the wild look in his eyes shifted to the more familiar loving kind that Aaron knew so well. Zeus reluctantly took a step forward.

"It's okay. Show me where he is. Where's Grandpa? Take me to him," Aaron said and walked up the steps as he'd done thousands of times before. Zeus raised his snout, sniffing the air, then turned tail and trotted into the house with Aaron in tow.

Aaron leaped up the last few steps and entered his grandfather's house. He called out, but there was no answer. Everything looked normal and in its place, but something felt wrong. The insides of Aaron's stomach twisted. There was a coldness in the air despite the warm weather outside.

Aaron followed Zeus through the house and down the back hallway leading to the study. He entered the room and found his grandfather lying on the floor.

Oh, no!

His grandfather looked up at him and sighed in relief. Aaron quickly knelt beside him. A trace of blood trailed down the side of his grandfather's mouth. His grandfather, who had always been a vibrant man—even into his eighties—lay helplessly on the floor. He looked wizened and old. Far older than Aaron could recall.

His grandfather gestured for Aaron to lean down. "Come closer," he whispered, placing something in Aaron's hands. "Keep it safe," he gasped.

"What's wrong?" Aaron asked.

His grandfather's face writhed in pain, and he sucked in ragged breaths. "Oh, Aaron. I'm sorry. I'm so sorry..." he said. His body convulsed violently, and his back arched while Aaron held onto him, crying out. Then his body relaxed with a great sigh. Aaron watched in silent horror as his grandfather stopped breathing.

Aaron heard others enter the room. He knelt there clutching his grandfather's lifeless body as the paramedics checked for a pulse. The paramedics labored to revive his grandfather, but nothing worked. He was gone.

Eventually, a gentle but strong hand gripped his shoulder. "It's time to let go, Son," his father beckoned. "Aaron, please," his father said.

Aaron carefully laid his grandfather's head down onto the floor. His father gently ran his fingers over Aaron's grandfather's eyes, closing them. Aaron kept watching his grandfather's chest, hoping that he would see it begin to rise and fall. That this was some sort of mistake. He wanted to believe it more than anything, but he knew the truth.

Aaron stood up and slowly turned, clenching his teeth, trying for all he was worth not to break down and cry. He was eye level with his father, who was also a man of great size, and the sight of his father's eyes brimming with tears made the breath catch in his throat. His mother cried out, and he watched helplessly as she collapsed over his grandfather. His father knelt down next to her and put his arm around her shoulders. Aaron stood there helplessly, watching his parents hold each other.

Aaron opened his hand and looked at the object his grandfather had given him. It was a silver medallion with a white pearl in the center and a carved relief of a dragon holding a rose curling around the front. There was a slight shimmer to it as it caught the light. After studying it for a few moments, he stuffed the medallion in his pocket and walked stiffly from the room.

The rest of the day passed as if it were happening to someone else. Aaron watched helplessly as the white coroner's van took his grandfather's body away. His thoughts raced in every direction, and he tried to get a firm grasp on the emotions welling up inside him. His pulse was racing and his chest felt constricted. He needed to do something—anything—as long as he was moving. He ran over to the stables and saddled Sam, a chestnut stallion, and put as much distance between him and the house as possible. Beyond the stables was a wide-open field bathed in sunshine. The gentle swaying of the grass and distant trees mocked him. Sam snorted anxiously, sensing Aaron's unrest. The trailhead on the far side of the field beckoned him, and he nudged Sam into a gallop.

Aaron glanced over to the side and saw Zeus plowing along next to him. Aaron gave Sam another prod, urging him faster. He wanted to fly, and Zeus flew with him. He veered off the trail and headed into the woods, dodging trees. Faster and faster, cutting each turn tighter until the branches tore at him, scraping through his shirt. He didn't care. He wanted to be reckless and rode as if his life depended on it. Zeus ran with him, darting in and out of sight like a spirit. He didn't know how long he rode, but the edge of the cliffs appeared before him in the waning sunlight, and he stopped. Aaron gazed out at the small valley before him, his heart pounding. Sam snorted and pawed at the ground, feeding off his need to keep moving.

Aaron stepped off his horse and fell to his knees, letting out a silent wail. He felt stripped bare before the world, the mortality that surrounds us every day becoming a reality for him. Grief overtook him, and he let out a piercing scream that echoed through the valley.

Zeus nuzzled his pocket, and he reached inside, taking out the medallion. Why did his grandfather give it to him? *Keep it safe*, he had told him. But safe from what? He traced his fingers along the foreign symbols that surrounded the creamy white pearl in the center. At first, he thought it was silver, but the way the metal felt and shined in the light led him to believe otherwise.

Aaron's grandfather had been his mentor. He had mourned the loss of his wife, Cassandra, who had died before Aaron was born. He had fought wars, but would not speak of them. His past, like his pain, was shrouded in mystery. Reymius was the type of man that when he spoke, you wanted to listen and earn his respect. His calming nature brought out the best in people.

With the sun beginning to settle and his shoulders slumped, Aaron started back to the house. He decided to walk, leading Sam, and Zeus followed. He knew the land well, but he was glad for Zeus's company. The long walk back to the house allowed him to calm down. By the time he arrived at the house, it was dark and deserted. He took care of Sam by way of brushing and giving him some food, and thanked him for the ride. He thought about going into the house, but decided to go to the sparring room instead.

The sparring room was adjacent to the main house, but was only accessible from the outside. He removed his shoes before entering—a habit instilled in him since before he could remember. Hanging along the walls was all manner of weaponry. From staffs to swords of all sizes, Aaron knew how to use them all. His father would say he knew them too well, but Reymius had nurtured Aaron's natural ability with the weapons in the room.

He walked to the center of the room and sank to his knees, facing a marble fountain against the far wall. Water fell gently upon smaller leaf pools, until at last it trickled to a pool at the base. The soft, rhythmic cascade of water soothed him and lulled him into a sense of inner peace. There were two wooden columns on either side of the fountain. His grandfather had carved the columns himself, and the shadows from the soft candlelight caressed the carved relief of roses spiraling up from the base of each column.

He closed his eyes and took slow, deep breaths. He felt a slight vibration through the floorboards. Opening his eyes, he caught a glimpse of something disturbing the water in the fountain. He crossed the room, stared down into the shallow depths, and noticed a small silver ring bobbing among the water plants along the bottom. He reached into the cool water and tugged. Sounds of pins driving into place could be heard under the floor as some unseen mechanism was put into motion. Aaron's breath caught in his throat as a gaping hole opened in the center of the room, revealing stairs that led down into darkness.

Aaron crossed the room and stood atop the narrow staircase, looking down, and a bluish glow emanated from below. He descended the staircase, which opened into a small room where a cylinder hung suspended in midair, surrounded by a blue, pulsing glow. Below the cylinder was a worn stone chest. Inside his pocket, he felt the medallion grow warm. He drew out the medallion and gasped as the white pearl began pulsing, growing brighter as he brought it closer to the cylinder. Aaron reached out to touched the cylinder, and there was a blue flash of light as the cylinder came to rest upon the chest. A lock clicked from within, and the lid groaned, sending a cloud of dust into the air as it opened. Aaron peered inside. Atop a white cloth bundle was a folded piece of paper with his name written on it. With shaky hands, he reached in and opened the letter.

Dear Aaron,

I fear that as I write this our time together has become short indeed. You have brought joy and light back into a heart that was clouded in darkness and despair. Your grandmother, Cassandra, would have been proud to see you become the man you are today and will rest easier knowing her sacrifice was not in vain. There are things that will happen with my passing that I am powerless to prevent, but I must have faith that you will overcome the obstacles ahead of you. There are things about me that I have never told you, about both my past and where your true home is. One day soon, you will discover that your life is nothing like you thought it would be. You have a power that will arise. I have seen the signs of its coming recently, and so will you when you quiet your mind. The training that I have provided will aid you in reaping the benefits of your coming gifts...and more importantly, will help you stay alive, for there is always a price to be paid for such things. Always remember that fate uses us to its own ends, but it will never take away our right to decide. Choose wisely, and choose quickly. Death comes swiftly to those who tarry in the middle of the road. The things you have found along with this letter are yours. The medallion is your birthright; keep it safe. Both your Faith and your Fate are tied into these items. The Falcon blades are your heritage. Use them well. Worlds will change, but in the deepest, darkest depths, remember who you are. The light of our souls never truly fades, and may the light shine forever upon your path.

Farewell, my grandson.

Reymius Alenzar'seth

Alenzar'seth? That wasn't his grandfather's last name. Frowning, he reached back into the chest to retrieve the cloth bundle. Inside, he found two swords, each resting in a black scabbard; both were the length of his arms. He drew each sword from its scabbard, revealing a strange form of writing along the center of the blades and holes running their length. The swords were surprisingly light in weight and balanced perfectly in his hands. Set in the base of each sword was a crystal. A calling came to Aaron in that moment. A force that had been sleeping within him suddenly rose from the pit of his stomach, filling his chest. He carefully slid the swords back into their scabbards, wrapped them in the white cloth, and picked them up.

The calling had him entranced, guiding him as he exited the sparring room and stepped into the twilight. Zeus walked beside him until the lights of the house faded away and the trees gave way to a moonlit clearing. There were horses grazing nearby. Aaron gazed up at the night sky as the clouds blew past the moon, allowing its light to dance upon the ground. He knelt and set the white bundle in front of him. Unwrapping the swords, he drew them from their scabbards, feeling his grandfather's presence all around him. That same calm and unwavering force that watched Aaron grow from a boy into a man. The swords warmed to his touch as if they, too, were alive.

He closed his eyes and tilted his head, listening. The medallion grew warm in his pocket. The crystals in the hilt of each sword emitted a faint glow. Aaron looked up, believing it was the moon, but the pure white light was coming from within each crystal, pulsating in rhythm with his beating heart. He heard the soft urgings of a thousand voices within.

Wield the blades.

Release the power.

Claim your birthright, Safanarion.

Slowly and with a certain amount of grace, he wielded the Falcons. The pure notes of the bladesong poured forth, ringing out into the night. A force awakened within him, as if the shield that had held it in gave way to an awareness of the world around him. Life's energy surrounded him, pure and simple; its elegant force blazed vibrantly, and he felt his connection to it strengthen. The crystallized light danced upon the ground at his feet. Among the pure notes of the bladesong, Zeus howled. Not a howl of despair, but a howl of triumph. Aaron became infused by his connection to everything around him, losing himself within the music coming through the Falcons. This was his song.

The clearing quickly filled with wild animals. The horses were drawn to this spot and formed a wide circle around him. A nighthawk cried from above. Life's wellspring burst forth inside Aaron, and the crystals in the blades flared brightly. His sorrow momentarily melted away to a brief respite at this gift bequeathed to him by his grandfather.

CHAPTER 2
THE THINGS A MOTHER KNOWS

It was the middle of the night when Aaron finally got back to his grandfather's house. His mother sat in one of the rocking chairs on the front porch with a solitary candle for a companion. Her long blonde hair was tied back in a ponytail. She stood up when he came to the bottom of the stairs with Zeus by his side. Relief shined in her red-rimmed eyes as she held her arms open to him.

With each step Aaron took he felt his will not to break down erode. He still saw the memory of her crying in his father's arms.

"Mom, I—" He choked, dropping the white bundle. He hugged his mother and for that brief moment, he was a boy seeking a mother's comforting embrace. "I can't believe he's gone."

"It's okay," she said soothingly. "He would have said it was his time."

"Do they know what happened?" he asked.

"No, they don't know why," she said. "If they did, would it really make a difference?"

Aaron frowned in thought. "No, I guess not."

"Come on, let's go inside and get some sleep," said his mother.

"You're staying here tonight?" Aaron asked.

"It's late, and I just feel like I need to be here tonight, don't you?" she asked.

"Yeah," Aaron agreed.

Zeus whined from behind him and pawed at the cloth bundle that held the swords. Aaron went down the stairs and retrieved the bundle.

"What have you got there?" his mother asked.

Aaron thought about telling her, but decided against it. "Just some stuff I found," he said.

Together they entered the empty house.

A few hours later, Aaron tossed and turned. He couldn't get comfortable despite being exhausted. His mind kept racing. Alenzar'seth, the name his grandfather had signed the letter with—what did it mean?

He gazed out of the window of the guest bedroom. Zeus lay on the floor next to the bed, but Aaron didn't think the wolf half-breed slept any better than he did. Why did his grandfather hand him that medallion? He had clutched it like it was the most important thing he had to give. Then there were the swords. What was he supposed to do with the swords? His thoughts drifted back to the letter.

One day soon, you will discover that your life is nothing like you thought it would be...

The sun was rising when a soft knock came from the door.

"Come in."

His mother opened the door and took a step inside. "Did you sleep okay?" she asked.

"About as good as you did," Aaron answered.

"I see," she said. "Come on down. Your father brought breakfast."

Aaron didn't think he could eat, but he decided it would make his mother feel better if he at least tried. He threw on a pair of jeans and a gray T-shirt and looked at the nightstand where the medallion lay. He considered just leaving it. A ray of sunshine peeked through the window, caressing the edge of the medallion. Aaron sighed, reaching out to grab it, and stuck it in his pocket.

The sweet aroma of cinnamon-raisin bagels wafted from the kitchen table. He sat down and took one as his father came in through the front door. His dad's great size filled the doorway without any effort. Being a carpenter kept him fit and trim.

"Morning," his father said.

"Does Tara know about Grandpa?" Aaron asked, buttering his bagel.

"Yeah, your sister will be out here later," his father answered, then looked at him in a way that made Aaron feel like he was an open book. "Are you all right?"

Aaron heard the echoes of the bladesong in his head, and the medallion warmed in his pocket.

"I guess," he said. "I'm numb really."

Should I tell him about the letter?

"There are no words that I can say that will make this any easier," his father said. "He was a great man, and he loved you. I'll miss him too. I keep expecting him to walk in at any moment. But you know what, it's because we loved him so much that mourning the loss will be hard. By the same token, we can count ourselves fortunate for having him in our lives for the time that we did." He paused and took a sip of his coffee, glancing out the window. "We don't have to talk about this now if you don't want to."

Aaron looked out the same window. The sun was shining with no hint of a cloud in the sky. It was a perfect day outside, and it mocked everything he was feeling. The room felt like it was closing in, suffocating him. He just wanted to run and not stop until he was far away.

"It's fine, Dad. I just need to get some air," he said, rising out of his seat and grabbing his bagel.

He stepped outside, not knowing where he was going, and before he knew it, he was standing inside the sparring room, gazing at the fountain. His breath came in quick gasps. It was dark with all the shades shut. He was taking deep, rhythmic breaths, finding his calm center, when the attack came. A slight shift in the air blared warning bells in his mind, and instinct took over as he tumbled out of the way and came easily to his feet. He ducked again as he heard a staff whistling through the air, missing his head. Aaron spun toward the wall and grabbed his own staff.

Aaron could only make out the shape of his assailant in the dimly lit room. He moved into the center of the room, meeting them head-on. The staff was one of the simplest weapons to use, and in the hands of the right person, among the deadliest. The way his adversary moved with the staff told him that they knew how to use it. His assailant rained attacks down on him. Aaron blocked the attacks and probed with a counter to feel out his attacker. Aaron's size was often deceptive because he was quick as well as big, but all his attacks were blocked. It was like he was practicing with his grandfather. He baited his opponent with an opening. As the staff came down, he shifted to the right and forward, rendering the blow useless, and launched a powerful front kick that sent his attacker across the room. He expected the grunt of a man, but heard the gasp of a woman.

Aaron quickly reached over and turned on the lights, only to see his mother resting on one knee, leaning on her staff. Her hair had been tied back and tucked into a black shirt.

"Reymius has taught you well," she gasped with a pride-filled smile. "I am my father's daughter, Aaron, no need to look so surprised."

"Are you okay?" Aaron asked, kneeling down and helping her to her feet. Aaron had never viewed his mother as anything other than a mother, and it was shocking to think of her as just a person.

"Yeah. You kick pretty hard," she mused, rubbing her side.

"I'm sorry," Aaron said, and left the unasked question hanging in the air for a moment. "But you've never been in here. Not with any of the classes or while he taught me."

His mother nodded. "There was so much I couldn't remember after the accident. What I can remember doesn't make any sense to me. It's like trying to see something through a thick fog," she said, regaining her feet. "One thing I did remember was how to defend myself. I know all of these weapons here, but I don't remember learning how to use them. I know all the forms for gaining flexibility and quieting the mind as you do, but evidently am not so well practiced."

Aaron's hand rested on the pocket of his jeans. He felt the medallion and was trying to decide if he should ask her about it. "When is the funeral going to be?" Aaron asked.

"The day after tomorrow. Tara should be here soon," she said while they walked back outside. Aaron took a last glance at the fountain and the center of the floor where the secret chamber lay hidden.

"Where has she been?"

"She's been away with Alex, looking at places for the wedding reception."

Aaron nodded. His sister had recently become engaged, and he was happy for her. Her fiancé, Alex, was a really good guy. Tara was just a few years older than he and had always looked after him.

"Do you have any exams left?" his mother asked.

"Yeah, one tomorrow. I was thinking of calling the professor to see whether I could have it changed," Aaron answered.

"Well, that's up to you," she said. "Life will go on whether we are ready for it or not."

"Carlowen," his dad called.

"We're out here," his mother called back.

"Jack is here with the paperwork." his father said.

Jack was a family friend who happened to be a lawyer. His mother left him and followed his dad back into the house. Aaron decided to drive to campus and see Dr. Kozak about the final rather than calling. He knew it was an excuse just to do something, but it gave him something to think about besides everything he preferred not to. As he pulled away from the house, he caught a glimpse of Zeus before he disappeared into the trees. Though there was no chill in the air, he shivered.

CHAPTER 3
NEW PERCEPTIONS

The drive to campus revived him. He had the top down on his Jeep, and the fresh air did him good. He walked into the humanities building where the sociology department was and went up to the fourth floor. He turned the corner, thinking about what he was going to say, when Professor Kozak came out of his office, heading in his direction. His steel-rimmed glasses caught the fluorescent lighting above, and he appeared to be muttering to himself. His gray hair was in its normal disheveled state.

"Hello, Dr. Kozak. I need a few minutes of your time."

"Sure, Aaron," Dr. Kozak said, looking up at him expectantly, and when Aaron hesitated, he added, "Oh, would you like to step into my office?"

"If that's okay; this is a personal matter," Aaron said.

The office wasn't much bigger than a closet and was jammed with all sorts of books and dusty objects. There was a picture of a mountain whose peak poked above a swath of clouds. The writing beneath it said, "Faith is taking the first step when you don't see the end. The truth is what you find once you get there."

"Do you like the picture?" the professor asked.

"Yeah, I like the caption," Aaron answered.

"Oh really, what do you think it means? I mean, it sounds good, but what does it mean?" the professor asked with a dubious tone.

Aaron paused, considering. "Sometimes in order to get to the truth, you need to take a leap of faith. I supposed it's how one gains wisdom."

The corners of the professor's mouth rose. "Ah yes, you're my philosopher, very good. I am always curious about what people think of that quote. Anyway, what can I do for you?"

Aaron told him about his grandfather's passing and that he wouldn't be able to take the final exam the next day. The professor nodded and conveyed his condolences to him and his family. Aaron liked that about Dr. Kozak: Some professors had an embedded disdain for anyone's lives but their own, but Dr. Kozak was a kindhearted person.

"It's certainly not going to adversely affect your grade if you do not take the final. Not for you, at least. You actually showed up and participated in my class. My goal the entire semester is to get students to think about the world around them, and not be so concerned about grades. The question I had proposed for the final is not far off from the quote you just analyzed for me, which I am happy to say you've hit dead-on. I had hoped you would consider majoring in sociology, but knowing that you are about to graduate, I see I'm too late to recruit you," he said, rising and extending his hand.

Aaron shook the professor's hand and thanked him.

Aaron left the office and took a quick detour to the bathroom.

While rinsing his hands, he felt a sick feeling in the pit of his stomach.

Rap!

Rap!

Rap!

The loud noise echoed from outside the bathroom. Aaron yanked the door open. The hallway was empty. The fluorescent lights went out, and all was eerily quiet. Sunlight shined brightly through the entrance at the far end of the hall, but his area was dark. A sudden chill crept down his spine like tiny spiders crawling down his back.

What the hell was that?

The medallion grew cool in his pocket. Aaron stepped out into the hallway and started walking toward the entrance. He felt a presence come rushing toward him, and he spun around, but the hallway was empty. He was all alone.

Aaron quickened his pace down the hallway. He kept looking behind him, but he couldn't see anything. Aaron tried to dismiss the sinking feeling, but was compelled to turn around one last time. He peered into the darkened hallway. There was a loud screech, and something knocked him backward, off his feet. He rolled and was instantly up again, his heart pounding. He scanned about, looking to see who was there. Another blow blindsided him, and he went down. He tasted blood in his mouth while he shook his head, bracing himself. He scrambled back and regained his feet. He leaned back against a glass display case. He scanned out with his other senses, but couldn't detect anybody there with him. In fact, he sensed nothing, as if this place were devoid of life. Then he felt it, the force gathering itself, preparing to strike. Aaron barely got out of the way in time as the blow meant for him shattered a glass display case behind him.

He turned and sprinted down the hallway with the shattering of glass trailing his wake. He reached the end of the hallway, gasping for breath. The lights came back on, revealing a mess of shattered glass as people drawn by the noise filled the hallway. He ducked out of sight, heading down the stairs, but he could have sworn that he'd heard an ominous cackle right before the lights came back on.

As Aaron exited the building, the campus police were rushing in. His chest ached where he had taken the brunt of the blow, and he glanced back at the building. *What the hell was that?*

He took the medallion out of his pocket and ran his fingertips over the carved relief of the dragon holding a rose. On the flip side were two swords, like the ones his grandfather left him. In the center was a white pearl. The medallion was cool now, but he knew that it had reacted to whatever it was back there. Was this what his grandfather's letter warned him about? *One day soon, you will discover that your life is nothing like you thought it would be...*

How could he face something that he couldn't see? But he was able to sense it for a second.

Aaron looked up and saw a hawk flying gracefully, circling to and fro. He followed the hawk's movements, its slight change in its wings to keep riding along the wind. And then he saw it, just a spark at first, but as he focused, he saw the impression of the life force of the hawk shining brilliantly. The hawk, as if sensing him, dived down hard, only to land elegantly on the roll bar of his Jeep. The hawk peered at him, cocking its head to the side, and Aaron calmly looked back.

After a moment, the hawk let out a cry and took flight.

Aaron climbed into his Jeep and noticed the thin leather cord he kept hanging from the rearview mirror. He picked it up, looped it through the eyehole on the medallion, and tied it around his neck. He then tucked it inside his shirt. His hands still shook from his encounter with whatever had been in the school. Sirens sounded from more campus police cars speeding toward the humanities building. Aaron put the Jeep in drive and slowly drove away.

***

Aaron's sister, Tara, waved to him as he parked his Jeep. She stood on the lowest rail on the fence while watching the grazing horses. Her long auburn hair spilled gracefully down her back. His sister turned more than a few heads, but her heart belonged to her fiancé, Alex. She had the ability to get the shyest of people to start talking to her. But today she looked sad. She was grieving just as much as he was, even though Reymius wasn't her true grandfather. His half-sister was four years his senior and remembered precious little of her own mother. Carlowen helped to fill that gap when she married their father, Patrick.

"What's going on?" Aaron asked.

Tara inspected him. "What happened to you?"

Since they were kids, she always knew when he was in trouble just by looking at him. Should he tell her what just happened? *Oh yeah, a freaky ghost attacked me at school today, and I have a medallion that seems to be an early warning device.* That made a lot of sense. Then he remembered the scratches along his face and arms from his wild ride last night.

"Nothing," he lied. "I kinda don't know what to do with myself."

"Yeah, I know the feeling. Don't want to be here like this, but I don't want to go anywhere else either," she said. "Bronwyn came by. She had heard about Grandpa."

"How nice of her," Aaron said.

"I thought so," Tara said, until she noticed him glowering. "Oh come on, Aaron. She's a nice girl. You can't stay mad at her forever."

"Sure," Aaron said. He didn't want to deal with Bronwyn now.

Tara stepped down from the rail and looked up at him in such a way that made him feel small and foolish. "One thing you will have to learn, dear Brother, is that sometimes people make mistakes. No one is perfect. Not even you. Forgiveness may not come easily, but when you care about someone, wouldn't you want a second chance?"

He clenched his teeth without realizing it. "I didn't do anything wrong. She's the one who had the lapse in judgement," Aaron said.

"Be that as it may. You need to make a choice." She paused until he looked her in the eyes. "Did it ever occur to you that the reason this tears you up inside is because you still care for her? Those feelings can't be turned on and off like a light switch."

"Yeah—" he began, but Tara cut him off.

"Look, I'm not condoning what she did, but you should at least talk to her and hear what she has to say. Then maybe you can move on."

Brother and sister faced each other, both unwavering.

"Maybe," was all he would say, and Tara rolled her eyes, muttering about the stubbornness of men while she walked away.

Aaron filled the rest of the day with mindless tasks just to keep busy. His parents were occupied with making arrangements for the funeral.

Aaron busied himself with the horses, seeing that they were exercised and fed. When his mind wandered, it kept going back to the same unanswered questions. What was happening to him? Try as he might to go about a normal day, he kept looking over his shoulder.

Often, his thoughts strayed to the swords, so much that he decided to keep them close to where he was working. He opened the white cloth sack to look at them and reached inside to feel them in his hands. They gave him a small measure of reassurance. His grandfather referred to them as Falcons in the letter. He couldn't determine what type of metal they were made from. As an engineering student with a focus in mechanics and materials science, this perplexed him. Certainly not steel, as they were much too light. But they were strong. Each time he held the swords, they felt more at home in his hands, which both comforted and scared him. After all, why would he need swords?

CHAPTER 4
DAY TO MOURN

The morning trickled away while Aaron's family prepared for the funeral. The whole idea of a church ceremony for his grandfather annoyed him; after all, his grandfather was not a member of any church that Aaron could remember. They never talked about it. He thought he should have known something like that about his grandfather, and he was beginning to wonder how much he didn't know about the man. An image of the Falcons flashed in his mind, and echoes of the bladesong emanated from within him. He glanced over at them safely tucked away next to his bed. He wasn't ready for them yet, but their calling whispered to him. *I can't exactly walk around with them strapped to my back,* he thought. He wore a dark gray suit and checked his appearance in the mirror before leaving his room. He went down to the kitchen to get something to eat.

"Good morning," his father greeted him.

"Hey," Aaron said. The absurdity of the whole funeral thing still whittled away at him. "Dad, do you think this is right, what we're doing?" he asked.

"What do you mean?"

"Grandpa wasn't even a Christian. I just don't think it's right. Is this funeral what he would have wanted?" Aaron asked.

His father set down his cup of coffee and eyed him for a moment. "Funerals are for the living, Son, as well as the dead," he said softly. "The truth is that your mother and I don't know what he wanted. He never told us. We thought a funeral would be best. Your grandfather touched a lot of lives, and many of them will want to pay their last respects." He took another sip of his coffee before continuing. "I know it's hard, and if you truly feel that this is not right then you do not have to be there. However, I would like for you to come."

Aaron sighed, feeling foolish. "I'll go," he said. How could he do otherwise?

***

The funeral was outside at the local cemetery. Aaron and his sister exchanged glances more than a few times at the large crowd that gathered. His grandfather had touched more lives than he'd realized, and it filled him with a sense of pride that his grandfather was beloved by so many. Aaron closed his eyes, soaking in the noonday sun. A soft breeze toyed through the air, and the voices of those around him drifted away on the soft eddies of the wind. He breathed in slow, easy breaths. With each exhalation, he sensed the energy of all things around him. He delved deeper within while projecting his own energy out. The energy danced all around and gathered to him. He felt the calling to move the way he did with the Falcons, and then a presence was suddenly there. Aaron's breath caught in his throat as something cold and dark washed over him, and his back stiffened.

Aaron knew it was the same presence that attacked him at the school. He didn't know what to do. The presence felt more potent. Aaron smelled its foulness stealing away the freshness of the air. He opened his eyes to scan the crowd. A hooded figure walked among the people gathered for the funeral. Thunder that no one else seemed to hear boomed in the clear sky. The hooded figure made his way to the other side of the casket, across from Aaron. The figure drew his hands up to remove his hood in a slow, deliberate motion. Aaron's heart thundered as the hood fell away. Soulless black eyes housed in a ghostly white head sneered at him. He had a strong imposing face of high cheekbones and a pronounced chin that dominated his chiseled features. He was completely hairless, and he carried an air of absolute arrogance. The shadows seemed to swirl around him, and Aaron grudgingly met his gaze.

"Ferasdiam has laid her mark upon you, scion of the house Alenzar'seth." His voice was like granite. "A pity," he said and made a show of studying his surroundings with disdain.

Aaron rose to his feet. The crack of a whip sounded, and the being stood directly in front of him. His massive hand reached toward Aaron, and the white pearl in Aaron's medallion flared to life. The being's hand recoiled, and he stepped back with a look of uncertainty flashing across his soulless black eyes.

"Beware, you have this day to mourn. Then you're mine." He screeched the last word with such vehemence that Aaron felt his breath rush past his face.

A hand gently gripped his shoulder, and he looked up to see his mother prodding him to get up. The people at the funeral were beginning to disperse. He got up and scanned the area, all the while hearing the echo of the being's last words, and he shuddered.

Later on he climbed into his Jeep, preferring to drive by himself than ride with his family. He loosened his necktie and tossed it into the center console. He lowered the soft top and tied it off.

"Aaron," a voice called softly from behind him.

The muscles in his shoulders stiffened when he heard Bronwyn call his name. There was a time when her smooth voice sounded like heaven to him, and despite all his efforts to banish her from his heart, her voice still affected him. Why couldn't he just forget her?

He took a deep breath and turned around. "Hello, Bronwyn," he said, and his heart twisted up in knots as she stared back at him with her honey-brown eyes and rich brown hair spilling down her back. She wore a simple black dress, which made her natural beauty appear to be anything but simple.

"I'm so sorry about your grandfather, Aaron. I know how much he meant to you. Are you okay?" she asked.

"My sister said you stopped by yesterday. Thank you, but you didn't have to do that."

"Yes I did," she said. "He meant something to me too, and your family has always been good to me." When Aaron did not say anything, she continued. "I've wanted to see you, but I know—"

All the anguish at her betrayal welled up in him. "Why did you do it?" he blurted out.

Bronwyn took a step closer and put her hand on his arm, her eyes brimming with tears. "I'm sorry, Aaron. I made a mistake. I was wrong and I'm sorry. She paused. "Aaron, please look at me."

Hearing his name from her lips cut his heart in two. Both halves were fighting, one wanting nothing more than to take her in his arms, the other wanting to get as far away from her as possible so the pain would go away.

"How can I ever trust you? I mean, you've taken everything we had and tossed it away the moment you cheated on me. I thought what we had was special and enduring, and you ruined it! You can't get that back!" The bitterness of his words cut him as he saw the pain in her eyes.

"It is special, that's why I'm here. I can only say I'm sorry. I want to be with you. Please, won't you give me another chance?" she asked.

It would be so easy to just take her in his arms and hold her. How he yearned to do that even now in the midst of all the anger and pain, but his anger would not relent. "I don't think you deserve another chance. You stay away from me!" he shouted, earning them some worried looks from the departing funeral procession. "All that we had is dead!" The words left his lips without any thought, his anger taking him to a place where reason and clarity had no sway, and the wisdom of his core began to rebel against grief's foolishness. *She doesn't deserve this.*

"That's not true. I can see it in your eyes," Bronwyn said.

He didn't say anything.

"What we have is not dead," she said.

"I can't be with you," Aaron said.

Those cruel words broke her resolve. Let her be the one to hurt for a while. He climbed back into his Jeep and sped off, leaving her there with tears streaming down her face. His own tears came in bitter defiance to his anger. *You are a fool,* he thought, and struck the steering wheel with his fist over and over again.

He looked into the rearview mirror, and soulless black eyes stared back at him. After a moment, they disappeared, but he heard an echo of mirthless laughter that drained the heat from his blood. The words from his grandfather's letter came to mind. *One day soon, you will discover that your life is nothing like you thought it would be.* Aaron glared at the rearview mirror, and his fist shattered it, and all the while mirthless laughter reverberated in his mind.

CHAPTER 5
ANOTHER WORLD

It was midday in the cursed kingdom of Shandara, but one would never know it. Life was all but forsaken, as the lands were covered in decay, and darkness reigned supreme. Whispers of a glorious past lived in the stone remnants found throughout this once lush and proud kingdom in the land known as Safanar. Now wasteland dominated it. The old kingdom of Shandara had been a jewel upon Safanar that was unparalleled, and the palace, a triumph of human and Hythariam kind. Now it was all but a cold corpse. A testament of Colind's recklessness. This was his prison. He was an outcast banished to this forsaken land where he had once been the guardian for all, but now he was just a shadow. It had been more than twenty years since Shandara had fallen. How he longed to feel the warmth of sunlight on his face, drink clean water, and eat food. Oh how he missed the taste of food. Even more, he missed the sunlight on his face, but his prison forbade both.

Colind was a shadow, his soul ripped from his body, which was still imprisoned in the earth, fiendishly preserved as a reminder of a prison he couldn't escape. Sunlight was deadly to him, as it could erase his very essence. The shadows were his home now, as they had been for more than a score of years. Despair claimed him in the beginning, then madness, where he roamed like any other specter, and now a bitter contempt for a prison that had no walls. He was cursed, forever to roam among the place of his failure. This was the price he paid for not being true to the Safanarion Order and not accepting the harsh truth about one of its members. But what parent isn't blind to a child's shortcomings? A feeble argument compared to the destruction it caused, and the silence from all those who had died at the fall of Shandara was his answer.

Here, in the land of shadow, he had little worry about the sun, which was safely tucked away behind a perpetual wall of clouds. Colind still remembered with unwavering clarity those last days. The days when his old friend Reymius had fled Safanar with his only daughter, Carlowen, to stop the evil that was unleashed. He again felt the faint stirrings of a heart that was no longer beat inside him. It had begun the day before, like an itch that needed to be scratched. Beckoning and constant, but gaining in urgency. *Come to Shandara. Return to the palace, Colind. Your role is not yet finished.* The resolute tone was reminiscent of Reymius, but how could that be? If Reymius had, in fact, returned to Safanar, that meant one thing. Reymius was dead. Only he could reach across the planes of death to Colind. A scant flicker of hope that the winds were indeed changing stirred within him.

He closed in on the palace and reluctantly looked up. The legendary ivory walls were scorched and riddled with cracks where they hadn't shattered altogether. Of the twenty towers, a mere six remained standing. He cast his eyes to the ground, unable to stand the sight of Shandara in such a state. He made his way to the sacred grove that lay in the heart of the palace.

Years of existing in the shadows allowed him to instinctively sense when the sunlight was near, and those instincts saved him. Within one pace, the line of darkness gave way to the light, and Colind looked to the sky in awe as shafts of sunlight dotted the once-proud city. His gaze drew downward to the heart of the sacred grove. A pang surged from deep within. The ancient tree of Shandara gleamed under the sun, and the sight of it almost caused him to run perilously into the light.

A glowing figure of a man sitting at the base of the sacred tree slowly looked up and smiled sadly. Colind stopped, unable to go any farther. A barrage of memories swept over him. *Reymius?* The wizened figure nodded in understanding.

"My friend, please tell me that you and Carlowen were spared, that you escaped the fall?" he asked, falling to his knees. The apparition nodded again, and Colind sagged with relief as a great weight lifted from his shoulders. Colind began to speak again, and the luminescent Reymius glided forth, coming before Colind's slumped form. His eyes were full of patient understanding and loving friendship that warmed Colind's lonely heart. For a few fleeting moments, he felt the ground beneath his knees and tasted the sweet air of the sacred grove once again. In one fluid motion, Reymius raised his hand to Colind's forehead, linking them. Images of a young man fanned through Colind's mind.

The heir of Shandara, my grandson.

The Dark One, Tarimus, was already on the hunt, and the trials were about to begin. Colind felt desperation through the link and backed away, knowing what he needed to do. He had to guide Reymius's heir in traversing the crossroads between worlds, facing the perils between life and death.

You are meant to guide, not to interfere. Colind, you are forbidden to interfere. Aaron must choose his own path if there is to be any hope. These are his trials to overcome if the Safanarion Order is to return.

Those cruel words echoed in his mind. Once again, he would be the observer. *Well, we'll see about that.* The specter of Reymius, as if hearing his thoughts, fixed him with a rigid gaze, then faded into the sacred tree and disappeared. Colind glared at the tree for a few moments. He would accept his charge despite his imprisonment. He was *still* a guardian of the land, and he had a debt to the house of Alenzar'seth.

Both he and Reymius had given an oath to protect the land. He would do all that he must in service of the Goddess, despite his loyalty to the house of Alenzar'seth, the keepers of Shandara.

Colind withdrew from the sacred grove and made his way to the gates of the palace. The journey would have been much easier had he simply traveled through the walls, but the part of him that clung to remnants of his humanity refused to give in. He had to travel to the crossroads in order to journey to the home of Reymius's heir. The Goddess saw fit to give him a second chance, and he could not falter. This could be the redemption that he had waited so long for. He now had a chance to set right some of the wrongs that occurred so long ago. To do this, he would need to confront Tarimus once again. Thoughts of Tarimus tore his heart in two, and a single name appeared in his mind with utter contempt: Mactar. *All roads of betrayal lead to your doorstep, and we shall meet again.*

CHAPTER 6
THE FOG BEGINS TO LIFT

Aaron looked up at a great marble statue of a dragon that cast its thunderous gaze down at him. Its massive wings were spread wide, and Aaron stood there, taking in the awesome presence before him. The fringes of his vision were blurred to his surroundings, as if he were peering through a window with water streaming down the edges. But the statue was clear and unwavering in his dream. Since he first slept with the medallion around his neck, his nights had been filled with dreams of places he had never seen before. But no matter the dream, sooner or later he would end up in a coliseum with marble columns running down each side, leading to a statue at the end. The statue would sometimes be a tree, intricate in its design and detail as if the stone were once a living entity. He heard the sound of a clock ticking, and the walls of the temple around him were stripped away, revealing a black void. Icy cold ripped the breath from his lungs, and the sinister laughter began.

"The time of mourning is over," a voice thundered from the void. A crushing blow sent Aaron reeling off his feet. The hooded figure that had been at his grandfather's funeral appeared. "I will drink from your soul, Ferasdiam marked. Alenzar'seth's heir," he spat.

Aaron quickly lashed out with his foot. He missed his mark, but was able to get to his feet.

They squared off. This was his dream, and no one had power over him in his own dream. "Who are you?" Aaron demanded.

Lifeless black eyes regarded Aaron. "You're going to have to do better than that."

"Fine!" Aaron said between clenched teeth and charged.

The being disappeared with a cackling laugh, and Aaron cursed himself for a fool. *Remember the hallway at school.* He closed his eyes, claiming the void within, and stretched out his feelings until he found the darkness. Their energies touched for a moment, and the hatred that emanated from this being almost broke Aaron's concentration.

"I found you."

"You know nothing," it hissed back.

Aaron kept a firm hold of his focus and a name appeared in his mind. "You are Tarimus; I know this is your name."

Tarimus howled in such a rage that Aaron's hands went to his ears in a feeble attempt to block out the horrible sound. For a moment, he teetered between wakefulness and sleep.

Aaron opened his eyes and found that he stood upon a dark surface barely visible through the mist that gathered up to his knees as far as the eye could see.

Tarimus floated in the air above him. "Now for your first lesson in power, boy," Tarimus spat, and then he swooped down with lightning speed and struck him.

Aaron felt himself begin to break apart and tried feebly to hold himself together. Then, with a flash of light, he found himself sprawled on the floor of his room. He sprang to his feet, circling around. His breath came to him in labored gasps. He looked at himself in the mirror and saw blood trickling down the side of his lips and two fist marks over his heart where Tarimus had struck him. The medallion lay coolly against his chest.

A hard knock came from his bedroom door. "Aaron, are you okay?" his mother asked as she came in, not waiting for an answer.

He quickly wiped the blood from his face and turned toward her. "Yeah, I'm fine." It was getting to be a habit telling people this.

"I thought I heard something..." She stopped suddenly with her eyes fixed on the medallion. "Where did you get that?"

"Right before Grandpa died, he placed this in my hands and told me to keep it safe."

Carlowen gasped for air, and her eyes grew distant. "Safanar," she whispered.

"What did you say?"

His mother frowned and looked as if she couldn't quite concentrate. "Safanar, our home," she said.

"Our home?"

"We'll talk more in the morning—" She paused, swallowing hard. "I just need some time, okay?" Her eyes darted back to the medallion.

"Do you know what it is?" Aaron asked.

"Yes. It's the crest of our family, but don't show anyone else. I mean no one, Aaron," she said firmly.

Aaron nodded.

***

Carlowen started to go back to her bedroom, but turned in mid-stride and headed down to the family room. Memories of places long forgotten danced along the edges of her mind, breaking through the walls built long ago. She was standing on a balcony of a palace, watching the sun set over rolling green hills. To her right was a black flag with a gold dragon holding a rose embroidered on it.

"Hey, what's going on?" her husband said, snatching her from her thoughts.

"Everything is fine, Patrick. I thought I heard a noise coming from Aaron's room."

Patrick joined her in the family room. "He's changing more and more every day," he said.

"Yeah, he's growing up," she answered, but in her mind she was still seeing the medallion. The creamy white pearl in the center, surrounded by a dragon clutching a rose protectively. Their family heirloom. The protective walls that had blocked off her memories were slowly crumbling, and she scrambled to make sense of it all. She had seen that medallion before, when it had been worn by her mother. Hazy images of a life long dead invaded her mind. A great white castle lay burning with the acrid smoke stinging her eyes and throat. She blinked back watery eyes. *Shandara, her home.*

Patrick watched the troubled thoughts flow through his wife's eyes. In some ways he knew this woman like he knew himself, but in other ways she was a complete stranger to him. A part of her had always been distant. *Like Reymius*, he thought suddenly. Here but not *truly here*. His death unlocked something in Carlowen, a key to all the memories that were sealed away. It had never bothered him that she couldn't remember her youth. Carlowen loved his daughter and was good to him. Something paramount was happening to both his wife and son, and he felt powerless against it. The only thing he could do was be there for her as he always had been and pray it would be enough. He sat quietly next to her and gently rubbed her back. Her untarnished elegance made the rest of the world fade away. Beneath the beauty was strength and wrought-iron will—the very same strength mirrored in his son.

"It's late," she said. "And you have an early day tomorrow."

Patrick groaned while getting up.

"Go on ahead. I'll be there in a minute," she said.

When she was alone once more, Carlowen knelt straight-backed on the floor. Her breath came in a smooth, even rhythm. The cruel fog in her mind that blocked the memories of her youth was thinning. Glimpses of a stranger's life flashed before her. A world nothing like the one she'd called home for so long. One moment, she was a little girl running through a courtyard with her father growling playfully for the chase. Next, she was in a sparring room much grander than the replica that her father had built at the farm. She squared off against a man dressed in black, whose face she didn't recognize. Next, there was smoke billowing all around her. And screams...

"Take her, Reymius, save yourself," a voice said.

"Cassandra, no!" Reymius pleaded. "There must be another way," he growled.

"There is no other way. You must go. You cannot face the Drake. Go, my love, and live. Protect our future."

Then she was gone, and the world went black. Pain that had been locked away gushed forth, and her world shattered. A lingering feeling touched her thoughts, and she sensed the presence of compassion, whose warm arms surrounded her. She knew this presence, but could not remember his name. His voice echoed in her memories.

"Mom, are you okay?" Aaron asked.

Carlowen opened her eyes to see Aaron above her. Whatever presence had been there, fled. Her son, scanning the room, had felt it too. *Have I been blind all these years?* she wondered. She saw the outline of the medallion beneath his shirt and knew that her son would be leaving her soon. She told him everything was going to be all right.

"Who are the Alenzar'seth?" he asked, his eyes never leaving hers.

"That is the name of our family," she paused, choosing her words. "Tonight, I began to remember all those years lost to me. For so long, I could only remember the time just before you were born, but not now." Her voice trailed off. "It's all right. There's still time." Precious little time, but yes. "We'll talk more in the morning."

As she walked by him he asked, "Who am I, Mother?"

Carlowen turned to look at her son. "No matter what happens, Aaron, you are who you've always been. Nothing will change that." And with that, she turned and left.

***

* * *

Colind watched in silence as Reymius's grandson walked back up the hallway. What a strange world Reymius called home for so long. The safety that once was awarded by this place was gone. It was only a matter of time before their world, Safanar, caught up with them. Colind sensed the impression of Tarimus's rage and utter contempt. The hound had found its prey, or so it would seem, but who would prove the better—the hound or the prey? He stayed at the house that night, dividing his time between Carlowen and her son, watching over them even though neither slept. He was drawn to Aaron and sensed the boy's potential. Power was drawing toward Aaron, but it was a power that he remained ignorant of. How was he supposed to guide Reymius's grandson? Colind couldn't help but think of Aaron as a snowball sailing into the fire as he wondered what Tarimus would do next.

CHAPTER 7
DECEPTION

The next day Aaron overslept. His father left him a note asking that he help out with tending to the horses at his grandfather's farm. Aaron had hoped to get some answers from his mother, but his house was empty. He headed over to the horse farm and noted that everything around him seemed clearer than before, as if he possessed a heightened sense of awareness of his surroundings. Even the horses, which he got along with fine before, responded better to him.

At the end of the day, he took Ginger, a honey-brown mare, out for a ride in a small meadow. It was off the beaten path, and he preferred its seclusion. He brought the swords to practice with them, melding the bladesong into the forms that were taught to him by his grandfather. Aaron suspected that his grandfather trained him with the Falcons in mind. These swords felt as if they were made for him. In light of current events, he wondered if his grandfather had always been preparing Aaron for what he was about to face. He just didn't know what he should do now. He needed to talk to someone about all this, someone who would understand, but who? His mother had avoided him this morning. She struggled with her own returning memories, and Aaron preferred to give her some space, but he needed answers. Who knew when Tarimus would strike again? With the Falcons in his hands he felt more secure, but he couldn't bring them with him wherever he went.

Aaron headed back, allowing Ginger to have her stride, and it wasn't until he came within view of the stables that he realized he wasn't alone. Another horse, approaching from one of the other trails, came up next to his.

Bronwyn!

She didn't look surprised to see him. The sun bathed the back of her head, giving her brown hair a reddish glow, and he felt his pulse quicken. The anger and resentment had faded to a dull ache as if he were finally exhausted from it all.

"Hi," Aaron said.

Bronwyn simply looked back at him, her eyes revealing nothing and everything at the same time. He'd acted like such an idiot at the funeral, and now he was the one who felt uncomfortable. *It's your own fault for losing your temper.* He looked back at her, forcing all his angst back. She was waiting for him to say something, and she had every right to.

"I'm sorry for what I said at the funeral," Aaron said.

She regarded him for a moment. "It's okay. I know how much he meant to you," Bronwyn said, easing her horse, Abby, next to Ginger as they continued on.

They rode together in silence, which Aaron appreciated, because for the life of him he couldn't think of anything to say. They guided their horses to the stables and began storing their gear. He watched her brush down Abby, her long slender arms moving in smooth, graceful strokes. The light streamed in through the windows, catching her honey-brown hair in a golden hue. When she noticed him watching her, he looked away, quickly feeling foolish, but he could have sworn he saw her smile. How could his heart yearn to reach out to her and recoil at the same time? *Maybe I just need to get away from this place for a while.* He was stowing his saddle, gathering his resolve to walk over to her, when she came up behind him.

"I'm not sure when a good time will be, but at some point we need to talk," Bronwyn said.

"Okay. It's been tough, you know. There's been a lot going on." He stopped, trying to decide whether he should tell her all the things that were happening.

"It's all right if you don't want to talk about it now," she said. "But I'm here in case you do."

Aaron pressed his lips together. "With his death, I am learning that my family has a history that I never would have believed possible." *Yeah, go ahead, tell her that you're from another world; she won't think you're crazy... Am I crazy?* He wasn't so sure anymore. "It's hard to explain."

"I'm sure you'll find the words when you're ready. Now just doesn't seem to be the right time. Just remember, no matter what your family history is, it doesn't define you," Bronwyn said.

Aaron nodded.

"Can I come by and see you later on this week?" she asked.

"I've been running things here, so this is where I'll be most of the..."

He grimaced. "I mean, yes, I would like it if you came by."

She smiled, clearly relieved, and for a moment, a glimmer of hope grew in her eyes. She said goodbye and left.

Aaron waited a few seconds, debating on whether he should go after her. *Screw it,* he thought. He came out of the stables, about to call after her, but Bronwyn was heading toward the sparring room. There was something in the way she moved that didn't seem quite right, leaving an icy feeling sliding down to the pit of his stomach. He watched her open the door and stop in the doorway. Her head cocked to the side. She turned around, and Aaron sucked in a breath. The lifeless stare of depthless black eyes hit him like a blow. She flashed a haunting smile and went inside.

"Tarimus," Aaron gasped, then sprinted to the sparring room. He came to the door and stopped. Blindly charging in would be foolish.

"Bronwyn?" Aaron called as he stepped cautiously through the door into the darkness beyond. Aaron reached over and flipped the light switch, but the lights wouldn't turn on. It was so cold he saw his breath. *It's the middle of June!* He halted just inside the door and was looking back at his Jeep, where his swords were nestled behind the backseat, when he heard a voice call his name tauntingly.

"Aaarrronnn. Come on inside, Aaron."

Aaron stepped inside and saw her standing before the fountain between the twin rose columns. She looked like death's mistress with her skin pale as moonlight and her lifeless black eyes regarding him coldly. She held a long black staff, resting one end on the floor.

"Leave her out of this, Tarimus. I'm the one you want."

Tarimus's sinister laugh escaped Bronwyn's lips, leaving their voices juxtaposed, and it sent shivers down his spine. Her beautiful face twisted into an evil cast. "Or what, Ferasdiam Marked? Will you hurt me?"

Bronwyn leaped forward.

Aaron took a step back in spite of himself. "I won't fight you like this."

Bronwyn brought the staff up. "That's good. All you have to do now is die!"

Bronwyn launched herself toward him quicker than he thought possible, raining down blows as she came. Aaron scrambled out of the way of the whirling staff. Her attacks came so fast he didn't have time to think. All his efforts were to avoid being hit as he maneuvered around the room. He couldn't take the attack to her. He had to find a way to free Bronwyn, but how? *Think, damn it!* Then an idea sprang to mind. He broke down the rhythm of attacks quickly in his mind and began grinning whenever Tarimus missed. The attacks became more out of control, and Aaron kept taunting the demon. Then he deftly caught the staff and locked his grip around it.

"What's the matter, Tarimus? Can't you hit me?" Aaron sneered, smiling wolfishly, then shoved the staff back.

Tarimus howled in rage and attacked in earnest. The dance resumed, taking them the length of the sparring room. The staff whirled in an exquisite medley of attacks that would have killed him had his grandfather not spent hours training him.

The goal here is not to fight, but to keep others from harming you and themselves. A true master can prevent someone from hurting them and keep harm from coming to their opponent as well.

He never appreciated that lesson until now.

Aaron laughed as he avoided the staff. With each miss, Tarimus's rage grew. It wasn't inherently obvious, but something kept nagging at the back of his mind. Tarimus possessing Bronwyn's body to try to kill him didn't make sense. Why her when he could have possessed any number of people throughout the day and struck out when he would have least expected it? They were alone...unless...

Aaron stopped abruptly as a piece of understanding clicked into place. He caught the staff again while looking into those nightmarish black eyes and tossed it aside. "You're not trying to kill me."

Tarimus studied him the way a game master regards a pawn, and his lips curled icily.

"What do you want from me?" Aaron asked.

Tarimus seemed to pause, considering. His gaze drew downward, and he whispered, "You couldn't possibly imagine what I want or what I will take from you."

The remaining warmth fled the room as Bronwyn casually walked over to the wall, grabbed a short sword hanging among the rack of weapons, and turned to face him. She slowly lifted her eyes, smiled, and in one fluid motion, plunged the sword into her stomach.

A strangled cry left Aaron's mouth as he rushed in to catch her. Her nightmarish eyes returned to normal. She looked at him in confusion and pain. The sword clanged on the floor, dropping from her bloodied hands. Aaron laid her gently on the floor, tore off his shirt, and tried to stop the blood. *This can't be happening!*

"Bronwyn, you're going to be okay," Aaron said.

This is all my fault. Please.

She let out a gasp and stopped moving.

"Bronwyn, wake up."

Aaron's fingers went to her neck, feeling for a pulse. He couldn't find a heartbeat. His mouth went dry. He drew deep into his core, and his awareness of the world sharpened. A mighty force built within him and remained clouded in mystery. The medallion warmed against his chest, spreading through his arms and legs. Aaron smoothed Bronwyn's hair from her face.

"No," Aaron cried.

He positioned his hands over her chest and started CPR. He counted down from thirty, tilted her head back, and blew a breath of air into her mouth. Aaron repeated this process a few more times and then stopped to check her pulse again.

Nothing.

Aaron leaned in to blow air into her mouth. Bronwyn's eyes opened, revealing sinister black eyes. Aaron scrambled to his feet, watching in horror as the thing that had once been Bronwyn slowly rose. A shimmering purple glow emanated from her body, flashing in waves of darkness until Aaron couldn't see it. An icy wind blew, becoming a ferocious howl that rattled the windows until they shattered.

The glass fragments were sucked into the black void. Bolts of deep-purple lightning flared brilliantly, coalescing around a dark orb. A beam shot forth from the orb and struck Aaron full in the chest. The force of the blow sent him through the windows and beyond the walls of the sparring room.

Aaron dangled in the air several feet off the ground. Sharp pain rattled his bones and he felt as if his life was being drained from him.

He gritted his teeth and tried to close his mind to the pain. The raw energy of the bladesong drew up mightily from within, enclosing him in an azure glow. The pain didn't subside; instead, it rose in ferocity, threatening to break his will, but his connection to the orb of blackness began to waver.

A hand reached inside his shirt, grabbed the medallion, and thrust it directly into the beam of light. The medallion flared to life, blazing, and the pain melted away from him.

Aaron looked up and saw his mother standing over him with the medallion thrust forward like a talisman, then everything went dark.

Chapter 8
FAMILY CREST

Carlowen Jace watched her son as he slept. Patrick had helped her carry him into one of the spare bedrooms of her father's house. She glanced out the window. Patrick was cleaning up the destruction of the sparring room. Carlowen shivered and she looked at Aaron. *They won't get you, my son.* It was as if two worlds collided in her mind and she was struggling to catch up. Her son was strong, but very young. He possessed his father's strength of character, and she feared he would need every bit of it to survive what was coming. He stirred and slowly woke up.

Carlowen had lit a few candles, allowing their warm glow to soothe her. In her lap, the Falcons rested. It had been a lifetime ago that she'd seen her father wield these blades. She ran her fingers methodically over the engraved blades and pommels.

Aaron pushed himself up, and she noticed the wince of pain he tried to hide.

"Next time, perhaps you should keep these a little closer," she said and gestured toward the Flacons.

"I'll try to remember that," Aaron said.

"Are you okay?" Carlowen asked, placing her hand on his arm.

"No, I'm not okay," Aaron blurted out. "Ever since he died, nothing has been the same. Things keep happening to me. Something... Someone keeps attacking me. Do you know what it is?"

Carlowen studied her son. "I'm not sure," she said.

Recent revelations about her life, like her son, left her grasping for a handle on the moment herself. Her life had been here. She had a son here. For her, Safanar was comprised of snippets of a life she was only now starting to remember. It seemed as if Safanar had finally caught up with them. Such an evil so great in its wrath that it reached across worlds to hunt her son down meant one thing—fate was calling her son to return to Safanar. Why else would the power that had been in their family for generations stir within him? Fate was calling him. There was no one else left to call. She took a breath and looked into her son's expectant eyes. They demanded an answer. Had her father known what would happen? Part of him must have suspected. Why else would he have set Aaron on the path to find the swords?

"We are from another world called Safanar. A year before you were born, we were forced to flee our home. Your grandmother sacrificed herself so that we could get free and you would have a chance to grow into a man. She knew I would bear a son who would one day return. Your grandfather almost never spoke of her, because the pain of her passing was always with him. The price of her death afforded us the protection that we so desperately needed, but is now gone with his passing. He must have suspected that Safanar would eventually catch up to us and that he would not be able to protect us any longer."

Aaron shook his head. "How is it that you know all this now, but not before?"

Carlowen regarded her son calmly and pointed to the medallion resting on his chest. "When I saw our family crest again, it was like a long-forgotten world awakened within me."

Aaron traced his fingers along the foreign symbols that surrounded the white pearl in the center. The carved relief of the dragon cradling a single rose caught the candlelight and danced mysteriously with the shadows.

"Who is Tarimus?" Aaron asked.

Carlowen's breath caught in her throat, but the suppressed memories poured forth. "He is a demon sentinel cursed to roam between the world of the living and the world of the dead. He is what stands between you and Safanar. It is he that hunts you."

"Safanar," Aaron said, standing up. "I'm not going to Safanar." He stood there for a moment, collecting his thoughts. "He seems more like an assassin, but even that isn't right. He wants something; otherwise, why wouldn't he just try to kill me and be done with it? With every encounter he seems more powerful, and I don't know how to face him."

Carlowen regarded her son helplessly. The things that were happening were only a reminder that she was powerless to protect her son. She stood slowly and resolutely walked over to him and held out the Falcons. "He needs you to be strong before he feeds upon you. Only then can he claim the power bestowed upon our family for himself."

"What am I supposed to do with swords?"

"Keep them with you. You've keyed them," she said. "What happens when you wield them?"

"I feel invigorated. Strong. I can sense the life force of all around me, filling me." He paused. "There's music when I wield them, and although I've never heard it before, I know the song is mine. It's part of me."

Aaron recounted everything that happened since her father's death. He left nothing out, and with his telling she felt the blood drain from her face. "I feel so alone," he finished.

"Son, you're not alone. Not ever," a firm voice said from outside the room.

The candles in the room flickered, and the bedroom door opened slowly as Patrick stepped in. They shared a look, and something unspoken passed between them. Then Patrick walked up to Aaron and gripped his shoulder. "No matter what happens, Son, we will stand by you," he said firmly.

Aaron frowned. "Did you find Bronwyn?" he asked.

Carlowen glanced at her husband.

"No, there was no one else," Patrick said.

"I have to go. I think he's taken Bronwyn," Aaron said.

"You don't know that, Aaron," Carlowen said. "He will try to confuse you. Use all that you love against you. He is a monster."

"You're right, but I need to find out. I need to know if she's okay. If he has her..." His words trailed off with a shiver. Then he rushed from the room without a backward glance.

***

* * *

Colind watched Reymius's daughter and her husband from the shadows beyond the candlelight. Carlowen's husband had a genuine quality about him that he knew Reymius approved of. He was a good man. It was the tragedies that befell good men that made him truly sick at heart, and on a night like tonight...he smelled blood in the air. Death was coming this night. It was just a matter of when and where.

***

Aaron barely lifted his foot off the gas pedal, and neither the screech of tires nor blasts of horns swayed him. All fell upon deaf ears as Aaron made his final turn down Orchid Street. Red lights flashed above two police cars parked in front of Bronwyn's house, and his heart sank to his stomach.

He slowly drove down the road and approached the house. Neighbors gathered on the sidewalks, speaking in hushed tones. He turned and looked up at the giant bay window of Bronwyn's house, and for a moment, Tarimus's cold, dead eyes stared back at him, sending an icy drip to the pit of his stomach as the medallion grew cool against his skin.

"Is she dead?" someone asked.

"They don't know. The ambulance just left. The daughter came home acting strange and started screaming frantically. Then she took off. The police are looking for her."

He was too late. Aaron shuddered as the voices trailed behind him. He gripped the Falcons in his lap, but when he looked back up at the window, Tarimus was gone. He closed his eyes and stretched out with his feelings. The life energy of all those around him became apparent, but of the malevolent force that was Tarimus there was not a trace. He needed to meet Tarimus on his own terms, but he didn't know where or when he would appear next. An idea popped into his head. Perhaps he could meet Tarimus on his own terms after all. With a plan formulating in his mind, he sped off.

CHAPTER 9
WHAT COMES NEXT

Aaron knelt before a small fire whose flames danced rhythmically before him. Zeus sat beyond the fire, watching intently and sensing the power that gathered around him. Was this how it was supposed to happen? Tonight, he would bring Tarimus to him the only way he knew how. Dreams. *You always have mastery over your dreams if you remember what they are.* Aaron stared at the fire as he gathered himself, converging all thought to separate his consciousness from the waking world. Fire became his world, and he fanned the flames that became his center. He drew deeper into a trance, the energy seeping from below the earth, filling him with a power that he channeled inwardly. Focusing all his thoughts, he let go of the last string keeping him in the waking world and entered the dream state.

Aaron found himself in a burned-out shell of a church. The proud walls held few remnants of their gleaming past, and the white pillars lining the main thoroughfare were cracked with broken pieces on the floor. The soft glow of moonlight entered through the broken remnants of the stained glass windows. His footsteps echoed in the cavernous hall as he walked the length of the main chamber. Before him appeared a great chalice, where a fire flared to life.

The medallion grew cold against his chest. Aaron blinked his eyes, and Tarimus stood before the great chalice of fire. In this place, Tarimus seemed more real than he had before, something more than a ghost. They were in the place between the waking world and the dream world, and Aaron knew by the triumphant smile on Tarimus's face that this is what he had wanted all along.

"Who pulls your strings, Tarimus?" Aaron asked, closing the gap between them.

Tarimus's gaze narrowed angrily. Clearly, he was used to men cowering in fear before him.

"Does a moth truly know fear while he draws helplessly toward the flame?" Tarimus replied coolly.

"Where is she?" Aaron demanded.

Tarimus slowly drew his sword, and a metallic echo rang throughout. "She's no longer your concern," Tarimus said, baring his teeth. "I've watched you, Shandarian. You spurned her. Do you treat all your women with so little respect? What do you care?" he taunted.

"Leave her out of this. Where is she?" Aaron asked through clenched teeth. "Tell me or..."

"Or what?" Tarimus spat. "You'll kill me? I'm already dead and well beyond the reach of the likes of you and your kin."

Aaron jumped back, barely avoiding Tarimus's sword as it whirled through the air, striking the ground where Aaron stood only a moment before. Aaron focused inward and called to the Falcons. He called up an image of the swords in his mind, building it to the tiniest detail, but the image shattered.

"This is no dream, boy," Tarimus spat before delivering a kick that sent Aaron sailing through the air into a stone column.

Aaron's thoughts scattered, and he scrambled to get out of the way. Tarimus was on him in an instant, delivering another crushing blow, sending him sprawling. A bluish orb of light rushed from afar to settle down between the two combatants, giving Tarimus pause, and drew close to Aaron, hovering before him.

A deep voice called from the orb. "Rise, Shandarian."

Aaron's eyes widened as the orb flashed, and the Falcons clanged into his lap. He grabbed each hilt and brought them up just as Tarimus's sword thundered down. Deflecting the blow to the side, Aaron kicked out, sending Tarimus back in surprise.

"NOOOOOO!" Tarimus howled in rage. "Watcher, you are forbidden to interfere," he screamed out to the void.

When Tarimus turned back, Aaron stood ready to face him. He smirked and then wielded the Falcons. The blades flashed into motion, filling the chamber with their mysterious song. Tarimus, for the first time, looked fearful, then he bellowed his battle cry and unleashed a mighty wave of attacks. Wild cracks of steel echoed throughout the church. The power of the bladesong gathered to Aaron and with it an awareness of something much older that lives within the depths of the soul. Visions danced through his mind of the lives of people he'd never seen before. He heard whispers upon the fringes of his hearing. The awareness became more acute and wild in the harsh majesty that binds nature together. The fierceness and golden beauty of the balance of life came to alignment within him, and he drew upon that balance for strength to do what had to be done.

Tarimus sensed the change and howled in denial. "*Ferasdiam*," he spat, and charged yet again. Aaron stood perfectly still. At the last possible moment, he dove to the side, taking a grand swipe with his swords, but his blades passed through Tarimus without making contact. Aaron reeled in confusion, while Tarimus merely laughed.

"I'm not that easy to kill." Tarimus cocked his head to the side. "Can I be killed? I wonder." Dead-black eyes regarded him coolly. "You fight me as if I am alive. I assure you I'm not. Death has no sway over me, boy."

"What about life? Does that sway you at all?" Aaron asked.

"Life," Tarimus said. "These are the halls of what could be your life. Shall I show you what comes next?"

Aaron lashed out with a series of vicious attacks, driving Tarimus back. He'd had enough of these games, and Tarimus was right in front of him. Aaron dove for Tarimus like a falcon on the hunt. He held nothing back and fought with everything he had. The medallion grew warm against his chest, and the Falcons glowed in his hands. Sparks emanated from the clashing blades. With a great sweep of his blades, a jagged cut appeared along the side of Tarimus's face. The demon held the side of his face in disbelief. Tarimus turned, and with a sweeping gesture, he heaved the great chalice of fire off its pedestal, hurling it toward Aaron.

Aaron dove out of the way and scrambled to his feet, putting the Falcons in motion. The bladesong echoed throughout the church. The Falcons were engulfed by a shimmering blue glow. Tarimus made another sweeping gesture, hurling a great oak bench at him. With blades glowing blue, he sliced through the oak bench, scattering it to either side of him.

"Life is what matters to you, isn't it, boy?" Tarimus asked, circling with the appearance of a lazy stride. But Aaron knew better. "What would you do if you knew those that you loved were in danger and no matter what happens, you will never get there in time to stop it?"

Aaron's heart pounded in his chest. Tarimus's words had the ring of truth to them. "Tell me," he said, trying to keep his voice steady. *What have I missed?* he kept thinking. He had been sure that facing Tarimus in this way would force a resolution. The fires in the abandoned church died out in unison, plunging them into darkness save for the moonlit glow through the broken windows.

"Fate has finally caught up with you, Heir of Shandara." Tarimus's voice seemed to echo from every direction. A cold wind blew. "Tonight, they shall weep in their own blood." Tarimus's voice came ahead of him in almost hushed tones. "I unleash *you*, Shandarian. See what has been hidden from you."

A blinding light burst forth from Tarimus's outstretched hand. The light coalesced into an image of Aaron's home. Fire raged throughout the house. Nine men dressed in black stood before the house, and screams came from the burning home. His father burst forth, charging through a window. The centermost man in black lunged forward, drawing his sword.

"Is this real?" Aaron cried. "What have you done? Is this real?"

Aaron screamed as the light shimmered then winked out, and he was once again kneeling before the burning embers of the fire he'd built. Without a backward glance, he dashed off toward his car, but he couldn't shrug off the arresting fear that he was already too late.

CHAPTER 10
ANOTHER WORLD

"Beware of the man who has nothing left to lose. You might push too hard, and he will be unable to fulfill his destiny," Prince Tye warned.

"On the contrary, Tye, it is a man who has nothing left to lose that can accomplish great things," Mactar advised the young prince.

"Think about it," Mactar continued. "The Heir of Shandara is within our grasp. Think of the glory that would bring if it were you who brought him before your father, the High King. This lone act will put you first among your brothers. Think of it, Tye, the last remnant of the house Alenzar'seth, holders of the keys to Shandara." He noted the slight tension building within his young companion with satisfaction. Young, power-hungry fools were the easiest to bend to your will with the right motivation, and this fool had means to fulfill this end. Tye was actually quite capable, but he had been forever shadowed by the deeds of his older brothers.

"Absolute secrecy is paramount, Mactar," Tye insisted. "Only my own men will be used for this. The Elitesmen will not be involved."

"Of course, my Lord." Mactar smiled. The Elitesmen could not know about the Heir of Shandara, not for the moment anyway. The utter bitterness he'd felt upon learning that Reymius escaped with that wretched daughter of his tried even his patience. The house of Alenzar'seth once again had cheated annihilation. It was a bitter pill to swallow, but did help to explain why the barrier between worlds continued to hold. Reymius's heir held the keys to great power, and he would be brought to heel and deliver what was due. He wondered how the Elite Grand Master would receive the Heir of Shandara? The complexities of the Elite Council were for another time, Mactar mused, and returned to the task at hand.

"When can we be underway?" Tye pressed.

"Soon, my Lord. Very soon," Mactar answered. "Make ready, and I will send for you shortly."

Tye took his leave, and Mactar strode to a darkened room whose sole occupant was a large mirror. The engraving that encircled the mirror held a powerful spell to allow someone to communicate through the ethereal planes between realities. It was dangerous and unpredictable, as he had learned through another's folly. Mactar lit the candles on each side and called forth to Tarimus.

"I am here, Master." Tarimus appeared instantly. Although Tarimus had answered to him in this manner for years, a new emotion roiled beneath those cold black eyes. Hope. Tarimus had never succumbed to his prison, but he had been leashed, so to speak. His stance betrayed a readiness for action and a hunger for Mactar's destruction.

"The time has come. Tye will be going through," Mactar said, narrowing his gaze.

"Are you sure?" Tarimus taunted. "He is not like the others. Do not underestimate Reymius's heir. He has grown strong. He is different...mindful."

Again, it was there, albeit the last of that statement was added grudgingly. An unspoken challenge and hope, an uncharacteristically human emotion that seemed foreign on Tarimus's now-demonic face. The pieces were falling into place, but what could have given Tarimus cause to hope?

"I trust you've done your part?" Mactar warned.

"Of course," Tarimus answered, stone faced.

"Then he will fall in line and perish when his usefulness is no longer apparent," Mactar said.

"Prince Tye, you say, is making the journey. Ahhh, the youngest son. How clever of you, Mactar."

"I'm glad you think so. He has the power to extract the keys to Shandara from Reymius's heir."

Tarimus appeared to have been on the verge of saying something further when Tye entered the chamber with eight of his men, all dressed in black, adorned with a silver dragon emblem on their chests. These were hard men. All of them battle tested and highly trained, but they were no Elitesman, with one exception. Darven, who had been cast out of the Elite order and had been Mactar's man ever since. Darven would be his eyes and ears on this journey.

Mactar turned back to face Tarimus, who now wore a sardonic smile. Disgusted with Tarimus's taunting, he gathered his will in crushing force and brought it to bear, encompassing Tarimus's essence. He was a hair's breadth from severing his feeble line forever, and Tarimus looked on, waiting to be released, even hungering for it.

But Mactar still needed him, and Tarimus knew it.

Mactar turned to address Tye and his men. "The crossroads of fate have brought us here, and each of you has a chance to achieve glory reminiscent of ages long past. As Tye has no doubt told you, the Heir of Shandara of the house Alenzar'seth has been discovered on another plane. Reymius escaped the destruction of Shandara to a world quite different than ours, but its people are no different than you or I. In order for us to obtain the keys, we must capture Reymius's heir, either in body or the essence of his soul. My Lord Prince, you know of what I speak. Let us begin. May Ferasdiam give her blessing to your journey." He almost stumbled on the last words; after all, Ferasdiam was not his god, but of the fools who stood before him. He harbored no faith in anything but himself. Mysteries were meant to be solved and could not be explained away by folklore. He smiled inwardly to himself and began the night's work.

CHAPTER 11
AMID THE ASHES

Aaron couldn't get the image of his burning home out of his head. He slammed his foot down on the accelerator as he frantically weaved around cars, blowing through stop signs and lights.

What would you do if you knew those that you loved were in danger and no matter what happens, you will never get there in time to stop it.

Never get there in time! The words were branded in fire in his mind. His family was in danger. All his thoughts were so fixed on getting home that he never once thought about what he would actually do when he got there. Would he see the horrifying visions that Tarimus had shown him? Could he even stop it? Clinging to a fleeting hope, he pressed on.

The tires of his Jeep CJ7 screeched around the corner of his street, and to his surprise, all was quiet. Eerily normal, the flickering streetlights betrayed nothing. He gunned the accelerator and skidded to a stop in front of his house. The medallion became like ice against his skin. Aaron grabbed the roll bar, pulled himself up, and stood there for a moment, scanning the area. A flicker of movement betrayed itself on one side of the house and another on the other side. Aaron drew the Falcons from their sheaths and jumped down. The front bay windows shattered, and his father tumbled onto the front lawn. His face was bloody, and his left arm hung limp at his side as he struggled to rise.

"Dad," Aaron cried, charging toward him.

His father looked up at his call. "Aaron. Behind you!" his father shouted.

Aaron dove to his left, feeling the hiss of a blade on the air where he had been, and was back on his feet instantly. A man in black came rushing toward him, his sword bearing down. Aaron crossed his raised blades and stopped his opponent's momentum through sheer strength. Aaron growled as he charged forward, pulling the Falcons in opposite directions, and sent a glancing blow into his assailant's face. The man cried out in pain, and Aaron kicked him aside.

He turned and saw another man in black standing behind his father. A gold cape hung loosely around his shoulders, and a sword hung casually in his right hand. Four more men in black with a silver dragon emblem on their chests fanned out to either side with blades drawn.

"Take him!" the leader ordered.

Aaron froze in horror as his father scrambled around and wrapped his arm around the leader's neck. The leader struggled for a few seconds, then reversed his blade and plunged it into his father, who fell with a deep sigh.

Aaron's stomach clenched, watching the blade sink in and his heart turned to ice. He screamed out to his father while charging forward.

The first black-clad figure rushed him with his sword out, but Aaron didn't slow. He lashed out with one blade, knocking it aside, then with the second blade, he smoothly sliced through his opponent's sword arm. His guttural scream was cut short as Aaron's Falcons took him through the throat.

Aaron cut through the remaining three men as if they were leaves writhing through the wind. All went down lifeless, bathed in red, and the bladesong burned in his mind.

"Well met, Reymius's heir," Tye said.

Aaron snuck a quick glance at his father lying on the ground and was relieved to see his chest slowly rise and fall. He wondered where his mother was. As if in answer to his unspoken question, sounds of a struggle came from inside his house. Aaron called out to his mother while edging his way forward. The leader brought his sword up and moved with leopard-like grace, poised to spring.

"I am Tye, Prince of Safanar. I am here to collect what your family has kept hidden for far too long," he said, and he lunged with his sword.

Aaron unleashed the bladesong into the night. Each probing attack by Tye was driven back in an ever-flowing motion of song and steel. He brushed aside the gnawing questions and brought the attack to his opponent. Tye was good and adapted well to whatever Aaron threw at him. Neither held the upper hand. Aaron felt the power of the bladesong coalescing in him, and he heard the whisperings of countless voices. Urges from within began guiding his hands, and he struggled to maintain control. Panic set in, and he tried to quiet his mind in a failed attempt to quell all that sought to distract him.

Struggling and fighting two battles at once quickly exhausted him, leaving him vulnerable to attack.

Tye pressed his advantage, driving Aaron back. Unable to block them out, Aaron opened himself up to the voices within, beginning to seek them out, merging the urges into his own fighting style. The medallion grew warm against his skin, and the crystals within the hilts of his swords began to glow. Tye faltered and was driven back, his sword knocked from his hands as Aaron swept him off his feet.

"Not so quick, boy. Put down your swords," a voice ordered behind him.

Aaron maneuvered to see where the voice had come from and keep Tye in his field of vision.

Mother!

***

Carlowen Jace stood with a dagger to her throat and an arm pinned behind her back. She would not allow her son to sacrifice himself for her. It was for a mother to sacrifice for the child, not the other way around. She had to act quickly. Her gift to Safanar would be her beloved son. *He will survive the journey there. That is his destiny. Like a bright shining star, he will drive the shadows from Shandara.*

Carlowen tightened up as Aaron lowered his swords, not seeing the dark figure rise up behind him. She drove her elbow back with stunning force, breaking the locked grip that held her. Zeus, snarling from the shadows, charged, tearing at the man. She turned swiftly, twisting the hand that held the dagger, and kicked out with her foot, driving the man into the bushes. She turned, poised to throw the dagger at her son's attacker, when a door of light sprang into being behind them.

"Down!" she cried, and without a moment's hesitation, Aaron dove to the ground.

***

Something whirled past him, and Aaron bounced back up, seeing his mother standing there, but it was a few moments before his mind allowed him to register that there was a dagger protruding from her chest.

Aaron glanced behind him and saw Tye, who had a dagger lodged in his own throat and a shocked look in his eyes as he sank to the ground. Without a second glance, Aaron ran toward his mother, catching her as she fell. She had blood trickling from her mouth, and his throat thickened. His mother looked up and smiled faintly, struggling to say something. Aaron leaned in to hear her.

"*Be...strong*," she said at last in a half whisper, then lay still and breathed no more.

Aaron knelt there, holding his mother's lifeless form, silently rocking back and forth. The image of his mother's lifeless glazed eyes burned into his mind. Her blood was on his hands. Aaron gently laid her down and slowly stood. The blackness that entered his heart yearned to do unspeakable things. He wanted blood.

The remaining members of the men in black gathered around Tye. Two of them hoisted Tye's body up, and a savage roar came from the door of light. The men hesitated, and one turned to face Aaron. His face was bloodied. He called out, and the rest of them turned to meet Aaron.

"Out of the way, you fools," a voice ordered from beyond the door of light. Then a fiery blue orb came hurling toward Aaron. He brought up the Falcons, and the crystals in the blades flared in a brilliant white light that shielded him. The fiery orb ricocheted from the shield and tore into his house, leaving a gaping hole. The men in black stumbled through the door of light, which was rapidly becoming smaller. Growling, Aaron pulled the dagger from his mother's chest and hurled it through the closing door to the sounds of screams, and then all was silent.

A small explosion came from within the house, and Aaron saw flames spread hungrily. He carried his mother's body away from the burning house and then returned for his father. He came up to his father, who lay staring at the house through the eyes of a broken man. Aaron felt his strength slip away seeing his father like that, but when his father saw him, the broken man disappeared, replaced with the unwavering force that was his father. He wasn't a broken man, but one who faced a journey that visits the doorsteps of all men who dare to live, and those who would die before their time.

Aaron tore off part of his shirt, rolled it up, and pressed it firmly on the wound in his father's chest. "I have to move you," Aaron said, lifting his father as much as he could, then dragging him away from the burning house.

"Your mother?" he asked.

Aaron shook his head, tears streaming down his face. "She's dead. I failed. I couldn't protect any of you."

"No." His father coughed. "You had no control over this, Son. You weren't meant to stop this."

"But Dad, I..." *Should have done something*, he finished to himself.

"No," his father said firmly. "This isn't your fault. There are no perfect solutions. Not in life, Son."

Aaron had no words for the life that was burning away all around him. Everything he had ever known was being stripped away.

"Aaron," his father called out weakly. "Protect Tara."

His father's grip hardened in his hand for an instant before slipping limply away. Aaron knelt, his shoulders slumped, stuck somewhere between shock and disbelief.

Get up, Aaron told himself.

He slowly rose to his feet and brought his mother to rest beside his father. If he focused on just their faces, he could almost fool himself that they were still breathing, but he couldn't stop seeing their bloody remains.

Aaron watched the firemen try to put the fire out, but their efforts were to no avail. The fire would not go out, leaving them to shake their heads in confusion. The EMTs checked him for injuries, and he spent most of the night recounting the events to a policeman, withholding a few facts that would have begged questions that he couldn't answer. When Tara arrived his resolve nearly crumbled. He numbly held her while she wept.

Against the advice of concerned policemen, firemen, and medics, Aaron and his sister stayed in front of his house all night, watching the fire raze his home. At some point, Zeus came up and sat next to him. Eventually, the firemen surrendered their efforts to put out the flames but remained vigilant in preventing the fire from spreading to the other houses.

Aaron kept going over the night's events in his mind. Despite his father's last words, he couldn't help feeling responsible for his parents' death and the danger that now threatened his sister. The danger she was in so they could get to him. He was the key to something, but what? There was no one else he could seek answers from.

Aaron decided that he owed Tara the truth. They shared the same father, and though Carlowen was not her biological mother, she was the only mother that Tara had ever known. Tara silently watched the flames next to him, and in hushed tones, he told her everything. She was in too much shock to do anything more than listen.

"I have to leave. If I don't..."

"Where will you go?" Tara asked.

"To find the men responsible," Aaron said. He yearned to hold the Falcons again, but his swords were safely concealed for the moment. "I don't care how long it takes or how far I have to go. I will make them pay."

"Aaron, you don't—" Tara began, but stopped as some people walked by. "This didn't happen because of you," Tara said.

"Yes it did. This isn't something the police or anyone else can handle," Aaron said.

"You're not responsible for the whole world. Just don't charge off and do anything stupid," Tara said.

Aaron sat there the remainder of the night, mulling things over in his head. He had to meet Tarimus where there was no escape for either of them. Looking back on the events that brought him here, he knew there was no other way. As dawn approached, the unquenchable fire that claimed his house completely and inexplicably went out in the span of a passing breath. Zeus let out a low growl, and the firemen began muttering to each other.

Smoking embers and a burned-out shell were all that remained of the home he'd grown up in, but Aaron wouldn't let himself turn away. He couldn't. He took in the scene in its entirety, allowing it to burn into his mind lest he forget the price of failure. A small voice from within cried out that it wasn't fair. How could he have known? But he should have known that an attack would come, and others paid the price with their lives. *Maybe if he...* He looked around, wearily avoiding the path of "what ifs" for now, and with heavy footsteps, he got in his Jeep and drove slowly away.

***

Faint stirrings of a heart long buried ached within Colind's chest at the tragedy before him.

Tarimus, what are you up to? Colind wondered, watching Reymius's grandson drive away. *A remarkable man, not at all the fool that Mactar believes him to be. But what does Tarimus believe?* Soon, he would have to reveal himself to Aaron. Power was drawing itself to Aaron, and he was learning to control the power of the Falcons. The balance of life on Safanar was a delicate thing, and the pendulum was swinging wildly out of control. Always the guardians like himself were there to lend guidance and to maintain balance, but he was the last, and he wasn't sure he could truly call himself a guardian anymore with his own dark betrayal haunting him still. Reymius's last days on Safanar were the darkest of both their lives. So much had gone wrong, and evil was allowed to endure. Colind launched himself into the air, riding along the shadows and easily catching up to Aaron. He kept pace while watching. Was Aaron strong enough to endure the path that he must walk? Colind didn't know, and his perceptions were clouded whenever he tried to think on it. Mactar would soon learn the extent to which he underestimated Reymius's heir and would double his efforts. Colind resolved to do what he must and hope for the best; at times, it was all one could do.

CHAPTER 12
PARTING

Aaron woke up to Tara calling his name. His whole body jerked awake, and he sat up, gasping.

"Are you all right?" Tara asked.

"Yeah, it was a bad dream," Aaron answered.

Barely two days had passed since their parents were murdered, and neither one of them had gotten much sleep. Tara's fiancé, Alex, stayed with them, lending support to his sister where he could, for which Aaron was grateful. Aaron had hardly let Tara out of his sight.

They were staying at his grandfather's house...their house now, since they had nowhere else to go. The funeral for their parents was today, and Tara had made him promise that he would stay long enough to attend, which he grudgingly agreed to. Tara didn't realize the danger she was in. Zeus, on the other hand, had hardly left his side these past two days. So Tara had double the protection. At first he'd expected another attack, but nothing had happened. He hadn't even felt the presence of Tarimus.

The funeral was peaceful and quiet and completely at odds with how Aaron was feeling. It was his second funeral in the past few weeks, and he didn't have any tears left. After burying three family members, all he had was smoldering rage, loitering beneath the surface, wanting to lash out at anything and everything around him. He yearned to have his swords in his hands to kill those men again, only this time he would arrive earlier and save his parents.

The funeral procession left, and Aaron was last to leave. He stood in front of the headstones of his parents' grave. Beloved husband and father etched on one and wife and mother on the other. Aaron knelt down and rested his hands on each tombstone. His throat thickened, but his eyes were dry. He stood up and balled his hands into fists. After taking one last long look he turned around and left.

After the funeral, Tara went with their family friends to Alex's house while Aaron slipped away. He changed into his good hiking clothes, which were extremely durable, and left a note for Tara. He advised her to go away for a while and told her that he loved her. He even left Alex a voicemail advising him to take Tara away somewhere on vacation for a few weeks.

The medallion pulsed with a warmth all its own and had done so since the night his parents were murdered. Aaron knew that it had protected him once and hoped it would again. His swords were strapped on his back. At one time he would have felt foolish with them on, but he didn't feel foolish today, just determined.

Standing before the doorway of the ruins of the sparring room, Aaron gathered his will, and then he stepped through. He struggled to quiet his mind. He needed to focus. He closed his eyes, taking deep, rhythmic breaths, and stretched out, feeling the life energy all around him. He felt the familiar presence of Zeus, sometimes savage, sometimes loving, as is all that is wild by nature. He delved deeper into the secret chamber where he had found the Falcons, the medallion, and the cylinder that glowed in a bluish light. He called it forth, and the floorboards shattered as it hovered in front of him, slowly spinning.

"There is no turning back from this," a voice said from the shadows.

Aaron glanced over at the dark corner, trying to see who spoke. "I know, but they will never stop hunting me if I don't do this, and I will find the men responsible."

"Vengeance is a path that you can follow, to be sure, but it usually leads to a place devoid of spirit," the voice answered.

"Who are you?" Aaron asked.

"My name is Colind. I was a friend of your grandfather Reymius. I am sorry for his loss and the loss of your mother. They were both very dear to me," Colind answered.

Aaron saw the old man more clearly. There was a hard edge to him, and his gray eyes carried a slightly worn and haunted expression. "How do I know you are telling me the truth?"

"You can't," Colind said, his lips curving, but the smile did not reach his eyes. "I understand your caution, I do, but as Reymius has told me on countless occasions, the choices we make are all leaps of faith. You will need to decide whether you can trust me or not. Just hear me out and then decide for yourself."

Aaron watched Colind, considering. "Fair enough," he said. "It sounds like something he would say."

It was Colind's turn to consider Aaron's response, and then he laughed. It was a sound that seemed foreign, ripped from the pages of another life. "You surely are your mother's son. She had a backbone to her too and a no-nonsense attitude when she set her mind to a task." The smile felt foreign to his lips and was gone quickly. "Time grows short, and the need is great, for you are in more danger than you realize."

Aaron watched silently, waiting for him to continue.

Colind looked at the cylinder as it hung in midair, slowly spinning, then fixed Aaron with a hard stare. "To travel the crossroads between worlds is perilous by itself, but for you the danger is tenfold, for Tarimus is waiting. Tarimus dwells in the planes between life and death with a foothold in each world, but is denied the release for which he yearns. I know you have unlocked some of the secrets to the Falcons, but believe me, you've only scratched the surface of what you are truly capable of." Colind sighed in frustration. "Your gravest obstacle is Tarimus, and he has played both sides of this battle masterfully. Through your confrontations with him, you have learned much and gained in strength, but when you face him on the crossroads, he will come at you in full strength. In his arena, he will be the master. As a parasite would possess a host, Tarimus will vie for your soul and gain a vessel with the power to return to Safanar."

"A vessel? You mean me?"

"That's really up to you, Aaron. He will try, and he may succeed if you don't find a way to stop him. He is still so full of hate and jealousy." Colind looked away with a pained expression. "He is lost," Colind whispered, and felt tears well up that could never come, because his anger forbade it—anger at Tarimus, at what he had become, and at himself for his gravest failure. Colind studied Aaron. By the Goddess, the last remnant of the shattered house of Alenzar'seth stood before him, stripped of family and the knowledge that was passed down generations.

"How do you know so much about Tarimus?" Aaron asked.

The question was simple enough, but Colind could tell from Aaron's gaze that he was testing him. He decided to be honest and cut straight to the point.

"Tarimus is my son and my greatest failure in life."

"Your son," Aaron hissed, stepping back from Colind.

"He was not always the monster you have seen," Colind said quickly. "Like all men, he was innocent as you are now. And his decisions and my unwillingness to see the truth cost the lives of many."

"There must be more you can tell me. How can I beat him? I wounded him once; I know there must be a way to do so again," Aaron pressed.

"He was once a man, and despite what he has become, the foundation remains."

"Are you alive or dead?" Aaron asked.

"I am banished. My body locked away in an earthen tomb. And my soul is tied to this realm, a punishment for my failure."

"I don't think so," Aaron said quietly. "You are alive. I can sense it in you."

"Don't tell me my own business, boy," Colind barked. "You don't know the half of it."

"I may not know what happened to you, but you have presence, an energy. All life is energy in one form or another. As you stand before me in one form or another. The fact remains that you are alive, and if you are alive then there is always hope," Aaron finished with an inner smile because he supposed he was speaking for the both of them.

Colind stared at Aaron in disbelief. Here was Reymius's grandson, with no knowledge of his lineage or their world of Safanar, lecturing him! He was banished. Banned from the realms of the dead and of life, yet here he was. A whisper on the winds of his mind pleaded with him to yield to this wisdom. Could Aaron be right?

"Now is not the time for this. We need to focus on you," Colind said.

"Okay. Is there a way that I can get through the crossroads without Tarimus knowing?"

"Not a chance. I'm afraid Tarimus is attuned to you as you are him. Both of you will know when the other is near. And there is no one who can guide you through." Colind stopped abruptly as Zeus let out a low growl and barked, looking at each of them. Colind studied Zeus as if seeing him for the first time. "Was this Reymius's companion?"

Aaron nodded, and Colind laughed. "Oh, Reymius, you sly dog," Colind bellowed.

"What is it?" Aaron asked.

"Tell me, Aaron, has Zeus left your side since your grandfather died?"

"Not for long."

"Zeus will be your guide. Reymius prepared him for this. He bonded Zeus to him, and when he died, that bond passed to you.

Wolves live in the world of the living, and their spirits roam other realms. He will be your spirit guide on the crossroads to Safanar."

"You can't be serious," Aaron said.

Colind understood Aaron's hesitation, but there was no time. By now, the news of the prince's death would have surely reached High King Amorak, and Aaron was not ready for that battle.

"Is it so hard to believe? Your grandfather surrounded himself with animals, all of which he loved. When I knew him, he had the uncanny ability to know exactly what they needed. He had this ability with people too, and they were drawn to him. He prepared Zeus to be your guide because he knew that there was a strong possibility that you would journey to Safanar. He suspected the protection bought by your grandmother, the Lady Cassandra, would cease with his death. The fact remains, Aaron, you are being hunted. They came once, and they will come again because you have something they want."

Protect your sister. His father's last words echoed in his mind. The best way to protect her was to leave, but part of him felt like a coward for leaving. He took a long look at his grandfather's house with the wraparound porch where friends and family would gather, often joking into the night. Then he turned to the various paths that led through the wooded estate. Pathways he and Bronwyn would take to pass the afternoon away. When he looked once again at the remains of the training room, he clenched his teeth hard. He would have his vengeance, and he would start with Tarimus.

"I will not hide from Tarimus," Aaron said. "But I will accept whatever help you have to offer."

"The crossroads is a place where time can be chaotic. So be mindful of which path you take. You will be drawn to Safanar, whose doorway will resemble the carved relief of those columns," Colind said, gesturing to the remnants of the mahogany columns sticking above the rubble.

"Let's say I make it through somehow, where will I come out in Safanar, and will you be there?" Aaron asked.

"Should you make it through, you will come in through the ancient ruins west of Duncan's Port." As Colind spoke the last word, the cylinder let out a shrieking sound, and a blinding blue light seared the floor. The light expanded with a rhythmic hum to the size of a doorway. Then Colind spoke again, but his voice sounded like it came from a great distance. "Seek Prince Cyrus. He can help—"

The rest of what Colind was about to say was cut off. Aaron scanned the area, but couldn't find him anywhere, nor could he sense his presence. The next two steps he was about to take would forever change his life. He stood rooted in place, watching the door of light. Whispers welling up from deep inside urged him forward. This place where he'd grown up had been his life and would always be part of him. He would carry his home in his heart and hope it would be enough to endure what was to come. For the briefest of moments, he seriously considered running as far as he could, but his parents deserved better.

Aaron slowly took a long look around at the home he loved, and a lump filled his throat. It was then that he saw Tara standing on the porch with his note in her hand. Her eyes were full of concern and brimming with tears. In a moment of unspoken love between the two siblings, they whispered goodbye.

Be strong, his mother's words echoed.

"*Come, Ferasdiam Marked, embrace your destiny*," a voice whispered from the door of light.

Aaron's eyes widened for an instant, then he took a giant leap through with Zeus in tow.

CHAPTER 13

THE JOURNEY

An icy charge washed over Aaron's skin as he leaped through the portal. He landed on hard ground and stumbled a few steps. Zeus burst through the door of light, and the cylinder dropped to the ground. Aaron bent over and retrieved the cylinder. He glanced around and found he was in a well-manicured forest. An old brick path stretched away from him. There was no sun or clouds, just a sky cast in perpetual twilight. Trees lining the path swayed gently, and Aaron noticed a natural progression to them. The same type of tree would appear as if it were in each of the four seasons, marking its cycle of life. He walked past the golden autumn leaves of a maple tree towering over the pathway. Then the same tree appeared again, devoid of leaves, and the air was colder.

"I don't suppose you know the way?" Aaron asked, but Zeus just sniffed along the ground a few times before looking back at him.

Aaron started walking down the pathway. The way ahead appeared to just keep going until the path met a distant horizon. Aaron wondered how far they needed to go before they came to the doorway to Safanar. It was quiet on the path. There were no birds chirping or flies buzzing. It was as if he and Zeus were the only ones alive. Something kept gnawing at the back of his mind. The more he thought about it, the more he knew that if he kept going the way he was, he wasn't going to get anywhere. Doing the same thing and expecting a different result is the definition of insanity (thanks, Einstein).

Zeus came to an abrupt stop as if their thoughts mirrored each other's, arriving at the same conclusion. But which way to go, he wondered. They stopped in front of an oak tree in its autumn season, and Aaron remembered the seemingly endless amount of leaf raking he and his father would confront each year. He smiled at the memory and immediately clenched his teeth at the loss of those better days. Both sides of the path appeared exactly the same, and Aaron didn't have a clue as to which way to go. He brought out a silver dollar he had stashed away in his pocket and held it out.

"I guess we'll let fate decide. Heads we go right. Tails we go left," he said, flipping the coin high into the air.

The spinning coin hit its apex, and the medallion grew cold against his chest. The coin remained suspended in the air until a great thunderclap shattered the silence and the coin came hurtling to the ground. The coin was embedded in the earth with heads facing up. A definitive answer if he ever saw one. He decided to leave the coin where it lay as a payment of sorts and headed off the path in what he hoped was the right direction.

Trekking through the forest, he eventually came upon an overgrown path. It was better than wandering aimlessly in the twilight of this place. He quickened his pace to a trot until he came to a clearing. It looked as if someone had drawn an invisible line and decided that this was where the forest would end. A sea of thick fog stretched out before him with an occasional shadow breaching the top of the swirling canopy. He walked to the edge of the fog and extended his hand and moisture began to collect on it.

Zeus eyed him through the savage eyes of a wolf and took a bold step toward the fog with a growing hunger in his eyes. *All right, my friend, I'll follow you.* Holding on to the dense fur on Zeus's back, he plunged into the fog. He held on as if his life depended on it. The fog thickened so much that he could barely see his hand in front of his face. The air grew cold around them, and Aaron stumbled blindly, holding on and trying his best to find his footing, but Zeus quickened the pace. The ground beneath him leveled off and hardened. He was sure they were going down a road of some sort, and there were buildings just beyond the swirling fog. Aaron closed his eyes and allowed his other senses to take the lead. The medallion grew warm against his chest, and he focused on the dragons around the white pearl at the center.

Zeus came to a stop and nudged his hand with his muzzle. Heat began to build in the pearl, and Aaron fed the heat with all his concentration. When he could no longer stand the heat, he reached into his shirt and pulled the medallion out, holding it over his head, but he didn't let go of the power gathering within. Faint whisperings urged him to give over and release his hold upon the power, but he held on a few moments more, until he could bear it no longer. Light rippled from the white pearl in bursts, burning up the fog around him, and Aaron found himself standing within a towering coliseum, all gray with worn stonework throughout. The ground beneath his feet held old dry dirt, stained with blood and the stink of death. A crisp wind blew, and Aaron looked up to discover the stadium full of onlookers, all eerily silent. Whenever he focused to get a better look at them, they went distinctly blurry, but from within his peripheral vision he knew they were there. There was something grim and silent watching him. Judging, leaving Aaron feeling undeniably exposed. Mutterings and hushed tones swept through the coliseum, breaking the silence, and he clearly heard *Ferasdiam Marked and Safanarion.*

"How quaint," a voice called from behind him.

Aaron spun to see a cloaked figure standing behind him, and Zeus let out a deep, rumbling growl.

"You are a long way from home. How honored I am that you've come to mine," Tarimus hissed.

Silence embraced the coliseum as a hush swept over its attendants. This was what he'd come for, to face Tarimus. It was inevitable, despite what Colind had hoped to achieve. Who was Colind trying to protect—himself or his son?

"I know what you want, and if you think you can take my soul, then go ahead and try," Aaron said.

Dead-black eyes regarded him frostily. "I see," he said.

Aaron expected more of a response than this. He knew to the depths of his soul that there would be no waking up from this nightmare.

"I am going to Safanar," he said.

"You walk a fool's path, boy," Tarimus muttered, and then made a waving motion with his hand. A bell clanged throughout the coliseum, and by the third gong, a columned stone doorway appeared at the far end, behind Tarimus. "There is the door. All you need to do is get past me," Tarimus sneered.

Aaron noticed that Tarimus still had the cut on his cheek put there from his blade. He had cut him, but how could he kill Tarimus? With his mouth going dry, he scanned the crowd of the coliseum. All the onlookers watched silently, like judges on a panel. He dropped his backpack to the ground and drew his Falcons.

Let's do this.

If this was going to be his end, then he would be sport for no man or demon.

Tarimus wickedly bared his teeth and drew his black sword, which drank the light. They each regarded the other, poised, and at the same instant, they both charged. The clash of blades rippled through the air.

Aaron spun and was ready for Tarimus. The demon spawn brought his great dark blade to bear. The fury of each hack from the dark blade rattled his hands and arms, but he numbingly held on. *How can he be so quick with a sword that big?* Scrambling, he managed to deflect or dodge the onslaught of attacks. Not blocking quickly enough earned him a shallow slice burning down his side, and a blurring kick sent him into the air. Aaron stumbled to get up, and Tarimus kicked him down again with a furious howl.

"Ferasdiam Marked or not, you will never survive this!" Tarimus spat. "This is no dream world, boy. Here, you are a master of nothing."

A thundering kick sent Aaron down again. Tarimus rained blow after blow on him, until it felt as if it were happening to someone else. Part of Aaron wondered when he would stop feeling the pain, and the other part of him raged for him to get up. That deep core where the greatest reserves of strength reside began to defy logic, and he struggled to his knees.

"Why do you do it? Why get up?" Tarimus stopped kicking him, breathing heavily. "Why fight a battle you cannot hope to win? Are you so eager to die? Would it be so bad to give yourself over to me?"

Aaron looked up, steeling himself for another blow. He hurt everywhere, but the fire within him hadn't diminished in the slightest. He planted his fist into the ground and rose to one knee.

"Why, why do you persist?" Tarimus asked through clenched teeth.

Aaron regained his feet. "Because I choose to."

Tarimus was right about one thing—this was a fight he could not win, not here in this place, but perhaps he could survive, and that was enough.

Tarimus dwells in the planes between life and death with a foothold in each world, but is denied the release for which he truly yearns. Colind had told him a golden truth, which became apparent to Aaron in this moment of bruised clarity. Tarimus needed to learn to let go. This truth gave him purpose, and with that, his strength returned in warm waves flowing through his body. The medallion grew warm against his chest, and a faint blue glow emanated from his discarded backpack.

"It's not too late for you," Aaron said, still hunched and feigning weakness.

"For what?" Tarimus replied contemptuously.

Aaron paused, giving Tarimus a long look, standing straight up before he answered. "To do the right thing. To let it all go and be at peace," Aaron said mildly.

A flash of disbelief crossed Tarimus's face before he began laughing with a mad glint to his eyes. Aaron expected as much, but sometimes words spoken have an uncanny way of coming back to haunt you.

"Do you seek to save me, boy?" Tarimus sneered.

"No, to remind you." Aaron brought up the Falcons and released the bladesong into a swirling harmony that comprised his soul's heartbeat. The voices and life force of those who had come before eagerly came to the brink, their knowledge readily available, but Aaron held them there. This was his fight. The crystals in his swords glowed, casting off a pure white light, blurring in the speed of Aaron's dance. The sound of the audience coming to their feet in unison echoed throughout the great space.

The Falcons felt weightless and required little effort to wield. Aaron poured all feelings, his memories, his rage, and his love into the dance. The faces of family and friends who had come and gone throughout his life flashed in his mind, but he was ever mindful of Tarimus. Random thoughts and experiences flashed by until he saw a shadow of Bronwyn standing before him, her honey-brown eyes silently begging him not to forget her. Her rich dark hair was unkempt, and her clothing was in tatters, but was she alive? She opened her arms out to him, and his throat tightened with the ache of regret. How could he have been such a fool? The love in his heart mocked him for what he'd tried to deny.

The bladesong unleashed a melody that he had never heard before, but fit him the way no other action ever had. He put his heart and soul on the altar and hoped it was enough to appeal to the little humanity that was left in Tarimus. Communication conveyed without words, but rather through raw emotion. The stone facade that framed Tarimus's cold, lifeless black eyes began to shake.

"What are you doing to me?" Tarimus demanded, becoming disoriented and covering his face with his hands in a feeble attempt at denial. "What sorcery is this!" he cried.

Truth. Life. That which you've forgotten. Aaron spoke the words in his mind, which were then conveyed through the dance. The pure white light stretched out its brilliance to encompass all.

Shaking from the struggle within, Tarimus peeled his hands from his eyes, and with a guttural roar, he charged, his dark sword attempting to swallow the light.

Aaron stood his ground, both blurring blades carrying a motion too fast for his mind to track. Thinking at this point was an obstacle. It was his training and awareness unlocked through wielding the Falcons that saved him. The ability to let go, to trust his feelings and to allow nature to take its course would determine this outcome. At last, a final lesson preached by Reymius was understood. No matter how hard he trained, this lesson could not be learned in a sparring room. He engaged Tarimus because there was no other choice, but in his heart he knew his fate lay with Tarimus upon these crossroads between the realms of Earth and Safanar, for Tarimus was the gatekeeper.

Each swing of the blade was countered, and Tarimus howled in rage, but no matter how hard he pressed, he couldn't break through the bladesong. Tarimus at last broke off his attack. Although Aaron stopped the bladesong, the power that gathered did not dissipate; rather it stayed with him, heightening his perceptions.

"Your father never gave up on you," Aaron said.

"Are you still trying to save me, boy?" Tarimus asked. "Don't speak to me of that fool. I have no father," Tarimus spat.

The word father echoed in his mind. Like thunder rumbling before a gathering storm, Aaron at last came for Tarimus. He unleashed the power of the bladesong with each blow, and Tarimus was thrown back, unable to stand against such a force that went beyond the strength of his arms. Aaron's blades cut him again and again, but no blood spilled forth from Tarimus. Their blades locked at the cross sections, and Aaron sent the dark blade spinning away. Sweeping out his leg, Aaron brought Tarimus to his knees. Aaron's vision was hued in red with the blood rage, but he stopped, poised to strike. He could strike Tarimus down with the power gathered and utterly destroy him, but he hesitated. Something wasn't right. If Tarimus dwelt between the realms of life and death, then what could Aaron possibly do? You can't kill what should already be dead. He was battling a ghost. To destroy a soul was something he knew nothing about, and if he did, could he use that knowledge, even on Tarimus?

Yes! a voice demanded. *Destroy him.*

Tarimus, he realized, was but a vessel for someone else's machinations. A prisoner desperately seeking revenge on his jailer. All Aaron needed to do was win his way past Tarimus.

"Colind spoke to me of Mactar. Is it he who holds you within this prison?" Aaron asked. "If I stop him, will that release you?" he pressed.

Tarimus regarded him with a mix of contempt and surprise, then with a fluid motion, he held his hand up. His sword flew to his hand, seemingly of its own accord. Though the coliseum's occupants were silent, their gazes were deafening. Tarimus sheathed his sword, driving it home, and a sense of finality filled the air. Aaron watched warily as Tarimus brought his hands together, and a purple orb of crackling light gathered with intensity above his head. The medallion grew cold against Aaron's chest. Ferasdiam was spoken in hushed tones throughout the coliseum. The gong of a church bell rang in cadence, banishing the whispers into silence. Zeus howled, eerily reminiscent of the night Aaron first tapped into the power of the bladesong. The howl held a calling, and Aaron wanted to heed that call. The columned stone doorway stood with its opening ajar, a shimmering curtain of silvery light blocking the view to the other side.

"I can settle it for both of us," Aaron said, and took a few precious steps toward his pack, where the cylinder glowed. He needed that cylinder if he was going to get to Safanar.

"What will you do in Safanar?" Tarimus asked.

"I seek those responsible for the murder of my family. They shall all pay. This *I swear*," Aaron said. "I will seek out Mactar."

"Vengeance is the path of death. I am responsible for the deaths." Tarimus turned his back to Aaron slowly shaking his head, the purplish orb hanging between them. Aaron wondered what ghosts haunted this demon who had once been a man, Colind's son. Tarimus abruptly turned toward Aaron. The words he spoke seemed reluctant to come out of his mouth, but his facial expression was oddly lucid.

"Perhaps you will succeed where I have failed." He paused, taking in Aaron's measure. "But perhaps not," he hissed, and a menacing glint overtook his face. His arms rose, and the purplish orb flared brighter. "I will have you, Shandarian!"

Aaron barely had time to flinch before the beam of light shot out of the orb, slamming him in the chest. The beam split between the pearl in his medallion and the crystals in the hilt of his swords, forming a blazing pyramid of deep purplish light. The medallion became the focus point, and blinding pain seared his chest, bringing Aaron to his knees. With all his might, he brought up his swords, cutting off the beam and sending it back to its source.

Tarimus stumbled back in shock, but before he renewed his attack, Aaron scooped up his pack and sprinted toward the door to Safanar. Tarimus howled in rage behind him, but Aaron didn't dare turn back. The door to Safanar was his destination. He ran as if the ground were falling away beneath his feet. Closing in on the door, Aaron brought out the cylinder, its bluish glow gaining in intensity.

Aaron thrust the cylinder out, the shimmering silvery curtain parted, and the stone doors began to close. He risked a glance back to Tarimus, but all he saw was the purple orb barreling toward him, screeching louder as it drew in. With the stone doors closing and with Zeus beside him, Aaron leaped through the door to Safanar.

The coliseum's mysterious occupants returned to their seats, and, as one, stared into the space before them. A dismissal hung in the air, and they were all swept away like sand blown in a strong breeze. Tarimus remained there for a few brief moments. "So be it," he whispered and disappeared.

* * *

***

The earth shook, snatching the attention of its people. As it was foretold, the Lords of Shandara would once again walk the lands of Safanar. Ferasdiam had left her mark upon him, and he would be her champion, but the path would be of his choosing. A cold wind blasted its way down, bringing an ounce of relief from the scorching heat of the deserts of Deitmar to the far off plains of the Waylands. Deep in an ancient forest, well protected from the realms of men, the old one stood. The wind carried a strange scent and swept his graying hair back. His eyes scanned the canopy of trees above. He was coming, finally. It set his mind at ease that Reymius did not fail in his task. The last of the ancient house of Shandara had returned. It was left to him to find Reymius's heir and keep him safe above all things, even from himself. Let the forces of shadow be wary, the Hythariam would once again enter the world of men. His golden eyes flashed briefly while he took his first steps on what would be a long journey.

CHAPTER 14
A HERO, A FRIEND

Aaron collapsed to the ground, writhing in pain. Coming through the doorway was like plunging into icy waters, but without getting wet. The cold was so sudden that the air was sucked from his lungs. He squeezed his eyes shut, hoping fervently that the pain would pass. The burning on his chest intensified. He struggled to remove his shirt and looked down at his chest, expecting to see blistering skin, but instead saw a perfect reproduction of the carved relief from the medallion. The dragon with his wings spread, holding a rose, and the white pearl in the center. The pain subsided, fading to a harsh, burning ache. The brand was more like a tattoo than a burn, because it had a silvery shimmer reflecting from the dragon scales. With each breath he took, it appeared as if the dragon were breathing.

Thunder rumbled, and he looked up at the dome-shaped ceiling covered with cobwebs. A shadow passed over an opening in the roof, then sunlight streamed lazily in. There were four statues in the room that were equal distances apart, like the points of a compass. A ray of sunshine set the fountain in the center of the room ablaze, and the water reflected the light in glistening waves that shimmered throughout the room.

Aaron slowly got to his feet, still getting his bearings. He put his shirt back on and bit back a gasp.

He'd made it. This was Safanar. The thought looped in his mind, and he had never felt so alone in all of his life. There would be no going home for him. He walked over to the fountain and eagerly dipped his hands in for a drink. Then, he filled the two metal water bottles from his backpack.

The statue on the far side of the temple caught his eye, seeming to glow of its own luminescence. The statue was of a man wearing robes with the hood drawn back, revealing a proud face. His right hand held the remnants of a staff, whose broken haft would have reached down to the floor. The pedestal beneath the statue was adorned with an intricate design of laurel work that drew the eyes to the center. Aaron traced his fingers across the patterns, and the faint whisperings of the bladesong began to awaken within him, urging him on. The center of the laurel work had a round impression. He glanced down at the medallion and held it up. It was a perfect fit. Aaron pressed it firmly into the impression. There was a faint click, and the white pearl in the center glowed. A stone doorway revealed itself off to the right. Aaron peered through the doorway. Faint glowing orbs grew brighter, lighting the pathway beyond. Aaron retrieved his medallion and whistled to Zeus, then went through the doorway.

The passageway sloped downward, twisting to the left. His footsteps echoed down the passageway until he came to the end. The passageway opened into a large, windowless room. Glowing orbs grew brighter as they sprang to life around the room. In the center was a long dark wooden staff driven into the rock floor, and a black cloak hung from the top. Runes were etched along the length of the staff, and a faint breeze toyed with the draping cloak. The musky air almost made him sneeze. Aaron stretched his hand out to the staff, and as his fingers closed around it, the runes flared to life. He tried to draw his hand back, but he couldn't.

"So, one of the Alenzar'seth has returned," a voice called out. "Do you dare claim my Rune Staff for your own?"

Aaron thought for a moment. The voice sounded familiar but different. "I just got here, and the road ahead is long. Please, I could use a good walking stick," he said.

The silence dragged on and then was replaced with a mirthful chuckle. "As did I when fate came knocking at my door, young one."

A ghostly apparition of an old man appeared before Aaron. The man's broad shoulders hinted at the powerful frame he must have had when he was young, but they now stooped with age. His eyes twinkled, showing no signs of age at all. His bushy white eyebrows moved as his face lifted into a smile. Something in his features seemed oddly familiar yet foreign at the same time.

"Uh...hello," Aaron said. "How do you know who I am, and who are you?"

"I had a name once, but that was long ago," the old man mused tiredly. "I am simply known as the Keeper. This staff can light the path of all, even among the darker places of this world. And there are dark places you will be traveling, to be sure. But know this. As with all things, there is a balance with the taking of this staff. To bring light invites the darkness to come take it from you."

"I'm already hunted. Keep the staff," Aaron said firmly, beginning to step away.

"You don't understand. This staff was meant for you as it was for me during my time. You cannot run from your destiny," the old man insisted.

"I walk my own path," Aaron said. "And I make my own destiny."

The old man smiled in a knowing way. "Fate uses us all, son. Failure to play in her game will cost you more than you know."

Aaron unclenched his teeth. "It has already cost me."

"Take the staff and use it well in your journey. That is all I ask. Ferasdiam has already marked you. Take with you another weapon to fight against the maelstrom arrayed against you. Think of it as a long-lost family heirloom." As the old man said the last, he faded away.

"Wait," Aaron cried. "Who are you? Please, tell me your name."

Silence hung in the air for a moment, but Aaron was sure that the Keeper was still there.

"I once was Daverim Alenzar'seth, your ancestor. I, too, served the Goddess once upon a time, and now I have a beloved whom I've kept waiting for far too long. Farewell and good luck."

His ancestor? What were the odds of that? This wasn't at all what he'd expected. Then again, what should he have expected? His life had been anything but normal since his grandfather died and a good deal more brutal. He carefully removed the black cloak from the staff and put it on. Aaron had never worn a cloak before, and it seemed to fit him well, not restricting his movements at all. His swords were well concealed on his hips, and the cloak would make blending in with the people here easier, or so he hoped. Donning his backpack, Aaron reached out for the rune-carved staff once again. At least his sister was safe. He had accomplished that much in coming here. He gripped the Rune Staff and easily pulled it from the ground. As the staff left the soil, a vision of a glowing, yellow reptilian eye seemed to lock onto him instantly. A mighty roar echoed in his mind as Aaron threw down the staff. He shook his head, gasping, then stared at the staff lying on the ground. Zeus eyed him intently, whining softly. Aaron looked back at Zeus, bewildered.

Well, I can't just leave it here.

He cautiously knelt down and picked it back up. The runes glowed briefly and then faded. He ran his hands appreciatively up and down the staff, which was a good weight and perfectly balanced. Aaron wondered how long the cloak and the rune-carved staff had been there as he retraced his steps back up the passageway. He inserted his medallion into the base of the statue, and the stone doorway shut with finality. After taking another drink of water from the fountain, he walked outside.

Aaron emerged from the temple entrance, which was nestled on top of a small hill that overlooked a meadow. The path leading away from the temple was mostly overgrown. He hoped the path would lead him to a town and from there perhaps he could find where this Prince Cyrus was that Colind told him about. Where was Colind? Did he know that he made it to Safanar? He'd hoped that the specter would show himself, but Aaron was alone.

Aaron left the temple, taking the path away. He was the Heir of Shandara. Did that make him some type of lord or a prince? His faint amusement at the thought quickly faded. He'd come here seeking all those responsible for the murder of his family, but he was starting to wonder if he would ever stop paying for things that his ancestors had done. He found himself in the middle of a war where the threat to his life was as real as the air he breathed. A cold shiver ran through him. Was the world always this harsh, or was it that his illusions of the world had been stripped away?

Being a seasoned hiker, he was able to set a good pace and cover a lot of ground. After a few hours, he found a dirt road. The staff helped. He noticed smoke rising in the distance and decided to set off in its direction, hoping to find a town. There was an oddness in the air that nagged at him for a while, until he finally realized it for what it was. The simplicity of it made him snort to himself. There was an enduring silence beyond the sounds of nature. There were no sounds of cars, trucks, planes, or cellular phones. All the things that made up his modern society were gone, leaving him wondering what technology was here. Even when hiking and camping, you brought portable technology with you and could see others with the same.

He went off the road a bit and sat on a fallen tree, taking his ease and closing his eyes. Simply soaking in where he was. The day was growing warm, and the shine of the sun peeked through the canopy of trees surrounding him. Zeus pawed at the ground anxiously, and then he heard the distant sound of galloping horses upon the road.

So much for technology.

Aaron pulled his hood up and crept toward the road, hugging the ground for a better look. The group of riders broke into view and slowed to a stop. All the riders save two wore brown cloaks and sat in their saddles with ease. The remaining two riders that led the group wore dark-blue cloaks. Aaron heard some of the men ask why they'd stopped, and they were answered with contemptuous silence as a blue rider held up his fist. The blue-cloaked riders scanned the area, and as one rider's gaze swept his way, Aaron felt a slight graze upon his senses. When the second blue-cloaked rider turned in Aaron's direction, a large shadow passed overhead, sweeping over them, blocking out the sun.

"Dragon!" one of the men shouted, and some men drew their swords and readied their bows.

"Hold," a blue rider shouted. "That is no dragon. It's a Ryakul. He's on the hunt, but not for us. Let's move out."

As one, the riders left. Aaron moved on as well, but stayed to the forest, following alongside the road rather than walking upon it. *Dragons? Ryakul? What kind of place is this?*

Before he knew it, the sun was setting. He found an old campsite, built a small fire, and ate some of the food he brought with him, but it wouldn't last more than a day. He cursed himself for not thinking to bring more than a day's worth of food, but at least he had water. Not thinking the food situation through left him wondering what else he hadn't thought through before charging headlong on this journey.

Zeus had come back, licking his chops, and settled down close by. Zeus was in his element out in the forest, but this place was still alien to Aaron, with different sounds than back home. He lay back and gazed up at the alien sky. The stars and their formations were all different, and there were two moons, one reddish in color and the other white like home. It was not his first time sleeping out under the stars, only his first time sleeping under them on another world. His first night on Safanar was filled with a dreamless sleep, as if the previous weeks had finally caught up with him. If he dreamt, he was blissfully unaware. He knew that with Zeus there he would be safe enough, and if not, he would at least be warned.

The next morning, he decided to chance walking upon the road, and before lunch, he reached a small town. The town reminded him of the old Western frontier towns he had seen pictures of in history books. Broad, dusty streets lined with worn, but well-maintained buildings—some more elaborately decorated than others. Some of the buildings were made of a type of stone masonry construction rather than wood.

The townsfolk bustled with activity, and although a few glanced at Zeus because of his great size, no one's gaze lingered for long. From under his hood, Aaron scanned the people and buildings as he walked by. He turned down the main thoroughfare to the town's square. A small crowd had gathered, but most walking by were determined to stare straight ahead, ignoring the activity of those around them. Then he heard screams.

Aaron was about to make a quiet withdrawal, but decided to press closer, gaining a better vantage point. A man plainly dressed in a leather apron was being held by the riders in brown cloaks that he saw yesterday. A gauntleted fist slammed home into the man's middle, and he sagged to the ground, gasping for air. Some onlookers cheered, but most looked on with fear, silently praying for a quick conclusion. A small boy that couldn't have been more than ten years of age burst through the throng of people.

"Please," the boy screamed, "don't hurt him. That's my father." Tears streamed down his worried face, and his eyes searched frantically through the crowd for someone to help. But most people in the crowd wouldn't meet his gaze. Those that did would never help by the look of it.

Aaron's pulse raced. *Why doesn't someone do something?* he thought. Another brown-cloaked rider ran up and launched a vicious kick at the man as he struggled to his feet. Aaron clenched the rune-carved staff in his hand.

"No!" the boy cried, and charged feebly to the man who was about to kick again. The rider spun quickly and lifted the child up by his shirt. The man on the ground screamed, struggling to get up, but two men pushed him down with their boot heels, while a third grabbed him by the hair, pulling his head up.

"This boy needs to learn some respect for the guardsmen of the Elite."

The boy's face paled in fear as the dreaded gauntleted fist drew back. The boy's father screamed.

Aaron pressed his way forward. "I don't think so," he growled, and swung the rune-carved staff into the face of guardsman holding the boy. The guardsman's nose exploded into a river of blood as he fell onto his back, releasing the boy to the ground. The other guardsmen were so stunned that, for a few moments, they stared at their companion writhing upon the ground while the crowd seemed to hold its breath.

The guardsmen recovered quickly and drew their swords, fanning out to face Aaron. These were hard men with the seasoned coldness that accompanies those who have faced death in their lives. The crowd quickly scrambled out of the way, and the boy ran to his father's aid.

Aaron held the staff ready and beckoned with his other hand tauntingly for the men to have at him. The first man lunged, and Aaron quickly sidestepped, allowing the guardsman to overextend, then paid him dearly with several crushing blows. While the other guardsmen were strong and skilled, they were no match for Aaron as he weaved in and out between them, delivering decisive blows until he was the only one standing.

He'd never thought his life would become anything resembling a daily life-and-death struggle, but it was becoming that way. He had enjoyed the sparring room back home because there it was competition, it was fun, and it was for learning. If a mistake were made, you worked to correct it next time. But here, if he made a mistake, it could be the end of him. He didn't know why the guardsmen were beating that man, but he couldn't just sit back and let them hurt a child.

"Well, what do we have here?" a voice hissed behind him.

Aaron spun and saw one of the blue-cloaked riders standing before him with his sword drawn. His sword was single edged with serrations on the opposite side, a vile-looking thing.

"I believe your men were out of line," Aaron replied.

The man regarded him coolly. "No, no that won't do at all," he said, circling to one side, dividing his gaze between the fallen guardsmen and Aaron. "But I cannot tolerate such insolence from one such as you. If I did, where would it end?" the man asked with the surety of one who would squash a bug. The arrogance of it darkened Aaron's anger.

"I didn't kill any of your men. I just taught them a lesson," Aaron said.

"You dare raise your hand against a guardsman dispensing justice, a deed punishable by death?"

"Beating a father and son in a town square is what you call justice? What were their crimes?" Aaron asked. "I suppose if I raise my staff against you, that is also punishable by death?"

The murmuring crowd watched the two of them with a sense of fear and of hope. There was no change in the blue rider's demeanor except for his body springing into action, spinning his terrible blade in an all-out attack. Although Aaron was ready for the attack, he was pressed backward by the sheer ferocity of the charge. Aaron remained vigilant in his defense, but would rather have had his swords in his hands than his staff. The man he faced was highly skilled. He anticipated Aaron's movements well and used that to his advantage. Aaron sought the calmness of his inner core until there was nothing left around him except for the man he was facing. His movements became quicker and more precise. The key to his survival was in the boundaries of his own mind. The medallion grew warm against the tender skin of his chest, and the whispers urged his movements. The rune-carved staff grew warm in his hands, and sparks burst forth as blade met wood. Through his opponent's shock, Aaron swept the man's legs out from under him. The remaining people in the town square gasped and looked at Aaron in awe, but none more so than the blue rider who was lying flat on his back.

"My Lord," said several townsfolk as they sank to their knees.

Aaron's mouth dropped open when he realized they were speaking to him. "Ferasdiam," he heard whispered from more than one person. The blue rider erupted from the ground, screaming in rage and flailing his blade. Aaron was ready; he became one with the urgings and whisperings that came from within and was able to move with a mastery he had never felt before. The flow of blade and staff resumed until Aaron struck decisively, sending the man several feet back in a heap. The blade clattered onto the paving stones, out of reach. The man gained his feet once more, with one hand clutching his chest and the other drawn within.

Aaron sensed the energy gathering within the man in a dark foreshadowing. He brought up his staff as the man shot his hand out, sending a cracking blue beam of energy burning toward him. The staff flared to life as a white light encompassed him. The blue lightning glanced off the staff and disappeared into the ground. There was the distinct sound of the snap of a bowstring, and a shaft protruded from the man's chest.

"You are either the bravest or the luckiest man I've ever seen," said a mirthful voice.

Aaron looked up, seeing a young man smiling down at him from his horse. He wore a dark cloak and a wide-brimmed black hat with a rather large feather sticking out one side, reminding Aaron of a Musketeer.

"Here, I brought this for you," he said, holding out the reins to a second horse behind him. "Not to worry. It was his. While you may be handy with a staff, I think we should make our way out of here before all this attention becomes a bit overwhelming." The young man's mirthful smile vanished as he turned to address the crowd. "Let it be known that the Elite are not as infallible as they would have you believe. There are those who can fight them. Spread the tale of this day, but for now, please empty this square. I can already hear the other guardsmen approach."

Aaron took the reins and mounted the horse. The young man regarded him for a moment, then nodded and extended his hand. "I am Verona Ryder, and it is my esteemed pleasure to make your acquaintance, but we must save further introductions for later, my friend. The road calls." And with that, he gave his horse a good kick and galloped away.

Aaron turned to see the boy helping his father to his feet. The father looked as if he were about to say something, but Aaron nodded, gesturing for him to leave. They waved appreciatively, then became lost within the scattering crowd. Hearing the shouts of the guardsmen, Aaron kicked his horse into a gallop, following Verona Ryder.

***

"You presume much," the Elitesman said, shifting his blue cloak, his disgusted gaze sweeping over both the disoriented guardsmen still gaining their bearings and his dead companion.

"It is more important that we inform Mactar and the High King." The old wizard had been on tenterhooks since Tye's unfortunate demise, but Darven suspected it was a theatrical performance.

"Darven, the Council of Masters must be informed as well. The taking down of an Elite is troubling, even one as pathetic as this one," he said, gesturing toward the dead man. "Do you truly believe that this man is the Heir of Shandara?"

"Oh yes, it's him. I was there the night that Tye was killed. I've faced him before." Darven paused for a moment. "Seth," Darven called, and one of the guardsmen detached himself from the rest. "Follow them. They are taking the same road as you to meet up with your party."

"My identity might be compromised," Seth replied, but Darven cared little for the pitiful doings of an average guardsman.

Fixing the man with a rocky gaze, he said, "Risk is part of the job."

The iciness of his tone betrayed nothing of the empty feeling he felt in his gut. The Heir of Shandara should be dead. He shouldn't have been able to come through the crossroads, not with the safeguards Mactar had in place. He watched Seth's eyes flash briefly in anger, but he schooled his emotions soon enough. Darven brought out two small crystals, both alike in appearance, and handed one to Seth. These crystals were a marvel; when keyed properly they allowed the bearer to communicate with whoever had the crystal's twin. "I want regular reports, but be wary of that man," he said, gesturing to the road. "His name is Aaron, and he is very dangerous." Before the other could raise any questions, he said, "Mactar has plans for him. That is all." He gave a brief salute, and Seth turned and stalked off.

Darven turned back to the Elitesman. "There are forces at work here beyond you and me. We must inform the right people and complete our mission," he said, making a silent prayer for the legendary Elitesmen singular purpose to not manifest itself today. He knew what the Elitesman wanted, and it wasn't as simple as Aaron's blood. Master Elitesmen were ever seekers of those who could be brought to their order, or the alternative, which was the challenge of the hunt. They were a class above men, and their order was a mystery even to Darven, who had been cast out, but he knew enough to show respect and a small amount of fear to those of the Elite order.

"Very well," the Elitesman said, tearing his eyes away from the road. He closed his eyes, his brow wrinkled in concentration, then brought his hands to his mouth and blew out a single melodious note. A raven appeared and shot forth in a blurring dark streak across the sky. "The Elite council will be informed and will pass the information on to the High King," he said to a very stunned Darven. "Let's go," he commanded. The guardsmen and Darven wasted no time in making for the road, for it was unwise to dally when an Elitesman's patience was being stretched.

CHAPTER 15
FERASDIAM MARKED

Zeus kept the pace, easily gliding through the surrounding forest, but he also kept his distance, appearing briefly ahead of them in silent beckoning. How long would Zeus stay with him? He had helped Aaron through the crossroads to Safanar—shouldn't he now seek to be with his own kind? They had been riding a short while when Verona asked if he thought they were being followed.

"Probably," Aaron answered. With his luck, it would be a certainty.

Verona eyed him. "Well, let's hope my luck proves true this day, my friend," he said as if hearing Aaron's thoughts.

"Thanks for your help back there," Aaron said.

"You seemed to have things well in hand, although why you would choose to tangle with an Elitesman is beyond me, but I'm glad you did. You've brought hope to that small town and allowed a father and son to escape the poorness of their timing," Verona said, frowning as he stole a glance behind them.

Aaron wanted to ask the obvious question about what an Elitesman was, but doing so would only confirm his proverbial "not from around these parts" status. Verona appeared to be close to his own age, and his instincts told him that Verona could be a friend. What would it cost Verona to be his friend? Aaron wondered darkly. He would gain nothing by being closed off from others, and he needed help if he was going to find this Prince Cyrus. Where was Colind? He had hoped to meet him when he came through.

"I am Aaron Jace," he said, extending his hand, but in his mind he whispered, *of the house Alenzar'seth.*

"Well met, Aaron," Verona said, shaking his hand firmly. "It seems as if luck is not with us, at least in regards to avoiding pursuit." Verona gestured behind them to the distinct dust plume of the riders who were on their trail. "Well, they won't find this fox such easy quarry. Are you with me, Aaron?"

"I'm the one being hunted; perhaps it would be better for you if we went our separate ways."

"Nonsense," Verona replied, shaking his head. "I've got my fair share of trouble following me. Besides, how can I abandon the first person in a generation to take down an Elite? You intrigue me, Master Jace, and it's not mere happenstance that fate put us in the pot."

Aaron looked doubtful as the dust cloud from the riders loomed ever closer. They needed to get moving.

"Colind sent me to find you. I can explain more later, but we have to go now."

"Colind?!" Aaron said. "Let's go."

They kept a sturdy pace for a time, occasionally walking their horses to conserve their strength. The forest grew thick around them, and the road faded to a barely discernible path in some places, but still they pressed forward. A shadow engulfed the sky above them and then disappeared just as quickly.

"Did you see it?" Verona asked, glancing up at the sky.

"No, but earlier I heard the Elitesman refer to something called a Ryakul flying the skies. The guardsman believed it to be a dragon," Aaron replied.

"I see. No, definitely not a dragon. The Ryakul have indeed grown bold if they venture here," Verona said. "Come, I'll tell you on the way. I'm due to meet with some friends in a couple of days, and we must keep moving." Verona took out his longbow and rested it on his lap.

After walking a short distance, Zeus came up silently and nuzzled Aaron's hand. Verona gasped, catching sight of the wolf, and Aaron quickly assured him that Zeus was a friend.

"There are not many men that a wolf would befriend," Verona remarked. "It's an allegiance that has faded with the passage of time, I'm afraid. And I fear our loss from it is greater than theirs."

"He was my grandfather's and has been with me since he died."

Verona nodded. "There are more knowledgeable people who can tell you a great deal about the Ryakul, but since they are absent, I will shamefully attempt to use my meager knowledge to shed some light on the subject."

Aaron couldn't help but smile a bit at the short speech; the man certainly had energy.

"The Ryakul kill indiscriminately, whether man or beast. Dragons appear to be their mortal enemy, but there are few dragons left, and many Ryakul remain, and no one knows for sure the reason why.

They do not belong here. There are stories that the Ryakuls came from another world and were released during the fall of Shandara." Verona paused, going around some branches. "Many things were released during that time, but most were imprisoned by Reymius Alenzar'seth before he died at Shandara."

Aaron nearly tripped at the casual mention of his grandfather.

"You know of Reymius?" Verona asked.

"I know him," Aaron replied, but before Verona noted the distinction, he added, "Tell me about Colind, please."

"Ah yes, Colind," Verona said, his eyes hardening. "Do you believe in ghosts, Aaron? Because I would doubt the validity of my own perceptions if I didn't see what I saw with my own eyes."

"It's not a matter of belief for me anymore. Recently the unexplained has a knack of finding me," Aaron said dryly.

"It was not three nights gone when Colind appeared to me, but at the time I didn't know it was him. You see, Colind, like Reymius, is a man upon which legends have been made, and he's been gone for a long time. He didn't seem like the man that all the stories claimed he was. He was withered and stooped with haunted eyes, but I swear I saw strength in them still. And anticipation. He told me that a new hope was coming to this land and I should watch for it at Duncan's Port. A stranger would appear and I should offer my aid to him. When I saw you in the town, I knew it had to be you," Verona said, watching Aaron. "He said he didn't have much time, but had a message for you, and these are his words exactly. 'Beware the beast that has slept with your family's leaving, for it will wake, yearning for the hunt upon your arrival.' That was all. I'm hoping that it makes more sense to you than it does to me."

Aaron stood in silence, taking in the message that both Colind and Daverim, his ancestor, had warned him about...that he would be hunted. "I had hoped that Colind would be here."

"He found us once; perhaps he will find us again. What did Colind say to you?" Verona asked.

"A great deal, but not enough, it seems. The last thing he said to me was to seek out Prince Cyrus, but I don't know who or where he is."

Verona's eyes widened at the mention of Prince Cyrus. "Do you have any idea why he wanted you to seek out the prince?"

He wasn't sure how much he should tell Verona, who was all but a stranger to him, but how could he expect Verona to help him if he didn't know at least something? "I am a stranger to this place, but I think it would be safer for both our sakes if we didn't delve too much into this right now. I don't know you, and you don't know me—" Aaron stopped himself. "Look, I appreciate all of your help, but if you want to change your mind and go your own way, I will understand. Just point me in the general direction so I can find this Prince Cyrus, and I will make my own way."

Verona stared at him with a look of honest bewilderment. "What kind of man would I be if I abandoned you out here?" he asked, sweeping his hand out, gesturing to the forest around them. "A man of legend asks for my help, which will probably be one of the most significant events to happen in my life, and you ask me if I want to walk away? A charge has been given to me by Colind of the Safanarion Order to help you on your journey. Fate has called upon me, Aaron. Who am I not to heed her call? I promise. Nay, I pledge," he said with his fist across his heart, "that I will see this through to the end and stand by your side as a friend."

The offer hung in the air between them. "You don't even know me. You don't know what you're getting yourself into. Are you willing to risk your life for the words of a ghost?" Aaron asked.

"In this you are mistaken, my friend. I've seen your quality when you stood up to the injustice at the town of Duncan's Port and spared a father and son a horrible end. The winds of change are upon us, and I know in my heart that they have to do with you. So where you go, I follow. As for the trouble that will come of it, well…" He paused with a small, inviting smile. "Trouble has a way of finding us all."

The look of conviction in Verona's eyes left little doubt in Aaron's mind that he meant every word. Back home, his reaction would be that Verona was crazy, but here in this place, he didn't have the luxury of time nor of beating around the bush. Life and death were present in everyday life, but here, out in this world, it seemed to be brought to the forefront. He had a feeling that Verona would prove to be the best friend he would ever know.

"Thank you," Aaron said, shaking Verona's hand firmly. In that single moment, Aaron felt some of the weight lift from his shoulders due to the comfort that only companionship could give.

A short while later, with the sun ebbing away, they reached a clearing. Verona stopped his horse. The woodland around them seemed to draw in its breath in silent anticipation. Aaron's horse snorted nervously, pawing at the ground. An ear-piercing roar came from across the clearing, rattling the trees in its wake and making them jump. A cavernous roar answered, and a dragon launched itself into the air with four Ryakuls in pursuit, their giant bat-like wings whooshing through the air.

The dragon, in all his majesty and savage beauty, reflected the sun, blazing like a star in the sky, and the Ryakuls pursued, swallowing up the light. The Ryakul were the antithesis of the dragon, sharing powerful arms and talons, but that was where the similarities ended. The hide of a Ryakul was glossy black, and its long neck ended in a gaping saber-tusked maw in direct contrast to a dragon's proud head. The dragon turned in midair, roaring its challenge, which the Ryakuls eagerly answered, rising up for their quarry. Aaron's heart thundered in his chest, but he couldn't tear his eyes away from the dragon. The tattoo on his chest throbbed, and the medallion grew warm against his skin. The battle that ensued had a ferocious brutality like nothing Aaron had ever seen. Two of the Ryakuls were brought down in a twisted heap, but not before extracting their toll on the dragon in the form of large gashes along his golden hide. The dragon fought with agility and blinding speed, flourishing teeth and talon alike. The ground shook with its landing, and the remaining two Ryakuls approached warily.

The dragon's gaze fixed upon Aaron, noticing them for the first time. Aaron took a step forward, enamored by the dragon's gaze and feeling utterly exposed at the same time. The Ryakuls lunged toward the dragon, which broke his eye contact with Aaron. Without a thought, Aaron drew his Falcons and charged. As he swept across the clearing, the wind raced past his swords, and a few notes of the bladesong were released. The Ryakuls stopped instantly and turned, their terrible green eyes fixed upon Aaron, who stopped in his tracks.

A small breeze tugged at Aaron's cloak. He was rooted in place, feeling nothing but the burning of the dragon tattoo on his chest and the stirring of power from the medallion. He began to wield the Falcons with a savage need to smite the abomination before him. The melodic tune from the bladesong bewitched the Ryakuls long enough for the dragon to seize the opportunity to strike. A powerful swipe with the end of its armored tail nearly severed a Ryakul in half, but instead of blood, black vapor hissed free.

The remaining Ryakul charged toward Aaron, its black wings spread, but it remained on the ground, propelling itself with giant leaps in reckless abandon. The dragon pounced mightily, driving the thrashing Ryakul into the ground. The two beasts were a tangle of claw and talon, each snapping at the other. Aaron closed the distance between them as the Ryakul's soulless green eyes fixed upon him, even with the dragon tearing the life from it. Aaron roared as he leaped, driving his Falcons through the eyes of the Ryakul, avoiding the saber-sized tusks from its mouth.

The dragon eyed him curiously. The boiling rage within him that demanded the death of the Ryakul had subsided, and calmness returned. Aaron sheathed his swords and held out his empty palms, showing the dragon that he meant no harm. He wasn't sure why he sheathed his swords, but it felt right not to arm himself in the presence of a dragon. Perhaps because they shared a common enemy-- the Ryakul could be nothing else to him. Verona was right. They were an abomination. The dragon snorted and turned, favoring one of its legs, and limped off.

"Are you okay?" Verona called behind him.

Aaron couldn't take his eyes off the dragon and tried to resist the urge to follow. The dragon looked back and cocked its head at them, then kept going.

"Let's follow him," Aaron said. Verona nodded, clearly at a loss for words. Aaron spoke soothing words to the horses, rubbing gently at their necks, and they calmed down enough to follow the dragon. They kept their distance at first, but with the passage of time, they grew bolder. The dragon turned to look at them a few more times, and when he was satisfied that they were following, he didn't look back again. As time went on, the dragon's breathing became more labored. All the graceful agility the dragon displayed in his battle with the Ryakuls was fading with each strenuous step. Aaron asked Verona if he had any idea where the dragon was taking them.

"I'm not sure," Verona replied. "What happened to you back there?" he asked, seizing the moment for conversation. "One moment you were next to me, and the next you charged. Where did you get those swords? They're like nothing I've ever seen before."

Aaron took a moment to gather his thoughts. He'd been thinking the same thing for a while. Why did he charge into that clearing? "I'm not sure what came over me. When I saw the dragon making his stand against all those Ryakuls, it was as if I had become the dragon and his fight became my fight," Aaron said, absently rubbing the dragon tattoo beneath his shirt. "These swords were bequeathed to me by my grandfather when he died."

Verona swallowed and glanced at the dragon. "There are stories, legends really, about men of the Safanarion Order whose connection to their souls was so in tune and strong that their connection to every living thing was amplified to a level of unspeakable proportions. They could feel the life force of all those around them. Many believed that they could read minds, but perhaps it was due to their heightened perceptions that they were able to know what was in a man's heart, even if that man himself didn't know. Not sure about that. They were more in tune with all forms of life and were therefore both shunned and rejoiced by man. In some cases, like in recent history, they were hunted by those jealous of their power. Legend says that the Safanarion Order's most gifted members were known to have the mark of the Goddess. Ferasdiam Marked, it was called. If what you are saying is true, then perhaps *you* are such a man," Verona said. After considering for a moment, he spoke again. "Who was your grandfather?" he asked in a tone that belied the seriousness of the question.

At some point during Verona's speech, Aaron had clenched his jaw shut and been about to reply, but the dragon had abruptly stopped, its labored breathing coming in gasps.

There is no time.

Aaron heard the words in his mind and looked to Verona for some confirmation that he too heard them, but there was none.

He cannot hear me. Only you as a bearer of our mark can speak and walk among us in this way. Only the bearer of the staff will have the power to aid us and drive away the spawn of shadow. You must come. There is no time.

The dragon swung its mighty head, his golden eyes peering at them intently.

"He looks hungry," Verona whispered nervously.

"No, he won't harm us," Aaron whispered back. He focused himself as he would if wielding the Falcons, and immediately his perceptions sharpened. The power was there at his call; all he needed to do was reach out.

What can I do to help you? Can I ease your pain somehow?

The dragon narrowed its gaze, turned away, and began taking great strides ahead, and they had to leap to catch up.

Just keep up. There is something you must see.

The pace the dying dragon set left them little chance for talking. All their efforts were to simply keep up. The horses grew increasingly nervous, and they decided to lead them rather than ride. They climbed a steep hill, and the setting sun filled the sky behind them in a brilliant orange blaze. Aaron could no longer see the clearing where they'd first encountered the dragon and was amazed at how far they had traveled. Thighs burning with every effort, they crested the hill and were met with a twilight sky on the other side. They stood at the ring of a vast crater where the trees grew thick, blocking their view of its mysterious interior.

Aaron peered down and noticed the occasional stone tower peeking out over the forest canopy. The towers looked old and worn down, as if slowly being consumed by the forest. The dragon thundered down the crater, making its own path, and Aaron followed. The thick gnarled trees gave way grudgingly to the dragon's hapless passing. There was something down there amid the ruins, hidden in the forest. The air felt vibrant with energy, and a sense of calm settle in all around him. He looked at Verona, who nodded his unspoken confirmation that he felt it too. He hadn't answered Verona's question earlier, but he knew sooner or later the subject of his lineage would come up again. A faint mist toiled on the ground as they made their way deeper into the crater. Verona produced a glowing crystal hanging on the end of a chain. The crystal gave them just enough light to see by. As they continued to follow the dragon, Aaron noticed a faint light glowing in the distance.

"What do you think it is?" Verona asked, breaking the silence.

"I don't know. Let's go see," Aaron said quickly.

He barely saw Zeus trotting ahead, the end of his bushy tail just catching the light. Aaron quickened his pace and they emerged into a clearing. A circle of white columns surrounded a pool of water lined with stone. Something in the water was glowing, sending shimmering waves of light dancing upon the trees and columns alike. The light grew brighter as they approached, revealing the statue of a beautiful woman seemingly standing on the water. The trick of the light made her flowing gown shift among the shadows.

The dragon heaved its body down behind the pool with its tail and head wrapped on either side. The light reflecting off its golden hide showered them in a rainbow of color. The eyes of the statue were startlingly lifelike, capturing an essence of pride and strength, making Aaron want stand taller. Through the shimmering light, her appearance changed from a beloved sister to mother to friend to lover, all in cyclical elegance. The darkness that dwelled in his heart inched back grudgingly, but the molten anger and sadness refused to give way completely. He held onto them as he would to a cliff to keep from falling into the void. He would have his vengeance.

Aaron stepped closer, and the rune-carved staff tingled in his hands, sending eddies of energy coursing through him. The dragon tattoo on his chest ached anew, and he winced. The eyes of the statue drew him in and he stood spellbound.

"*You are in the presence of the Goddess,*" the dragon said, and Verona must have heard him, because he sank to his knees, muttering a prayer.

Aaron tore his eyes away from the statue, and the dragon stared pointedly back at him.

"It's a statue," Aaron said.

It's a symbol, the dragon replied.

The tattoo on his chest flared anew, making Aaron wince at the sharp, burning pain.

Cleanse the mark of Ferasdiam with the sacred waters.

The burning intensified, and Aaron scrambled to get his shirt off. He plunged his hands into the cool water and quickly brought them up to his chest over and over until the burning subsided. The pain was completely gone. The dragon markings on his chest no longer appeared fresh, but looked as if they had always been there. Perhaps they had, and coming to this world made the mark of the dragon come forward. He wondered if his grandfather had known about this. What could they have done, regardless? He turned to snatch up his shirt when he heard Verona gasp, staring wide-eyed at him.

"You are one of the gifted, a member of the Safanarion Order. You are Ferasdiam Marked," Verona said, pointing at Aaron's chest.

Aaron snatched his shirt from the floor. His medallion was safely hidden in the folds of his shirt. He put them both on at the same time, keeping the medallion hidden. The medallion had his family crest, which would surely announce who he was, and he didn't want that known until he knew more about the Alenzar'seth.

"I didn't have this mark until yesterday. I don't know where it came from or what it means," Aaron said.

Gaze into the sacred waters and allow the Goddess to show you her vision, the dragon said.

Aaron slowly stepped up to the water's edge, bracing himself for what he was about to see. Verona and Zeus joined him, and he was comforted by their presence. He steadied himself, taking a deep, focusing breath, and gazed into the calm waters. The light deep within the water flared brighter, beginning to pulse, becoming more intense. Aaron looked up, his eyes transfixed on the statue in silent anticipation. Then, in a space between moments, the eyes of the statue opened, revealing an orchestra of images so vast that he felt as if the world both faded away and collided with him at the same time. A dark and dismal land devoid of life, where a lone beacon of light blazed, drawing him closer. He found himself surrounded by the ruins of a vast castle, whose craftsmanship and sheer majestic qualities were clearly evident, even in its dilapidated state. He focused in on a tower, which had a massive carved relief of a dragon caressing a single precious rose, and his mind reeled in recognition of the Alenzar'seth's family symbol. The images shifted to a lone white tree amid a courtyard, which stood in stark contrast to the shadow lands about. Aaron knew immediately that he had to go there. A series of images swept by too fast for him to register, but he recognized Colind and a lone hand bearing the mark of a leaf on its palm.

The land needs a champion. Time is short, and already the sickness spreads. Ryakuls are just the beginning of what was unleashed at the fall of Shandara.

The words and images were synonymous in his mind, and all begged the question of what he could do about this. He was a stranger to this land. This was not his home. The remains of his home were nothing but a burned-out shell devoid of anything to mark the passing of better days. He came here seeking vengeance and to protect those he loved.

The fate of the land falls upon the house of Alenzar'seth, of which you are the last. Guardianship of the land is a legacy shared with the Safanarion Order, who have all but vanished. Fate has chosen you for this.

"I make my own fate!" Aaron shouted at the dragon. "They brought this battle to me. I didn't ask for this," he said, drawing his swords and throwing them down to the ground. "They murdered my—I want Mactar, and in order for me to get to him, I need Colind. Where can I find him?"

The fury erupted like a deadly viper, turning his molten blood to acid. He had been here before, the place where the fires of his rage took him, where he hated everything, including living. His life meant nothing in the face of vengeance; so dark was his vision that everything turned gray and meaningless around him. He struggled against the tumultuous darkness threatening to reign supreme inside him.

Remember who you are! His father's deep voice filled his ears. A lone voice of reason amid a furious storm. This wasn't who he was, he told himself over and over again, and like a spark to a flame, his sense of self returned, but the echo of dark rage remained imprinted upon the edges.

The dragon stared at him pointedly. *Your quest for vengeance will consume you if you let it.*

"It's all I have," Aaron said.

The dragon regarded him, looking exhausted. *The choice is yours. The wanderer dwells in his prison among the ruins of Shandara. Seek him out there if you will, but be warned he is not as he once was.*

The dragon laid his head down with a great sigh and breathed no more. A golden hue surrounded it, his body becoming transparent and then transforming into countless golden sparkles that ascended into the night sky. Aaron's shoulders slumped and his throat thickened. Dragons were the stuff of legends back home, and a real-life encounter with such a majestic creature was awe-inspiring to say the least. They were creatures of high intelligence and purpose, not simpletons ruled by animalistic passion.

The eyes of the statue closed once more, and the light coming from the waters diminished to a soothing glow. While Aaron stood staring at those waters, Verona had built a good-sized fire. Aaron went over to the fire and sat down across from Verona, who absently stoked the flames.

"I can tell that you have experienced a great loss, and for that I convey my sincerest condolences," Verona began. "What passed between you and the dragon I do not know because he gave me my own message. Every man harbors secrets for his own reasons. Fear not that I will press you for yours. I said it before, and I'll say it again— where you go, I will follow. Our paths are connected."

Aaron nodded, not knowing what to say. "Can you tell me about a place called Shandara and what you know of the man Reymius Alenzar'seth?" It was the first time he'd said the name aloud, and it made his heart pound to say it.

"I've never seen Shandara. I was a small boy when Shandara fell, and most of what I know is just stories. You would do well to ask the lore masters when we reach Rexel or Prince Cyrus himself. He was the one whom Colind said you should seek," Verona said.

"That's right, but the dragon said that Colind dwells in his prison among the ruins of Shandara," Aaron replied.

"Shandara was described as a truly wondrous place, home to the Safanarion Order. The Alenzar'seths were of royal blood and keepers of the great seal, a gift from the Hythariam folk, who are themselves legend, but have withdrawn from the world of men. The Shandara that exists today is a land devoid of life and consumed by shadow."

"Not all of it," Aaron said quickly and a bit defensively, which surprised him. "The dragon showed me a white tree that grows among the ruins of a vast palace. That is where I need to go." He could feel the compulsion within fueled by his need for revenge. He would do what must be done, but at what cost?

Verona eyed him. "We will need help if that is our road. We should do as Colind advised and seek out Cyrus, the prince at Rexel. Now about Reymius Alenzar'seth. He was there at the fall of Shandara. In some ways, he bore responsibility for its collapse, and in other ways, he saved the rest of us by staving off what was unleashed there. Misguided use of power and betrayal is what my uncle tells me. Much of what transpired is a mystery to all but those who were at the heart of it. I wish I knew more, but history was never one of my strengths. What I know of Reymius is the stuff of heroes and stories. Despite his birthright, he was ranked high in the Safanarion Order and was something of a diplomat with the Hythariam folk. Now and again there are whispers from small towns about a trapper seeing some of the Hythariam, but they always disappear, some vanishing right before their eyes," Verona finished, stifling a yawn.

Aaron yawned himself. "That's all right. Tell me more tomorrow. We have enough to go on, I think," Aaron replied, settling back on the ground. He rolled up a blanket for a pillow and gazed up at the brilliantly clear night sky. Though his thoughts were not idle, sleep soon came to him as his second day in the land called Safanar drew to a close. Under the watchful eyes of the statue of the Goddess, the weary travelers slept.

CHAPTER 16
THE SUMMONS

The mirror's empty reflection hung in silent defiance that gnawed at him. Mactar mulled the whereabouts of Tarimus, staring fixedly into the mirror, which had been empty since the shaking of the earth that announced the coming of Reymius's heir. The blood of the house Alenzar'seth held the key to Shandara. He called to Tarimus through the mirror, but it mocked him again with its silence.

"Prisons don't last forever, nor do prisoners for that matter. Sooner or later, they break or escape. You have much to answer for," a silky voice purred from the window.

Mactar turned, seeing a veiled face, but no one could mistake those depthless blue eyes framed in creamy skin that had made many a foolish man go willingly to his death. Those icy eyes were transfixed upon him and for a moment gave even him pause. Of all High King Amorak's heirs, it was his daughter, Sarah, that was a step above the rest and would not be swayed as her younger brother had been. All the difference a mother can make. This one was a hunter at heart, and the world was her quarry. Not a pampered princess by any means, she possessed a single-minded determination to rival his own. Stepping away from the window with her leopard-like grace, the golden-haired beauty removed her veil. Arrogance was a fitting word to describe all Amorak's heirs, but unlike the bravado of her brothers, she either had true potential or was a grave threat. He couldn't decide which.

"My father will receive you now," she said, holding a purple travel crystal.

"So you've risen in the ranks to the king's messenger?" Mactar taunted, but he knew that Sarah would never give in to so menial an insult. "So be it. I have something for your esteemed father in the other room."

Sarah eyed him coolly, following him. "What are you playing at?"

"Trust me," Mactar said, gesturing to a dark cylinder suspended in the air above a small pedestal.

Sarah waited patiently, her face impassive, and Mactar applauded her for not rising to the bait. Dangerous indeed.

"Your fool's errand cost Tye his life, and no amount of *gifts* will quell my father's anger."

"Perhaps, my dear," Mactar replied patiently. "We will see. Regardless, there are forces at work here beyond the son of the king. Besides, he has two more sons ready to inherit."

A momentary flash of anger arrayed itself across her eyes, but instead of continuing their verbal sparring match, she activated the purple travel crystal, all the while fixing him with a stony stare.

"Won't you be joining us?" Mactar asked, raising an inquisitive brow.

"As much as I would enjoy watching you squirm before my father, I have other duties to attend to and nothing you need concern yourself with."

"Ah yes, would those duties require you to travel to the east? South of Rexel, perhaps?" Mactar replied in a sunny tone. He had gotten the Elitesman report as well when it came to the Council of Masters. The report of a mysterious stranger who had taken down an Elitesman was intriguing to say the least.

The golden-haired beauty regarded him with a look of utter boredom. "Grovel well, my Lord," she said, and then activated the travel crystal, cutting off his response.

Arrogance indeed was his last thought before the flashing of light.

***

The princess stood among Mactar's vile furnishings and could no longer mask her utter contempt for the home of the Dark Wizard. His slippery fingers were in everything, but so far she had not fallen prey to one of his schemes. She had heard the report about the mysterious stranger who had taken down an Elite, but it wasn't that which drew her attention. It was a restlessness she had been feeling of late. She sought solace at an abandoned church devoted to the Goddess located along the fringes of her father's kingdom. It was one of the few things she clung to in her mother's memory. She'd been there when the earth shook and a soft voice whispered in her ears, *One of the old blood has returned.* That was all that was said, and it happened so fast that she might have imagined it.

She stood silently regarding the mirror that Mactar had watched so intently. There was no reflection, only an inky black void.

Sarah, a slithering voice taunted slowly. *Beware the man marked by dragons*, it hissed.

She grasped the travel crystal and disappeared in a flash of light, but not before she heard a mirthless cackle coming from the mirror.

CHAPTER 17
HIDDEN AMONG THE SHADOWS

Aaron snapped awake, gasping for breath, and the dark dreams that held him abated. The sun was chasing away the morning fog, and the lingering unease slowly retreated just below the surface of his thoughts.

"Are you all right?" Verona asked. "Those must have been some dreams. You were muttering most of the night, but I guess that is to be expected given the circumstances," Verona said, glancing at the statue.

Aaron wondered what he had been muttering, and for a moment he considered just telling Verona everything.

"We should get moving," Verona said.

The two men broke camp. They kept a good pace, rotating between riding and leading their horses, each of the mindset that if the time came when they truly needed to run, they could. But avoiding conflict would be preferable. Aaron kept weighing whether he should tell Verona who he was. Caution and honor were warring within him. His life was in Verona's hands just as surely as Verona's was in his own

—hadn't he already proved that?

They decided to rest for a bit.

"Who is Bronwyn, if you don't mind me asking?" Verona asked.

Aaron was taking a sip of water and began coughing. "Bronwyn is a girl I knew," he said.

"You mentioned her last night. She was important to you," Verona said.

"Aren't they all?" Aaron asked. "Yes, she was important to me." His tone hardened. "She and others near me were all in danger, but I was too blind to see it and didn't act fast enough. She is dead now." He stood up, drew his swords, and slowly began to wield them. The bladesong whispered on the breeze, aligning the energy around him.

"These were bequeathed to me by my grandfather...*Reymius*," Aaron said, staring directly into Verona's astonished eyes. "I am the grandson of Reymius and Cassandra, and son to Patrick and Carlowen Jace. I am of the house Alenzar'seth." He quickly sheathed his blades in a single fluid motion. "I'm sorry I concealed my identity. I didn't think it would be fair for you to travel with me and not understand the risks that come with it."

Aaron watched as Verona gathered his thoughts.

"I knew there was something about you, Aaron, when I first laid eyes on you. You are the Heir of Shandara, and I vow that your identity will stay with me until you give me leave to do otherwise," Verona said with a fist across his heart. "I understand your caution. How could you know whether you could trust me or not? I said it before, and I say it again—I will see this through and stand by your side as a friend even in the face of our death."

The man must be crazy, Aaron thought, but he believed every word Verona said. In this world, there could be no time wasted on foolishness.

"Well, well, if you haven't given us a great chase, my Lord," a voice boomed out from the surrounding trees.

"Surrender now and you will only be a little light on coins," another gruff voice called out.

Verona grinned. "If it's more of a chase you want, just say the word, and we'll be off again, you dogs," Verona shouted. The silence was broken by the hearty laughter from the men concealed by the surrounding forest. "Vaughn, Sarik, and Garret, I know it's you. I would advise you to come forward for I'm afraid my friend here has a rather large wolf for a companion who likes to feed on dogs. Even one as great as you, Vaughn."

Three men extracted themselves from the surrounding trees, all with broad smiles. "Well met, my Lord," said the man in the middle, grinning.

"Well met, Vaughn," Verona said, extending his hand to the bear of a man, who had traces of gray in his hair and beard. "May I introduce you to Aaron Jace, another such as we who has a talent for attracting trouble." Aaron shook each of their hands in turn, and all returned a firm handshake. "Where are Eric and Braden?" Verona inquired.

"Camp is set up a few miles north of here. We were hunting for dinner when we quite literally stumbled onto you," Vaughn said, leading the way. "I had expected to meet up with you much sooner and at the wayward point," he said, raising an eyebrow. "Did you get sidetracked again? What was her name?"

"An old friend came to me with a request that I couldn't refuse," Verona answered with a twinkle in his eyes.

Vaughn frowned. "There has been word of some trouble in one of the smaller towns and some cursed Ryakul activity to the east," Vaughn replied, giving a slight glance overhead.

"We don't have to worry about the Ryakuls for now. Aaron and I witnessed an epic battle between a dragon and four Ryakuls." The word dragon was echoed by the other men while Aaron listened silently. *News travels fast, it seems.*

Vaughn glanced at Aaron. "A knack for finding trouble indeed. Dragons are rarely seen during these times. Though it's troubling that the Ryakuls have ventured this far. I wonder what brought them."

Vaughn happened to be looking at Aaron when he said the last, and it got him thinking. Were the Ryakuls hunting him? Hadn't Daverim Alenzar'seth said beasts of shadow would be drawn to him if he took the cloak and rune-carved staff?

"It could mean that the shadow lands are extending beyond Shandara's borders," said the wiry young man called Sarik. It took almost all of Aaron's concentration to not look at Verona at this point, but he felt the tension in the air between them. Instead, he scanned their surroundings as they made their way up the path.

"Peace, Sarik, you speak of what you do not know," Garret said gently.

"It was just a thought," Sarik replied. "The Ryakuls grow bolder with each passing season," he said, adjusting the quiver of arrows poking over his shoulder. "I'm going to see if I have any more luck finding a decent meal for us without you lot plodding through the forest. I'll see you back at camp," Sarik said, trotting ahead of them.

Vaughn picked up the pace, speaking with Verona as they took the lead. Aaron was just as happy to walk and not be on the saddle of a horse for a while. He watched the two men ahead of him and kept an eye out for Zeus, whom he hadn't seen in a while, although he did hear the sounds of other wolves in the distance. Perhaps Zeus had found a home in this place. As soon as the thought came to mind, he caught a glimpse of the smoky gray wolf through the trees, stopping occasionally to peer at him.

"So there really is a wolf," Garret said.

Aaron nodded.

"How did you end up traveling with Verona?" Garret asked.

"I met up with him in a small town south of here," Aaron replied. "He helped me get out of some trouble."

"Well, that sounds about right. Verona can hardly resist a bit of mischief when the opportunity presents itself," Garret replied in a knowing sort of way. "Is that trouble still following you?"

The question was simple, direct, and straight to the point, which Aaron liked. "Yes," he answered.

Garret nodded as if he had expected nothing less. "Not to worry, Aaron, trouble has a way of finding us all from time to time, and it usually doesn't let up easily once it has arrived."

That's putting it mildly, Aaron thought, and he heard the echo of his father saying that you couldn't always avoid trouble when it came, but you could do your part to prepare for it as best you can.

They traveled swiftly to the camp, where Aaron was introduced to Eric and Braden, who were brothers. Both men were like picturesque warriors taken straight from a Greek sculpture, towering above most men and wearing their swords with the graceful ease of one married to the blade. There was no arrogance in their eyes or mannerisms, which instantly commanded Aaron's respect.

Sarik made it back shortly after them, and luck was with him, Aaron noted, since there was a good-sized deer being prepared for dinner. Aaron had worried that he would be looked upon with suspicion as a newcomer to the group, but all of them trusted Verona, and it was by his leave that they reserved their judgment, which Aaron thought was fair enough. When they all sat down to dinner around the fire, Zeus boldly stepped out of the twilight, his eyes locked upon Sarik, who was portioning out the meal. There was no mistaking the wolf's intent. He expected his share, and it was Garret who directed Sarik to set some aside for the wolf. After Zeus devoured his meal, he moved to Aaron's side and lay by his feet.

"So, Aaron," Braden said casually, "Verona tells us that you took down a member of the Elite order."

The rest hushed to an abrupt silence.

"I stopped some men from hurting a father and his son. I've never heard of this Elite Order before I met Verona," Aaron answered, absently stroking Zeus's fur. Most of them masked their surprised reactions well, but all stole a quick glance at Verona, who gave no reaction at all.

"You must be among the luckiest of men," Braden said, taking out a dagger and sharpening it, his powerful arms making precise thrusts with the stone.

"Luck had nothing to do with it, I can assure you," Verona put in quickly. "There is another Elitesman who has been tracking us, so with all possible speed, our road must take us to Rexel."

The men all spoke at once, but it was Vaughn who silenced them. "The prince advised, no, warned you to not return, family or not. We should consider heeding this warning for the time being," Vaughn said.

"Oh, come on now, Vaughn. It has already been a while; perhaps the old man is in a forgiving mood." Verona smiled mischievously.

"Not long enough, I think. He had the guards chase us out of the city the last time," Vaughn said, smiling, and the others laughed. "Why there? Why to the prince? What business is so important that it requires us to go back there?" Vaughn asked.

"Colind the Guardian is alive," Verona said. "He has been a prisoner all these long years, but it's a prison unlike anything I've ever heard of before."

During the ramble of questions, it was Garret whose deep voice spoke up above the rest. "Where is he?" the older man asked.

Verona took a long look at Aaron, who nodded before he answered, and the others noted it. "In *Shandara*," he answered.

Pandemonium. All agreed that it would be impossible to free Colind from his prison because they could never survive the journey. Absolutely no one in their right mind entered Shandara. Aaron wondered if this would be the reaction of the prince as well. He hoped not. Colind was certain that the prince could help in some way, but he never got to say how or why the prince would help him.

"Don't tell me you honestly mean to trek into Shandara to free him," Vaughn said. "That is a fool's errand if ever I heard one; tell him, Garret."

Aaron cleared his throat and drew the others' attention. "No, it's not Verona's intent to trek into Shandara. It's mine," he said, letting the words hang there for a moment while he met all of their eyes. "I am going to Shandara to free Colind, but I was advised to seek the counsel of Prince Cyrus before I go, by Colind himself. So if it's a fool's errand, then I am fortune's fool, for that is my road."

"And I am going with him," Verona finished.

The silence was deafening; Braden even stopped sharpening his dagger in mid stroke with his mouth open. Garret recovered first. Being the oldest among them, he seemed to be the most levelheaded. Aaron did note the concern in Vaughn's eyes; clearly, he looked on Verona as an uncle would look upon a nephew, and their bond was strong.

"That's quite a declaration, Verona," Garret said evenly. "Why would you agree to go on what many of us would consider a suicide mission? Are you that eager to face your final judgment?"

"Did you not hear him?" Verona said, gesturing toward Aaron. "Colind appeared to him just as he did to me. That's what took me away to Duncan's Port. That's where I met Aaron. Colind's own words were that I should offer my aid to a stranger in the town. One who will stand out from the rest, and I believe that taking down a member of the Elite Order is enough to announce that this is who Colind had in mind. Tell them, Vaughn. You were with me when Colind appeared."

Vaughn stood staring at the fire for a moment. "I saw," he began. "I came at the end, but I did see an apparition vanish before my eyes, and I thought I heard his voice. It could have been Colind."

"It could have been dark magic," Garret said. "We've never attracted the notice of the Dark Light Master, but if this one has attracted the Elite's notice," he said, gesturing toward Aaron, "then it will not be long before it brings Mactar's notice as well, and the High King for that matter."

"Gentlemen, please," Verona said. "I won't ask any of you to go farther than you will. But this is where my path goes, with this man for good or ill. I trust in time, if you will allow, that he will earn all of your trust as you have all earned mine. At least travel with us to see the prince; from there, if you feel that we should part ways, then I shall bear no ill will against any man who does so."

There was a brief moment of silence before Braden sheathed his dagger. "I'm not about to abandon you, my Lord, and I believe you have good reasons for this. My sword, as always, is yours." His brother, Eric, nodded in affirmation.

"As is mine," echoed Sarik.

"To Rexel then," Garret said.

"What say you, Vaughn?" Verona asked.

Vaughn sighed. "I say you're all fools. We shall go to the prince at the very least." Vaughn's eyes strayed toward Aaron, and he noticed the hardness within them show for just a moment.

Aaron let out a small sigh and took his leave. He had his work cut out for him if he was going to earn the trust of Verona's companions and find acceptance within the group. All things in time, he supposed, but he hoped he'd be fortunate enough to have the same loyalty and camaraderie that these men showed to each other.

The next morning, the men woke early and ate a quick breakfast before setting out. Zeus set off on his own, occasionally coming into view. According to Vaughn, traveling by horseback they were about five days away from Rexel, home to Prince Cyrus. This puzzled Aaron, who was wondering what type of technology was available in the world of Safanar. When he was at Duncan's Port, he didn't have the time to take note, but all he had seen so far were people traveling by foot or on horseback. Had the people of this world managed to create anything like a car or plane?

He traced the runes along the black staff. A tool against the shadow, but it would also draw their attention. A wizard and his staff, Aaron mused, only he was no wizard. Perhaps the staff wasn't meant for him at all. He could just be its keeper, but for whom, Aaron wondered. He hoped Colind would know what he was to do with the staff. He needed Colind if he was going to stop those who were hunting him. It was thoughts such as these that were both alien to him and also becoming a daily occurrence. He hoped his sister was safe and had managed to find some peace. His throat thickened at the thought of home and all that he'd lost. He lowered his gaze and set a quick pace.

In the days that followed, their path took them through a gnarled old forest, which eventually gave way to grasslands. They passed a few farms along the way. The farmers were friendly enough once they discovered that they were just passing through, for which Aaron couldn't blame them. Living so remotely would require that they keep their guard up. It wasn't until the shoes of his horse broke that they decided to head to a nearby town.

The mood among the men had lightened considerably, especially when Garret took it upon himself to teach Aaron the bow, which he had never shot in his life. His grandfather had taught Aaron many weapons, but a bow wasn't among them, and unlike his swords, he had no apparent affinity toward the weapon. Good old hard work would have to suffice, which suited Aaron just fine, but it did become a joke among the others that he couldn't fire a bow with any degree of accuracy. Nobody would be standing in front of a tree with an apple on their head as a target for him to shoot at any time soon. They were, however, well aware of his accuracy with throwing knives, much to Eric and Braden's delight since they were fond of having contests after supper. Vaughn had adopted the wait-and-see approach, but he watched Aaron closely, and it was becoming increasingly difficult for Aaron to conceal his identity. He began to question Colind's advice in hiding who he was, and he could tell that Verona was caught in the middle. At least there were moments when the anger and pain left him, but they were few and far between. He wondered what would happen if the darkness in his soul consumed him. Who would he become if that happened?

They arrived at a small town by midmorning, and the local blacksmith informed them that he would take care of their horses before midday. This gave them time to resupply, and Aaron used the time to explore the town. All streets led to the town square, where merchants had set up their wares, but what was most notable was an old fountain in the middle of the square. A worn statue of a woman stood gazing up to the sky, reminding him of the statue that he and Verona encountered in the forest. The hot sun blazed down upon his head, feeling like tiny pinpricks on his scalp and reminding him of his need to acquire a hat.

"Do you like the fountain?" an old woman asked, appearing as if by magic beside him.

"Yes," Aaron replied.

The old woman gazed at him intently. "You have kind eyes, child," she stated. A small smile stole itself onto Aaron's face at her bluntness. "I'm sorry to see that you bear so much pain. Perhaps being in the presence of the Goddess's fountain will bring comfort to a troubled soul, even if it is only for a moment."

Some children began playing games around the fountain, drawing his attention away. When he looked back, the old woman was gone. He gazed at the fountain, allowing his eyes to drink in its splendor, and for that moment at least, he did feel better. He made his way over to a booth where a dusty, black, wide-brimmed hat lay among the wares. Aaron shook the hat, patting it against his side, then tried it on. It fit perfectly. The woman tending the booth eyed him kindly. He wanted to purchase the hat, but had no idea about the currency used in this world. The paper money he had wouldn't be worth much except for kindling the campfire, but the quarters he fished out of his pocket brought a broad smile to the woman's face, and they disappeared quicker than Aaron's eyes could follow. It was good to get the sun off his head.

***

"Who *is* he, Verona?" Vaughn asked.

"I've already told you all I am permitted to say, my friend. Any more than that would not be appropriate," Verona replied as he watched Aaron from across the square.

"There is something you're not telling me about this man," Vaughn said, his hand gesturing toward Aaron. "Any man who attracts the trouble of the Elite Order we should be wary of and perhaps keep our distance from."

Verona fixed Vaughn with a stern glare. "Aaron will reveal what he wants you to know when he is ready, and until then, you should respect his wishes. He asks nothing of anyone and offers aid when he can." His gaze softened a bit as he put his hand on Vaughn's shoulder. "Perhaps you should consider this, that it is he who is trying to protect us all by only revealing so much. He has his demons to face as do we all, but by and by, I've pledged my friendship, and my word is my bond. What are we without our honor? Nothing but bloodless barbarians and chaos driven at that."

"Vaughn," called Garret as he and Sarik ran up to them from the adjoining street. "Riders approach bearing the black uniform of the High King's guard. They are accompanied by a member of the Elite Order." As Garret said the last, they heard echoes of many horses approaching.

Verona cursed. "Go find Eric and Braden quick. Sarik, stay out of sight and keep your bow ready," Verona ordered. He turned toward Aaron, who had heard the horses and was staying in the shadows as the procession of riders passed. He watched Aaron's face grow grimmer with each passing rider until he saw undeniable recognition followed by a coldness that Verona felt across the way.

The black riders bearing the silver crest of the High King filled the square, and the lively town square hushed to a few low murmurs. The uniformed soldiers stopped in militaristic precision, lining their mounts and surveying the people in the square.

"People of the town, you have among you a stranger who is wanted for crimes against the High King's guards. We know he came this way and is still here. Turn him out, and we'll be on our way. Harbor him, and I'll order this place burned to the ground. The choice is..."

"Murderer!" Aaron sneered, stepping boldly into the street, his black cloak trailing behind him like a swath of midnight.

Vaughn gasped. "What does he think he's doing?"

Watching, Verona strung his bow.

***

"No need to hold the town by the throat to get to me. You harbor a murderer among yourselves," Aaron said, drawing his swords and stepping boldly forward. A casual breeze toyed with the fringes of his black cloak. "Are you man enough to stand before *me*, murderer?" Aaron taunted, speaking directly to the scar-faced rider to the left of the leader.

The leader looked to the rider and then back to Aaron. "You dare challenge us! Who—form ranks *now!* To arms, men," their leader barked.

The two figures at his side remained motionless. Other men dismounted and drew their swords as one. Two archers remained in the saddle and drew their bows, arrows locked in with deadly precision.

Aaron's eyes were locked on one of the few men still remaining in a saddle. The man's surprise betrayed him. *That's right, you bastard. I'm coming for you.* He still saw the man's eyes that night as he held his mother by knife point and the bold look of determination upon her face as she made her last courageous move to save his life.

None of this was supposed to happen, damn it. She should be alive! I should be home! Aaron's muscles quaked with anticipation, and a subtle, irrevocable truth entered his mind.

I have no home anymore. The thought fanned the flames of his rage.

"By my word, I will order my men to put you down should you not do as I say. Now lay down your swords. We're not here to kill you," the leader said.

Aaron remembered the heat of the fire that took his home. The musky smell of ashes was stuck in the recesses of his nose. *I have no home anymore!* His predatory gaze swept over the men arrayed against him, and they all wore the same scarred face. They were *all that* bastard who cowardly stayed upon his horse, and they would all weep in blood. Seizing the power of the bladesong, he hurled out notes of rigid fury.

Arrows heaved from their bows, furiously seeking their mark, but Aaron was too quick and swept them aside like toothpicks. With the power of the bladesong in him, everything slowed down, giving him ample time to react. The rule when outnumbered was to keep moving and keep striking in order to survive. Movement was life, but it was not survival he sought, but to kill. He cut through three men before they had a chance to counter. In the midst of the other men's hesitation, Aaron saw arrows take down the two archers on horseback and knew Verona was with him. Aaron plunged headlong into the remaining men, whirling his blades into a vortex of death and dismemberment. Compared to the power growing within him, the unenlightened men were as children and died as easily. The whisperings of countless lives filled him with their knowledge, for the soul was an old vessel that never truly died. With each life he took, the fire in his blood roiled in protest. The five soldiers left alive looked fearfully at their fallen companions and threw down their weapons, running past the remaining three on horseback despite their captain's screams of protest.

Aaron charged. His eyes locked on the man whose face had been upon all those he had killed this day. The one who was among those that butchered his family. But before he could make contact with his mark, he was swept aside by an unseen force and knocked from his feet.

"I will deal with this upstart myself," a venomous voice rasped.

Aaron heard mutters of Elitesman from the crowd of onlookers. As he regained his feet, he told himself that what stood before him was just another man like himself, nothing more and nothing less. When one makes his opponent more than what he is, he has already lost, and Aaron would suffer no fear in his heart. The fire inside him yearned for the blood of the scarred man's face, but he knew that he must be wary of these Elitesmen.

The Elitesman drew a slender, curved black blade that appeared to be a distant cousin of a Japanese samurai sword. Aaron brought his Falcons to bear and lashed out with a thunderous attack. If he didn't fight with all that he was, then he would be dead. He moved smoothly and harmoniously, his Falcons an extension of himself, but each swing of his blades was met by the Elitesman's blade, and so the dance ensued. Banishing thoughts of victory and defeat, survival and death, he focused all his efforts on movement, bringing him to a place beyond thought. And in freeing his mind, he achieved a greater awareness that turned the tide of this deadly contest with the Elitesman.

Aaron gained on his opponent, slowly driving him back in a blur of whirling blades. The Elitesman's swordsmanship, like his composure, unraveled as the pattern of his attack became apparent. The Elitesman betrayed surprise as a long slash appeared, running across his chest. Aaron moved with deadly patience, taking the pose of the waiting dragon with his swords held like giant talons waiting to tear at his prey.

The grim-faced Elitesman took his sword with both hands, angling the point of his blade directly at Aaron. Blood flowed freely from the deep slash down his chest. For all his tricks, he was just a man, and he was beaten, a fact they both knew, and yet he would not yield. The Elitesman embraced death like a waiting lover and charged, rushing toward his fate.

Swords clashed with a wild crack of steel, and the Elitesman's blade shattered into pieces. Instead of delivering the killing blow, Aaron kicked out with his leg, sending the Elitesman hurtling off to the side.

Aaron closed in on the guardsman. The man threw down his weapons, crying out for mercy.

"I beg of you. Mercy!" the man said, falling down to his knees. "Don't kill me," he pleaded, his face crumpling in fear.

Aaron stepped forward, his blood running like ice through his veins as he regarded this murderer before him. "You ask me for mercy. There was no mercy from you with a knife held to my mother's throat." He spat, and with a quick flip of his wrist, a shallow cut appeared on the man's face, mirroring the other scar.

"No! No! Please don't kill me. I'm sorry. I was under orders. Mercy!" The man's eyes were wild with fear as tears streamed down his face.

"You are not worthy of *mercy*," Aaron sneered. "I have come for you as I will to all who have brought this war to my doorstep and stole those I loved," Aaron said with his swords at the ready. His will was like iron, and the vengeance gripping his heart yearned to be unleashed.

"Under whose orders were you so compelled to obey?" Braden asked, coming up beside Aaron, his sword drawn as Eric materialized beside him.

The man's eyes were both fearful and defiant at the same time.

"You have but one chance before you die. Who sent you?" demanded Aaron, who was answered with a silent glare of open hatred. This man felt no remorse. Without hesitation, Aaron plunged both swords through the man's chest, and as the life drained out, he grabbed his shirt, holding the dying man up, growling as he did so. His withering glare never left the dying man's eyes. "The others will join you soon," Aaron said, and roughly cast the body aside.

He turned his attention to the Elitesman, who had regained his feet, if a bit wobbly. Upon seeing his approach, the Elitesman plunged his hands into the depths of his robes and brought out a shimmering purple crystal. An aura of light surrounded him, and he vanished.

Send my regards to your masters, Elitesman, Aaron thought bitterly.

Aaron surveyed the carnage around him. Dead men littered the street, and blood was everywhere. The air stank of it. He had allowed his hunger for vengeance to turn him into a monster. The innocence within him cried out in despair from the dark corners of his mind, but his pain yearned for more. Is this what he had become? Was this the purpose for which he had been trained? His eyes swept all the dead men's faces, and he saw them for what they were instead of what his rage demanded they should be. He felt soiled in such a way that no amount of washing would ever get him clean enough. His skin crawled with death. He looked down at his hands still clutching his bloody swords; the gleaming blades were covered with blood. He flung them to the ground in disgust. Sinking to his knees, he vomited. The rage-induced tunnel vision fled, and the truth of what he had done to these men left him disgusted. It was them or him, a colder part of himself said. No, he would not condone his own actions as a mere act of survival and vowed to himself to face men as men and not as what his anger demanded they be.

He heard the sound of a bowstring straining with an arrow notched, and he looked up from his knees to see the leader of the soldiers taking aim at him. Braden and Eric blocked his view by standing in front of him.

"You might want to think that move through," called Verona with his own arrow notched, ready to take flight.

"I'm quite certain we'll get you first," Sarik called from the rooftop of the nearest building.

The leader released his bow and returned the arrow to its quiver.

"The king shall hear of this," he shouted, turning his horse and leaving the town at a full gallop.

Aaron slowly got to his feet. The wave of nausea left him, and numbness settled in. He nodded gratefully to Braden and Eric, who had put their lives in harm's way to defend him, a fact he would never forget. The crowd of townsfolk gathered and slowly approached.

"Brave warrior," someone said.

"Took down an Elitesman," said another in a loud whisper.

"Who are you, stranger?" the blacksmith asked.

Aaron glanced at Verona, who regarded him in silence, then gave a small nod. Though Colind had strongly advised that he conceal his identity and at one time he'd conceded the point, he just could not hide who he was anymore. It was not fair to those who traveled with him, nor did it feel right to himself. Never in his whole life had he needed to hide who he truly was, and in these dark times, he refused to give his enemies that power over him. They would hunt him regardless of who knew the truth.

"My name," Aaron began, and the crowd leaned in seemingly of its own accord, "is Aaron Jace. Son of Patrick and Carlowen, grandson of Reymius Alenzar'seth. I am the last of the house of Alenzar'seth of Shandara." His eyes swept the crowd, but lingered for a moment on each of the men he traveled with, who over a short span of time he'd come to count as friends and hoped they would remain so. Verona gave him an approving nod, but the others looked shocked. Sarik, who had raced down from the rooftop, turned to Garret, who pursed his lips and nodded to himself.

"The Lords of Shandara have returned," someone gasped from the crowd. "The keepers of the sacred trust have returned."

Eric and Braden shared a brief look before going down to one knee with a fist over their hearts. "By my life or death, I pledge myself to the house of Alenzar'seth and the Heir of Shandara, as was my father's place before me," they said in unison. "We are descendants of the De'anjard, the Shields of Shandara, and our swords are yours." Their words echoed off a stunned crowd, and without exception the onlookers shouted their approval.

The cheering soon died down, and Aaron looked down at the two men kneeling before him, not knowing what to say.

"Please. Please get up," Aaron said quietly. Men shouldn't kneel before other men.

Eric and Braden rose as one, and while their warrior-like demeanor held a resolve to cope with whatever a harsh life saw fit to throw their way, now their eyes brimmed with a hope and purpose they'd not had before. Aaron found himself face-to-face with Vaughn, who looked fearful and shocked as his eyes darted back and forth from Aaron to Verona.

"I want to believe you," Vaughn began, but then words failed to come. "Prove it," he said simply.

It's a fair request, Aaron thought, and he could expect nothing less from the likes of Vaughn. He untied the laces of his shirt, his eyes never leaving Vaughn's, and the dragon tattoo shimmered, dancing amid the rays of the sun under the medallion bearing his family crest.

"By the Goddess," Garret gasped. "He is Ferasdiam Marked. One who is—"

"Marked by fate," Vaughn finished. "And he bears the mark of the house of Alenzar'seth, the Lords of Shandara," Vaughn said in a shaking voice, fearing the truth before his eyes. "My Lord, I have wronged you. Please forgive me."

"No," Aaron said, "you were protecting that which matters most to you. I would count myself fortunate to have someone such as you looking out for me. Verona kept his silence at my request." Aaron extended his hand, and Vaughn shook it firmly. It was liberating to finally reveal who he was to those he wanted to trust so badly. The darkness within him retreated, and even if it was only for this moment, perhaps it would be enough. The others regarded him silently. "We should go. These people are in danger as long as I am here."

"Yes, he's right. We must make haste," Verona agreed. They gathered their horses, and the townsfolk promised that they would hide the dead soldiers. That it would be their honor to aid the Heir of Shandara.

As they came out of the town, Aaron noticed a cloaked figure standing by the edge of the road. The cloak mostly hid the person's face, but Aaron caught a glimpse of the unmistakably beautiful feminine eyes and slender neckline of a woman. Their eyes locked for a moment, and neither looked away. Aaron frowned. He didn't understand why the others rode past her without seeming to notice at all. Her eyes searched his, and he felt as if his soul was laid bare before her. Aaron began to speak but couldn't, and part of him was grateful that he couldn't break the spell over both of them. She took a step toward him and exhaled a breath, her eyes looking regretfully at him, then there was a brief flash of light, and she was gone.

Aaron exhaled the breath he had been holding, searching all around him. "Did you see that?" Aaron asked quickly.

"See what?" Verona asked, puzzled and looking back at him. Eric and Braden drew their swords and immediately started scanning everywhere at once.

"The cloaked woman who was over there," Aaron answered, gesturing toward the far side of the road.

The men exchanged glances. "There was no one. The road is empty as it was moments before."

Aaron was about to protest, but it seemed pointless. Clearly, they hadn't seen her. He still saw her eyes in his mind, and his heart raced. "Do you know how the Elitesman disappeared with a flash of light?" Aaron asked instead.

"He had a travel crystal. Pieces taken from a whole crystal allow the traveler to always return to the source or any place that they know the pattern to. They are not that common," Verona answered.

"That would be useful to have," Aaron mused. "Is there any way we can get to Rexel faster than horseback?"

"Use of an airship would allow us to reach our destination much quicker, but all the Ryakuls in the area make for dangerous skies. Not for pirates, mind you," Verona answered with a twinkle in his eye. "Fear not, my friend, we will make it to Rexel soon enough."

"I just wonder how the Elitesmen are able to track us so easily. There was that group behind us at one point, but now they appear to be coming at us from every direction. Do they all have that travel crystal?" Aaron asked.

"They are a group shrouded in mystery," Verona said. "That is one of their strengths, but it could also mask weakness. I'm sorry, my friend, but I simply don't know."

They rode on in silence after that, chewing up the road quickly as they made their way ever closer to Rexel, where he hoped to find some aid. When he wasn't thinking about the mysterious woman, he knew his companions' questions were mounting up. The first of which came to him from Sarik as they were making camp.

"How did you do it?" Sarik asked. "How did you best that Elitesman?" The other men, including Verona, stopped what they were doing to hear Aaron's answer.

"Are they not 'just' men?" Aaron asked.

"Yeah, but..." Sarik began. "Men I can face, but an Elitesman knows things, just like you know things. How else would you be able to stand your ground against them?"

Aaron had given these Elitesmen a great deal of thought since his first encounter, when he'd met Verona. They had an arrogance to them that he equated to being slapped in the face. Just the thought of them made him tuck in his chin stubbornly.

"My grandfather, Reymius, trained me for as long as I can remember. He, with my father's help, built a school and taught many people, but he never mentioned anyone called an Elitesman. He would drill into me the importance of quieting the mind and moving without thought," Aaron said, smiling a little in remembrance of better days. "He said that sometimes our brains slow us down, and that in order to tap into the greatest strength within, you must let go of all thought. There is knowledge and power to be gained from the spirit, which is far older than the vessels that house it for a time."

Sarik said nothing for a few moments and then got down on one knee and asked, "Will you train me?"

Sarik's question was self-evident in each of their eyes. A sense of hope to stand against a monster that had haunted their footsteps for longer than Aaron could imagine.

"I've never taught anyone. I'm no teacher," Aaron said quickly.

"You carry the lost art of the Shandarian masters within you. We would honor anything you would teach us," Braden said, also going to one knee, followed by Eric.

"Please get up. You are men, for God's sake," Aaron said gently. After a few moments, they did. "It's not right for men to kneel before other men."

"Perhaps it will allow us to stand with you against the next Elitesman, for sure as the sun will rise in the morning, there will be more of them coming after us," Verona said.

Us? Aaron thought. He searched the eyes of all his companions and within them saw something unique and unyielding. Aaron could see the pattern laid before him. These men would be the first to learn what many might come in search of: Reymius's teachings. Was this the reason his grandfather was forced to flee his home? Was this knowledge the reason why war was brought from Shandara to his home? *Keepers of the sacred trust, that's how the townsfolk referred to me.* What sacred trust? He needed to know why his grandfather had to flee this world in the first place. Aaron looked back at Sarik and the others and nodded; he would teach them.

CHAPTER 18
FEAST OF SHANSHERU

The city of Rexel stretched extensively upon either side of a river. Even from a distance, Aaron could tell that the city was well thought out in its layout of roads, allowing for efficient commuting from different parts. However, nothing prepared Aaron for the sheer size of the place. On the western side was a palace whose pale spires reached longingly toward the heavens. There were no walls that surrounded the outer city, and the roads led to a main thoroughfare that went straight to the river. He was to seek out Prince Cyrus, who, according to Colind, would be able to help him, but Colind hadn't had a chance to tell him how. *Where is Colind?* Aaron thought for the hundredth time. He was beginning to wonder whether he was on a fool's errand.

"Verona," Aaron called, "I presume that the prince resides in the palace."

"Your presumption is correct, my friend, but I bet you're wondering whether the guards will grant us an audience with the prince," Verona said.

"Something we are all wondering," Vaughn said dryly, "considering how we left the last time."

"Indeed," Verona replied with half a smile. "Aaron, how would you proceed knowing that our…no that's not right, my reception may not be the warmest?"

"I think I'd take my chances knocking on the front door," Aaron replied.

"Ah, the direct approach. Excellent." Verona grinned. "Perhaps you should go first when we arrive." Verona paused for a moment. "Not to worry, my uncle has been kicking me out of the city since I was sixteen years old, and never once has he actually had me thrown into the dungeon upon my return."

"He also never had the guards chase us from the city like the last time," Braden said, nodding to his brother Eric.

"What happened the last time you were here?" Aaron asked.

"A simple misunderstanding concerning a very attractive young lady. Unfortunately, she was betrothed to a pompous peacock of a princeling from the neighboring kingdom of Selapan," Verona replied, and Vaughn grunted something inaudible under his breath.

"It was just a dance," Verona continued, ignoring Vaughn.

"You made the princeling look so much the fool that he challenged you to a duel," Vaughn finished impatiently.

"And taught the peacock a well-deserved lesson," Verona answered. "He won't be bragging about his mastery of the bow anytime soon, or the sword for that matter."

"You also strained the already fragile relations with Selapan," Vaughn responded. "There are consequences for such actions, Verona."

"I'm sure it's all blown over by now," Verona said. "And besides, I'm sure there are other things that hold my uncle's attention at this very moment, given the time of year," he finished with a raised brow.

The dawn of recognition took hold of Vaughn, who quickly looked at Aaron and then back at Verona. He pressed his lips together, considering, but said nothing, waiting Verona out. Aaron wondered what Verona had up his sleeve.

"Coincidence or fate, my old friend?" Verona asked in a flat tone, and Vaughn nodded in understanding that was clearly beyond Aaron at the moment.

"The Feast of Shansheru, which is an ancient celebration to honor the guardians of the ivory tree," Verona said, clearly enjoying himself as understanding registered itself with each of the men, who all looked at Aaron.

"And who would like to inform our newest friend who the guardians of the ivory tree were?" Verona asked, glancing around at the rest of them, grinning. "For seventy years, the ivory tree was safeguarded in Shandara by the noble ruling house of Alenzar'seth. The ivory tree is a symbol of balance given as a seedling by the Hythariam people to Shandara, who repelled the first Ryakul incursion." Verona stopped, smiling at his friend. "So you see, as you are the only living heir of the house of Alenzar'seth, it would be poor manners indeed should my uncle, the prince, deny an audience with *you*, Aaron."

Vaughn shook his head. "All those years of tutoring, and that's all you can remember of the Ryakul incursion and symbolism of the ivory tree? You would think that the incursion was just a few flying beasts and not hordes of monsters. Not to mention when the Hythariam first came to Safanar," Vaughn said.

"Isn't that the gist of what happened?" Verona countered. "I'm sure you and my uncle can speak on this subject for days on end, but we don't have that kind of time, do we?"

Aaron was keenly interested in what they were saying, but became distracted by the flags lining the main thoroughfare into the city. They were of a dragon with his outstretched wings, cradling a rose in his talons. The center was white and pearl shaped, with the etching of a tree. They matched both the medallion and the tattoo on his chest, which he rubbed absently. Shouts of greetings could be heard as they made their way down the street, and a few soldiers cast a wary glance in their direction but waved them on. Aaron noticed a soldier was sent on ahead, no doubt to inform the prince that Verona had indeed returned.

"I don't see any of the airships you mentioned earlier," Aaron said.

"Look over toward the far side of the palace and on the outskirts of the warehouses along the river," Sarik said, urging his horse next to Aaron's. "That's where you will see them take off and land."

Aaron kept a wary eye where Sarik pointed, and he saw something cylindrical rise into the air gracefully, with lines attached to a ship. Wings extend from the main body, and small propellers drop down. The balloon and ship were of equal size, which left Aaron wondering what was being used to fill the balloon because hot air and helium weren't enough to raise a ship that size.

"Do you know how they work? How they can rise straight up into the air? How they are powered?" Aaron asked.

"The crystals are powered through magnified sun beams, which are stored in the crystals. They are rotated as they reach capacity, and energy is drawn from them as needed. As long as sunlight is available, then there is plenty of power," Sarik answered eagerly. "Garret, can you tell Aaron how the engines work?"

"The energy stored in the crystals can be used for more than just lighting the way," Garret began. "Some can be used to ignite a propellant for short periods of time, which can push the vessel in any direction. There are limitations—mostly with storing and tapping the energy, as it is not entirely without risk. There have been fires and explosions known to happen when certain precautions are not met. Airships are relatively new to the world and come with their own share of problems."

"Perhaps we can persuade the prince for a closer look at one should you desire it," Verona added.

"I would like that. Traveling by airship would be much faster than by horse," Aaron replied.

"Indeed, in that you are correct, and they are much more comfortable," Verona said. "I'm not sure if my uncle will be amiable to parting with one of his precious ships, though."

Aaron noted the slightly bitter tone from Verona, which begged the question of how many times Verona had tried to make use of the prince's airships. They both noticed that Vaughn kept looking down the street and behind them.

"Stop fretting, Vaughn. If my uncle intended to have us arrested, the guards would have been upon us already," Verona said confidently.

"Then you don't need to worry about the squad making a beeline right toward us," Vaughn said.

Verona turned, saw the approaching guard, let out a broad grin, and waved to them as they approached. "Well, no use running. We want to get to the palace, don't we?"

"That is indeed our goal," Aaron said with half a smile.

Verona grinned back at him. "Well met, my friend."

Twenty weathered guards approached calmly, and the leader waved back to Verona. "The prince would like to see you, my Lord." His tone was half casual and half stern, but Aaron noticed a slight smile as if he'd had to collect Verona several times in the past.

"I am, of course, at the prince's service, but I must insist that my companions accompany us, for I have urgent news for his grace," Verona answered.

"Of course," the guard said. "After you, my Lord."

The crowds on the streets parted to allow them quick passage, and Aaron quickly lost track of where they were in the sea of city streets. One thing that stood out to him was how clean the streets were and how well kept the buildings. All the people he met were quite friendly, which was a change from the reserved receptions from the smaller towns. Not that the people from the smaller towns weren't friendly, but there was a general mistrust of strangers and a feeling of vulnerability. The realization made him appreciate his home more and more and demanded respect for how far people had come. How would the prince feel about the Elitesmen victimizing the people of the smaller towns, and would he be able to do anything about it?

The walls surrounding the palace grounds had been visible since they had entered the city, and as they got closer, their tallness became much more apparent. They were met at the gates by the palace guards, who took over as escort. The sight of the palace left Aaron's mouth hanging open at the sheer size and meticulous detail of the architecture down to the smallest window. It was not only a place of power, but of beauty as well, and Aaron couldn't help but feel a little intimidated as they got closer.

A steward came to collect them and escorted them through the palace. They didn't need an armed escort because there were guards everywhere Aaron looked, and they were hardly prisoners. The steward brought them to the great hall, which was a cavernous room filled with floor-to-ceiling windows that gave a beautiful view of the palace grounds. Once again, the sheer wealth of the place continued to impress upon him whom he was meeting.

The prince glanced up as they approached and raised his bushy brow quizzically, then he returned his attention to the group of people already before him. A palace guard, of some rank judging by the adornment of his uniform, moved to stand between them and the prince surveying them. Verona spoke a few hushed words to the steward and the guard, but the guard seemed bothered by the sight of Aaron.

"Knight Lieutenant, I will vouch for him upon my honor," Verona said.

"With all due respect, my Lord, the safety of his grace is my responsibility, and I cannot have a stranger so heavily armed in his presence," the lieutenant replied.

"I'm sorry, is there a problem?" Aaron asked, coming next to

Verona.

"Yes sir. I must request that you remove your weapons prior to meeting with his grace," the lieutenant answered.

"Why?" Aaron asked before Verona could interject.

The lieutenant narrowed his gaze pointedly before answering. "You represent a security risk to his grace. I must insist that you disarm yourself at once," he said, and grim-looking guards moved in to surround them.

"I see," Aaron said, nodding in understanding and pursing his lips. "I'm sorry, I cannot comply with your request. You see, as all the heavily armed guards here represent a clear security risk to myself and my companions, I would be remiss in my duty to them and myself if I were to let such a risk go unchecked," Aaron countered calmly, returning the knight lieutenant's gaze.

The guards surrounding them gripped the handles of their swords, ready to draw them upon the knight lieutenant's command.

"Come now, what is the hold up over there?" barked the prince from his throne behind them.

The lieutenant turned and bowed. "Your Grace, this man is refusing to disarm in your presence."

The prince's gaze shifted to them.

"Uncle, I will vouch for the quality of this man upon my honor. I humbly ask that you hear us out in your private chambers for I have a tale to tell that I believe you will find most interesting." Verona stopped as the prince held up his hand.

"Ah, my dear nephew Verona, as poetic as always," the prince said with half a smile that vanished instantly when he looked directly upon Aaron. The prince had a hard look to him with his graying beard, like a person who commanded respect. Much like his grandfather Reymius's presence commanded the respect of those around him. "Who are you, sir, that inspires such poetry from my nephew's lips?"

Aaron felt his mouth go dry as he gazed back into the eyes of the prince. "I am Aaron Jace—"

"Uncle, I must insist that we discuss this matter in private," Verona stated again.

The prince's eyes searched the faces of the men standing with Aaron. "Vaughn, I see you've been looking after my nephew these past few weeks. It's good to see you, sir."

"Likewise, your Grace," Vaughn replied. "But I must agree with Verona upon the urgency of the matters we need to discuss with you."

"I see," the prince said. "Yes, it must be of grave importance for you to have returned so quickly after my guards chased most of you out of the city upon your last visit. Don't think for second I've forgotten about that little stunt, Verona."

Sarik would not stop looking at the floor, his ears red. Eric and Braden calmly surveyed the room. Vaughn and Garret simply nodded, but before Verona could speak, Aaron stepped forward.

"Colind of the Guardians bid me to seek out your council, sir. Please, if I may have a few moments of your time. I've travelled a long way to get here," Aaron said.

The prince looked at Aaron, considering. "You look quite familiar to me. Have I met your father perchance?" he asked.

"I'm quite certain you've never met my father, but you knew my grandfather, Reymius Alenzar'seth," Aaron said.

The prince's gray eyes hardened as he rose from his seat, taking a few steps to stand before Aaron. "That's a bold claim or a fool's claim," he said quietly.

Aaron calmly met the prince's gaze. "The situation calls for both at times, but I assure you Reymius was my grandfather." He had come this far because Colind's last words were that Prince Cyrus could help him get to Shandara. He must journey to Shandara to free Colind from his prison. He needed Colind's help to avenge his family, or he would continue to be hunted—or worse.

The prince studied Aaron for a few moments. "Okay, Verona, we shall do as you requested and retire to my private chambers." He glanced back at the steward. "Please have some food brought up, as I suspect we will be talking for a long time."

The steward bowed and left the great hall. The rest of them followed the prince through a doorway off to the right and entered a smaller room.

They spoke at length, with Verona and Aaron taking turns recounting the events since they had met. The prince was particularly interested in Aaron's home and where Reymius had been for the past twenty-five years, but Aaron could tell he was doubtful. Even showing the medallion and tattoo did little to sway the mind of the prince.

"Surely you must know something about why Reymius left? How he left and why he stayed away?" Prince Cyrus asked.

"I'm sorry, I don't know why he left. Maybe he couldn't get back. My mother's memories were gone, and only bits and pieces returned after he died. All he left me was..." Aaron paused. He had almost forgotten and cursed himself for not remembering sooner. "Would you recognize Reymius's signature if you saw it?" Aaron asked.

The prince waited a few moments, pacing the room, then turned to Aaron. "I believe so, but I can go further than that. I have documents in my possession that bear his signature," the prince said, smiling, and then asked, "You mentioned your mother—is she here?"

Aaron felt like he was punched in the stomach and slowly shook his head. "She died."

The prince's eyes softened. "I'm very sorry for your loss."

Aaron dug into his pack and took out the letter his grandfather had left for him. The letter was folded and worn because he had constantly reread it hoping to glean more information. He carefully opened the letter and passed it to the prince, who took it gently and looked at it intently. After a few moments, he looked up at Aaron.

"You seem like a genuine person, Aaron. I realize this could not have been easy for you. There is a close likeness in this signature," the prince said, and he held up his hand before Verona could interject. "Enough for me to have my scribes pull the documents I mentioned before from the archives so we can compare. However, this will take some time, and I must insist you remain as a guest and attend the celebration this evening." The prince handed Aaron's letter back to him and requested that Verona stay behind a moment.

Aaron nodded, and an agreement was made to speak more tomorrow. They all left the room except for Verona and Vaughn. The prince took a long swallow from his goblet of wine and regarded Verona.

"Do you realize what you're getting yourself into, Verona?" the prince asked. "His likeness to the house of Alenzar'seth is remarkable to say the least. His stance, the way he speaks, all remind me of Reymius when we were young, but I also see Carlowen in him," the prince said with a pained expression.

"Then why don't you believe that he is who he says he is, Uncle?" Verona asked. "Why won't you acknowledge the truth before your eyes? He is a good man, and he is in need of our aid. He challenges the might of the Elite."

"Because if this is true, it will mean war," the prince said in a hardened tone. "War with the High King and the Council of the Elite. Not to mention Mactar the Dark Light Master and his twisted, evil ways. If what Aaron says is true and he is of the house of Alenzar'seth, then he will be the herald of death for many. War of the likes we've never seen."

"My Lord," Vaughn began, "the Alenzar'seth protected the lands of Safanar from shadow for generations. If they are in need of aid, then we should give it to them. They are owed at least that much, regardless of the circumstances surrounding the fall of Shandara."

"I understand what you are saying, Vaughn, but the repercussions of this will be felt by all. Some would argue that it's the Alenzar'seths' failure that cursed the kingdom of Shandara in the first place. I'm not saying I do, but we all need to tread carefully, for this is a slippery slope to be upon."

Verona stood up. "Uncle, I respect your counsel, but I have given Aaron my word. I will see this through with him to the end, wherever that may take us. Right is right. Who are we if we are not men of honor? No better than the High King, the Council, or the dreaded

Dark Light Master," he finished quietly, and then he left the room.

The prince was silent for a few moments, deep in thought. "That boy can certainly find trouble wherever he goes. Verona is an idealist. Who will stand with us should we choose to go down this road?"

"Cyrus," Vaughn said gently. He called the prince by his name in private, for they had been friends for a long time. "I've watched over Verona as you've asked. He is a man trying to live up to his principles, much like Aaron. While Aaron may have had a darker time of it recently, or so I gleaned from my charge, it sounds as though he was perfectly happy until Reymius's passing, which leads me to believe that he was safe. Carlowen was safe, and Cassandra's sacrifice was not in vain. Perhaps when the night is darkest, it's the idealists of the world that can light our way and bring others to our cause. It is something to consider." With those words, Vaughn quietly left the prince to his thoughts and the memories he'd helped dredge up from a distant past.

***

Aaron shook his head, feeling a little frustrated. On some level, he understood the prince's caution because he had literally shown up on the prince's doorstep with this fantastical story. It had all happened to him, and he was still struggling to believe it sometimes. They were being escorted to a suite of rooms for their use, and Aaron found himself walking quietly next to Garret.

"Patience, Aaron. This is a lot to digest for the prince," Garret said. "Your grandfather and the prince were close friends in their youth, and he mourned the loss of your family for a long time. The events surrounding the collapse of Shandara are shrouded in mystery, leaving the most ancient and bright spots of Safanar in darkness," Garret said, placing a gentle hand on Aaron's shoulder.

"I guess I understand," Aaron answered. "But we may not have the luxury of time. I feel that everywhere I go, I place people in danger. If we linger here too long, then something...anything is going to happen," Aaron said with his teeth clenching. He had to keep moving, and yet he was so tired.

"Again, patience. Rest. I'm sure you know the importance of a clear mind when it comes to making decisions. The baths are this way, and I will see that a fresh set of clothes is made available to you," Garret said.

Aaron thanked Garret and grew excited at the thought of being clean and actually sleeping in a bed.

CHAPTER 19
A DANCE

The baths were pure joy, and a surprising amount of dirt was left in the pool-sized marble tub. A pretty young girl brought towels and the clothes Garret had promised. Aaron blushed a little at the offer to wash his back, which he politely refused. He did, however, note her slight pause and lingering stare at the dragon tattoo on his chest. Eric poked his head in the door and asked if there was anything he needed, to which Aaron replied something about privacy. Either Eric or Braden was always outside his door. Neither had left his side since entering the palace. When he asked why they were outside his room, they politely smiled and said this was their place. If the room he was in was considered a "guest" room, Aaron wondered what the rest of the palace looked like. The room was cavernous, with tall ceilings, windows with laurel carvings of simple elegance, and a four-poster, king-sized bed. The soft mattress seemed to swallow him up. He fell asleep the moment his head rested upon the pillow.

Later on he woke to a soft knock at the door and noticed the sun was setting.

"Well rested?" Verona asked. He had taken time to clean up as well.

"Very much so. What did the prince want to speak with you about after we left?"

"You," Verona said and chuckled. "You made quite an impression upon him." Verona took in their lavish surroundings. "They don't give these rooms to just any guest. Regardless, I think he wants to believe but is afraid of what it will mean. The world has been limping along since the fall of Shandara. The Council of the Elite and the High King have remained unchecked for far too long. But," Verona said, holding up his hand before Aaron could say something, "they are but a smaller part of a much bigger problem. The Ryakuls aren't the only beasts of shadow to roam the lands, and it is believed by some that they are coming from somewhere within the land of Shandara."

"I'm no prince or king. I am one man. One man cannot keep nations in balance."

"I apologize if I gave that impression. I didn't mean to imply that this falls upon your shoulders. I simply meant that the time for these tyrants is at an end. People will rally behind you because of who you are, regardless of how you view yourself," Verona said.

Rally behind him? Who did they think he was? A few months ago, he was a kid finishing his last year of college.

"Verona, I'm not sure what to say. I came here because I am being hunted and Colind appears to be the only one with the knowledge to help. He is imprisoned in Shandara, and I need to find a way to free him so I can stop those who are trying to kill me. I know nothing of the politics in this world. The High King, Council of the Elite, and this Mactar meant nothing to me until a few days ago." He tried to keep the bitterness from his voice at the mention of the Elite and Mactar. Circles within circles. How far would this journey pull him in?

Verona smiled reassuringly. "I know this is all foreign to you, but it's important that you realize the impact the return of the Alenzar'seth will have on Safanar. Enough of this talk. There is a celebration to attend, and it will be something to behold, even if no one knows that a person in attendance is of the house they are honoring," Verona said with a wink and ushered Aaron out the door.

The clothes he wore were quite comfortable. Brown pants and a midnight-blue shirt that felt light and flexible upon his skin. They walked the corridors of the palace, and Verona joked with Eric and Braden, whom he nicknamed Aaron's Shadows, and for the briefest of moments Aaron wondered how Zeus was doing. He hadn't seen him since before entering the city, but he had no doubt that he wasn't far from him now.

Glowing orbs lit the corridors that led to the great hall, which was awash with light and color reflecting off chandeliers hanging from the ceiling. Giant doors more than twice the size of a man were open to the gardens, where more orbs hung in the air, lighting the party grounds along with the setting sun. The city was alight with color, as the feast extended beyond the palace walls. He had left his swords and staff in his room, but he still had a few throwing knives placed around his person. It never hurt to be prepared. The great hall was lavishly decorated with fresh flowers hung along the walls and tables. Brightly colored banners were arrayed along the way with some depicting the Alenzar'seth coat of arms. The flag of Shandara, he thought, and rubbed the medallion that rested coolly against his chest.

With a few men in his wake, Sarik joined them from among the sea of people who filled the Great Hall and the pavilion set up outside the gardens. While Verona was greeting the men, Aaron seized the opportunity to leave them behind. Aaron went outside to walk among the people, and some nodded in friendly greeting as he passed by. A group of musicians played a gentle tune near a large fountain of the Goddess that matched the one where they had camped a few nights ago. Glowing orbs from within the fountain left the place awash in shimmering light. He wondered how the orbs gave off light because he didn't see any electrical cords to power them. Now that he thought of it, he didn't see any form of electricity here. There were some accoutrements of a modern civilization, like plumbing and those glowing orbs, yet they still used the sword and spear.

He looked around taking in the faces of the people around him and stopped upon a stunningly beautiful woman. Her blue eyes and full cheekbones were unmistakable, for he had seen them before under a hood in a small town. Their eyes locked, his chest tightened, and blood rushed to his face. She had been like a dream on the edge of his thoughts that would disappear if he dared look too closely. The rest of the world around them faded away as he took a step toward her. Her golden-blonde hair was swept up away from her neck, and her eyes calmly searched his, almost challenging him in a way. She wore a gown of deep-sea blue that clung to her form and was both simple and elegant, putting her worlds beyond any girl he had ever seen in his life. The moments ran like quicksand, and his breath quickened as he stepped closer. She held something small in her hand that she kept casually by her side. Aaron silently prayed it wasn't one of those travel crystals.

"Hello," Aaron said, and she regarded him silently for a moment before her lips curved into a small smile. "I've seen you before."

"I've been watching you," she said. They were alone amid a crowd of people, and Aaron couldn't get any words to come out of his mouth. "You have kind eyes," she said, her fingers toying with whatever was in her hand.

Aaron smiled and held out his hand. "Would you like to dance?"

The question slipped out of his mouth without any forethought. She seemed as surprised by the question as he was and stared at his extended hand. Whatever she had been holding was gone when she gently placed her smooth hand in his. The musicians began a song with a slow tempo, for which Aaron was grateful because he only knew one type of dance. His mother had drilled the waltz into him in preparation for his sister's wedding. He placed his right hand on her hip and guided her into the simple elegance of the waltz. After a few moments, he stopped counting the steps in his head. She picked it up quickly, and couples in the area followed their lead. They smiled at one another in the gentle spin as the rest of the world faded away to gray.

"You are not at all what I expected," she said.

"What is it that you expected?" Aaron asked.

"I don't know," she admitted and let out a small laugh.

"I'm Aaron," he said.

"Sarah. It's nice to meet you, Aaron," she replied with a dazzling smile that made his heart melt.

"Sarah," he said, savoring her name in his mouth. "Why have you been watching me?" He asked the question hoping she wouldn't disappear with that cursed travel crystal.

"I want to know more about you," she said. "You've become a person of great interest, even if the people here don't realize it yet. Your actions at the town are even now circulating among powerful people."

Aaron frowned. "Who are you, Sarah?"

"I could ask the same of you, Aaron," was her retort. There was no harshness in her tone, just a determination to stay on equal footing.

"What would you like to know?" Aaron countered.

If she was surprised by such a direct question, she didn't let on.

"Where do you come from?" Sarah asked.

"I'm sure you've never heard of it," Aaron answered. "Earth," he said. He'd never thought he would answer a question quite that way in his life.

"You're right. I haven't heard of it."

"Well?" Aaron asked.

"Yes?" Sarah said with her blue eyes twinkling.

"Where are you from?" Aaron asked.

"Oh, I'm sure you've never heard of it either," Sarah said, her eyes alight with humor. The song ended, and they stood facing each other, but Aaron wouldn't break the silence. He just looked at her expectantly. "Khamearra," she said at last.

"Never heard of it," he said, smiling. "But I assure you, I'm not that interesting."

What am I doing? Aaron thought. He should walk away right now, but he couldn't, and for the first time in a long time, there was no darkness in his heart. The overwhelming desire to keep running was banished as he gazed into Sarah's beautiful blue eyes. They walked, slowly weaving their way through the gardens.

"On the contrary, Aaron, I think you're the most interesting person here. Do you make it a habit to humble Elitesmen wherever you go?" Sarah asked.

"Someone should," Aaron said.

"I'm sure you realize that they will be hunting you even now," Sarah said. "Even here."

He was pleased to hear the concern in her voice, as it was the first indication that she felt one way or another about him. As far as the Elitesmen were concerned, they could stand in line to hunt him.

"They aren't the first," he replied.

They walked in silence, making their way back to the fountain. His heart was at war with itself. He was cursing himself a fool for indulging in this fantasy, for he knew this was something that could never be, whoever Sarah truly was. Yet there was a part of him that defiantly clung to this moment.

"Perhaps with the right help, you'll be able to outrun them all," Sarah said.

"Are you offering?" he asked. After a slight pause, he said, "Well, I don't plan on making it easy for anyone. Perhaps now you can tell me something about yourself, since you seem to know an awful lot about me."

Sarah sighed and looked back at him. He saw uncertainty in her beautiful eyes, and he wanted nothing more than to hold her in his arms and feel the press of her lips upon his. Unless he was an utter fool, he saw a similar desire in her eyes. What was she hiding?

"Maybe another time then," Aaron said after a few moments, hiding his disappointment, but she wasn't fooled.

"I'm sorry," she said at last, pushing a rebellious strand of hair away from her face and taking a step closer to him. "It appears we both have secrets that bind us."

"A harsh prison should we choose to stay within its walls. Do these secrets hold power over us, or we them?"

"All things in time," Sarah said, gazing up into his eyes.

They stood there amid the shimmering golden lights by the fountain. Aaron reached out to Sarah's hand. They stood inches apart from each other, their eyes speaking the words that their mouths refused to say. He leaned in, their lips met, and his heart thundered in his chest. Sometimes a kiss spoke volumes. His thoughts became lost in the alluring embrace of her mouth upon his. Then he heard Verona call his name as he walked around the fountain. Aaron pulled away reluctantly from Sarah, each sharing a small smile with the other. He turned to his friend and was alarmed at seeing sheer shock in Verona's eyes—not directed at him, but at Sarah. Aaron turned back to Sarah as her hand left his arm. She whispered that she was sorry, and then she disappeared before his very eyes.

"It can't be," Verona said in disbelief, with Eric and Braden standing at his shoulders and Sarik bringing up the rear.

"It can't be what?" Aaron asked quickly.

"Unless my eyes have failed me, my friend, you were just kissing the daughter of the High King Amorak of Khamearra. Also, head of the

Elitesman Council of Masters. All rulers in our corner of the world are forced to swear fealty and pay homage to his kingdom," Verona said.

Aaron was stunned. "She was the woman I saw as we left the town. She told me her name was Sarah and that her home was in Khamearra," Aaron said. "She wouldn't tell me much." But her kiss told him enough.

Verona nodded. "Did you tell her who you are?" he asked. Aaron shook his head, and Verona sighed, clearly relieved. "Shandara was the kingdom that balanced the power, keeping the High King in check. In essence, you were kissing the daughter of your worst enemy. One of those directly responsible for the fall of Shandara."

Aaron had to steady his breath, allowing his mind to catch up. The daughter of his enemy? Was the High King the one pulling Tarimus's strings?

"She wasn't trying to hurt me," he said.

"That much is obvious," Verona chided, smiling broadly and glancing at Eric and Braden, who laughed in earnest. "I turn my back for a few minutes," he said to them, shaking his head. "Come, Aaron, we should take our ease this night. There is a cask of Rexelian ale that has our name on it," Verona said, patting him on the shoulder.

"She has one of those travel crystals. I think she was feeling me out for information," Aaron said. "Oh, would you stop," he said when they erupted in another bout of laughter. "It felt more like I was being interviewed. Weighed and measured." And with that, the rest of them started laughing so uncontrollably that he had no choice but to join in.

"Well, if that's true, I wish more beautiful princesses would interview me," Braden said, chuckling.

As they walked away, Aaron kept glancing back at the spot where Sarah vanished, hoping that she would return, but she didn't. They found a table and began drinking and telling stories into the night. There were many toasts given in honor of Shandara, to which Verona would give Aaron a nod and a wink. Those who knew who he was would raise their glasses in his direction much to the ignorance of the crowd. There was a single mournful toast of silence for the fall of the house Alenzar'seth, which felt surreal to Aaron. The celebration in its entirety stopped, and silence set in. After a few minutes, the celebration picked back up, but Aaron couldn't help but wonder what his ancestors had done to warrant such respect. Throughout the remainder of the night, Aaron's thoughts returned to Sarah and the way she looked at him with those blue eyes. He found himself remembering the soft curve of her full lips on his and wondered if he would ever see her again. What would he say to her if he did? Daughter of the High King.

***

The next morning, Aaron gathered his belongings and stuffed them in his pack. He grabbed his cloak, staff, and swords and exited the room to find Sarik waiting outside his door.

"Good morning," Aaron said.

"Morning," Sarik replied. "I'd like to start training today."

There was such enthusiasm in Sarik's eyes, and Aaron hoped he wouldn't disappoint him.

"Good. Me too. Do they have a place that we could use?" Aaron asked. In a place this big, how could they not.

Sarik smiled, clearly excited. "Oh yes. There is an entire courtyard devoted to the martial arts that the guards and guests can use to exercise."

Aaron's stomach let out a loud growl. He was famished. "Breakfast?"

Sarik nodded.

"Lead the way."

Sarik led him through the palace to the kitchens, where they were able to get some food, and then they ate in one of the smaller dining halls. They were soon joined by the rest of the crew.

"Aaron has agreed to start training us today," Sarik said excitedly to the others, who, to Aaron's surprise, looked pleased by this news.

"As I said, I've never trained anyone before, but I'll do my best to pass on the knowledge that my grandfather instilled in me," Aaron said evenly. They all nodded, including Verona, and finished their food.

They soon came to the training grounds, which were easily the size of two football fields. The racks of practice weapons along the walls reminded Aaron of the sparring room back home, only on a much grander scale. There was a section of practice dummies, stumps for uneven footing, walls for climbing, and much more. Prince Cyrus took the conditioning of his soldiers seriously. There were a few groups already there, so Aaron's group walked over to a clear spot for general training and were joined by Vaughn, who looked at Aaron's backpack and said, "Are you going somewhere?"

"Doesn't hurt to be prepared," Aaron said. "Regardless of what is found in the prince's archives, I will be leaving soon."

Vaughn looked the most surprised by this. "I'm sorry. I didn't realize you meant to leave so quickly. I think it's only fair that the prince is aware of your intentions."

"I would appreciate it if you could tell him," Aaron said earnestly. "I mean no disrespect to him, and I am grateful for his hospitality, but I can't afford to loiter anywhere for very long until we find Colind. My presence here puts everyone at risk, and I won't risk the lives of innocent people."

Verona stood between them. "I'm ready when you are, but I urge you to be patient. I suspect we haven't learned all that we could to aid us in our journey."

"Thank you, Verona," Aaron said and then turned to address the rest of the group. "I appreciate all of your help in getting me this far, but I urge you to consider carefully before deciding to come on this journey to Shandara. While I am of the house Alenzar'seth, I am not Reymius," he said, looking at them each in turn. What he saw staring back at him were men resolute of purpose. They really were going to come with him.

"You'd think he was trying to get rid of us," Braden said, glancing at his brother.

"It's okay, Aaron," Garret said. "We're well aware of the dangers, probably more so than you, but we appreciate you giving us the opportunity to leave with our heads held high."

"Now, are we going to stand here talking or train?" Eric asked.

Aaron surrendered; Garret was right. They had more knowledge of what awaited them than he did, but he'd needed to say what he did. He hoped this journey would not end with some or even all of them dead.

"Okay, let's line up," Aaron said, and they warmed up, loosening their muscles as Aaron began with some of the slower forms.

"The most important rule when doing any of these forms is to not think beyond the next move. Push all thoughts away. Breath and body must become one. Even the most basic of moves is worthy of all your attention," Aaron said, pacing up and down the lines. "Each move leads to the next through the natural progression. These forms are used to strengthen your ability to focus your mind. Your mind is the most important weapon and the key for surviving an encounter with an Elitesman." Aaron stopped surveying them as a few passers-by stopped in their tracks at the mention of the Elitesmen.

"That is why you're here, right?" Aaron said. "The Elitesmen are shrouded in mystery, you've told me. Very skilled to be sure, but they are men just the same." They stared back at him, and Aaron could tell they were not convinced.

"Men!" Aaron barked. "Flesh and blood the same as you or I. Men with weaknesses just like you or I. No one"—he paused—"no one is infallible. Any strength can be used against an opponent. Eric and Sarik, come forward." He couldn't have picked men who were more on the opposite sides of the size spectrum. Sarik was all wiry and speed, while Eric was tall, heavily muscled, and strong as an ox.

"A focused mind will measure your opponent in moments and unravel the pattern of their attack so that you can press your own. Or leave. What is more important? The goal you are working toward or victory over the man who stands in your way? Sometimes a way past is all that is required. Sarik is wiry and quick and will use his speed to his advantage at every opportunity, as well he should. Eric is very strong and will swing whatever weapon he holds with mighty force. Each has their place, and it takes a focused mind to survive the encounter." Aaron gestured to Sarik and Eric to return to the line. "As we travel, we will explore the different fighting forms and their applications toward not only self-preservation but the protection of others. Perhaps you may find yourself facing an opponent that you do not wish to harm," Aaron said, and a vision of Bronwyn with the dead-black eyes of Tarimus stared back at him. He swallowed hard. "Believe me, it's not as outlandish as it sounds."

"What happens when we face someone who is more skilled than us?" Sarik asked.

"I'm glad you said when and not if. Return to the basics. Focus and be in the moment; that is the foundation upon which you must build," Aaron said. "There will always be someone who is quicker, stronger, and more experienced out there in the world. Do not let fear or anger overwhelm you. Those are weapons that can cut as deeply as the sharpest sword or knife."

The next few hours were filled with practice and sparring. Aaron was surprised by how much he had to teach. It was like everything that Reymius had ever taught him was there in the back of his mind, eager to be shared. While he couldn't forget where he was given the grandeur of the training yard, he couldn't help but think of the hours spent in the sparring room at his grandfather's house.

The training yard had steadily filled, and as the time passed, they had gathered an audience. Most notable was a boy who couldn't have been more than seventeen years of age, dressed in clothes a bit too fine for the training yard. His companions were two rather large bodyguards that looked to be Eric and Braden's cousins. The boy's expression was of someone who smelled something foul under his nose. When he wasn't watching them and making hushed comments to his companions, he spared a few venomous looks at Verona, which made Aaron wonder what history was there.

Aaron picked up the rune-carved staff. "Let's talk about weapons for a few minutes. Sometimes the simplest of weapons are the most effective. Expensive swords or flashy axes or anything with a lot of finery can be overly complex and come with as many disadvantages as the advantages they offer in combat. A staff is the most common weapon available to anyone and is one all should have a cursory knowledge of."

The boy laughed. "A common weapon for common folk will not stand against a trained swordsman." The boy sneered, drawing everyone's attention and more than a few raised eyebrows.

Aaron smiled patiently at the boy. "A weapon is only limited to the hand that wields it. A farmer with a stick defending his home will most certainly fight harder than any hired soldier."

"A trained swordsman is more than a match for any commoner with a stick," the boy replied.

"I see," Aaron said mildly. "Are you such a trained swordsman? Do you have a name?"

One the bodyguards stepped boldly forward. "You have the honor of addressing His Exalted Highness, Prince Jopher Zamaridian."

"Would you be willing to put your theory to the test?" Aaron asked, never taking his eyes off the prince.

"You will address his highness by his proper title, Prince Jopher Zamaridian," the guard said harshly, placing his hand on his sword, and Aaron noticed Eric and Braden shift their position.

Aaron kept his gaze upon the boy prince, waiting for an answer. He would be damned if he was going to address this boy by any "proper" title.

After a few moments, the boy held up his hand to the guard. "It's okay. We are guests. I have no issue with putting my theory, as you say, to the test."

"Good, since I am neither a lord nor a prince or a king, I guess I'm as common as they come. Would you care to match your sword against my staff?" Aaron asked and noticed Verona shifting his feet. He would not claim any such title, regardless of his lineage.

The guard was about to protest, but the prince held up his hand, and he reluctantly fell silent.

"A friendly exhibition," Aaron said, and this time he looked at the bodyguard, who fixed him with a hard stare.

"Who will judge this friendly exhibition?" the boy prince asked.

"I will," said a much older voice at the rear of the crowd. Prince Cyrus calmly walked to the front as people made way. "I trust that will be sufficient for you, my Lord," the prince said, addressing the boy with a slight bow.

"Of course, your Grace. I appreciate your taking the time out of your day for this business," the boy said with a respectful bow.

"I think it will be truly enlightening," Prince Cyrus answered, inclining his head. He nodded to Aaron, and he and the boy took up positions facing each other.

While Jopher's sword was indeed flashy, the boy held it as one at home with the blade. When the prince signaled, the boy unleashed a barrage of attacks meant to overwhelm an opponent. Aaron allowed the boy to come at him, giving ground until he sidestepped and gave the princeling a good kick in the backside, which sent him tumbling forward.

Aaron ignored the snickers from the crowd and calmly waited for the boy to gain his bearings. Jopher attacked again, his moves more precise and calculated. Aaron blocked and parried each attack, guiding the boy around in a circle, but he kept coming. The boy was strong, and he was skillful with the sword, at least in that he wasn't mistaken, but his fighting was composed of his arrogance and therefore revealed his weakness. Aaron quickly stepped inside the boy's attack and swept his feet out from under him with his staff. He brought the point of the staff to rest upon the boy's chest.

"Had enough?" Aaron asked calmly.

The boy spat, signaling to his bodyguards. Aaron was waiting for this, but he had hoped the boy had some shred of honor. The two bodyguards charged at the same time, and Aaron moved fluidly against them with a leopard's grace. The whirl of the rune-carved staff humming through the air could be heard as he dealt decisive blows to the bodyguards, sending them sprawling. Aaron spun in time for the boy's attack. Blade met staff only once before Aaron disarmed the boy prince. He swept his feet from under him again with much more force than the first time and planted the end of the staff none too gently upon the boy's chest. Aaron took a quick glance behind him and was relieved to see that Eric and Braden held the bodyguards in place.

"Only a person without integrity dishonors the circle," Aaron said coldly.

The boy feebly struggled to rise, but Aaron held him down.

"You stay there," Aaron said. "Princes and kings can be born, boy, but only men can be made."

Aaron released the boy, who slowly got up rubbing his chest. Eric and Braden released the bodyguards at the same moment. They eyed Aaron as if weighing whether they should seek retribution, but instead came to the boy's aid, guiding him away.

CHAPTER 20
COUNCIL OF COMPLACENCY

Sarah needed to think. Aaron's almond-colored eyes flashed in her mind. So enticing. So...sincere. There'd been a few moments where she'd felt like she would tell him anything he wanted to know. And when they'd danced, it was as if they were the only two people in the world. She felt heat rush to her face and chastised herself.

Most of the men in her life had political motives and would only see her as the daughter of High King Amorak. Not all the men in her life had been bad though; some were good friends, but none had made her feel like her heart would race out of her chest. The few brief times she had seen Aaron, he had threatened to suck her into his wake. Even now she wouldn't mind being swept away. She hoped things wouldn't change when he learned who she was. Her thoughts drifted to the small town where he'd revealed he was a descendant of the house of Alenzar'seth, the Lords of Shandara, who were, by her father's account, the sworn enemies of Khamearra.

She wanted to be at his side and found her hand straying to the travel crystal she kept. She snatched it back, knowing that the crystal needed to be recharged. The more sensible part of her warned of the grave danger that would be certain to come by involving herself with Aaron. Would he even accept her once he learned who she was? She had always stood apart from her family, with her three half-brothers always plotting her demise and her mother long dead from an incurable illness. Her father had little time for the daughter he had never wanted in the first place, and when he'd remarried, she was all but forgotten. Sarah brushed those old hurtful thoughts aside. She had felt the change in the air when the ground shook and had almost exhausted her travel crystal tracking him. It was difficult to believe that Aaron was of the house Alenzar'seth. They were an ancient family aligned with the Hythariam people, who themselves were another matter entirely. The voices in the council chambers droned on as they discussed the very person who occupied her thoughts so much of late. She was in a private alcove where she would normally be able to observe without notice, but she sensed someone close by.

"My dear sister, what is the occasion for such a visit?" her half-brother Primus said behind her.

"Primus, how predictable to find you scurrying about," Sarah said. She loathed all of her half-brothers. They were malicious and cruel as boys and only showed signs of growing more evil and power hungry the older they got. Tye was the youngest of the three, with Primus and Rordan being twins.

"Indeed. I myself was on my way to the council when I noticed someone here, and Rordan is already in there. Perhaps I will stay here and spy...excuse me, casually observe from here," Primus sneered.

"Go to hell, Primus. Leave now before you embarrass yourself,"

Sarah said, brandishing a throwing knife that danced fluidly between her fingers.

"Tisk. Tisk. Such language is unbecoming for *a princess,* even one cast aside and not much more than a brooding mare at that. I'll be sure to send Father your regards," he said, retreating through the doorway.

Sarah took a few moments to calm down, because she really wanted to throw the knife. While she was above such cowardly acts, she knew her brothers were not, and she'd had to keep a watchful eye for as long as she could remember.

Just leave.

She had thought of it before. To just up and leave and never return, but that was before Beck had elected to train her. Beck was an Elitesman, one of the oldest of the order and from a time when it truly was something of which to be proud. Not like it was now. She knew how the Elitesmen were feared, and for good reason—they were among the deadliest warriors of Safanar. Beck would train her at night, away from prying eyes. He trained her in the old ways, from when the order was a sect founded by the Shandarian masters. Now most of the order was power hungry and tyrannical to all those who were not their superiors. Although her father was High King, he was just a member of the Council of Masters, but his word carried much weight. When her mother died, her father changed. She was swept to the side and was all but cast out, except for the occasions where her father was inclined to show her off like some broodmare. She was no man's property, even if that man was the High King. At the age of fourteen, she withdrew to the sidelines and was watched over by Beck at a minor holding outside the capital of Khamearra. That was seven years ago. She once asked Beck why he took care of her, and his only answer was to honor her mother. She never fully understood what that meant, and Beck, being a man of few words, had never explained. She returned her attention to the men in the council when she heard the silky voice of the Dark Light Master himself speaking.

***

"You have more to add to these proceedings, Mactar," Elite Master Gerric said.

"Indeed, I do. You must acknowledge the evidence points to the return of the Alenzar'seth to Safanar," Mactar said, striding around the room.

"We will be sending a small contingent of Elitesmen to investigate this man and bring him before this council," Gerric answered, his deep voice carrying throughout the chamber.

"A small contingent, you say," Mactar said with raised eyebrows. "Considering what he's done with previous Elitesmen unfortunate enough to cross his path, perhaps the contingent should include a few masters."

"As always, your council is very much appreciated," Gerric began, but Mactar cut him off.

"Underestimate this man at your own peril," Mactar said, his gaze sweeping the chamber.

Gerric clenched his teeth. "This matter is finished. The contingent is already underway, and from our reports there are few places where he could be heading."

Mactar surveyed the council room. The High King was absent, but his son Rordan was in attendance, and the other masters were so blinded by their arrogance that he almost felt sorry for them...almost, but the trap wasn't quite set...yet.

"One more thing if I may. I have another matter to bring forth to this council." When Gerric and the other masters nodded in succession for him to continue, he took a moment and let the silence hang in the air. "The Drake has awoken," he said simply.

Pandemonium.

Mactar waited patiently for Gerric to restore order, but it was long in coming. "It has been reported being seen south of the midland mountains toward Rexel."

Now they will believe, Mactar thought.

"The line of Alenzar'seth is dead. They have been hunted down and dealt with. Reymius is gone," Gerric said, echoing the others. "And..."

"The Drake will not awaken unless the Alenzar'seth has returned to Safanar," Mactar finished. "The keys to Shandara are once again within our grasp, and it appears that the death of Reymius was gravely overrated."

***

Sarah's breath caught in her chest. The Drake, a demon brought forth when Shandara fell. It had hunted all of the Alenzar'seth down, with one exception it seemed. None of the mighty house could stand against the beast. Reymius had escaped, but where had he gone? Shandara was a place beyond dangerous, and with that thought, she knew that was where Aaron would go. She rose quickly and left the room, leaving the trailing voices of the council behind her. She had to warn Aaron of the danger he was in. Sarah swept down the halls of the palace to gather what supplies she needed, all the while hoping she would get there in time.

CHAPTER 21
ESCAPE

"Well, that was an interesting lesson," Verona said, walking with Aaron. "I think you will prove to be a very effective teacher, my friend."

"Thanks. Jopher appeared to know you."

"Indeed. I knew his older brother, whom I had the privilege of teaching one of your lessons to the last time I was in Rexel. Maybe it runs in the family," Verona said, smiling.

"Are all these nobles so arrogant?" Aaron asked, giving voice to his frustration.

"Not all of us," a voice answered behind them.

Aaron turned to see Vaughn and Prince Cyrus. The prince gave Aaron a half smile.

"I meant no offense," Aaron said, inclining his head respectfully. "Where I'm from, we believe all men to be created equal. The rule of law applies to any man, regardless of the assets he calls his own or the armies at his command."

Verona began coughing, and even Vaughn looked slightly alarmed, but quickly got hold of his features. The prince merely smiled, nodding to himself.

"A man's quality is often revealed through his actions and the things he says. In this brief time, I feel confident in saying that the heir of Alenzar'seth is indeed here before my eyes. It is a miracle that you stand before us," Prince Cyrus said. "Whatever aid I may give you on your journey, I will. Your grandfather was a very dear friend of mine, and I'm sad to hear of his passing, but happy to hear that he did find some peace in his life. Please walk with me a while and tell me about Reymius and your mother, Carlowen."

The tension drained from Aaron's shoulders. He told Prince Cyrus about his home, about his grandfather as he knew him, and about his mother and father. Speaking of them was bittersweet, because it reminded him of the home he had lost, but he was grateful for the life he still had.

They eventually made their way to the office of the prince. While the others took their leave, Verona and Vaughn stayed with them. The room was large with windows overlooking the gardens. The prince had lunch brought up, and when they finished eating, he signaled to his steward. The steward walked over carrying a tray with a few documents yellowed with age.

"There is something I would like to show you, Aaron," the prince said, selecting one of the rolls of parchment and unfurling it. "This was written by your grandfather," he said, waving Aaron over. "Please read this here."

Aaron came around the table and examined the parchment. The elegant and precise flow of the script was unmistakably his grandfather's handwriting, which itself was enough to get his attention, but what was written left him speechless. It was a letter to the prince from his grandfather. He turned to the prince, who smiled reassuringly, and Aaron read aloud.

Cyrus, my friend and brother in everything but blood. I urge you to consider what we have spoken about at length. If we are to lead and rule over men, women, and children, then the rule of law must protect them, regardless of home or hearth. The rule of law should be equally applicable, whether commoner or king. I know this is not desirable to those who rule through fear, but at some point we must unite against the tyrants of this land. I have written several volumes on the subject, which are here at the White Rose, that I would like to share with you on your next visit. Cassey believes I may be moving too quickly, but has grown to appreciate that the provinces of Shandara have people at the capital to represent them. This freedom has given birth to such innovation of the likes we haven't seen before. We don't need to rule over the people, but embrace and protect them. Let them be masters of their own destiny.

Your friend,
Reymius

The room was silent.

"Reymius sent me this letter a few weeks before the fall of Shandara. So you see it makes sense that he helped instill in you an appreciation of the law and the freedoms that can come with it. Sadly, I've never seen the volumes that contain the words of which Reymius spoke."

"Was this the reason for the fall of Shandara?" Aaron asked.

The prince shook his head. "There is a power in Shandara that the Alenzar'seth were the custodians of. But it was their innovation that arrayed many against them. They designed the first airships, for example. The concept of people having a say in how they are ruled had spread like wildfire, but has since been suppressed in most kingdoms. What do you intend to do, Aaron?"

The prince didn't exactly dodge the question, but Aaron knew he wasn't being told everything either. "I have no desire for power of any kind. I intend to go to Shandara to seek out Colind. He is the only person who has the knowledge to help me. Even now, I am being hunted. Just me being here puts you all at risk."

They were interrupted by a commotion outside the door, followed by men shouting. Braden was closest, and with his hand on his knife, he opened the door. Zeus charged through and came to Aaron's side, his fur bristling.

"How did a wolf enter the palace?" the prince asked the steward, who stood panting at the door.

"We don't know, your Grace. One moment the hall was clear, and the next moment it was there," the steward said.

"He is with me," Aaron said. "We must leave. Danger is coming. That's the only reason why Zeus came here from the forests outside the city."

Verona turned to the Prince. "Uncle, please allow us the use of one of your airships. It can't have taken the Elitesmen long to figure out where we were heading."

"But the Elitesmen wouldn't dare travel here." The prince looked up in surprise and then motioned for the guard. "Send out word, and ready the Raven for immediate departure." The guard saluted and quickly left the room. "Gather what supplies you need and meet me at the airfield."

The prince told Verona that he would guide Aaron to the airfield himself.

"Aaron, I wanted to speak to you without the others around," the prince said, and Aaron nodded for him to continue. The prince took a quick glance at Zeus, gathering his thoughts. "I get the feeling that you haven't told us everything," he began. "I'm not saying you've been less than truthful, but I've been a prince for a long time. Long enough to know when someone isn't telling me everything." The prince looked Aaron straight in the eye. "Now, Colind sent you to me because he believed I could provide you with some help, which I fully intend to give, but I also believe that his purpose was twofold. He also wanted me to know that the Alenzar'seth have returned to Safanar. In order for me to really help, I need to know more. Who else besides the Elitesmen Order is hunting you?"

Aaron swallowed, considering how best to answer the prince. "Reymius didn't flee to some distant land on this world. He found a gateway to another world entirely. When he died, the gateway was opened once again, and something evil began to attack me. Tarimus."

"Colind's son!"

"Yes, but he is now enslaved to someone named Mactar," Aaron answered.

For the first time, the prince looked frightened, taking a quick look around them. Then he hardened himself and gripped Aaron's shoulders tightly. "Tread carefully. There is a reason so many fear the Dark Light Master. While you are journeying to Shandara, I will send out word to those who would stand with you, but there is one group that I cannot reach. It must be you who finds them, for they will be powerful allies and will be able to help you against Mactar and the Order of the Elite."

"Who are they?" Aaron asked.

"The Hythariam. They are another race of beings that withdrew from the world of men when Shandara fell. They live upon the edges of the wild, beyond the northern borders of Shandara," the prince said.

"How am I supposed to find them?" Aaron asked.

"I suspect that they will try to find you, and I believe that although they have withdrawn from the world, they are always watching," the prince answered. He quickened his step. Aaron lost track of how many corridors they walked and the different turns they took. At times, he suspected they were underground. When they emerged at the airfield, the sight of the airship made Aaron's mouth drop.

The ship hovered a few feet above the ground, painted black with two silver-and-blue stripes running the length of the ship. Most of the ship was some type of metal with polished wood furnishings. They were joined by Sarik and Garret, who also stood in silent awe of the airship. Verona was already on board with Eric and Braden.

"I never thought I'd get to ride in an airship like that," Sarik exclaimed, rushing forward to get on board with Garret close behind.

A grizzled bear of a man in a silver-and-blue uniform with a golden collar approached the prince respectfully.

"Aaron, I would like for you to meet Captain Nathaniel Morgan. Morgan, I'd like for you to meet Aaron Jace of the house Alenzar'seth."

The captain raised an eyebrow at the mention of Aaron's name, but quickly schooled his features and firmly shook Aaron's hand.

"A fine day for sailing the skies, lad. The Raven is among the finest of airships," Captain Morgan said proudly.

"Captain, if I could have a word," the prince said, and he and the captain walked a few paces away, speaking in hushed tones. A shipman climbing on board offered to take Aaron's pack and staff, which he handed over. His swords were attached to his belt, which he had kept on since the practice yard.

The Raven was immense, and Aaron wondered how many crew there were to fly such a ship. The ship was even more impressive than the airships they had watched take off as they approached Rexel the previous day. They had been here such a brief time. Thinking about last night brought Sarah and the kiss they'd shared at the fountain to his mind. She hadn't been more than a moment away from his thoughts since. He wondered if he would ever see her again.

The captain saluted the prince and nodded to Aaron before walking up the ramp to the airship.

"Aaron, I hope you find what you seek in Shandara, but be warned, while it was once a jewel of the free world, it is now a place of darkness. Safe journey to you," the prince said, reaching out to rest a hand on his shoulder.

Aaron was about to reply when the medallion grew cold against his chest. A second later, he heard Zeus's low growl. Aaron spun, scanning the shipyard.

"Get behind me, your Grace."

No sooner had the prince moved than three identical flashes of light and three figures appeared across the yard.

"You would violate the treaty, Elitesmen!" the prince said.

"We have our orders, your Grace. This one is coming with us," said the center Elitesman, his dark cloak billowing behind him as he pointed directly at Aaron.

"Like hell you are. This is my kingdom, and you have no authority here. To arms, guards!" the prince yelled. Three more flashes of lights erupted with Elitesmen standing some distance behind them. They were surrounded.

Aaron laughed loudly and took a few steps out into the open, drawing everyone's gaze to him. The soft wail of alarm bells could be heard from outside the airfield.

***

"Is he insane?" Vaughn said aloud to no one in particular.

"No, he's buying time for the guards to arrive. Sarik, get your bow ready and stand over there," Verona said. "No!" he hissed toward Eric and Braden, who stopped in their tracks as they were about to head down. "He's buying time for the prince to escape and needs cover from here. Captain, ready this ship to take off at once. Garret, help him. If we can escape, the Elitesmen will have no reason to stay. Eric, Braden, grab that rope over there and be ready to toss it down." Verona whispered a silent prayer to the Goddess and strung his bow.

* * *

***

"Six of you," Aaron said tauntingly and spared a glance at the prince. Guards began pouring in through the airfield entrances. "Your Grace, please take cover. It's me they want. I will distract them."

He didn't give the prince any time to protest and put more distance between them.

"Well, here I am," he challenged, drawing his swords, further increasing the gap between himself and the prince. As he expected, the Elitesmen remained focused on him.

As one, they Elitesmen drew their weapons. They expected fear, but Aaron refused to give in even though the six that stood around him all had the look of veteran fighters.

"What are you waiting for? I'm right here!" *If it's a fight they want, then let them come.*

The Elitesmen closed in on Aaron, and the first attack came from behind. Aaron quickly dropped to one knee and rolled away, leaping into the next attack. He unleashed the bladesong, and the power coursed through his veins with the whisperings of warriors past echoing in the depths of his mind. He was one with the blades now, and movement in battle was life. Aaron attacked and drove each of the Elitesmen back, becoming the living example of the lesson he had taught his friends earlier. He had no thought beyond the next block, dodge, and attack. His body moved with deadly grace, but he didn't seek the death of these men. Nor they him. They sought to capture him. Then, as suddenly as they had started, the Elitesmen broke off their attack. The leader brought his hands together, and a violet orb formed, crackling with energy. With a powerful push from his arms, the leader sent a beam of energy directly to Aaron, who barely got the Falcons up in time. The force of the blast rattled his bones and had no sign of relenting, but still he held his blades crossed, deflecting the attack. The other Elitesmen circled around, coming closer, and Aaron knew he was in trouble. He couldn't block the beam and fight the other Elitesmen at the same time. He could chance moving, but he wasn't sure if only one of his blades was sufficient to ward off the attack. There was another flash of light from a travel crystal, and a figure in black emerged and attacked the Elitesmen closing in on him, drawing them away.

The relief he felt was short-lived, as he had to stop the Elitesmen's attack and get out of there. He focused his will on the beam as it hit his swords, and the glow of the crystals in the hilts spread the length of the blades until it covered his arms and surrounded his vision. The power gathered around him, eager to do his bidding, and when he could contain it no longer, he hurled it toward the Elitesmen. A beam as bright as the sun sliced through the Elitesmen's attack, violently knocking him off his feet.

Aaron felt momentarily drained, but looked to the left, seeing that his mysterious protector was overwhelmed by the remaining Elitesmen. With his blades still imbued with energy, he made a broad swipe through the air, sending a rippling wave that sent three of the Elitesmen sprawling and left one engaged with the figure in black. Aaron raced toward them as the figure in black was knocked unconscious, but the Elitesman didn't press the attack. Instead, they turned to face Aaron.

The guards continued to pour into the airfield, circling all of them. Archers filled the ranks between the guards and drew their bows.

"I doubt even an Elitesman will survive a full volley of arrows at this range," the prince warned, joining the guards, and a wall of swords formed around him.

"This doesn't concern you, Prince Cyrus. Call off your guards. There is no need to shed any blood," the last Elitesman on his feet said, with the others beginning to rise.

Aaron heard the humming of the airship's engines grow louder, but he didn't take his eyes from the Elitesmen. He felt a rope hit his shoulder, and he chanced a look above to see Eric and Braden calling to him to grab it. Without any thought, he wrapped his arm around the figure in black and grabbed the rope. The airship quickly lurched into the air with the ground racing away from his feet. Aaron saw flashes of bright light from below, and he knew that the Elitesmen had left. Eric and Braden pulled them onboard.

They gently laid his unconscious protector in black on the deck. Aaron was relieved to see that there were no wounds. He unwrapped the black cloth from around the head and gasped when a swath of golden-blonde hair spilled out onto the deck. His protector in black was Sarah. She opened her eyes, and Aaron sighed with relief.

"You know there are easier ways to get to know me, but I'm grateful that you came when you did," Aaron said, breaking the silence. "Are you all right?" he asked, and he noticed her lips curve into the slightest of smiles before she nodded. Aaron offered to help her up, but she stood up on her own.

"I hope you'll stay longer this time," Aaron said, but before she could reply, Vaughn gasped in surprise and bowed.

"Your Grace," Vaughn said, clearly speaking to Sarah. She nodded with practiced grace and dignity.

"Please," she said, "I would prefer a bit of anonymity for the time being."

Vaughn nodded.

"I'm not going anywhere," Sarah said to Aaron. "But is there somewhere we can speak with a little more privacy?"

Aaron looked to Verona, who answered, "Of course. The captain has some rooms set aside for us to use, and I'm sure it will suit your purposes."

She's here. Aaron kept repeating it in his mind as Verona led them below deck. Why had she returned? How did she know to come to the airfield? Would she disappear again? She said she wouldn't, but... The questions tumbled through his mind, but when she turned to look at him, he decided he didn't care why she was here, he was just happy that she was.

They followed Verona through the ship to a room that was like a lounge, with several chairs and a few desks along the wall. Aaron let Sarah enter the room first and stuck his hand out, blocking Verona and the others from entering.

"I need a few minutes alone here," Aaron said and closed the door in Verona's surprised face. He smiled to himself as he heard them retreat down the hall, grumbling. They were all well intentioned, but there were things he wanted to know from her in private.

"Thank you for coming when you did," he said quietly. "I'm not sure how it would have ended otherwise."

Sarah smiled back at him. "I'm sure you would have thought of something. You really are quite resourceful."

Aaron let out a small laugh. "You took quite a hit, are you sure you're all right?" he asked, taking a step closer to her.

"I'm fine," she replied, pushing a rebellious strand of blonde hair away from her face. "Aaron, I need to tell you..."

Aaron took another step closer and reached out, taking her hand. "Sarah, it's okay."

"No, it's not, there are things that you don't know. You are in grave danger."

Aaron was a bit shocked by how scared she sounded. This had to be something other than the Elitesmen.

"Okay, let's just sit down, and you tell me what you came to tell me," he said, sounding more calm than he felt.

They sat together on a couch by the wall, and warm sunlight streamed through the windows. The day was so calm compared to mere minutes ago, and when she looked at him with those eyes of hers, he felt his heart grow warm in his chest.

"I am the daughter of High King Amorak of Khamearra, where the Elite Council resides. My father was among those who brought destruction to Shandara," she said. "And I know who you are." Her voice cracked. "You're Carlowen's son. Reymius's daughter of the house Alenzar'seth."

Aaron took a few moments before answering her. "Yes, I am, Sarah. Although it seems there were many involved with the fall of Shandara, and I'm afraid there is only one person who knows the whole story," Aaron said, thinking of Colind.

Sarah searched his eyes. "You don't hate me?"

"Hate you! I could never hate you," he said. "I'm not here to avenge Shandara. I'm just trying to stay alive." Aaron smiled at her. "You've risked a great deal to come here, and I can't help but wonder whether you're going to disappear again."

"I'm not going anywhere," she said. "I didn't come here to warn you about my father." She then told him about the Elite Council and how they weren't entirely convinced of who Aaron really was. At least, not before this last attempt to capture him. Then she told him of the Drake. "The Drake was brought forth around the time of the fall of Shandara and the extermination of the Alenzar'seth."

"But what is it exactly?" Aaron asked. He knew there was something he should remember, and it was tugging at the edges of his thoughts.

"It's a beast that is not of this world," she replied. "The last battle invoked a curse that allowed the beast to traverse between worlds. Mactar orchestrated events to allow this to happen, knowing full well what it would do to the kingdom of Shandara and to the Alenzar'seth. Their hearts were the source of their greatest strength and their ultimate weakness. The beast hunted down and murdered them down to the last woman and child. Then it just disappeared."

Aaron's mind raced. He had more questions than he could speak aloud at the moment. "Yeah, but how could me being here awaken this...beast? Where has it been all this time? How would it even know I'm here?" As he said the last, the warning bells in his brain grew louder. There was a knock at the door and in walked one of the crew returning the rune-carved staff.

214 | ROAD TO SHANDARA

The staff! "That's it!" he exclaimed, and thanked the crewman.

"I was given this staff shortly after I arrived on Safanar." Given wasn't the right word since his ancestor more or less forced it upon him. He looked back at Sarah and knew she had questions, but she was patient enough to wait him out. "In order for you to understand, I need to tell you...ah, everything," he said, rising.

"Aaron," she said, "how do you know you can trust me?"

Aaron looked at her for a long moment. "Can't I? I know we barely know each other, but when I look into your eyes, I know you would never betray me," he said.

Sarah's breath appeared to catch in her chest. She closed the distance between them, caressed his face with her smooth hands, and pulled him in. Their lips met, and if Aaron could have flown, surely he would have been floating over the rooftops of this world. He felt like there were fireworks exploding brilliantly all around him. They pulled apart from each other, smiling.

"I will never betray you," she said, looking deeply into his eyes.

He wanted to swim for eternity in those bottomless blue eyes, and wondered if he would ever get used to merely standing beside her without his knees getting weak.

They sat together on the couch by the ship's windows. Clouds passed by, and Aaron told Sarah everything. He started at the beginning, when his grandfather died. How his life had changed. He told her about his home and his sister, Tara, who thankfully must be still alive now that he had gone. At least he was able to honor his father's dying wish. He told her of the death of his mother and father, and how they had died to protect him. Aaron turned away from her, his throat thickening with grief. He had gotten so used to carrying it that in these rare quiet moments the weight threatened to crush him.

"You can't protect everyone from everything," Sarah said.

He knew the truth in her words, but he still felt that he should have been able to do more. He should have been able to save his family and Bronwyn. He could have done more, and the cost of not doing so still weighed heavily upon him. Instead of answering Sarah, he told her of meeting Daverim Alenzar'seth and the taking of the rune-carved staff. The beast he saw must have been the Drake waking from wherever it had been sleeping, and now...it was coming for him.

"I need to tell the others about the Drake. Perhaps Vaughn or Garret might know more," Aaron said.

"Aaron," Sarah said, holding on to his hand while they stood up. "Thank you for trusting me."

He took a moment, gripping her hand purposefully. "Thank you for saving me," Aaron replied solemnly and stepped quietly from the room.

After a few minutes, he returned with Verona, who'd been loitering not far from the door anyway. They were later joined by the twins, Eric and Braden, as well as Garret, Vaughn, and young Sarik. As Sarik went to close the door, Zeus nuzzled his way through and settled at Sarah's feet. She was alarmed at first, but when Zeus nudged her hand, she scratched him behind his ears.

"My friends, this is Sarah," Aaron said, making the introductions around the room.

Verona bowed formally to Sarah. "My Lady, it's not that we don't appreciate your timely arrival, but given the circumstances, one could argue that your arrival was a little too timely to be above suspicion," he said without a hint of disrespect.

"You are right to be suspicious," Sarah said, rising and meeting their gazes. "I did not come here expecting that my motives wouldn't be questioned. In fact, I hardly gave any thought to it as I had just learned that a detachment of Elitesmen had been dispatched to capture Aaron. By now, the council will know of its failure and will be better prepared next time they come."

"So why help us?" Vaughn asked.

"I'm here for Aaron," Sarah replied. "I heard a report of a mysterious stranger who took down an Elite, which caused quite a stir. Unlike my father and half-brothers, I still show respect for the Goddess Ferasdiam, like my mother before me. I was meditating at a secret temple that escaped destruction in Khamearra when the Goddess spoke to me."

"What did she say?" Aaron asked, and her gaze softened when she looked back at him.

"She said one of the old blood has returned. I knew I had to search for this mysterious stranger, and I eventually caught up to you in that small town. Prior to that, in another town, I talked to a father and son who spoke very highly of a man who stood up to the injustice of the Elitesmen," Sarah said.

Verona raised an eyebrow and looked at Aaron. "You did see someone outside the town that day. I thought...I don't know what I thought, but I apologize for not believing you, my friend." He turned to Sarah. "How did you appear to Aaron, but remain hidden from the rest of us?"

Sarah smiled at Verona with a hint of a challenge in her eyes. "We all have our secrets."

Verona and a few of the others chuckled. "I had to try. Fair enough, I guess."

"She came to warn us of something called the Drake," Aaron said, and an immediate hush overtook the room.

"The Drake has returned? I had hoped..." Garret spoke first, sharing a glance with Vaughn, but Aaron noticed the shaky note in his voice.

"Mactar believes so, and Aaron confirmed it for me," Sarah answered.

Aaron told them of the events that occurred when he'd first come to Safanar and how he'd come to be in possession of the rune-carved staff. Then he told them of the beast he saw waking when he first put his hands upon the staff. "Daverim Alenzar'seth said the staff would help in the days ahead."

"Perhaps he knew of the Drake and gave you a weapon to fight it with," Vaughn said.

Aaron shook his head. "I'm not too clear on the timeline, but my guess is that the Drake came after Daverim's time."

"He's right," Garret said, "but this was a lost relic of the Safanarion Order. They were the only ones who kept the Elitesmen in check."

"I have something else I need to tell the rest of you. When Verona and I encountered the dragon, it led us to a fountain with a statue of a woman. The dragon said we were in the presence of the Goddess," Aaron said. "It was then that I heard a voice in my head." He stopped, shaking his head slightly, and considered his words. "I'm sorry, but hearing a voice inside my head is not exactly a common occurrence where I come from." He let out a small laugh that the others shared.

"It's not common anywhere, Aaron," Sarah said, and the rest of the room faded to gray while they looked at each other.

Aaron swallowed and continued. "She told me the land is sick and needs a champion. The responsibility for the fate of the land falls upon the house of Alenzar'seth, of which I am the last. Guardianship of the land is a legacy shared with the Safanarion Order, who have all but vanished. Fate has chosen me for this. It's why I was marked. Ferasdiam Marked. Tarimus knew from the onset."

"Tarimus!" Sarah exclaimed. "That's the name Mactar was calling out to." She stopped abruptly, apparently remembering where she was.

"What do you mean exactly?" Vaughn asked.

"Mactar has an ancient mirror in his castle. When my father bade me to summon the Dark Light Master for his role in my half-brother's death, I found Mactar standing before a mirror, calling out to Tarimus, but there was no reply," she answered. "How do you know of Tarimus, Aaron?" she asked.

He knew more about Tarimus than he cared to admit. "He came after my grandfather died. He came for me in my dreams, while I was awake, and used people I care about to get to me." He couldn't keep the bitterness from his words. "I had to face him upon the crossroads between worlds, but"—he paused again, gathering his thoughts—"I haven't sensed him since coming through the gateway."

"A gateway," Verona said. "Between worlds? You've come from a place a good deal more distant than I originally thought, my friend."

Before Aaron could reply, there was a sharp knock on the door. Sarik opened the door, and a crewman entered.

"The captain wishes a word with you, my Lord," he said, speaking to Aaron. Aaron nodded and began following the crewman out of the room, but stopped and turned to Sarah.

"Don't worry, lad, we'll see that she gets settled in her quarters," Vaughn said, smiling. Aaron let out a small smile and followed the crewman from the room. The others began leaving the room, and Sarah rose from the couch when Verona asked to have a word with her.

"She'll be right there, Vaughn. This won't take but a moment," Verona said. He turned toward Sarah, and she wondered what he was going to say.

"Aaron is a good man," Verona began. "Fate has delivered him a tough hand to play, but a blind man would notice the way you two look at each other. Despite that, I'm still not sure why you're here. Your reasons are your own, and I can respect that, but"—Verona took a moment before continuing—"he's my friend, and he doesn't yet know the ways of this world. It's my job to watch out for him. If you are here for Aaron as you say, then I welcome you with open arms, but I will be ever watchful."

Sarah wasn't lying when she'd said the act of coming was on impulse, but in her heart she knew this was where she was supposed to be. The more time she spent with Aaron, the more she knew she could never go back to her old life.

"You are a good friend, and I have no doubts where your loyalty lies. It's interesting, your comment on Aaron not knowing the ways of this world. I think that could be one of his greatest strengths." What could she possibly tell Verona to put him at ease where Aaron was concerned? "I care for him, Verona. Fate has been pulling on all of our strings it seems."

"Indeed it has," Verona agreed. "Aaron has a way of seeing right to the heart of a matter. Whether he realizes it or not, he is a natural leader. I have but one more question."

"Then ask."

"Your travel crystal?"

"Is depleted," Sarah said, taking out the now-dark crystal.

Verona nodded. "Sarah, I sincerely hope your intentions are true where Aaron is concerned. He could be our greatest hope against"— he stopped, taking a measured look at her—"well, against the darkness springing from Shandara and the tyranny of Khamearra."

Sarah met Verona's gaze evenly. "I understand," she replied, and Verona nodded, leaving her with Vaughn.

CHAPTER 22
TRUTHS ACCEPTED

The council chambers of the High King were cold and silent, with the men in attendance not daring to speak. The Elitesmen squad had finished reporting their failed attempt to capture the apparent Heir of Shandara.

"Where is your sister?" High King Amorak asked, but none of the men in attendance was fooled by the calm tone.

"I last saw her outside the main council chambers of the Elite, Father," Primus answered.

The High King regarded his son as a lion observes his prey moments before unleashing his fury. "And you kept this information to yourself," he said coldly.

"I...I didn't think it warranted any attention," Primus stammered.

The High King came before his son. "It's the littlest things that can have the most impact. For example"—the High King made a grandiose gesture to the others present—"it can be a fine line between victory and defeat when there is a breakdown of the perceived importance of an event. Rordan?" the High King called out to his other son.

"Yes, Father," Rordan answered.

"Are the council meetings of the Elite open to the public? Can anyone come and watch them?" the High King asked mildly.

"No, Father, they are not," Rordan answered, pointedly not looking in his twin brother's direction. "But Father," he continued, "Sarah surely is not the one who thwarted the squad's attempt to capture this man."

"Perhaps," the High King answered. "Perhaps not."

"The plan was doomed from the start, your Grace," spoke a hooded figure entering the chambers, who was followed closely by another.

"The only thing learned was that this man can hold his own against six senior Elitesmen, and quite honestly, I think they got off lightly." Together, the men removed their hoods, revealing themselves to be Mactar and Darven.

The Grand Master of the Elite sneered at Darven, who coolly returned his gaze. Darven was the only living former member of the Elite.

"Your Grace, despite my warnings, the council sent these men to Rexel, alerting not only this man, but also Prince Cyrus that we know that the Heir of Shandara—" Mactar's words were cut off as the High King raised his hand.

"You speak out of turn, Mactar. I have not invited your council," the High King said, holding Mactar at his mercy. The lighting in the room dimmed by an unseen force, and the breath caught in Mactar's throat. He looked toward Darven with panic-stricken eyes.

Darven immediately sank to his knees. "Please, my Lord, release him. Hear what he has to say."

The High King brought his hand up higher, and Mactar's body rose off the floor. "Dark Light Master," he uttered with contempt, letting Mactar's writhing form hang in the air. "Many fear you, but I grow tired of your meddling. I should give you the death you so richly deserve. You have seconds to speak your case, but if you speak in riddles, I will kill you where you stand." The High King's bellow echoed throughout the chamber, and Mactar's body dropped forcefully to the floor.

Mactar gasped for breath. "Thank you, my Lord. As you well know, with the fall of Shandara it was assumed that the line of Alenzar'seth was finally extinguished. The Drake withdrew from the realms of men, and until a few months ago, I believed it as well—that is, until Tarimus appeared, unbidden, in the Mirror of Areschel with news about Reymius Alenzar'seth. Tarimus said a great many things that night, but what was most striking were the words: 'The Lord of Shandara has finally passed from the world of the living through the gateway of an unknown realm and takes his respite in the lands of shadow, awaiting the return.' Tarimus, being a creature between the worlds of the living and dead, could now sense the presence of the Alenzar'seth in this unknown realm. Two of them, in fact." Mactar paused again, watching the High King's expression turn even grimmer.

"Tarimus had enough power to traverse to this realm and was compelled to hunt the heir of Alenzar'seth, but as time went on, he changed, growing madder so that it became almost impossible to control him. I couldn't dissuade him from the hunt. It was almost as if he didn't have a choice. His nature forbade him from not seeking the two. He spoke of a young man who is Reymius's heir, and the second was Princess Carlowen, Reymius's daughter. Tarimus was fixated on the young man, and as he grew in strength, so did Tarimus's power in the place between worlds. This man must have traversed between realms to Safanar, and it was at this moment that the Drake awoke with the shaking of our world, thus proving that this stranger is of the house Alenzar'seth," Mactar said.

"Give us the room," the High King said quietly, and the council chamber quickly emptied, save for his heirs, Mactar and Darven, and Gerric, the Grand Master of the Elite.

"It appears that Tye's strike force wasn't a complete failure after all. And you were there," the High King said to Darven.

"I was, your Grace. I can confirm that Princess Carlowen was in this unknown realm. The last thing I saw before leaving that realm was the knife that left my hands and buried itself into her chest."

The High King nodded and shoved his anger at Mactar to the far corner of his mind. What he was offering was too good to refuse. "How is it that Tarimus did not sense the presence of the Alenzar'seth?"

"All roads lead back to Shandara, your Grace," Mactar said quietly.

"Shandara!" Primus exclaimed. "Are you mad?"

"Take hold of your fear, Brother," Rordan admonished, looking to his father.

"But none can travel to Shandara. The place is cursed. All who go never return. Entire armies have disappeared," Primus responded. Both princes looked to their father. Their eyes demanded an answer, but the High King nodded to Mactar.

"Shandara is the final destination for the heir of Alenzar'seth," Mactar said.

"It is no ordinary hunt of an assassin who lies in wait in the shadows to strike. The Drake can see into the heart of men and will first destroy all those they love, driving the soul mad with despair until it devours their essence," the Elite Grand Master added.

The High King turned his towering form toward Mactar, and a look of understanding passed between them. The heir was key to the true power of Shandara. "I think it's time we set up another force to go to Shandara. I have a present I want delivered to Reymius's heir."

"Father, I will lead the force that will go to Shandara," Rordan said without hesitation, and the High King nodded with approval.

"Both of you will go, but Rordan will lead with Primus as his second. The force will be made up of Elitesmen," the High King said, and then he pointedly looked at Mactar.

"Of course, your Grace, my services are at your disposal," Mactar replied.

CHAPTER 23
THE RAVEN

Aaron was led through a series of hallways that ran the length of the immense airship proudly named the Raven. The crewman leading him spoke of the layout and how Aaron would be able to find his way around in no time. Windows along the hallways provided ample lighting during the day, and Aaron noticed dormant orbs along the walls for the night. The interior of the ship was a mix between metal and wood, both polished and ornate. They came to the wheelhouse, and a guard politely opened the door. Captain Morgan was quietly speaking with one of his men when he noticed Aaron and waved him over with a friendly nod of his head.

"My Lord." The captain addressed Aaron formally.

"Please, call me Aaron."

Captain Morgan nodded. "As you wish. Shortly after our auspicious takeoff, one of my crew found an extra passenger hiding among the cargo."

Captain Morgan gestured toward the guards at the door, who immediately brought in a man with a cloth sack pulled over his head.

The guards held him firmly. Just then, Verona entered the wheelhouse.

"Well, what do we have here?" Verona asked with half a smile and a wink.

"We're about to find out," Aaron said.

"Indeed, as I was saying," the captain continued, "normally we would set down and send the extra passenger away with the local magistrate, but given the urgency of our trip, we may have to just throw him over the side." The crew laughed hungrily. The man with the cloth sack over his head sagged a little before standing up straight again. "That is, of course, before he said he was with you." The captain raised his hand, and the guard drew off the cloth sack.

It took a few moments for Aaron to realize he was staring at "the Exalted Royal Highness" Prince Jopher.

"My Lord Prince," Aaron said, and Jopher flinched. "I didn't realize you've decided to be with us commoners. What do you think, Verona?"

"It is a peculiar development to say the least," Verona began. "It might be easier to adopt the good captain's policy for unwanted passengers and toss him over the side."

"Please!" Jopher cried, falling to his knees, his disheveled black hair falling into his face. "I have wronged you, sir. My anger got the better of me, and I must atone for my offense. Please let me travel with you to repay my debt."

Of all the things Aaron might have expected to hear, this was not among them. "With me?" Aaron asked, and Jopher nodded vehemently.

Aaron leaned in closer. "What about every other person your royal arrogance has wronged?"

Jopher sagged to his knees, again not meeting Aaron's gaze, and the wheelhouse grew silent.

"It is not me you must atone to, but to people as a whole. Be a better person, Jopher. People were not born to do your bidding, despite what you may have been told. The wrong you've done is to yourself in believing that you are better than everyone else because your father happens to be king in some far-off land."

Jopher took a deep breath. "I will. I promise!"

Aaron regarded the prince and said, "If you were in my shoes, what would you do with someone like yourself?"

Jopher knelt in silence, staring at the floor for a few moments, hardly breathing. "Please," he whispered. "I want to be a better man, and I believe traveling with you will help me achieve that while I aid you in your journey."

"Aaron," Verona whispered, "I know that of which you speak, but the arrogance in him is taught from birth. Consider carefully. He may prove to be an asset."

"More than likely, this journey will bring his death," Aaron replied.

"Perhaps. It's the journey that builds the man, does it not?" Verona asked loudly enough for Jopher to hear.

Aaron narrowed his gaze, studying Jopher, and Captain Morgan cleared his throat.

"I might have a suggestion," the captain said with a wicked gleam in his eye. "We could always use some help in the galley. Perhaps a few days peeling potatoes or scrubbing dishes will go a ways in paying his debt and give you time to consider the boy's offer of aid."

Anger flashed in Jopher's eyes, but he quickly banished it.

Verona laughed out loud. "A fine idea, my good captain."

Aaron nodded, and the guards escorted Jopher from the wheelhouse.

"I hear the same treatment worked on you, my Lord," Captain Morgan said to Verona with a broad knowing smile, and Aaron couldn't help but laugh.

"Oh, my uncle never tires of the tale. We were all young once, weren't we?"

"Some of us were," said the captain. "Now, I have a ship to run, but the prince said you would give me a heading once we were airborne." Before Aaron could reply, the captain interrupted. "The prince filled me in on some crucial details, and the battle with the Elitesmen convinced me of the rest. Perhaps you would join me in the map room as we plot our heading?"

"Of course," Aaron replied, and followed the captain out the door.

The map room was a few doors down from the wheelhouse. The room hosted a desk and a large map as tall as a man that ran the length of the room. The map of Safanar was surprisingly detailed, and it took Aaron a few minutes to find Rexel, which was located almost in the middle.

Verona stepped up to the far side and pointed to a darkened spot on the map. "I believe this is our destination, Captain."

Aaron looked where Verona was pointing and saw Shandara marked in an area of the map that was deliberately darkened, with the words *Land of Shadow* written across the border.

The captain raised an eyebrow and looked surprised, but it passed in an instant. "So it's true then. You are the Heir of Shandara?"

"You make it sound like I'm some sort of king or something. Reymius was my grandfather, and after he died, it was revealed to me that I am of the house of Alenzar'seth," Aaron answered.

Captain Morgan looked sharply at Verona. "He doesn't know?"

"Oh, he knows, my good captain," Verona said with a slight smile. "He just refuses to accept."

"I've told you before, Verona, whatever anyone's plans are, I am no king," Aaron said.

What did his grandfather have in mind for him and the future? Did part of him believe he could run forever? That his mother would never regain her memories? He wished he could talk to his father one last time. Did he know about any of this before marrying his mother?

He turned to the map again, looking at the extremely long distance they would need to travel to reach Shandara. "I didn't realize the road would be this long. How long do you think it will take to reach this border?" Aaron asked.

The captain pursed his lips in thought for a moment. "A few weeks, maybe less, provided we have a good wind and clear skies to sail. As we get closer, we will need to travel only by night to avoid the Ryakuls. They are mostly active during the day, but at least we won't be so visible at night."

Aaron raised an eyebrow, looking from Verona to the captain. "I didn't think of that. Does this ship have a means to defend itself from a Ryakul attack?"

The captain drew himself up. "The Raven has teeth of its own. I'll have my first officer show you around so you and your companions will be able to lend a hand should the need arise."

"Garret told me a little about the crystals used to store energy from the sun. Can this energy be released?" Aaron asked.

"Against the Ryakul, you mean," the captain said, raising an eyebrow in thought. "It might be possible. I would suggest you speak with Hatly. He's the ship's engineer and is the real expert. I've heard some captains play at using the crystals as a weapon and blow themselves up in the process, which is why I've never explored the option. Since Shandara is our destination, though, I think it might be worth the effort and the risk."

"I will speak with Hatly and see if there is a way we can experiment safely," Aaron answered.

"A large crossbow bolt to the chest tends to work the best in my experience, but if you think you can work up something better, then give it a go."

Aaron nodded and left the room with Verona, eager to speak with Hatly. He was extremely curious about the crystals they had here. They had different properties than back home. He was no expert in crystals by any means, but he was fairly certain that they weren't used for storing energy from the sun back home. His hands drifted to his swords with his fingers gliding over the crystals inlaid in the pommel. They seemed to absorb energy, which had been extremely useful on occasion, even saving his life. He also suspected they came into play somehow when he wielded the blades to make the bladesong. Beyond the blades being bequeathed to him by his grandfather, they were as much a mystery to him as everything else in Safanar.

Aaron spent the next few hours speaking with Hatly, who was an easygoing, roll up the sleeves and get the work done sort of man that reminded him of his father. Crystals here in Safanar were a wonder and of a different breed than back home. A combination of different-colored crystals, when powered by yellow crystals, allowed steel to retain its strength but with less weight. However, the base yellow crystal had to be recharged, otherwise the weight of the steel bones of the ship would bring it crashing to the ground. These crystals were found throughout the hull of the ship, embedded in the wooden support beams because if they came in contact with metal, the metal would eventually dissolve into a rusty powder. Hatly assured him that there were many safeguards in place to prevent accidents.

Verona was able to fill in some of the blanks for him regarding the crystals. The richest sources were found in Khamearra and were controlled by the High King. There were stories of a great fire in the sky and how these special crystals were found in small deposits throughout Safanar. Aaron surmised that this planet experienced a large meteor shower that brought the crystals here. When Aaron explained what he had in mind for repelling the Ryakuls, Hatly was interested. The problem with releasing the stored-up energy was focusing its direction. If they broke, they would explode, which was something they all wanted to avoid even with the smallest of crystals. Aaron jokingly mentioned using a slingshot to hurl the crystals into the mouth of the Ryakuls, and Verona's eyes lit up.

"Not a sling, my friend. How about arrows with the shards fastened behind the tips? They won't be able to fly very far or accurately, and I'd wager we would need to wait for our target to get close to conserve our ammo," Verona said.

"That's a good idea, but how will they ignite?" Aaron's question drew a blank stare from Verona, and they both looked to Hatly.

"The crystals we use here on the ship are selected because of their durability. Only fragile crystals run the risk of exploding when they break. But..." Hatly paused, considering, and then reached over to his workbench, uncovering a wooden crate. He withdrew a dark crystal from the bunch and set it down. "This is a spent crystal. All the stored energy has been used up. Perhaps we can break it into the pieces we need and make them a bit more fragile. Then we could allow them to store power in the charging chamber, but we'll need to monitor the time, otherwise they will overload." Hatly went on muttering to himself, seeming to forget that they were still in the room. After a few moments, Verona nodded toward the door, and they quietly left Hatly to his work. In the hall, they met Braden, who was coming to collect them for dinner.

They dined with the captain and his senior officers. The mood was light considering where they were heading. Aaron wondered if Captain Morgan had informed his crew of their destination. The chef had prepared boar, for the tradition on a ship's first day of voyage was to feast in the evening. The food was delicious, with a variety that would surely satisfy even the most finicky of palates. The ale was dark and strong, leaving him feeling more relaxed than he had in a long time. Eric and Braden had resumed their roles as his shadows, never straying far from him. Garret and Vaughn were speaking with the captain, and periodically they would each glance in his direction.

"I see the old men are busy plotting," Verona said, bringing Aaron another pint of ale.

"Thanks, this ale is good," Aaron said. "They don't know what to make of me."

"Possibly," Verona answered. "Perhaps not. Old men talk, and young men drink." Verona smiled and raised his tankard.

"I guess." Aaron snorted, and as he raised his tankard to his lips, Sarah sat down in the seat next to him. He felt his heart quicken in spite of the ale-induced calmness. How did he feel about her? He didn't ignore her, but they both spent a fair amount of time not looking at each other throughout dinner. He felt that everyone must have noticed them not looking at each other. The few times their eyes did meet, Aaron felt heat rise from his chest.

"My Lady, you've found me again," Aaron said with a smile.

"To chance encounters," Sarah answered, raising her glass.

The three of them drank in unison. "What are the odds that the three of us would meet and be here at this particular moment?" Aaron asked.

"It does seem beyond mere coincidence," Verona said wistfully. "Right place, right time." Verona took another swallow of ale, raising an eyebrow.

"I have a question for you," Aaron began. "If I hadn't shown up, what would you be doing right now, you think?"

"That's easy, my friend. I would be looking for trouble. Or is it that trouble would be looking for me and succeeding more than failing," Verona said with a grin.

Aaron laughed with him. "No, seriously. Surely your life is more than looking for trouble."

Verona frowned in thought. "A starlit sky, good ale or wine depending where I am at the moment, and a beautiful lady to share the evening with. That is, of course, until I'm pulled back into the family business."

Sarah laughed, and the sound was music to his ears. Both he and Verona looked at her expectantly.

"I see it's my turn now," she said. "I'll tell you what I'd like to have been doing. Exploring a part of the world people haven't seen before. Where no one knows me. And you, Aaron?" she asked.

The question tumbled through his mind. What would he have been doing if none of this had ever happened? "Back home, I would have been in college, studying mechanical engineering. I like to work with my hands, so things like this airship fascinate me."

"Indeed, I could hardly get a word in edgewise when we spoke to Hatly," Verona said. "The ship's engineer," he said to Sarah.

"Sarik told me that you plan to train with him in the morning," Sarah said.

"He did, did he?" Aaron asked, glancing toward Sarik, who sat at another table with a guilty smile. "Yes." Aaron nodded. "I will be."

"I would like to join him if you wouldn't mind. I'd like to get some exercise," Sarah said with the candlelight caressing her face.

Aaron wondered if she had any idea how beautiful she was when she looked at him like that. Probably not. He would gladly dump Sarik over the side of the ship to spend more time alone with her.

"Of course," he answered, deciding he would thank Sarik instead.

"Good. I'm going to turn in for the night. Until tomorrow then," she said and left the room with more than a few glancing in her direction.

"Do you believe this lot?" Verona mused. "I'd say she only has eyes for you, my friend," Verona continued, and ignored Aaron as he nearly choked on his ale. "I'll admit I'm not entirely sure of her motives for being here, but when her eyes meet yours, well, let's just say there is more than friendship in them. I'd say the same for you, as well."

Aaron felt heat rise in his cheeks and silently cursed himself. "I can't," he muttered.

Verona smiled at him. "I think you already have," he chuckled. "There are times when the heart overrules the mind because it must. I believe this is one of those times. Why don't you go get some sleep? You look dreadful."

Aaron was about to protest, but he was feeling the ale in his veins, and his muscles were like water. He nodded silently and left. Instead of going to his room, he headed out on deck for some fresh air. Sailors nodded in greeting as they went about their tasks, and the cool night air revived Aaron as he stood gazing at the moon. The craters dotting the surface were clearly visible on this night. On the far side of the deck, a door opened, and the princeling, Jopher, appeared wearing a dirty apron and an angry expression. He met Aaron's gaze and took a few steps toward him before a deep voice called him back. Jopher glanced back at Aaron, who calmly looked back at him. Frowning, Jopher returned through the door. *A touch of humility indeed for that one.*

He dismissed thoughts of Jopher while sweeping his gaze across the night sky, taking in the view of the stars. Their clear and vibrant light speckled the sky with foreign patterns, leaving Aaron to wonder whether one of them was Earth. Was he even in the same universe? His passage to Safanar was shrouded in mystery, and these rare moments of stillness left him wondering what connection, if any, there was between Safanar and Earth. Could he ever go back? Would he want to if he could? How did his grandfather and mother go through the gateway between worlds? Could he travel to other places if he wanted? He wondered what his sister was doing and hoped she was safe. They had always been close, and he missed how they used to tease each other. In the midst of all the danger that surrounded him, the bright spot that repelled the darkness within him was Sarah. Despite how he tried to push such thoughts away, they returned in earnest when he least expected them to. Was there a perfect time for love, knowing that death would probably claim him in the near future? The thought tasted bitter in his mouth, but there it was. Unless Colind had an ace up his sleeve, Aaron had no idea what he could do against all that were hunting him. How far could he run? How much could he really fight? The mere thought of it all threatened to overwhelm him at times. Verona and the others looked to him to lead against the High King because of his lineage. When Tye killed his father, he had said he wanted to capture his essence. He had no idea what that meant, but being the last of the Alenzar'seth made him the key to something. All roads led to Shandara, it seemed. He hoped Colind had the answers he sought to thwart Mactar and the High King. Other than who he was, what could he possibly possess to drive these men to murder an entire family? Who were the Alenzar'seth? If they were like his grandfather, surely nothing they would have done would warrant such action against them. Based upon the letter that Prince Cyrus had shown him, his grandfather had wanted to shift the power from the nobility to the rule of law and allow people to govern themselves. At least, he implied as much. The High King and the Elitesmen were tyrants, holding these people by the throat. It was completely foreign for Aaron to even think of a world in these terms, but was Earth so different? Maybe in some places, but upon the fringes of civilization, the rule of law was fragile at best and most often nonexistent. People deserved better or at least the right to choose for themselves.

CHAPTER 24
THE FIRST LESSON

The next morning, Aaron awoke while it was still dark outside. He
quietly dressed, gathered his things, and with Zeus in tow, headed
immediately for the deck. The sun was beginning to rise, and the
brisk morning air drove the remaining sleepiness from him. The deck
had a wide expanse of space, which afforded him much room. He put
his staff and swords down and warmed up with the fighting forms to
increase flexibility, loosening up his muscles. He focused on his
breathing and perfection of movement with his body. It wasn't long
before Sarik approached silently and copied Aaron's movements
without saying a word. Sarik was a quick study and was able to mimic
his movements with ease. They worked silently, and a few of the
sailors watched from the side. Between forms, Aaron waved an
invitation for them to join. A few came over while the others kept
watching. He kept to the basic forms, allowing for a good warm-up,
and despite the chill of the morning air, beads of sweat formed on
him. Before long, they were joined by the others, including Sarah,
with whom he shared a brief smile in greeting. Aaron was surprised to

see Garret and Vaughn among the group of men that came to train and nodded to each in turn. He noticed Jopher watching among the men who stood to the side. He looked at Aaron with a hopeful expression, which Aaron ignored.

"Good morning. It was customary for my grandfather to begin each training session with a few words, and while we train together, I intend to continue with that tradition. Please, if you will form a circle and take a moment to look at those who stand among you," Aaron said, pausing while they formed a circle.

He took a few moments, considering what he wanted to say. If he was to change things here, he must start with planting the seeds of ideas among these people.

"You all come from different walks of life, from all corners of the world. Each experiences the world in his own unique way and with his own challenges. While we form this circle, we are all equals, and when we break off into smaller groups, the circle stays with us. The circle is how we should embrace the world around us, with neither disdain nor complacence, but with an open mind and compassion. Respect for your fellow man begins with respect for yourselves and thus provides the balance of life. We all breathe the same air and move basically the same way. Breath and movement is life, and this is where we will begin our first lesson..."

Aaron trained with them for the next few hours. Men who worked throughout the night asked if he wouldn't mind having a second training session for those who were duty bound and could not attend. He said that he would and was moved by all the words of praise and appreciation for sharing his knowledge with them.

"Teaching suits you," Sarah said, coming to his side while the others were dispersing. "Now are you up for a bit of a challenge?" she asked with half a smile, holding two pairs of wooden practice swords, and before he could reply, she tossed one at him.

"If you insist. I take it this won't be like our last dance," he said.

"You never know." She smiled back, and then she attacked.

Instincts took over as Aaron barely blocked her attacks. If this was practice, he would hate to face her when she was angry. Sarah broke off her attack, her eyes flashing angrily.

"You will do us both a disservice by not engaging fully. I'm no delicate flower wrapped in silk. Don't hold back, because I won't."

"I apologize, my Lady."

He brought up his swords and decided to dance with Sarah after all. He attacked first, bringing his swords to bear, and Sarah blocked with the grace and agility of a swan skimming across a lake. When Sarah lashed out with her swords, the attacks were quick and powerful, but she never overextended herself. *She's good.* They each probed the other's defenses and thus far were not able to exploit any weakness.

Aaron sensed she was leading him into a trap, as the pattern of her subtle defense taunted him into being more aggressive. Then he felt a tingle upon the edge of his senses, and he found her eyes searching his expectantly. The empty void within gathered essence as if he were wielding the Falcons and invoking the bladesong. His medallion grew warm against his skin as the tingle upon his senses persisted, growing more powerful. Sarah took full advantage of his distraction and swept his feet out from under him. He was flat on his back for an instant before he tucked in and rolled backward, away from the inevitable sword strike that crashed into the spot he occupied a second earlier.

Aaron sprang to his feet, and his wooden blades met Sarah's blinding whirl of attacks. He picked out the pattern and pressed her back with even, purposeful strides. His blades became a moving wall of defense and attack. Sarah was a really good fighter. She gave ground, studying his attack and adapting her own to counter his style. Then the tingle came back as a push on his senses. There could be little doubt that Sarah was doing something to him. He immediately stepped in close, sweeping her outstretched foot toward him just enough to bring her off balance. Their blades locked, and he could feel her breath on his face while she struggled against him.

"What are you doing?" Aaron demanded.

Sarah became still. "You've only scratched the surface of what you're capable of."

Aaron released her, and they stood facing each other, catching their breath. "What do you mean?"

"The lore masters of Shandara were legendary in the feats they performed. It might be safer for you not to discover these skills in the heat of battle," Sarah replied.

"You could have warned me," Aaron said.

"Are you always warned before being tested?"

Aaron's mouth hung open as he was about to reply. Feeling foolish, he closed his mouth quickly. "Point taken," he said. "All right, what do you want to show me?"

"I've felt you take in and harness the energy within yourself," Sarah said.

"When I focus, I can feel the beating hearts of those around me regardless of whether they are human or animal."

"That's because all life is connected. The Elitesmen choose to exploit the bonds of life to bend those to their will. Only the Shandarians, being led by the Alenzar'seth, kept them in check. The bonds of life give you strength, heal your wounds, but there is always a balance. Pull too much, and you will burn yourself out," Sarah said.

"I felt you pushing against my senses. Can anyone do this?" Aaron asked.

"Some—it's been known to manifest only within certain bloodlines." Sarah replied with what she'd learned from Beck, her unorthodox Elitesman teacher.

Aaron frowned, thinking of the whispering voices he heard when he wielded the Falcons and invoked the bladesong.

"I'm not so sure. My grandfather always said that all life is connected and that we can draw knowledge from the soul."

"Let's not get distracted. I said before you've only scratched the surface of what you are capable of, and I meant it. Normally, novices who show promise are given an amulet to help them become more attuned to drawing energy and in some cases store it as well."

"So an amulet would make me a better conductor," Aaron said, rubbing the medallion beneath his shirt. "Something like this," he said, withdrawing the medallion.

Sarah's eyes widened. "I'd say that is a little more than what a novice would be given. And you said you'd never seen this before your grandfather died?"

"No," Aaron said, shaking his head. "It was well hidden."

"Can you tell me what happens when you focus and draw the

energy within yourself?" Sarah asked.

Aaron described his heightened sense of awareness and sharpened senses. His connection to living things in his vicinity, as if they were all beating of the same heart. He decided to tell her about the voices he would sometimes hear with the bladesong. "This must sound crazy even for this place," Aaron said.

"No. No," Sarah said, shaking her head and smiling. "It's not crazy at all. It's something wonderful. Something beautiful. You're hearing the voices of past lives. There are those that believe that we live many lifetimes to help us grow."

"If I didn't experience this for myself, I would say that you're a little crazy. The voices aren't speaking directly to me. They're more whisperings and mutterings. Like I'm being urged, but not insistently so. It doesn't invade the void, but complements it. They helped me unravel the pattern of the Elitesman attack."

Sarah reached out and put her hand on his. "To hear so many means you have an old soul. Perhaps ancient, but you will never know who you may have been in another life. Your soul is also made up of pieces from your parents, so each time you are born it's unique."

"That's good I guess, because the implications of that could be scary. It still seems strange though," Aaron said.

"Trust yourself, Aaron. In the end, it's all we really can do. When you draw energy in, you can use it to give you an edge in most endeavors. You can move faster and jump farther than a normal person. You have already done so without realizing it when you faced the Elitesmen in the small town."

"I did? How? I just faced them as I would anyone else," Aaron interrupted, unable to contain himself.

Sarah smiled at him patiently. "Your honesty and integrity serve you well, Aaron. I suspect that when you faced the Elitesmen, you met them as equals. As men. You leveled the playing field, but you were moving just as fast as they were."

Aaron remembered the shocked looks of Verona and the others when he had killed all those men and took down the Elitesmen in the town. He'd been consumed by rage and had thought it was just adrenaline, but perhaps it was something else. "Maybe, but at some point, someone will just be faster or stronger. I wonder what the price is for being able to do such things," Aaron said.

"You could burn yourself out. When you release the energy, your body could release its life essence, leaving the body without a soul. The energy you draw in is meant to be used," Sarah said. "Stand up. It's better if I show you."

"Here?"

"There is no time like the present," she replied earnestly. "Your swords help you channel energy, but you can do it on your own as well."

"Wait a minute. What about the others?" Aaron asked.

"In time, perhaps," Sarah said quietly, answering the rest of his unspoken question.

Aaron glanced over at Verona and Sarik, who were speaking at the far side of the deck. "What do you want me to do?"

"We'll start off with something simple. I want you to clear your mind and begin drawing energy within you," Sarah said.

"Where does this energy come from?" Aaron asked.

"Can you feel the wind blow? There is nothing that you can see that pushes the wind, but there are underlying forces at work that cause the many currents of air to move. It's the same kind of thing. You are tapping into the underlying forces that give life to, well"—she paused, looking around—"everything."

Aaron's brow furrowed as he thought about this. How could something sound so bizarre and make sense at the same time? He cleared his mind, and in his mind's eye he wielded the Falcons, invoking the bladesong. He felt energy draw into him and his senses sharpened.

"Very good, Aaron. I can sense you. Can you sense me?"

Aaron allowed his senses to stretch out from himself, and he saw a faint, golden aura that surrounded Sarah, pulsing with the rhythm of her heartbeat. Then he caught a faint scent. "I smell jasmine," he said suddenly.

Sarah's eyes flashed in surprise. "Jasmine is my favorite flower. It grew near where..." She stopped suddenly and eyed him. "When I was a little girl, it grew near my window. The warm summer night air would fill my room with its sweet scent," Sarah said.

"Elitesmen can sense this?"

"No, their training is twisted. They draw their strength from elsewhere. We will discuss them another time," Sarah replied. "You can use the forces gathering within you to strengthen your body. Specifically, your bones and muscles and all that joins them," she said, looking at the cables that attached the ship to the balloon high above them.

"Then you push," Sarah said, launching herself into the air, jumping over twenty feet and catching hold of the cables that the crew would use to repair the ship.

Verona and the others stopped their conversation and looked up at Sarah in awe. "Well?" she called down to him.

Aaron could feel the energy build within and tried to focus it into his muscles. He squatted down, preparing to jump, and pushed with all his might. He rose about two feet into the air and came back down. His concentration broke, and his hold upon the energy within dissipated. *I'm an idiot.* Aaron glanced at the others and saw a few of them were trying their utmost to keep from grinning.

"I think you need a little more practice," Verona said, smiling as he walked over to Aaron. "Nice to see that you are indeed human like the rest of us."

Aaron shrugged his shoulders and grinned in spite of himself. He looked up at Sarah, and she stared back expectantly. He sighed, getting back on his feet. He then spent the better part of the next hour trying to match Sarah's rather impressive jump. Despite getting up to a whole three feet, he gave in to frustration and stopped.

Sarah assured him that he would be able to jump as high or higher eventually and to give it time. Despite Sarah's assurance, Aaron was frustrated. He put on a brave face, but inside it gnawed away at him. He needed to be prepared for whatever the Elitesmen threw at him—and the Drake. He glanced over at his swords. Perhaps if he were to...

"I want to see him! Get out of my way."

Aaron heard Jopher's shouting amid the crowd of men and a crash of things falling to the ground. Eric and Braden were blocking Jopher's path. Nearby was a deckhand quickly picking up the stacks of tablets that had crashed to the floor. Jopher glanced at the boy, and when he saw Aaron, he took an immediate step in his direction and began to speak. Aaron ignored Jopher as he stepped past him and squatted down to help the deckhand retrieve his tablets. A hush washed over the men on deck. Aaron smiled at the boy reassuringly and handed the remaining tablets to him. The boy thanked Aaron and quickly went on his way.

"Do you know why I won't allow you to be trained, Jopher?" Aaron asked, turning around, and Jopher for once was at a loss for words.

"It's because you don't see people. People are things to you, and until you not only see people, but learn to treat them with common courtesy, then you have no place with me or those around me." Aaron's cold eyes bored into Jopher until he looked away.

"I'm sorry," Jopher muttered, then quickly withdrew back to the kitchens.

The apology was unexpected and surprisingly sincere; perhaps there was hope for Jopher after all. Aaron glanced around and saw Sarah and Verona nodding approvingly.

"If the boy learns the lesson you are trying to teach him, he will be the better for it," Verona said.

"We'll see. It's really up to him," Aaron said.

CHAPTER 25
THE HUNTER

Over the weeks that followed they had good travel weather, and Aaron settled into a routine of teaching the men on the ship. After some prompting from Sarik, he even allowed Jopher to join in.

Jopher had put forth a great amount of effort to help those around the ship with any task, and Aaron observed the noble arrogance retreat from his gaze. He didn't think Jopher had ever had any true companions other than servants, and Aaron was glad to see some changes in him take root.

The ship headed steadily east and with each passing day brought him closer to Shandara. What would it look like? Was it really a land of shadow, a place where monsters roamed, a blight upon this world? He stood at the railing with his hand resting casually on his swords and watched the darkening clouds roll steadily in.

"Looks like we might see some weather today," Verona said, coming up next to him. A few sailors shuffled by, securing equipment and making ready for the storm.

"Looks that way."

"Hatly wants to demonstrate the progress he's made with our idea using exploding crystals against the Ryakul," Verona said.

"That's good news. I was in his lab earlier today, and he was extremely close. I've left him some arrows, but we're going to need to think of something better moving forward," Aaron said.

"You're right about that. I doubt an arrow burdened with enough crystal dust to do any sort of damage to a Ryakul will fly more than twenty or so yards," Verona replied, pursing his lips in thought.

Sarah emerged on the far side of the ship, her golden hair cascading down her back with the wind toying playfully at the ends. She smiled at Aaron and walked over.

"You're a lucky man, Verona said. "Normally, I would say she's beyond your reach, but I daresay she has taken a liking to you, my friend."

Aaron laughed and gave Verona a playful shove. "I've got to be crazy, Verona. This can't lead anywhere good for either of us."

"It seems as if your head and your heart are at war with themselves. A monumental struggle fought throughout the ages, to be sure. But, would you like to know a secret truth that many a man pays dearly for and yet still never learns?" Verona asked, his eyes twinkling. Only when Aaron nodded did he continue.

"Love is just love, there is no perfect time."

Aaron chuckled. "That's it? That's your great advice?"

Verona simply shrugged his shoulders, growing silent and using Sarah's arrival as an excuse not to answer. Sarah's blue eyes and smile drove Verona and his sage advice far from his mind. She nodded in greeting to Verona, who said he was going to Hatly's lab.

"Please tell me you're not going to have me try to jump again? I'm still recovering," Aaron said, which brought a small laugh from Sarah.

"No, I promise," she replied, and then her eyes grew serious. "It's up to you now."

"I know," Aaron said. He turned to scan the rapidly approaching clouds, feeling his medallion grow cool against his skin. In the back of his mind, he heard a great swath of giant wings cutting through the air. He glanced at Sarah, who was silently scanning the sky with him. He looked around the deck, and the sailors were going about their normal duties.

"Do you hear that?" Aaron asked.

"Hear what?"

Aaron peered into the sky, but saw nothing except the dark clouds blotting out the sun. He was hearing multiple beating wings now closing in. "Something is coming."

Sarah narrowed her gaze. "I don't hear anything," she said, her hands resting on her sword.

A crash of thunder and lightning tore through the sky, and amid the flash, he saw great winged shapes, dark and sinister, surrounding the ship.

"Ryakuls!" he shouted and was immediately echoed by the sailors of the watch.

There was an flurry of activity as the veteran sailors flew into action. The sailors threw back levers at key points around the ship, and sections of the flooring gave way. Giant crossbows rose from the depths of the ship. The sailors, in teams of four, made ready to fire upon any Ryakuls that breached the clouds, but none came. Ear-piercing roars erupted from above. Eric and Braden were immediately at Aaron's side, their bows at the ready. Captain Morgan arrived on deck, barking orders.

"How many of the beasts have we got?" the captain shouted.

"I see five of them, Captain," Sarik shouted back from the other side of the deck.

A team of sailors near Aaron cursed as they struggled to get a giant crossbow unstuck mid-rise from below the deck. Aaron hopped down the shaft and was immediately joined by Jopher. Without a word, they began searching for what was keeping the gearing stuck. The roars of the Ryakuls pierced their ears as they probed the ship's defenses. Aaron was rocked to the side as something big collided with the ship. Shaking his head, Aaron returned to his feet and began yanking and kicking away the debris from the gearing, until finally the crossbow platform rose to the decks.

A Ryakul slammed onto the deck and roared a challenge. The giant crossbows turned in unison and unleashed a deadly barrage of log-sized arrows, slamming the creature through the chest, forcing it over the side. The turrets were turned back to defend the ship, but no shots were fired as the Ryakuls proved too quick to track in the air. Aaron stumbled as the ship rocked under his feat.

"They're under the ship," a sailor cried.

Aaron ran to the side of the ship and tied a lifeline around his waist, and without a backward glance, he jumped over the side. The wind rushed past his face, and he tensed his muscles, silently praying that the rope would hold. The rope jerked, rattling his bones, sending him toward the armored underbody of the ship, where a Ryakul was clawing away. Aaron raised his heels, using the momentum of his jump, and blindsided the Ryakul, knocking a few talons loose from the ship's bottom.

The Ryakul shook its head and turned viciously toward Aaron with its gaping saber-tusked maw opening for the kill. Aaron drew his sword as he swung back toward the Ryakul, knowing that he was about to die. He roared in his suicidal charge, and Aaron felt the heat of his medallion burn through his shirt, sending a beam of light into the Ryakul's face, blinding it. Aaron barely dodged the rows of deadly teeth and slashed out with his sword, cutting deeply into the beast's long neck. It dropped from the bottom of the ship. Aaron felt a sharp tug on his rope as he was hoisted back up. He heard a swoosh through the air and turned to see another Ryakul closing in, its gaze fixed upon him.

Still hanging by the rope, Aaron kicked away and ran along the side of the ship. He felt heat blast from a great explosion behind him. He turned to see the charred remains of the Ryakul's body falling toward the ground far below them.

A horn blared from within the clouds, and the remaining Ryakuls screeched in reply, breaking off the attack. Aaron looked back up and saw Verona grinning from the side of the ship as Eric and Braden hoisted him up.

"Your idea with the crystals worked," Verona said, holding an arrow whose tip caught the light of the orbs around them.

Aaron thanked Eric and Braden and looked around the deck to find Sarah on the far side. She smiled in relief. Large talons slowly gripped the railing next to her and Aaron's breath caught in his throat. Sarah's perplexed look turned to terror as a great claw gripped her entire body and yanked her over the side.

"There!" Sarik screamed, pointing from above.

The Ryakul flew from under the ship, and Aaron's eyes found Sarah's as the blood pounded in his ears. He reached out, grabbed the crystal-tipped arrow from Verona's hands, and took a few steps back from the railing. He took a moment, gathering the energy from the wind currents into him as Sarah had taught him, and exploded into movement, hurtling toward the side of the ship. He jumped as he never had before. The energy strengthened his muscles beyond the constraints of ordinary men. He mightily pushed with his legs and shot away from the ship like a bullet, gaining on the fleeing Ryakul.

The wind roared past his ears as he reached out and grabbed the beast's leg. He held on with one hand as the beast plunged toward the ground with his added weight. Sarah struggled against the talons, but they held fast. Aaron clenched his teeth around the arrow, not giving a thought that at any moment it might explode, then drew his knife. The ground was rapidly approaching as he slashed deeply across the Ryakul's hamstring, causing black blood to gush forth as the creature howled in pain. The talons around Sarah grudgingly opened, and she fell from the creature's grasp. Aaron followed, turning in midair as he hurled the crystal-tipped arrow into the Ryakul's maw. The explosion pushed Aaron faster, and he caught Sarah in his arms. He summoned the energy from the storm into himself, steeling his muscles and bones to withstand the landing. The impact of his feet slamming the ground sent a wave of dirt into the air. When the air cleared, he placed Sarah on her feet, but she held onto him, gasping for breath.

"How did you—you jumped!"

Aaron shook his head, trying to get the world to stop spinning.

"I guess I needed the right motivation, but please let's not try that again." Lightning streaked across the sky, and the wind howled. The storm had arrived in earnest. They watched the Raven being blown away, unable to fly against such powerful winds. He saw the remaining Ryakuls swarming in the clouds above with one large Ryakul standing out from the rest. Another blast of thunder and lightning revealed a rider upon the Ryakul's back. The gusty winds blew the smaller Ryakuls away, but the large Ryakul struggled to stay in the storm's torment while its rider scanned the ground for them. After a few moments, the rider blew his horn, and the Ryakuls fell into formation, heading away from them.

They took a collective sigh of relief and jogged to the nearby trees to escape the wind and rain.

"Did you see that?" Aaron asked.

"That Ryakul had a rider. I've never heard of that before," Sarah said.

"This wasn't some random Ryakul attack. Someone is controlling them. Could the Elitesmen do this?" Aaron asked.

Sarah shook her head. "The Elitesman cannot control the minds of Ryakuls. Not even Mactar can do that."

Aaron rubbed his medallion, which lay coolly against his chest. It had flared to life when he fought the Ryakul, and he couldn't figure out how it happened. "Could it be the Drake?"

Sarah looked visibly shaken by the question and silently shrugged her shoulders, scanning the sky. "I can't see the ship anymore."

"We'll need a place to ride out this storm. Then I think we should head this way after it passes," Aaron said, pointing to the east. He had studied the map of Safanar in the navigation room on the ship every day since his first day on board, and he knew that heading east would bring him to Shandara. "We can't just sit here and wait for them. Not with that thing looking for us, and besides, when the others don't find us here, they will head east to look."

"You're right. Let's go," Sarah said.

CHAPTER 26
AN UNEXPECTED MEETING

After a couple of hours, the storm let up enough that they were able to keep relatively dry if they stuck to the forest. On any other day, Aaron would have enjoyed a hike in the woods, rain or not, but today, without any supplies, he was worried that they would feel the lack of food before long. Sarah, he noticed, didn't share his worries. She knew how to survive in the forest and seemed genuinely amused that he did not.

"Do you not have hunters on your world?" she asked.

"Of course we do, but most people aren't required to hunt. They buy their food at a local market," Aaron said.

"What happens if the local market doesn't have food that day?"

Aaron's thoughts stumbled a bit as he tried to imagine a local supermarket having no food, but he just couldn't imagine it. "It wouldn't happen. I mean, sometimes they might run low because a bad storm was coming, but there are enough markets to sustain people until more food and supplies can be delivered. Sometimes, the food comes in from far away."

"I see," she said and continued to walk.

He had always taken for granted that food was readily available back home. He'd never given more than a passing thought to what he would do should he have to hunt his own food. Why would he? Most people only kept enough food at home to last a few days or a week tops.

"It does seem foolish to me now that I think about it," Aaron said.

"Why would you say that?" Sarah asked. "That is where you came from. If something like food has always been available, then it's easy to see why people wouldn't learn basic hunting skills."

"Basic hunting skills," Aaron repeated. "Not something I would expect a princess to know anything about."

"I assure you my home was not all made of silks and ribbons," Sarah replied frostily.

Aaron looked up in alarm. "I meant no offense. I've never known any princesses before you, but hunting wouldn't seem like something a princess would know anything about. Most girls I've known don't know how to hunt. Then again, most can't handle a sword."

Sarah's gaze softened. "It's okay. Perhaps that's because you've finally met the right girl. The life of a princess for me has been anything but what the stories say. I grew up far from my father's court after my mother died. It was a small manor, and the reason I know anything about how to take care of myself is because of Beck." She stopped, turning to face Aaron. "Beck was an Elitesman. A very old Elitesman before they became the vile sect that you have had the unlucky happenstance to cross paths with. Beck left the order and would train me at night. He understood the danger I was in."

"Danger? From what?" Aaron asked.

"From my brothers and father...the world," she muttered. "I remember my father being kind until my mother died. Then he changed. He became bitter and never had time for me. I don't know why. I was just a little girl. Eventually, he sent me away. Soon after, news came to the manor that he remarried and had more children. Then Beck showed up at the manor one day and asked if I wanted to control my own destiny."

"That's a funny thing to ask a child," Aaron said.

"I was extremely sheltered at the manor, and news from the outside world was slow to arrive, if at all. The manor had a nice library, and I was eager to learn. Beck, in turn, taught me for years. Not just how to defend myself, but how to survive. I once asked him why he came to the manor, and his only reply was to honor my mother since no one else would. I never had many dealings with the Elitesmen, and Beck was more of an outcast. He was already very old when he came, and he died quietly in his sleep a few years ago. I decided to return to Khamearra. I thought that if I could prove myself useful, then my father would look kindly upon me as he once did. I returned to the court at Khamearra, where I was greeted by three younger half-brothers and a father who was all but a stranger to me. The time apart made him more bitter, and the light in his eyes was completely gone. I was tolerated at first, and my father was impressed with how I handled my half-brothers' attempts to have me meet with several unexpected accidents."

Aaron shook his head. "They tried to kill you for simply showing up?"

"They tried but never came close. It amused me for a while to thwart their attempts until my father became bored with the whole mess and ordered them to stop."

"How many brothers do you have?' Aaron asked.

"Three. Primus and Rordan are twins and a year younger than I." She stopped suddenly and looked at Aaron with concern in her eyes. "Tye was my youngest brother."

Hearing the name was like a freight train screaming in his ears. "Tye was your brother," Aaron said quietly.

"Yes," she whispered.

Aaron stomped down the trail in silence with Sarah following. "Did you know what they were planning?"

"No one knew what Tye was up to except Mactar," Sarah replied.

"He murdered my parents," Aaron said through clenched teeth. "Burned my home!"

"I know," she whispered. "I'm sorry, Aaron. Tye got what he deserved."

They walked on in silence, Sarah giving him the time he needed to calm down. What did it change knowing what he knew now? He had no choice now that they were hunting him down. What did this mean for Sarah and him? Regardless of what Sarah had said, they were still her family, and this was going to tear them apart.

"You know where this will lead?" Aaron asked, turning to her suddenly. "It's going to be them or me. Does this change anything for you?"

"How can you be so sure?"

"They're hunting me, Sarah! Mactar, Tarimus, the High King. All of them. It won't stop until either I'm dead or they are. Things are going to become real complicated between us."

"Maybe for some of them. Mactar certainly, but you don't know the whole story. Perhaps there is a way that this doesn't need to end in bloodshed."

"Not end in bloodshed?"

Sarah looked away. "Not everything is black and white, Aaron," she said sharply.

"Not from where I see it," came his terse reply.

"There will be fighting. No one is denying that, but must everything end in death? Must there always be killing?"

"What are you afraid of?" Aaron said, shouting now.

Sarah said nothing at first and took a deep breath. "For you," she said gently, reaching out toward him. "Of what this will do to you. What it already has done to you. I can see the toll it has taken. I've seen good men become twisted in the name of vengeance and survival. I don't want you to lose the good man that you are inside."

Aaron didn't know what to say. She knew there would be fighting but asked why everything had to end in death. Then he remembered the town where he had killed all those guardsmen. In his mind, he'd made them all as evil as the one man among them who had been with Tye that night his parents died. Something dark and sinister was unleashed within him, and perhaps this is what Sarah was warning him about. The dragon had warned him that the path of vengeance led to death. The dragon had not meant death of the body as Aaron had thought, but death of the soul. What choice did he have? The guardsmen from that town would still be dead.

Then it dawned on him.

I'm an idiot.

Had he faced all those men as men and not as what his rage demanded they be, would it have been different? Not to the men who died, but to himself, and that would make all the difference in the world.

"I'm sorry for shouting at you," Aaron said finally. "The dragon Verona and I met warned me against walking the path of vengeance, but the pain of their loss is always with me. When I close my eyes, I see the silver dragon emblem on the black uniform of those men who came to my home. I can still smell the smoke. I can still feel the weight of my mother dying in my arms." It was pure luck that his sister was not at home when the attack came. Fate had been kind enough to grant that much at least. "I don't know if I will ever find peace," Aaron choked. "Would it surprise you to know that prior to a few months ago, I'd never used any weapon to take a life or defend my own? None of this was supposed to happen."

"I'm so sorry this happened to you," Sarah said.

She stood by his side with her hand gently rubbing his shoulder. It felt good, her touch whisking away the dark thoughts. She gave him a smile of understanding. "It hasn't been all bad, has it?"

His lips curved of their own accord. "No, not all bad, and I've met some pretty great people." The burden of the dead still weighed heavily upon his shoulders, but he felt he could bear it better now, and for that he was thankful.

"Present company included?" she asked.

Aaron reached out, taking her hand. "Meeting you was the best thing that ever happened to me, but part of me wishes we had met under different circumstances," he said, imagining what life would have been like if Tarimus had never come.

"Better than not meeting at all," she said, squeezing his hand, and the sparkle in her eyes sent waves of warmth rippling deep within him.

They hiked through the woods, keeping an ever-watchful eye upon the sky, hoping for a glimpse of the ship, but the skies were just a misty gray. The forest grew thicker, and the canopy of immensely tall trees all but blocked out the sky above. Sarah stopped and looked up, scanning the surrounding trees.

"You know we could cover a lot more ground if we used the trees." Sarah winked, then launched in the air, jumping from branch to branch, reaching dizzying heights.

Aaron stared up at her from the ground. He had jumped before in the heat of the moment but wasn't sure he could do it again.

"Are you coming?" Sarah called from above.

Aaron closed his eyes and stretched out with his senses, feeling the energy from the ground beneath him. He called it into himself and felt his medallion grow warm against his chest. He launched into the air and continued to push off the air beneath him. Where Sarah needed three jumps to reach the treetops, he only needed one.

"Let's go," he said.

"Try and keep up, Shandarian," she said, and took off, barely touching one branch before launching to the next.

He launched after her, and slammed into the tree he was aiming for, his shoulder taking the brunt of it. After a few more jumps and with his shoulder only slightly bruised from his collision with several trees, he gained on Sarah. He had to admit that it was fun. He felt as if he were running, taking great strides catching up to Sarah, albeit more clumsily than her graceful leaps. When he caught up to her, she sped ahead of him.

The treetop canopy kept most of the rain at bay, but the damp wind slicked his hair back. He was working, but not breathing all that hard. His body was the conduit tapping energy from wind and the trees. He drew it into himself and released it so fast that it was like a river rolling through him. They soared through the trees like two eagles on the hunt. He focused himself as if he were calling the bladesong with his swords, and the forest ceased blurring by. He could see clearer and with heightened perceptions. He finally passed Sarah and came to halt atop a large branch midway up a tree, which was still over fifty feet from the ground.

"This is amazing," Aaron said.

"Your instincts are really good. The first few times I tried to do this, I crashed," Sarah admitted.

"I nearly did a few times. You make this look so easy. I bounced off a few trees just trying to keep up with you."

Sarah smiled at him. "All things with time, Aaron."

"I wish the others could do this," Aaron said.

"Maybe some of them can. Each person is unique and has varying degrees of ability," Sarah said.

"What do you mean?"

"Your bloodlines are ancient, with ties to the Hythariam folk. You have strength that few achieve, and you learn quickly. This is a good thing to have. The others' abilities will reflect directly upon their personalities and strengths of character. Not everyone is meant to jump so high, nor would they want to. Could you imagine Garret doing such?" Sarah asked.

Aaron thought about it for second. "Not really, but Verona and certainly Sarik."

"Perhaps," she said. "For some, the effect is subtle. All people draw energy from the world around them. It's just that some are more in tune with it than others."

"Who are the Hythariam?" Aaron asked.

"They are strange race of men that many believe are from a place across the ocean. They have a darker complexion, almost reddish bronze, with golden eyes, or so the stories say. Many kingdoms sought to align themselves with them because of their knowledge and ingenuity. They were highly skilled craftsman that would make all the grandeur of Rexel seem like the work of children. They allied with Shandara and contributed greatly to building the first airships, but have since withdrawn from our world. They are a secretive race, but occasionally there are sightings among the fringes of settled lands."

"Any idea why they allied with Shandara?" Aaron asked.

"Nothing concrete. More speculation, but I would have thought you would know more about them than I," Sarah answered.

"My grandfather didn't tell me anything about Safanar, much less the Hythariam," Aaron said bitterly. "It's like he deliberately kept me in the dark."

"I'm sure he was trying to protect you. It is possible that he believed that the doors to Safanar were truly closed."

Aaron thought about this for a few minutes, trying to put himself in Reymius's shoes. Reymius couldn't have told him anything—without revealing everything.

"I just wish I could understand more," he said finally.

He wondered what, if anything, his father had known about Safanar. Knowing his father, it wouldn't have mattered to him—he would have taken it all in and dealt with it one thing at a time. They made camp and ate a dinner of nuts, wild berries found nearby, and rabbit courtesy of Sarah's trapping ability. Having no desire to remain wet, they built a small fire to keep warm and dry out their clothes. Each took turns keeping watch, but the night was quiet.

They set off the next morning to a clear sky before the sun had fully risen. There was still no sign of the ship or the Ryakuls, so they continued east, hiking their way through the woods. The trees were much smaller, and traveling as they did yesterday wasn't an option unless one wanted to be impaled. Aaron learned that even though he pulled energy from nearby sources, it was still taxing. He wondered how he could wake up this power in others.

"I wish we could signal the others somehow," Aaron said. "I know they will head east eventually, but I was hoping to see some sign of them by now."

"Your captain is quite experienced. I'm sure he got them through the storm. We need to be patient," Sarah said.

They stopped to rest by a stream later in the day. Although the water was cool and refreshing, Aaron couldn't shake the feeling that whatever had launched the Ryakul attack yesterday was closing in on him. He scanned their surroundings, and all was as it should be—

from the crickets to the gentle swaying of the trees. The warnings about the dark things that would hunt him began with Daverim, his ancestor. He had told him to keep the staff close, as it would provide protection, only now the staff was safely aboard the ship and beyond his reach. He'd never taken the time to explore the rune-carved staff. More like never had a chance, but the beast he saw when he first grasped it must have been the Drake. Aaron suppressed the shudder that ran through him. At least he still had his swords, the Falcons, which were no ordinary blades. The Drake hunted the Alenzar'seth to extinction, but how? By all accounts, they were an ancient and powerful family with strong allies. How did the Drake track and kill all of them?

Aaron watched Sarah, who was refilling their only water container. The sun blazed along her blonde hair, giving it a radiance all its own. He had failed to protect Bronwyn from Tarimus, would he be able to protect Sarah from the things arrayed against him? Did she even need his protection? She must have felt his gaze on her, because she turned to him and smiled. He had no choice, because he couldn't deny what was in his heart. He would protect Sarah until his dying breath. What was hard was protecting her from the price she would pay for his love. Though they hadn't spoken the words yet, what was in her eyes was unmistakable.

"I can see smoke rising over there. We should check this out," Sarah said.

"Are you sure? Maybe it would be better if we go around," Aaron said.

Sarah chuckled. "There are good people in the world, I can assure you. We'll be cautious and besides, perhaps those on the Raven will see it too."

Aaron nodded. The campfires were farther away than they looked, and it took the better part of the afternoon to reach the camp. The smell of cooking food made his mouth water as they approached. Aaron counted about thirty wagons constructed as small houses on wheels. All were painted with bright colors that stood in stark contrast to the forest around them. There were children running around playing, and people went along doing their daily chores. Echoes of wood being chopped could be heard on the far side of the camp. They were greeted by a bald older man blessed with a symmetrical head that his lack of hair enhanced. He was followed by a grizzly-looking man with a beard that reached down his chest. He looked as if he could chop down an entire tree with one swing from the axe he carried or wrestle a bear, Aaron couldn't decide which. The older man smiled in greeting while the other looked on calmly.

"Greetings, strangers. I'm Tolvar," the older man said.

"Hello, Tolvar, I'm Aaron," he said, shaking the man's hand. "And this is Sarah."

Tolvar's eyes lit up. "Truly a sight to behold. You surely are the queen of beauty," he said with a slight bow, gently taking Sarah's hand. "This is my son, Armel." Armel nodded to each in turn. "What brings you to our little neck of the woods?"

Aaron and Sarah shared a quick glance. "Chance, I'm afraid," Aaron said, and told Tolvar of the storm and how they became separated from their ship during the Ryakul attack. They were approached by an older woman whose black hair showed streaks of gray.

"Margret," Tolvar called in greeting. "Tonight, we have honored guests. Victims of the recent storm and a dastardly Ryakul attack."

"Good sir," Sarah said, "we seek not to impose upon your generosity. Perhaps there is some way that we may offer aid to your people in exchange for a place by your fire."

"By the Goddess, the sound of her voice is enough to still this old man's heart," Tolvar said, elbowing Aaron's arm. "Or perhaps this young man's, eh?" he said, letting out a hearty laugh.

Aaron's face flushed in embarrassment, and he noticed Sarah's cheeks reddening as well.

"Enough, Tolvar," Margret said. "Of course you are welcome. Courtesy is not dead, now is it? Come along with me, dear, I'm sure the men can find something to occupy their time until supper."

Aaron watched as Sarah allowed herself to be guided away by Margret.

"Women, wives in particular," Tolvar sighed. "I've called that woman wife for more than thirty years, and she still thinks of all men as misbehaving boys. Very well, come with me."

"Aren't you worried that the Ryakuls will see your campfires?" Aaron asked.

"Nonsense, these are no ordinary fires, my boy," Tolvar answered, but didn't say anything more.

They headed in the opposite direction with Armel bringing up the rear. They came upon a smaller wagon that held casks of which one was tapped. Tolvar grabbed three steins and filled them with dark ale. Armel accepted one silently and took a hearty swallow, allowing the foam to gather on his mustache. Aaron took the proffered stein and sipped the dark ale. The rich, bittersweet chocolate liquid rolled through his mouth, leaving hints of malt in its wake. He took a bigger sip, nodding in appreciation to Tolvar.

"That's good," Aaron said.

"Hits the spot, doesn't it?" Tolvar said, and Armel sighed in agreement.

"I have a question about the fires. The ones you say won't draw the Ryakuls," Aaron said.

"Let's just say they burn with a little something extra to keep the beasts at bay," Tolvar answered aloofly. "Why are you so concerned with Ryakuls?"

"Let's just say they have a knack for turning up wherever I happen to be," Aaron answered.

"Ahh, that is unfortunate, and I now understand your concern. You're worried that your presence here will put the camp and my family at risk."

Aaron nodded.

"Well, fear not; we have ways to shield us from unfriendly eyes. You may take your ease here this night without worry."

"Where were you heading when the Ryakuls attacked your ship?" Armel asked.

"Armel," Tolvar admonished, "we mustn't impose upon our guest's privacy."

"It's okay, really. We're heading east," Aaron answered.

Tolvar nodded. "I'm afraid you're heading in the wrong direction if you wish to avoid the Ryakuls."

"I know this, but it's where I need to go," Aaron said, drinking the last of his ale; it was quite good.

Tolvar's eyebrows raised for a moment at Aaron's answer, then he looked at Armel. "Armel, please put that axe away. Perhaps now that we've had some refreshment, you are up for a bit of fun? A game?" Tolvar asked, rising.

"Sounds good."

After refilling their steins, Tolvar led them to a gathering of men who were throwing knives and hand axes. Armel picked up a couple of axes and handed one to Aaron.

"Care for a go?" Armel asked. When Aaron nodded, the big man launched the axe with blurring speed and it buried itself in the center of the target.

Aaron tested the weight of the hand axe and noted that it was pretty well balanced. He held the axe before him, lining it up with his target, and calmly sent the axe into the target, landing alongside Armel's axe, albeit not as deep.

Tolvar laughed with delight. "Not one for brute strength I see."

"Only when the occasion calls for it," Aaron answered, retrieving both axes and handing one back to Armel.

"How about the one over there," Armel said, gesturing toward the farthest target, which was a good sixty paces away. He lined up his shot and sent the axe sailing into the target, where it stuck perfectly center. Armel made it look easy.

Aaron lined up his shot, then brought his arm down, sending the axe just wide of the target. Some of the onlookers laughed, and he looked back at Tolvar and Armel and shrugged his shoulders.

"Try again," Tolvar urged, handing him another axe.

He took a breath and then blocked out the noise of the camp until it was just himself and the target. A slight breeze toyed with the branches overhead, but Aaron was fixed on the target as he brought the axe up. He focused himself, and the bladesong filled his mind, sharpening his perceptions. The familiar tingle spread throughout his limbs as he summoned the energy from the ground below, allowing it to course through his body. He hurled the axe with such force that the tree stump exploded in a shower of splinters. The men around them gasped aloud, but Tolvar nodded to himself and studied Aaron thoughtfully.

"Not bad," Armel said, appearing not to be surprised, and motioned for Aaron to follow.

Aaron was shocked; he hadn't meant to throw the axe like that. He hadn't even known he could do that. They walked to the remains of the target and retrieved their axes. Two men came with a new target and mounted it in place of the old one.

"How about we make this more interesting?" Armel asked. "Do you think you can keep my axe from reaching the target?"

"Are you serious?"

"We know you have strength, but do you have control, I wonder," Armel answered. "It is possible, I assure you. If you like, I will block your next throw even if you throw as you did before."

Aaron looked back at Tolvar, who nodded. He picked up his axe and called the bladesong in his mind. The power answered his call more eagerly than before. He brought up the axe and hurled it with all his might toward the target. A flash of light and a loud clang echoed as the axe buried itself into the ground well short of the target. Laying only a few feet away was Armel's axe. Aaron looked at Armel in surprise, and the man simply smirked back at him and held up another axe tauntingly.

Armel threw his axe five more times, and each time Aaron tried to knock it out of the air like Armel had done to his, only he missed by a wide margin. What was he doing wrong? Armel had made it look so easy. Even when he hurled the axe with all his strength so that the axe blurred from sight, Armel's axe still hit the target first. The big man said nothing but held up another axe, waiting for the next throw with an amused glint in his eyes.

"Might I offer a bit of advice?" Tolvar asked quietly beside Aaron. "Your mind is divided. Focus on one target at a time."

He already was focusing on the target, Aaron thought bitterly, grabbing another axe. He needed to keep Armel's axe from the tree stump, which meant watching Armel's axe and the target...his thoughts scattered as Tolvar's point was driven home. He summoned the bladesong to his mind, and his perceptions sharpened. Taking a deep breath and holding it, he nodded to Armel. When the big man sent his axe sailing to the target, Aaron drew in the energy until he felt he would burst and focused on Armel's axe. Time seemed to slow down, and Aaron saw the pattern of the axe's flight. He unleashed the axe, focusing his energy on its flight, using the air to guide its path. Like a falcon dive bombing his quarry, Aaron's axe forced Armel's into the ground in a cloud of dirt.

"Very good," Tolvar shouted, clapping. The men who watched nodded in approval.

"Well done," Armel said simply.

"Thank you," Aaron said.

"We haven't seen anyone block Armel's axe in a long time, and to be quite honest, his axe needed it," Tolvar said with a smile toward his son. "You know, I haven't seen it done in many years, since before the fall of Shandara, I'd say. Right, Armel?" Tolvar asked, and Armel thought for a moment, then nodded back. "That's right. It was the night we hosted that crowned prince if you can believe that. What was his name?" Tolvar rubbed the back of his neck, and Aaron's heart pounded. "Hmmm...Romus or Ryan? No, that's not right. When you're as old as I am, you lose some of the details," Tolvar said with a furrowed brow.

"Reymius?" Aaron asked quietly.

"Yes!" Tolvar exclaimed, his eyes lighting up excitedly. "It took him many more tries to block Armel's throw," Tolvar said, and Aaron glanced back at Armel, attempting to calculate his age. While the man was older, it didn't add up in his mind.

"Did you know Reymius?" Tolvar asked.

"Yes," Aaron replied, and images of his family played through his mind, from his grandfather's kindly face to his mother's endearing eyes and his father's strong demeanor. A lump grew in his throat. No matter how much time passed, he would never stop missing them.

"Haven't seen his like in a long time. That is"—Tolvar paused, looking at Aaron pointedly—"until today."

Aaron stiffened, and Tolvar put his hand on Aaron's shoulder. "It's all right, son, you are among friends here. Especially a scion of the house Alenzar'seth."

Aaron gaped at him. "How did you know?"

"Trust that some of us see with eyes beyond that of ordinary men. Perhaps in time you will as well." Tolvar smiled sincerely. "It gladdens my heart to know that at least some of you escaped the destruction of Shandara. But it breaks the wanderer's heart not to be able to traverse the lands of Shandara, for they were among the most beautiful in all the world." The sun had dipped low in the sky, and the men started heading back to camp. "Be at ease this night, and know that you are safe here." Tolvar spoke in such a way that Aaron believed him.

The lone roar of a Ryakul drew Aaron's gaze to the sky. It was too far to see, and Tolvar again reassured him that the Ryakul couldn't find them here. Having convinced himself that the mysterious rider of the Ryakul was in fact the Drake, Aaron wondered if the protection of the camp would thwart even the Drake. It was a short walk back to camp, where wood was being piled high for several bonfires. Tolvar took Aaron to a place where they could wash up, and while it wasn't a hot shower, it did feel good to be clean. Aaron kept scanning the crowd for some sign of Sarah, but couldn't find her. They took their ease on one of the many benches that surrounded the bonfires, and Margret walked up and whispered into Tolvar's ear. He smiled and nodded back to his wife.

"Not to worry, Aaron, she'll be along shortly," Margret said, smiling in reassurance.

The sun had set, and the brilliance of the firelight filled the air with a comforting flare. Smells of cooking food made Aaron's stomach grumble as Armel and some others joined them, bringing food that tasted as delicious as it smelled. Sarah's absence kept gnawing away at him, and while he suspected no foul play on the part of his host, the lack of her presence was grating his nerves.

"Aaron, I must take my leave from you at this time, but you should stay here with Armel and the other unmarried men," Tolvar said, and he quickly departed before Aaron could inquire.

Aaron noticed a group of men setting up a variety of drums off to the side, who were soon joined by others carrying different sorts of instruments. A hush swept over the crowd, and he glanced at the other men, but their attention was focused across the way, beyond the bonfires. The drummers beat their drums in unison with their sticks gliding effortlessly through the air. Each beat of the drum was precise and at times so fast that it was chaotic in its harmony.

Colorfully dressed dancers appeared between the bonfires. All the dancers were female, and as they spun, their skirts flared, showing a rainbow of colors and a good portion of their legs. He spotted Sarah spinning and stomping her bare feet in time with the others. Her dark shirt clung to her skin, leaving her bare midriff caressed by firelight. Her long blonde hair rode the air in waves, following the rest of her body as she moved with grace few could hope to achieve. Their eyes locked, and her smile made the heat rise in his chest and melt his heart. He followed her movements, unable to tear his eyes away until she faded from view, going to the far side of the bonfire.

Aaron could feel the rhythm of the music course through him, quickening its pace, and his beating heart rose to keep time. The bonfires flared brilliantly as the dance continued. A familiar presence tickled the edges of his senses. His eyes found Sarah's once again, and she smiled. Aaron extended his senses and was swept away amid the torrent of energy emanating from the crowd as it focused on the dancers. *See with eyes beyond that of ordinary men.* Tolvar's words echoed in his mind. Aaron searched the crowd and found Tolvar and his wife watching him.

A hand gently gripped his shoulder, and Armel nodded toward the dancers. "The choosing is about to begin." Aaron looked at Sarah and back at Armel with raised eyebrows. "Tolvar didn't tell you? You've come to us on a night of the choosing, celebrated with the solstices. Where a woman may choose a man she finds worthy, and if he accepts her laurel crown, he will be with her for as long as they both wish."

Aaron's breath quickened as he turned back to Sarah, swimming in her deep-blue eyes swathed in golden firelight beneath the starlit sky. She smiled at him in that way of hers, and the world around them faded to gray as Aaron finally accepted what his heart had been telling him since they first met. With Sarah, he would always be playing for keeps. He loved her, despite the worlds that separated them and being so far from everything he had ever known. In this place, Safanar, he had found his other half, and in a span between moments, a single wave of truth purged all doubts as he saw the very same reflected in her eyes.

The women resumed their circuit, weaving through the bonfires, and the men fought to keep themselves from giving in to their urges to join in the dance. Aaron wondered if Sarah understood what this dance meant.

Did he?

They had known each other for such a short time, just a few weeks aboard the Raven and a few brief moments in time before that. Was that enough? His father would have told him you only needed a few key moments to realize how you felt about someone.

How do you feel when you look at her, when she's looking back at you?

How do you feel when you watch her, when she's not looking?

And probably the most important, how do you feel when you kiss her? All the rest is whether you want to admit it to yourself.

Aaron recalled the conversation as clear as day. It had been when he had asked his father how he knew that his mother was the one. He smiled a bit in remembrance of gentler days, and then Sarah stood before him, glowing with the firelight caressing her silhouette. She held out her hand to him, and he stared at it for a moment before rising and taking her hand in his. Other men who had been chosen rose and removed their shirts, and Aaron followed suit. The tattoo of the dragon shimmered in the firelight, a living replica of the medallion in his pocket.

The bonfires grew in an unearthly brilliance, releasing bursts into the night sky. Sarah reached up and removed a crown of laurels from the flowers in her hair, and Aaron knelt before her. She gently placed her laurel crown on his head, and he felt an invisible shroud of warmth rest on his shoulders, cascading down his back. Aaron rose to his feet and moved in rhythm with Sarah, and the rest of the world was gone from his mind.

Love is just love, Aaron. There is no perfect time. His father's voice whispered in the back of his mind, and Aaron clutched to this moment. He had never felt happier or more at peace.

The rest of the camp rose to join the chosen, but for Aaron and Sarah the world resided in both their eyes. Aaron felt a hand clamp down on his shoulder.

"Congratulations," Tolvar said, with his wife grinning next to him.

Aaron's reply was cut off as a Ryakul's shriek pierced the night above them, sending a hush over the camp as they looked up in alarm. He could hear the wings beating the air in great swaths as the Ryakul circled the camp. Sarah's hand found his and squeezed in gentle reassurance. A shadowed figure rode the Ryakul, searching, seeming to look upon the crowd but not seeing any of them.

"Are you sure the protection will hold?" Aaron asked.

"It will not breach the protection of this camp," Tolvar replied firmly.

"Are you sure? Whatever that thing is riding the Ryakul, it can sense that something is not right here. Perhaps you should get your people to safety," Aaron said.

The Ryakul stopped circling directly above them. The rider's long howl sawed through the air, causing them to cover their ears in a feeble attempt to block out the piercing sound. Aaron collapsed to the ground, clutching his chest. The dragon tattoo burned and shimmered silver in the darkness. His vision burned red as the pain in his chest threatened to overwhelm him.

"Fight it, Aaron. It calls to you," Tolvar said as he and Sarah crouched by his side.

Aaron braced himself with one hand on the ground and the other clutching his chest. He felt it then deep within the fires of pain, a summons. This was the Drake, and its call stirred something sleeping inside of him. The silvery light of the dragon tattoo pulsed with his heart's rhythm, and Aaron glared up at the sky, feeling the building energy within him as if he had keyed a bladesong of pure molten rage. The voices of his ancestors screamed for vengeance on the Drake, who had robbed them of their lives. He felt his will erode away, wanting to be swept up in the torrent, and at the same time a small voice pleaded caution.

The Drake's call sawed through the air again, and Aaron stood up, firmly answering the call. The dragon tattoo shimmered brightly, sending glowing waves of light into the air. Summoning the energy of this world and the wind into his muscles, he prepared to launch into the air, but Sarah grabbed his arm, forcing him to look into her eyes.

"Stay with me," she pleaded.

Aaron glared back up at the sky, his thoughts scattered by the rage of his ancestors and Sarah's plea.

"It's what he wants. Look at me!" she screamed. "Face this enemy at a time of your choosing and not simply because he calls. Deny him." Her voice pierced him as no other could, and he held onto that rational thought by a string, slowly forcing the power of the bladesong away. He looked into her eyes and just breathed. With each breath he took, he stepped further away from the brink. The voices and urgings had only guided his will until now. They had never risen up to demand action. This new revelation both scared him and reminded him that this power came with a price. A dragon's call answered in the distance, and the Ryakuls gave in to their instinctual hatred and abandoned their search as the Drake struggled for control, flying away from the camp.

Aaron kept breathing, not trusting his voice to speak. He wondered what would have happened had Sarah not been there. He would have rushed to his death. All of those voices...all of that anger, even the echo of it still called out to him. If all of the Alenzar'seth perished against the Drake, how would he be any different?

"Ferasdiam has marked you," Tolvar whispered. "I suspected but..." He stopped in mid-thought. "It's good that fate brought you to us, Aaron. We will spread the word of your coming through the lands. It will reach those who have kept themselves from the world of men for far too long."

"The Hythariam?" Aaron asked.

Tolvar smiled. "Yes, son," he answered quietly.

Aaron could still feel the echoes of voices crying out just beneath the surface of his thoughts and shuddered. He delved deeper, beyond the anger, looking for the root of such hate, and there it was. *Betrayal...Despair...Anguish.* All standing helplessly before a force that one could neither avoid nor fight.

"I was told the Drake hunted down all of the Alenzar'seth and murdered them. Do you know how I can defeat the Drake?" Aaron asked.

Tolvar shook his head regretfully. Aaron frowned, knowing that it was too much to hope for, but he'd had to ask.

"I need to get to Shandara," Aaron said.

"Then it's good that a ship is even now bearing down upon us," Tolvar said, looking up at the night sky.

Aaron looked up and saw the dark outline of the Raven descending toward them.

"We are only shielded from unfriendly eyes," Tolvar said.

Aaron waved up to Verona, who was at the bow of the ship, calling out to the others. A crewman threw down a rope, and Captain Morgan appeared at the side.

"Mr. Jace, my Lady, if you don't mind, I don't know how long the beasties will be gone, but I aim to put as much distance as possible between them and us now that we've found you."

Armel appeared at Aaron's side, handing him two small curved axes. "Two in case you miss with the first one." He winked.

"Go on. We'll spread the word," Tolvar said, and Aaron grabbed the rope and climbed up.

CHAPTER 27

REUNION

"I must say it took us a while to find you. Never would I have imagined that you could cover so much ground," Verona said.

"I picked up some new tricks along the way," Aaron replied, sharing a look with Sarah.

"Indeed," Vaughn said. "We saw you leave the ship—" Vaughn paused, looking pointedly at Sarah. "I'm glad that you are safe, my Lady."

"We had to set down to make repairs after the storm finally blew out. We found the remains of the Ryakul. I must say our project using crossbow bolts and arrows laced with crystals is quite effective at keeping the Ryakuls at bay," Verona said.

Aaron recounted the events after he left the ship, leaving Sarik barely able to contain himself with a question as to whether he could fly.

"No, I'm afraid I can't fly," Aaron answered, feeling a bit foolish. "What Sarah has taught me, some of you may be able to do. I barely understand it myself. Sarah is the real expert. But I have something else I need to tell you," Aaron said, waiting for them to settle down. "Some of the Ryakuls are being controlled by the Drake. At least those that attacked the ship were controlled by it. It came for us while we were at the camp."

Vaughn and Verona gasped, while Eric and Braden swallowed hard and Sarik looked questioningly at Garret.

"I need your help. The Drake is responsible for hunting down the Alenzar'seth, and it is coming for me." Aaron shared a brief look with Sarah before continuing.

"I think I speak for everyone here. We will stand with you for the duration of this journey," Verona said.

"I know." He smiled. "I'm not being clear. The Drake's call affects me in ways that you wouldn't feel." The ancestral voices stirred briefly, causing his stomach to clench.

"How does it affect you?" Verona asked.

"It has often been said to me that I am Ferasdiam Marked. One who has been marked by fate with the Goddess's blessing, which is curious because where I come from, there is no Goddess. Apparently, belief is not a prerequisite. When I invoke the bladesong, I feel the blood of my ancestors within me. Calling to me. Their teachings have saved me in the past, but when the Drake called to me, something else happened. I almost lost control to an overwhelming hatred that demands that I kill the Drake."

"No one is doubting your courage, even against the odds of all those arrayed against us," Vaughn said.

"It's more than that. The calling from my ancestors was for the blood of the Drake. I don't know how I'm supposed to fight this thing and survive when they all failed," Aaron said.

"He needs for us to keep an eye on him when the Drake is near to keep him from charging off to his death," Sarah spoke up, sweeping all of them with her steely gaze.

"Sarah," Aaron said quietly, "at some point, I'm going to have to face this thing."

"Like hell you do. And certainly not alone," Verona said.

The air seemed to solidify around them all until Vaughn spoke up.

"Peace, Verona," Vaughn said. "The fall of Shandara was a confusing time, twisted by dark betrayals and many fleeing for their lives from the place that we are destined to travel to. It didn't become apparent to anyone that the Alenzar'seth were being hunted until it was too late. We were preoccupied with taking in refugees and keeping the High King at bay. What are the odds that after the immediate family was killed, the distant cousins faded to obscurity and the beast that hunted them disappeared?"

"Then we head to Shandara as planned, free Colind, and get some answers to light our way. To face the beast now would be to face the darkness without any hope of success," Verona said.

Aaron looked at his friend. "Poetic as always."

Verona grinned and the discussion died down to a few murmurs. Sarah left, saying she would find him later on deck. She knew that's where he would be. Was he really that transparent? Aaron headed to the deck, into the crisp night air, with Verona in tow.

"Did you bring it?" Aaron asked.

"Of course," Verona answered, reaching behind a lockbox on deck and pulling out the rune-carved staff. "Safe and sound."

"Thanks," Aaron said, taking the staff. "Daverim said this would help. When I found it, it was stuck in the ground with his cloak hanging there. I swear, when I first touched it I felt the Drake awaken, but didn't know what it was at the time. It can't be coincidence."

"That's to be sure of. I can't imagine that your long-dead ancestor would insist that you take this staff if he knew that it would draw the attention of the Drake," Verona said.

"You're right. I think he believed that things would be drawn to me no matter what," Aaron said.

His grandfather had said as much in his letter. Surely the Falcons and the rune-carved staff could help him against the Drake. The blades were able to cut Tarimus. Why not the Drake? The only problem was that he would need to face the beast in order to find out, and he suspected that to truly face the Drake wouldn't be as simple as crossing swords with the thing.

"Looks like I missed quite a celebration at that camp. A crown of laurels?" Verona said, snapping him away from his thoughts.

Aaron couldn't help the smile that played across his face. "Yes," he mumbled.

"And Sarah with flowers in her hair. Never thought I'd see the day," Verona said.

"Can I ask you to watch over Sarah? I'm afraid that she will be a target now." How had the Drake known to take her from everyone that was on deck?

"Indeed. As if she needs watching over." Verona chuckled. "The lady more or less threatened that I keep an eye on you. It's strange there was a time such a short while ago when I questioned her motives for even being here. But now I see the way you two look at each other, even when you aren't looking at each other." Verona winked. "Well, it gladdens my heart for you both, but be warned I still suspect that Sarah has secrets that she has not told you yet."

Aaron thought the same thing sometimes, but he had no doubts that she would stand with him. "People have the right to keep some things private. Regardless, I truly believe that if there is something that Sarah needs us to know, then she will tell us at a time of her choosing. Now, speaking of secrets, what about you?" Aaron asked. "Surely there has been a woman who has caught your eye."

"If there was one of such quality as your lady Sarah and she wasn't in love with my dearest of friends, perhaps," Verona finished.

They said nothing for a few moments, both chewing on their thoughts. "Thank you, Verona, for everything."

"No thanks necessary, my friend. The world would be a far lesser place without you in it, of that I'm convinced." Verona gave him a playful shove before walking off.

Aaron stood there, counting himself lucky to have found a friend here in this strange world. He ran his fingers along the staff, tracing the strange runes. Then held it off the ground, feeling its weight. The grain of the dark wood was fine, and the staff itself was balanced. How was he supposed to use this against the Drake? He rested the staff back on the deck and lifted his gaze to the moonlit sky, keeping watch and silently praying that they would go unnoticed.

***

* * *

Sarah watched him cradling his staff from across the deck. The pull of one Aaron Jace was almost too much for her heart to bear. She absently tucked a strand of hair away from her face and with her other hand smoothed out an imaginary wrinkle on her clothing. She must have checked her appearance twenty times before coming out on deck where she knew he would be. Her appearance never concerned her much before, but now things were different. She liked the way Aaron watched her, even more so when he thought she wasn't looking. A smile played over her face, and she sighed. Speaking with Margret and the other women of the camp had helped her come to terms with her feelings for Aaron. She had always kept men in general at arm's distance. Aside from Beck, who was more of a father figure and was the only man she'd allowed into her confidence. Aaron was altogether different. Just being near him made her never want to leave his side. He now held her heart in his hands, and she couldn't even remember giving it away. He was only just starting to accept that he was the last scion of the house Alenzar'seth. He hadn't asked for any of this, and to have it thrust upon his shoulders... She understood all too well how the loss of a loved one could turn your life upside down. Most of her life, she had to contend with what the men in her life would do to her, but with Aaron, she was truly afraid of what would happen if he were to ever leave her behind.

She watched as his hands traced the markings, trying to gain some insight into what the staff could do. Aaron wanted to protect everyone, which was commendable but not always possible. She stepped quietly beside him and rested her hand on his broad shoulder. He looked up at her touch, genuinely surprised, and smiled warmly at her. She felt heat rise from the pit of her stomach, and her heart raced.

"You know, when I first came here I wanted revenge..." He trailed off, looking down at the floor. "And to protect my sister."

"In that order?" she asked.

Aaron seemed startled. "No," he answered quickly. "Maybe. My father's dying wish was for me to protect her, and since I failed up to that point, I wanted to honor his wish. They were after me, so leaving seemed to be the best choice. I don't regret leaving."

Sarah gripped his shoulder firmly. "None of this is your fault. There was nothing you could do to stop what happened. You had no idea what you were dealing with, and you should take comfort in knowing that she is still alive." Aaron stared at the ground stubbornly, and she hoped he saw the truth of her words.

"I hope she is safe. Tara is my half-sister, so they have no reason to take her." His voice shuddered, but the truth passed unspoken between their eyes. They could take his sister to get to him.

"I think you're right but for different reasons," Sarah said gently. "Mactar's hold on Tarimus is fragile at best, and he was only drawn to you when the protection from your grandfather was gone. Your sister, while dear to you, is not Alenzar'seth."

"Thank you," he said. "They wouldn't need to travel so far to get to the people I care about." He turned toward her and reached out, caressing the side of her face. "I love you, Sarah, which both fills me up and scares the hell out of me."

Sarah hushed him to silence with a kiss. "There is no safer place for me than at your side. My heart is yours, my love."

"And mine is yours," he whispered back and kissed her.

They stood together on the deck of the ship, bathed in the pale moonlight, keeping silent watch. Both wayward travelers had found a home in each other, and as their arms intertwined, they basked in the moment for however long it would last.

CHAPTER 28
SHANDARA

In the following days, Aaron watched as the land grew more desolate and dark, as if the sun had forsaken this place. He knew they were closing in on Shandara, but he hadn't been prepared for the dreary landscape, as if winter's hold kept the plants dormant, but without the cold. The captain kept the ship along the tree line, hoping to avoid notice, but doubling the watch all the same. Aaron saw shadows moving among the trees and heard the howling of wolves in the distance. Zeus's ears perked up at the sound as he studied the landscape intently beneath them. Aaron caught glimpses of ruined towers along a river below, while abandoned villages and farms dotted the land.

"What drove the people from their homes?" Aaron asked.

"There are dark beasts that roam the land now. They weren't always this far, but they've never ventured farther than Shandara's borders," Verona answered. "Well, to be honest, not many live near the borders of Shandara anymore."

"Dark beasts?"

"Something sickens the land. Like the life is being sucked away."

Aaron pursed his lips and looked at the gray skies around them. "Or it's something underneath that's causing all this. Like a volcano."

"And driving what normally lives underground to the surface? I've never heard of a volcano so widespread as that," Verona said.

"You're probably right about the beasts, but a volcano could darken the skies like this," Aaron said.

"The land has been this way for twenty-five years. It's a bit of a long time for a volcano to produce cloud cover like this."

"It was just a thought," Aaron said.

"Regardless, perhaps when we meet up with Colind, the answers that elude us now will be given," Verona said.

"I hope so."

Sarik walked up and gestured to the far side of the deck where the others were waiting for them. They joined the others, and Verona took his place next to Sarah. Sarik stood between the brothers, Eric and Braden, while Vaughn and Garret stood off to the other side.

"I have an idea that I would like to share with you," Aaron began. "I don't know what we're going to encounter when we finally reach Shandara, but I have no doubt that the Elitesmen are following this vessel. I've asked the captain, and there have been no sightings reported of any other ships in the air, but it's just a feeling I have. Sarah assures me that the travel crystals won't work at the remnants of the city, but they could teleport closer to our destination and beat us there."

"Good enough for me," Braden said, and the others echoed their agreement.

"Through our training sessions, I've been trying to pass along the knowledge I have to help you stand with me against the Elitesmen. I think they're helping, but Sarah has helped me with some new abilities that may not be limited to me. However, they will not manifest the same way for everyone. I'll let Sarah explain," he said, nodding toward Sarah, who joined him.

"The Elitesmen use focused medallions to help quicken the process for an initiate to tap into the energy around us. Until recent years, this was a practice used sparingly because of the danger it poses to an undisciplined mind. However, the irregularities produced by this practice gained weight with the Council of Masters, and now it is encouraged," Sarah said.

"Irregularities?" Verona asked.

"Yes, to open oneself to life's energy is to tap into your soul, and the body is the conduit. Most souls are young, while others are quite old. When you open yourself up, you will be subject to the influence of the experiences of your soul's past, which can be both a blessing and a curse. Only a strong sense of self will shield you from those influences, but within the depths there is knowledge to be gained," Sarah continued.

"Some knowledge is best forgotten. If what you say is true, then you could be opening yourself up to great evil," Vaughn said.

"Only if you were greatly evil in another life," Sarah replied.

"There is a risk that comes with this, Vaughn," Aaron said. "My experience prior to the Drake's challenge was gentle urgings that guided my hand in combat. I was able to gain enough insight to unravel the pattern of attacks that the Elitesmen threw at me. Haven't you ever had a keen insight into a critical situation, and you couldn't pinpoint where the solution came from? Reasoning and experience account for much, but sometimes, when things matter most and the stakes are high enough, you need to go beyond the ordinary."

"Yes, but I suspect Reymius didn't impart any of this knowledge to you. My guess is that he had reason not to," Vaughn said.

"I don't know what he intended, to be truly honest with you. I believe he prepared me as he thought best on the chance that Safanar caught up with him in the end. Sometimes, I wonder if he ever thought he would go back. Opening yourself in this way will allow you to use the currents of energy all around us, but it will reflect on who you are as a person. If you're a physical type of person, then channeling the energy into feats of strength or speed may be possible. If thoughts and strategy are your forte, then greater clarity of thought may be achieved."

Vaughn nodded, conceding the point.

"The danger I was referring to earlier comes from a fractured mind and reckless use of this ability," Sarah continued. "The Elitesmen target certain individuals for advanced training beyond what their martial skills may be. Looking for certain personality traits such as a lack of empathy, being prone to violence, and the use of cunning brutality to accomplish goals."

"That explains my instant dislike for them," Aaron said.

"They can be quite charismatic too," Sarah continued. "Their followers want nothing more than to serve them." Sarah looked as if she were going to say more, but she stopped and shook her head. "We're off topic. Let's continue. The body is a conduit for the connection to the soul, and if it is overloaded, you can burn yourself out, which is why we train. The focus medallions heighten the sensitivity of the user, but we don't have any of those, and honestly, I wouldn't recommend we use them even if we did have them. When Beck trained me, he would have me meditate under various conditions, which allowed me to gradually become more sensitive. Aaron has started you all on a similar path. Practicing the slow fighting forms is a type of meditation for focusing the mind."

"Hold on a minute." Garret spoke up for the first time. "Let's go back to the irregularities you mentioned before with the Elitesmen's use of these medallions. I think it's important to know what we may be facing."

"Please understand that my knowledge is secondhand. I didn't actually train with the Elitesmen. I was trained by Beck, who left the order and was someone who kept himself apart," Sarah replied.

"Fair enough. Anything you can share though would be useful, I think," Garret said.

"Beck spoke of the Council of Masters trying to create a group of specialized Elitesmen who could affect the elements. Like creating fire where there was none. Our perception of fire, for example, is not as acute as someone who constantly obsesses about it," Sarah said.

"Did they succeed?" Garret asked.

"To a certain extent. They learned that the elements had their limitations. The mind-body connection is easier to manipulate than the world around them."

"That's why you had Aaron try that jump before the attack," Sarik said.

"Yes. I had very little doubt that he could achieve it, as he was already using these abilities when facing the Elitesmen, albeit in a more subtle way," Sarah answered.

"When my grandfather died, he left me these swords," Aaron said, drawing the Falcons from their sheaths. "The holes in the blade carry a melody when wielded. The bladesong helped heighten my connection to life's energy all around me. I think I can do something similar with all of you if you're willing to try."

Verona and Sarik gave their assent quickly and were followed by Eric and Braden. Vaughn and Garret, however, exchanged a few glances, and while Vaughn still looked skeptical, Garret then nodded as well.

"Come, Vaughn, let us see if an old dog can indeed learn new tricks, shall we?" Verona prodded with a grin.

Vaughn let out a small laugh. "Perhaps."

"Great," Aaron said. "All right then. Have a seat and close your eyes. Focus on your breathing. Close your mind to all distractions. When you hear the bladesong, try to open yourself up."

When the others sat upon the deck, Aaron was somewhat surprised to see Sarah join them. She regarded him with a slight smile and closed her eyes with the rest. Aaron took a deep breath, focusing himself, and began wielding the Falcons. He felt as if it had been an eternity since he first rode out to that clearing back home in a torrent of sadness and loss while mourning his grandfather. The first time he wielded these swords, the bladesong sending waves of melodic sound through the air had helped him become whole. He and the blades were one, but the connection was deeper than mere metal upon skin.

The blades came to life in his hands, and a warmth spread through his core as his perceptions sharpened, seeing the currents of energy surrounding the ship and in the air around them. The more he gathered the energy, the deeper it plunged into his own being. He turned his attention to the others, who resonated a shadowed light of their own as they waited for him to help open the door. He pushed the energy out to each of them, surrounding them with calmness, knocking on the doors of their souls. Sarah's presence filled him up and pulled him in almost to the point where he forgot all else. He had to resist that which he yearned for with all his heart. *Another time...*

He managed to pull himself away and focused on the others. The lifebeat of the others was present, but diminished in vibrancy, and he had to figure out a way to reach them. He swung the Falcons in slow, rhythmic motions, sending eddies of melodic tones into the air. Delicate tendrils of energy reached across the space between them, and he bound the group together. Aaron brought his attention to Sarik and Verona, hoping that youth would allow their minds to be more open than the others'. Sarik's youthful energy burst forth almost instantly, pulsating with vibrant intensity, and Aaron heard Sarik's sharp intake of breath as his awareness of the world around him heightened like never before.

Aaron shifted his attention to Verona, a man of many levels, fiercely loyal to his friends and the ideals of great men. His natural lively manner made one want to engage with him in any gambit conceived at the time. He reached out to Verona, beckoning with the excitement of a great game, and Aaron saw Verona's lifebeat surge forth as his friend broke through. He moved his attention to the brothers, Eric and Braden, and gave more of a warrior's edge to the bladesong. He reached out to Eric and Braden as he had to Verona, but without any response. He pushed out with his blades, sending a thrum of air, which bounced off their chests. He called out to them to rise up and heed the code of the De'anjard. Defend the helpless. Stand the watch. Honor your brothers of the shield. Sacrifice for the greater good. For the briefest of moments, Aaron saw their lifebeats pulse brighter, but they immediately diminished. They were not ready.

Aaron moved on to Garret and Vaughn, both men of some rank, as their word carried weight in Prince Cyrus's court and they were charged to watch over Verona. While Vaughn was clearly loyal to Prince Cyrus, it was Garret that Aaron believed was loyal to Colind. Through the bladesong, he reached out to the older men with an open hand, but there was not a flicker of change in their lifebeat at all. He stopped wielding the Falcons, bringing them to his sides. A lone shaft of sunlight momentarily blazed upon the deck where Aaron stood before being shut out by the perpetual cloud cover. He kept hold of the bladesong in his mind and looked at his companions. Verona and Sarik scanned their surroundings with eyes wide open. Eric and Braden gave him an acknowledging nod, while Garret and Vaughn's attention were on the others. Sarah caught his eye and nodded approvingly. Reaching two out of the six was more than he had hoped for, but Aaron was a bit disappointed that he couldn't reach all of them.

"You mustn't blame yourself," Sarah said, quietly coming to his side.

"You can't make blind men see."

"This is amazing!" Sarik exclaimed.

"Is this what you see whenever you wield those swords?" Verona asked.

Aaron swallowed. "Sometimes. I don't need them anymore to focus myself."

"Why is it fading?" Sarik said in disappointment.

"It's not gone. Trust me. You will learn to maintain the connection longer now that you know what it feels like. Try to focus," Aaron said, and turned to scan the sky. "There, focus on the hawk. Take a deep breath. Can you see it?" Sarik's brow furrowed in concentration. "Can you feel its beating heart?"

"I can see it," Verona said in an exhale of breath.

"I can, too," Sarik said.

"But it's not as clear as before," said Verona.

Aaron was about to reply when Eric and Braden stood before him. "We have failed you, my Lord," Braden said.

"No, you haven't. This is only the first time. We will try again. I promise you," Aaron said

"For a moment, I thought I felt something but..." Eric's voice trailed off.

"It will be different for everyone," Aaron said.

Alarm bells shrieked throughout the ship, snapping their attention, and the sailors rushed to their posts.

"My Lord." A shipman approached, gasping for breath. "The captain requests that you join him in the wheelhouse."

"Of course," Aaron answered, and they all fell in behind him.

"Cursed Ryakuls," Captain Morgan grumbled, speaking in low tones with one of his officers. He turned toward Aaron and the others as they entered the wheelhouse. "I hope you have more tricks up that sleeve of yours. Markus!" the captain barked. "Signal below to charge auxiliary engine burst."

"What's happening?" Aaron asked, seeing the crossbow turrets rise from the depths of the ship.

"The watch reports that Ryakuls are following this ship. They are off the stern and on either side, staying just out of crossbow range," Captain Morgan replied.

"They are herding us," Vaughn said.

"Yes, but to where?" Aaron said. "Are they keeping us from Shandara?"

"No, but having them so close and not attacking is enough to set everyone on edge. This is not normal for Ryakul," Captain Morgan said.

Aaron and Sarah exchanged glances. "The Drake. It can control the Ryakuls."

"Yeah, but wouldn't it want to prevent you from reaching Shandara?" Sarik asked.

"If it's herding this ship, then it forces you to get there at a time of its choosing," Sarah said.

Aaron suppressed a shiver as he felt a familiar stirring underneath the surface. He'd held off the blood lust of his ancestors only barely at the camp, and now the Drake was closing in.

"Aaron?" Verona asked.

"This changes nothing. We head to Shandara as planned. We should stay on guard in case the Ryakuls change their mind and attack. How much longer till we get there?" Aaron asked.

"According to the charts, the towers of the White Rose should be visible in the next few hours or so," Captain Morgan replied.

Aaron looked out the windows at the gathering Ryakuls crowding the already darkening skies. At this rate, they weren't going to make it, and he saw that fact reflected in all of his companions' eyes. "Can we outrun them?"

"Only in short bursts. The auxiliary engine burst releases energy stored in the power crystals, which will surge the ship forward, but the Ryakuls will catch up eventually," Captain Morgan answered.

"How many bursts can they handle?" Aaron asked.

"Depends on how quickly the Ryakuls catch up. Sequentially, maybe five before they're blown, and then we're either blown up or stranded. They are an emergency measure at best," the captain answered.

Aaron was silent for a moment, considering. To come this far and die within sight of Shandara would be such a waste.

"Then we fight," he said. "Captain, do the controlled bursts, but don't blow the engines. Perhaps there will be a place within the city walls where we can put down and hold out against the Ryakuls."

"There might be a place if it's still standing." Garret spoke up for the first time. "The Dragon Hall. If we set down within its walls, maybe we could use some of the defenses there."

"The Dragon Hall is big enough for this ship to land in?" Aaron asked, unable to keep the disbelief from his voice.

Vaughn nodded. "You could put the whole of the palace of Rexel within its walls. That is, of course, if it's still standing."

They were interrupted by a shrieking Ryakul that rattled the windows at it passed. "We're out of time. Garret and Vaughn, stay in the wheelhouse. Help the captain find the Dragon Hall," Aaron said.

"Good hunting, Shandarian," the captain said, saluting with his fist across his heart, addressing him in the ancient form for those of the Royal House of Shandara. Aaron nodded back and left the room.

Aaron headed toward the bow of the ship with the rune-carved staff in hand, surveying the number of Ryakuls surrounding the ship. They could really use some help right now. Sailors rushed with practiced efficiency, manning their stations.

"I hope you have a plan, my friend," Verona said, notching one of the special arrows glowing with crystallized dust as Sarik did the same.

"How about not dying?" Aaron said.

The floor beneath their feet shook, and they turned to see the wings extend from the main hull of the ship. Spaced every ten feet were pods swinging into position. The pod caps opened in unison, revealing rows of glowing crystals. Aaron grabbed hold of the side and followed the sailors' examples as they all tied lifelines around their waists. He called Zeus over and tied a lifeline to the wolf, putting crossing loops around his chest so the line wouldn't hurt if it had to be used.

The Ryakuls circled their quarry with ruthless enthusiasm, patiently waiting for the perfect time to strike. Aaron focused himself, drawing upon the energy around them, and his perceptions sharpened. He scanned the sky, looking for some sign of the Drake.

An alarm bell ringing in increments of two from the wheelhouse went off and then the Raven shuddered, groaning under the force of the engines.

"The first burst," Verona shouted over the roaring wind.

The Ryakuls moved in a frenzy to block the advancing ship, swooping dangerously close to the lines securing the balloons and the wings. Aaron grabbed one of the small curved axes given to him by Armel and tracked the approaching group of Ryakuls. He sucked in the energy from the wind, feeling it rapidly spread throughout his limbs while never taking his eyes from the lead Ryakul. The black beast closed in, aiming its talons for the ship's wing. Aaron unleashed the small curved axe, sending it streaking toward his target. The axe shattered the armored tusk below the mouth, causing a small explosion of black blood. The lead Ryakul spun in midair, screaming in pain, and the small group that followed collided, sending a tangled mess toward the surface.

The sailors cheered as the Ryakuls fell behind and the ship broke free of the dark beasts. A call spread among the men on the deck. Alenzar'seth! Alenzar'seth! Alenzar'seth! The call spread throughout the entire ship, and Aaron faced the men while holding the rune-carved staff up in triumph. When the chanting stopped, Aaron saw Jopher making his way through the crowd, holding something in his hand. He knelt before Aaron, holding a broken shard, which he recognized as the remains of the axe he'd just thrown. Aaron thanked Jopher, who bowed and took a few steps back, watching Aaron with wide eyes.

"That was one hell of a shot," Verona said. "Picked up a new trick while you were away?"

"You like that? Unfortunately, I only have one more left," Aaron replied.

"Well, keep it handy."

The engine burst lasted for another twenty minutes, and the Ryakuls became lost in the darkening skies behind them. Verona assured him that the crystals would recharge over time. Aaron stayed at the bow of the ship, gazing over the landscape. In the distance, he saw the faint outline of buildings in the perpetual twilight. His hand traced the rune-carved staff, remembering the dying dragon and his message.

The land needs a champion. Time is short, and already the sickness spreads. Ryakuls are just the beginning of what was unleashed at the fall of Shandara.

The dragon, even Tarimus, had warned him of the path of vengeance. He had been so filled with molten anger that it had consumed him—and now? He looked back at Sarah with her long blonde hair cascading in the wind, glowing with a light all her own. Was she the reason for the change in him? Daughter of the High King. The High King who, along with Mactar, was largely responsible for the destruction of Shandara. Who even at this very moment hunted them. Would this fight tear him and Sarah apart? Cut their hearts until only bitterness and regret remained? He hoped not, but at the same time, he knew he couldn't run from this. Fate was indeed pulling on his strings, and when fate pulled on your strings, there was no choice but to play the game. Walking away was never an option. He knew it when he went through the portal, leaving everything behind to come here.

Sarah tied back her hair and turned toward him with those eyes of hers that stilled his heart. It wasn't fair to think about what he would alter if he could go back and change the course of time, and he shouldn't feel guilty for finding love, but part of him did. As if finding a shred of happiness was an affront to all those who had paid the ultimate price that led him here. They silently gazed at each other, speaking volumes but not saying a word at all.

"Stay close," Aaron said quietly.

"I will," she answered.

Aaron released his breath, nodded to himself, and then waved over Verona and the others. "When Verona and I encountered the dragon, it took us to a fountain with a statue of the Goddess. The dragon showed me images, saying it was the Goddess's message. A glowing white tree standing amid the ruins of a castle is where we will find Colind's prison. There is a tower with a massive carved relief of the Alenzar'seth's family symbol: a dragon caressing a single rose."

"We could use the help of a few dragons," Verona said, looking back at the already gaining Ryakul.

"It's not as if they were numerous to begin with," Sarik said.

"Do you know of the tower?" Verona asked Eric and Braden.

"The towers were part of the main complex of buildings, and if they are still standing, then we should be able to see them," Braden replied.

"Have you ever been there?" Aaron asked.

"We were children, but our parents told us stories. They were among those who escaped the fall, but they believed that the Alenzar'seth would return and that they would be called upon to serve again," Eric replied.

Once again, Aaron was impressed by the level of loyalty and belief the people of Shandara had for the Alenzar'seth. Even though the family had disappeared for over twenty years, the people still persevered, believing that they would one day return.

They decided to spread out and keep an eye on the horizon. Verona divided the explosive arrows between himself and Sarik. Aaron kept tracing his fingers along the rune-carved staff. He had felt stirrings of power emanating from it when he first picked it up and again at the fountain of the Goddess, but nothing since. Not that he'd had much time to spend with it.

He kept thinking about the White Tree and finding the tower. The landscape thus far held the bones of trees and hardly any vegetation, but Aaron could feel energy coiling beneath the surface, wanting to break the bonds that held the trappings of winter firmly in place. A winter without the cold. Colind had said his soul was stripped from his body, which was in an earthen tomb. Was there a way to reunite both body and soul and set him free from this prison?

He focused himself, drawing the energy within as he invoked the bladesong in his mind's eye. The image of the White Tree was brought to the forefront along with his need to find it. The runes on his staff flared brilliantly, sending a beam of light out slightly north of their current easterly heading.

A solitary spot amid a land in twilight was bathed in a lone shaft of sunlight. The Ryakuls' howls were close now, and the rear-mounted crossbows unleashed a volley of special bolts courtesy of Hatly, who was becoming legendary among the Raven's crew. The bolts tore through the sky, streaking into the Ryakuls and exploding.

The beam of light coming from the rune-carved staff stopped, but the runes retained their glow. Aaron felt tendrils of energy along the staff, and the Ryakuls' guttural roars pierced the sky as the shadowy mass of tusk and teeth enveloped the ship. For every Ryakul shot down, another took its place.

A Ryakul emerged from beneath the ship and perched itself on the railing. The Drake's call sawed through the air with such force that all activity on deck ceased. It locked its glowing yellow eyes upon Aaron, and its dark armor drank the light. It clutched a giant, twin-bladed axe that any normal man could barely lift with two hands. Verona and Sarik fired two glowing arrows, which it deflected, sending them flying harmlessly away from the ship. A soldier dropped from above, swinging his sword in a deadly arc, but the Drake swung its axe up, biting into the soldier's armor and sending the already dead man over the side.

Aaron felt the dragon tattoo twinge along the edges and the medallion grow warm against his chest. A single alarm bell rang through the silence. He yelled to Eric and Braden to step back.

"This is not your fight," he said, thundering past with the rune-carved staff clutched in his hand. Aaron stepped down to the main deck, where the Drake waited, poised as doom's herald. The ancestral voices stirred, but Aaron clamped his will down, not giving their bloodlust any footing.

"Here I am," Aaron shouted, and another alarm bell rang in the background. *One more.*

The Ryakul lashed out with its great tusked head at the end of its long neck. Zeus leaped at the same instant, his jaws locking onto the Ryakul's throat, holding on for all he was worth while the Ryakul thrashed about.

The Drake swung down from the Ryakul's back and hammered at the wolf with the haft of his axe. Zeus cried out as the blow sent him across the deck. Aaron brought up the staff, but didn't attack. The Drake studied him as he stood with one hand on the Ryakul as it shook its head, dark blood gushing from its wound.

God, this thing is big.

The Drake was a head taller than Aaron, who was usually among the tallest wherever he went. The third and final alarm bell rang, signaling the imminent engine burst, and the Raven lurched forward.

Aaron flourished the staff, the glowing runes streaking into view, snatching the Drake's attention. At the same moment, two explosive arrows plunged into the Ryakul just as the ship shuddered, gaining speed. The explosive crystal dust blew the Ryakul from the deck, sending the Drake over the side. Aaron rushed to where Zeus struggled to his feet. Zeus took a step and then dropped back down to the deck.

"It's okay. You got him," Aaron said, gently rubbing the wolf half-breed behind his ears. Zeus came to his feet once again and favoring one side, stood ready to go. Aaron gently grazed his hand over Zeus's ribs, and Zeus whimpered. He snatched his hand away and the wolf half-breed lay on the deck.

"He must have broken some of his ribs," Aaron said to Sarah, who came to his side. Seeing Zeus hurt made a lump grow in his throat. He couldn't lose Zeus, who had been his companion since the beginning.

"Aaron, come up here. You must see this," Verona called.

Sarah nodded for Aaron to go, promising to stay with Zeus. He leaped up the steps to the bow of the airship. The Ryakuls were in complete disarray, falling behind as the Raven sped away. The great towers of Shandara reached toward the sky. Some were jagged and cut short, like the spires of a broken crown, but even at this distance, Aaron saw that the capital city of Shandara was immense. The city stretched out, desolate and without a hint of life, and he wondered what the place must have been like when it was bustling with activity. In another life, he would have been born here.

Sarah joined them, taking his hand and silently scanning the city ahead. Zeus stood to his other side, still favoring one of his legs. He felt the energy within the rune-carved staff surge and flash, sending another beam of light toward the center of the city where a space beyond sight was illuminated briefly, until the beam melted away. Someone from the wheelhouse must have seen the beam, because the ship's course changed to head in that direction. There was a great expanse of wide paved roads leading to the city that at one time must have been well kept, but had fallen into disrepair. Aaron looked on, impressed by the amount of traffic the roads must have been able to accommodate.

"For a while there, I didn't think we were going to make it," Sarik said, joining them.

"There are forces at work here beyond any of us," Garret said as he and Vaughn joined them.

"You truly are touched by Ferasdiam," Vaughn said. "I believed wholeheartedly that you were the grandson of Reymius...but..."

Aaron slowly nodded. "Does any of this look familiar to you?" he asked.

"It was ages ago when I was here...as a young man. Don't look so surprised, Verona. I too was young once," Vaughn said. "You would be pleased to know that it was the one place in the world where the legends did not do it justice. The Alenzar'seth believed in the gathering and sharing of knowledge. There were colleges here, where people could learn and more. Gardens were planted throughout the city. To see it like this...so ruined."

"I never thought I would see the towers again," Garret said with slow tears brimming in his misty gray eyes. The rest of the group traded glances while the burned-out shell of a city loomed before them, whispering hints of a gloried past.

CHAPTER 29
WHAT SLEEPS MUST AWAKEN

A loud explosion rocked the ship, causing it to list to one side. Orders were given to retract the engine pods for repairs. The crackling of damaged crystals could be heard from within the pods, and the ship lost altitude.

Sailors scurried around the deck, making repairs and gesturing toward the balloon that held the ship aloft. There would be no escaping the Ryakuls a third time, once they caught up again. They needed to land the ship and make repairs within the confines of the city if they were to have a chance.

"Do you think we'll make it to the city?" Aaron asked.

"It's going to be close," Verona answered. The great city loomed before them like a sleeping giant.

"We need to be ready to drop into the city near that tower, but I'm thinking perhaps some should stay behind to help guard the ship—" Aaron began.

"With all due respect, none of us are going to stay behind with the ship," Braden said, his deep voice resonating with his icy glare.

"They have a job to do," Verona said, gesturing toward the sailors, "and so do we, so let's be about it. We're the real targets here."

Aaron surveyed the group, all of whom calmly, but defiantly, returned his gaze with the exception of Sarah, who looked slightly amused. He knew she had no intention of staying behind.

"Nathaniel will have things well in hand. The good captain did serve in the military, which is why the prince selected him for this voyage," Vaughn said. "And most of these sailors have served as members of the guard."

There was a soft clearing of the throat, and Aaron saw Jopher standing behind him. Jopher had his swords and travel pack at his feet, and he wore the common garb of a sailor. His notorious princely arrogance was clearly absent in his sincere gaze. A small group of sailors swung down from the higher observation decks, and a bucket of tools overturned, spilling its contents on deck. Jopher immediately squatted down, helping the sailor retrieve his tools.

Prince Jopher Zamaridian has learned a touch of humility it seems, Aaron thought.

Jopher slowly turned back toward Aaron with his hand across his heart. "Please allow this son of Zsensibar to aid your journey to Shandara," he asked quietly.

"He's earned it," Sarik said quietly, and Aaron could sense the general consensus from the others, who were either indifferent or leaned toward allowing the boy prince to come.

Has being on board the Raven for a month truly changed the boy prince? Aaron wondered. "Okay, you can come. But you follow my lead and take orders when given," Aaron said.

Jopher nodded eagerly and began strapping on his weapons.

The immense city walls rose before them. Their smooth surfaces were made of a light-colored stone. How could any army hope to breach those walls? The others gasped their surprise at the sheer size and thickness, echoing Aaron's thoughts. The walls between what remained of the towers contained massive carved reliefs depicting the Alenzar'seth coat of arms. He studied the damaged sections and noted how the debris dotted the landscape outside of the wall.

"This city fell from within," Aaron said. "Whatever took this city couldn't have come through the walls. So how did they get inside?"

Just beyond the walls, the burned-out bones of the city stretched before him. How many must have died trying to escape what happened here? The mere thought sickened him.

"Could they've used travel crystals to get in?" Aaron asked.

"Only small groups, but there were no travel crystals around during the fall of Shandara," Sarah answered.

The Raven drew steadily closer to the ground, unable to hold its altitude any longer. Aaron scanned the roadways. From the corners of his eyes, the shadows seemed to move, but each time he looked closer he saw nothing out of place. The chill in the air seeped through his clothes, and he shivered. Whatever this place had been, it was now a place of death. A tomb from an earlier time. Though it was the middle of the day, the only light in the area came from the center of the city. Zeus whined, sniffed the air, and then let out a low growl while pacing the deck. The wolf still favored one side, but otherwise looked alert.

Captain Morgan set the Raven down near the Dragon Hall, a large octagonal building in the center of a complex of other buildings. The building was ornately carved to complement the gardens that were part of the complex. Everything appeared functional and beautiful all at the same time. The pride of craftsmanship radiated from it, down to the smallest detail. Shandara made Rexel look like a small country town in comparison. Aaron couldn't shake the feeling that the capital city of Shandara was modern by any measurement back on Earth. What really had him perplexed was how they'd achieved these marvels. The ship landed, heaving its bulk to the ground in a final thud, and a lone howl echoed in the distance.

"I've delivered you to Shandara as promised," Captain Morgan said, coming on deck with an officer behind him.

"As good as your word, thank you," Aaron said. "How long will it take to make repairs?"

The captain surveyed the workings of his crew as they moved about the deck. "How long do you need?" he countered.

"As much time as you can give me," Aaron answered. "If you have any tricks up your sleeve, we'll need those as well. We're not alone here."

Nathaniel nodded. "Good hunting," the captain said, and went off to supervise the repairs.

Aaron and the others descended the gangplank to the surface. Large cracks ran down the walkways, with some extending to the rubbled remains of a building. They moved as quickly as they dared coming out of the complex, leaving the Dragon Hall with its gaping roof behind.

The musky dry air became more apparent the deeper they moved into the city. Deep fissures scarred the roadway, and there were no signs of life among all the scorched remnants. The streets were empty, without a single blade of grass trying to claim what had been made by man. There was a stillness to the air that was only disturbed by each echoing footstep they took. Faint Ryakul howls could be heard far off in the distance. They drew steadily on, not speaking, as if an unspoken agreement had descended upon them to make their way to the towers as quietly as possible.

Seeing the land and the city of Shandara, Aaron wondered if he would have ever been able to make this journey without the help of his friends... *His friends...* Somewhere along the way, they had become more than traveling companions. He looked at Verona, whom Colind had tasked with finding and helping him. He wouldn't be standing here right now if it weren't for Verona. He had hoped that Colind would reach out to him once he was closer to Shandara, but so far he had not.

They turned down another street with a massive tower a short walk away. Aaron gripped the rune-carved staff in his hand and kept scanning the area. So much destruction. Seeing the burned-out buildings that had collapsed on themselves reminded him of his own home. The acrid smoke stinging his nose while he held his sister as she wept on his shoulders. The fires burning away what he'd failed to protect. Watching as the firefighters gave up trying to stop the blazing inferno that consumed his home. The same thing must have happened here in Shandara, but with considerably more destruction. Some of the fissures ran deep into the ground, and Aaron shuddered to think of what escaping from this place must have been like.

How could Grandpa let this happen and then just leave?

He knew that the past haunted his grandfather, but he'd had no idea just how deep those scars really were. To lose your wife and the home you labored to protect in so short a time. Part of him understood his grandfather's need to protect the one remaining person who was wholly dependent upon him. Now that he thought of it, his mother hadn't escaped Shandara entirely unscathed. Something had wiped her memories of this place. Something, or someone, Aaron corrected himself. The stale air of decay invaded his nostrils, and the dark side of anger roiled beneath the surface. So many lives lost for other men's greed, and he was thrust into the middle of their war. Seeing the state of Shandara, how could he not want to fight against all those who were responsible for this? Vengeance in and of itself was not enough anymore. What he wanted was a reckoning, and the two were completely different in his mind. This place was out of balance and spiraling toward destruction that went deeper than the city. He could feel the unrest crawl through his skin. The air felt energized, as if a storm were about to break out at any moment.

Eric stopped in his tracks, motioning for the others to halt. He stepped through the doorway of a building left mostly intact. Braden was peering through the doorway when Eric returned with a broad smile, carrying two metal rods about two feet in length. Eric tossed one to his brother. Each rod had a handled cross section just off-center. Eric grasped the handle, triggering a mechanism that sent small bands across his forearm. The rod extended and then fanned out, forming a golden shield. The shield was adorned with an etched carving of a tree. Braden triggered his shield, which formed in the blink of an eye.

Aaron walked up to Eric and ran his hands along the shield. The seams of the interlocking pieces weren't visible and the smooth solid surface felt cool beneath his fingertips.

"The shield of the De'anjard," Eric said proudly.

Aaron nodded, grasping his shoulder. They collapsed the shields, which returned to their original form just as quickly and silently, leaving Aaron slightly in awe of the craftsmanship used to construct such a thing.

"Aaron," Verona whispered. "It's not that I don't appreciate the calm reprieve from people trying to kill us, but isn't this a little too easy?"

"He's right. I would have thought we'd have seen something by now," Garret said.

The Elitesmen were here, they just hadn't shown themselves yet. A dark shape swooped overhead, and they scattered out of sight. The Ryakuls couldn't have caught up to them that quickly.

"We have to keep moving," Aaron said, and continued toward the tower.

The others followed silently, and both Sarik and Verona had arrows ready to be drawn quickly if needed. The rest had their swords drawn with the exception of Sarah, which didn't fool Aaron in the slightest, as she was among the quickest of them. They rounded the corner of the gateway, passing underneath the tower and heading toward the interior courtyard.

Aaron stopped in his tracks. Beyond the tower, the scarred landscape gave way to a grove of trees, and the smell of fresh pine penetrated the stale air. The runes in the staff pulsed, and he could feel a slight tugging at his core, drawing him into the grove. Aaron focused himself and tried to reach out for Colind, but he couldn't sense him. Zeus whined slightly, perking his ears with all his attention on the grove. A gentle hand touched his shoulder.

"Are you all right?" Sarah whispered.

Aaron nodded and continued forward.

Come on, Colind. Give me a sign.

The gnarled trees of the grove stood tall, lining a straight path, where a white glow radiated. Aaron jogged to its source. The grove gave way to a clearing where a lone white tree stood solitary and majestic, glowing from its own luminance. A border of light surrounded the tree. Zeus pushed ahead, limping past the border, where he seemed to phase out, becoming transparent. A soft rush of air blew back through Aaron as Zeus passed through the border, and the wolf half-breed came to a stop at the tree, wagging his tail. He stood straighter, not favoring his injured side anymore, but something was off. Extreme coldness rolled through Aaron like something had been cut from him. He reached out with his senses toward Zeus, but there was nothing but an expanse of cold.

Sarah caught his arm, reaching toward the barrier, shaking her head. "Death lies beyond that barrier. I can feel it, can't you?"

Aaron called out to Zeus, not bothering to keep quiet. He reached out, but was careful not to touch the barrier. Zeus started to come, but something else grabbed his attention, as if he were being called back.

A hooded figure appeared in a golden cloak, and a hand reached out to gently pat Zeus's head. Aaron's heart stopped in his chest. The stance of the figure was unmistakable, because he had seen it many times while growing up. The figure in the golden cloak was none other than his grandfather, Reymius Alenzar'seth.

He clenched his teeth, feeling the heat rise to his face as he fought blaming his grandfather for leaving him so ill prepared to face the perils that had come with his passing. Then a great weight settled into the pit of his stomach. A deep sadness as the lives lost to bring him here flashed through his mind.

Be...strong... There are no perfect solutions. Not in life, Son. The last words whispered by his parents were always with him. Aaron looked at the shade of his grandfather, no longer with the eyes of youth, but with those of a man in silent understanding. As someone who had walked a few steps along a similar path. *Sometimes, we can only do our very best and leave the rest to hope.*

Aaron stepped forward, and Sarah grabbed his arm.

"It's okay. This is something I must do. Wait for me," he said. When she nodded, he turned to Verona and the others. "Guard the way. This is something I must do alone."

Verona looked questioningly at Sarah, who nodded. He motioned for the others to fan out around the tree, but they kept their distance from the barrier.

Aaron lifted the rune-carved staff and brought it thundering down just outside the barrier, and the runes pulsed to life. Aaron stepped through the barrier leaving the staff behind. He was instantaneously engulfed in a blazing white light as the world faded away around him.

***

* * *

"Where did he go?" Sarik asked.

"He needs time," Sarah answered. "We must give him time." As she said this, shadows descended upon the grove, spilling beyond the tree line.

"Well done, Sister," a sneering voice called, emerging from the dark. "We couldn't have done it without you."

The shadows retreated, leaving them surrounded by too many Elitesmen to count, but it was her brother Primus who spoke.

"The company you keep nowadays. I must say, Father would not approve. Where is the Alenzar'seth dog? He was here just a moment ago."

Sarah met Verona's cold gaze as she was sure he was weighing whether she had betrayed them or not in his mind. She would not leave. Not when Aaron asked her to wait for him. She wouldn't leave even if he hadn't asked her to stay. Rather than waste time with words, she sent two throwing knives streaking toward Primus and Rordan. The Elitesmen at her brothers' sides easily blocked the knives, but the shock in their eyes was indisputable. If they came for her now, blood would be spilled. The lines had been drawn. She drew her sword with the ease of one married to the blade, its sharp edge gleaming in the light of the Shandarian tree behind her.

Sarah focused her mind, drawing in the energy from this once-proud city. Beck had given her the tools, and the Resistance throughout the land of Khamearra, her purpose. Her brothers drew their weapons, and the Elitesmen surrounding them followed suit. It was time to make a stand.

"Let us not be too hasty." A figure stepped forward, his black cloak billowing behind him. "We care not for any of you. Step aside, and I promise that I will let you walk free of this place," Mactar said, his oily voice dripping with poisonous reassurance. Although Primus and Rordan looked to disagree, they kept their silence.

Eric and Braden brought the shields of the De'anjard to bear and stood poised to attack. Sarah looked at the others and felt a surge of pride as all of them stood rooted in place with fierce resolve in their eyes.

"I believe you have your answer, my Lord," Sarah said.

Mactar looked amused and brought his hands up. A blue orb grew from his hands, crackling with energy. He thrust his hands out, sending the orb blazing toward the twins, and the orb bounced off their shields harmlessly. Gasps of surprise slipped from the mouths of the Elitesmen while Eric and Braden glanced at each other and back at Mactar challengingly. Mactar furrowed his brow, summoned forth an orb of dark energy, and hurled it directly in Sarah's path. An invisible barrier swallowed the blast. Then a voice echoed around them.

"You were a fool to return here, Mactar."

The deep voice of Colind, guardian of the lands, spoke out, echoing around them. Small tendrils of energy seeped out from the rune-carved staff and latched on to each of the defenders. Sarah felt a shield move in place around her and knew they were protected from Mactar's attacks. The Elitesmen drew their weapons in one single motion that spoke volumes of their discipline and training, their black armor making them appear more demon than man.

"Remember what Aaron has taught you. They are men. Face them as such," she shouted.

Verona pulled back a crystal-tipped arrow and sent it streaking toward the ground at Mactar's feet. The explosion sent the Elitesmen into disarray, but Mactar remained untouched, erecting a barrier of his own. Another explosion echoed behind them from where Sarik's crystal-tipped arrow found its mark. Without a backward glance, Sarah charged.

***

Purpose...

A voice like slabs of granite chafing together spoke.

The land needs a champion... The fate of the world rests upon the last scion of the Alenzar'seth.

The dragon's words echoed in Aaron's mind, weighing down on him. He opened his eyes to a shimmering world of twilight, and the shade of his grandfather stood before him.

"Why didn't you tell me?" Aaron whispered. His grandfather nodded in understanding, but remained silent.

"He can't answer you, Aaron. Not anymore," Colind said, his voice everywhere and nowhere at the same time. "Search your heart for the answers Reymius would have given."

Aaron knew Colind spoke the truth, but he would have liked to hear the answer from his grandfather himself. Reymius was dead, and with Zeus at his side, he knew that Zeus had carried out the last of his master's orders. Zeus was to help guide Aaron to Shandara and with that task complete, could now rest. His only link to the world he knew was severed, leaving him feeling truly cut off from the life he had always known. But he was not alone, and the solace he had found would sustain him.

"I've come to free you, Colind," Aaron said.

"I told you before, boy, I cannot be saved," Colind said coolly.

Aaron heard bitterness in his voice, tinged in a hopeless certainty of one's fate.

"Whatever you may think, you are alive. I can feel it. I can feel your life beat even from this place," Aaron said, and silence answered him. "We need you, Colind. This world needs you. I can't do this without you."

"Your friends need you, Aaron. Even now they are being attacked," Colind countered.

Sarah!

He shifted toward the barrier.

Stay focused, he told himself and stopped.

"Where is your prison?" Aaron asked quickly. He had to leave this place. Time was running out. "I don't know everything that happened at the fall of Shandara, but I know you had a part. Don't you want to help set things right?"

"I have helped!" Colind shouted. "I've given everything. A lifetime of serving the higher cause, and what did it get me? A dead wife and a son who became a monster. A gatekeeper for a pathway between worlds who is also responsible for unspeakable evil."

"Those sound like reasons to fight to me," Aaron replied.

"Those are reasons for vengeance and despair," Colind said bitterly.

"Vengeance will only get you so far, and despair is all I have. When Reymius first called me to come aid you, I thought my redemption was at hand, but the more I saw of this world, the more I knew its people have moved beyond the guardians. They need to fight for themselves. Reliance upon a powerful few has left them firmly under the tyrant's boot."

"You're right. They do need to learn to fight for themselves, or all is lost, but there is something you've forgotten. Something that the most stalwart servant of the light can forget. This place has sapped it even from you... Hope," Aaron said.

Silence hung in the air between them, and then Colind replied quietly, "Even for Tarimus?"

Aaron felt bile rise up his throat, and for the briefest of moments he thought of abandoning Colind to his fate. Like Shandara, Colind had spent too much time in the shadows. Who was he to deny a father's hope that his child could be redeemed?

"Tarimus walks his own path, but if he chooses to follow the light, then yes, even for Tarimus."

Colind appeared before him on the cusp of the light barrier, dark smoke billowing around him so thickly that Aaron wondered how he could see. Aaron felt the presence of his grandfather stir behind him.

It's time for you to step back into the light, my friend.

The voice of his grandfather spoke, and a vine of light shot forth from the tree, wrapping itself around Colind's wrists and pulling him in. Colind erupted into screams as his shade made contact with the light, but the vines pulling him forth were relentless, and two more wrapped themselves around his torso. The thrashing shade was pulled forth fully into the light, and bit by bit, the shadow was burned away until only a luminous being remained. Colind's screams ceased, and the shade hung in the air as if he were sleeping. Then, in a flash of light, his shade shot forth beyond the grove to another clearing, into the center of a massive stone prison composed of boulders.

Aaron was pulled back, and the shade of Reymius slowly faded into the tree, beckoning him closer. He stepped forward and put his hand upon the bark. Of all the questions tumbling through his mind, there was one that kept coming to the forefront, demanding to be answered. He had to know why. What was the sacred trust that was imparted upon the Alenzar'seth?

Images spewed forth in his mind of a place where a dark rift hung in a valley. Something pressed against the edges of the rift, desperate to break through. As Aaron drew closer, whatever was struggling ceased its efforts. The rift hung like a dark-stained glass window before him. As he looked through, he saw a gathering horde of creatures in armor, the likes of which he had never seen, swirling like shadows in the dark, poised to come through. The land beyond was barren and dark. Those in front noticed him looking through, sending them into a frenzy with the promise of death and destruction. Whatever was on the other side was definitely not human. A large, heavily muscled creature filled the space just outside the rift, its long neck the size of a tree trunk. It swung its head into view, and wild yellow eyes regarded him with barely contained rage. Aaron jumped back and watched as the creature struggled against the rift, which barely held it at bay. The edges of the rift appeared to fray under the barrage of attacks from the creature beyond it.

Aaron was pulled away from the rift. This was the pledge of the Alenzar'seth. They were guarding the pathway from another world, where an invading army lay in wait, poised to attack. What was keeping this army of darkness from overrunning Safanar? He needed Colind. Was this why he was being hunted? Was this what Mactar had wanted all along?

Aaron pulled his hand from the tree, and the light diminished until it barely surrounded it. The currents of energy he felt were fading fast. He was thrust back into the torrent of the battle surrounding him. The others were cloistered around the tree save for Sarah, who danced between the Elitesmen like twisting death, keeping their attention off the others.

Not so far, Sarah.

The Elitesmen, as if hearing his thoughts, surrounded her. Sarah jumped and was met by multiple black-armored Elitesmen cutting her off. After a few more attempts, she simply stopped and held her sword at the ready, breathing heavily.

Aaron drew his Falcons and called upon the bladesong, summoning the energy from the tree. Immediately, his perceptions sharpened. He took a few steps, leaped up into the air, and landed beside Sarah, who looked at him with both shock and relief.

"I thought I'd even the odds," Aaron said. Not waiting for a response, he engaged the charging Elitesmen.

Aaron became a whirlwind of death, and the Elitesmen fell to his blades. The bladesong coursed through him, and its song assaulted the Elitesmen to the point of distraction. He was able to move as they did, only faster and with much more strength. He tapped the knowledge of his ancestors, who had fought many more battles than he ever could in a lifetime, and their knowledge was his for the taking. He unraveled the pattern of their attacks with increasing ease until they broke off and turned their focus upon his friends. As fast as he was, it would be impossible to protect them all. He shouldn't have expected that the Elitesmen would fight with any semblance of honor. What would he have to sacrifice so that they could survive this? Colind was now buried in his earthen prison, which he must reach. Time was slipping away.

Vaughn and Garret were disarmed first, despite Sarik's valiant attempts to keep the Elitesmen at bay. Sarik was driven back, as was Verona. Eric and Braden fought with their backs to each other with sword and shield, but were quickly surrounded. Jopher managed to get near Sarah, but they too were encircled by a wall of swords.

"Hold!" commanded a man in a violet cloak. "Or they die."

Aaron stopped in his tracks, taking a moment to gather himself. *Think slowly, there must be a way out of this.*

"I'm the one you want," he offered.

"Indeed, the stories are true. You are of the house Alenzar'seth," said the man, whose facial features and blond hair looked oddly familiar. Then he glanced at Sarah, and the family resemblance became apparent.

"You know so much about me," Aaron replied, stepping slowly toward Sarah and Jopher, who were the most heavily guarded.

"I am Prince Rordan. Interesting blades you have. I don't believe I've seen their like before," Rordan said.

Great, another prince. Rordan had confirmed his suspicions that he was Sarah's brother.

"I have, your Grace," Darven said, emerging from the shadows to the prince's side.

Aaron saw the man for the first time. "I know you," he said coldly, remembering the man who had dragged Tye's body through the portal. "You and I aren't finished; before this day is done, I swear I'm going to kill you." As much as he wanted to charge in and claim his vengeance, he also knew that would be the quickest way for his friends to die. They were trying to distract him. It was the only reason the prince came forward. "I would see the face of my enemy."

There was a brief moment of silence before a voice answered. "Your guardian protector is gone. You are all within my power now," Mactar said, appearing as if by magic at Rordan's side. What little light there was in this accursed kingdom of Shandara diminished even more.

For all that he had heard of Mactar prior to this meeting, Aaron had expected more than the wiry man with slicked back oily hair before him. Mactar reminded him of a bad used car salesman, appearing harmless but with an agenda to get the better of you. It was the eyes that didn't fit, appearing dull and dimwitted, but when Aaron peered closer, they became cold and calculating. The man looked directly at him, seemingly aware of everything at once. This was the man who had helped orchestrate the events that drove his grandfather and mother from Safanar? The one who engineered the fall of Shandara? If Aaron had passed him on the street, he wouldn't have given him a backward glance. Many must have underestimated this man to their demise, and the irony was not lost upon Aaron as to how the same applied to him.

"He's not gone," Aaron said with a small, knowing smile.

Mactar frowned, considering. "Well then, time is short for you if the Wanderer has indeed found his way out of shadow, as it were," he said, glancing in the direction of Colind's prison.

He knows.

Aaron continued to take Mactar's measure and added gambler to the list of attributes he was compiling for his enemy. Mactar could be nothing else. He was a puppet master of grand proportions, with the appearance of someone supremely inept.

Beware, a venomous voice whispered along a chilling breeze that danced across his neck, and Mactar's eyes widened in shock as well.

Tarimus!

Aaron tried to sense his presence, but it was gone in an instant. *Why now? Focus. The presence of Tarimus has put Mactar off balance.*

Rordan frowned, looking from Aaron to Mactar. "You speak in riddles, Mactar. Speak plainly if you must speak at all."

A Ryakul screech pierced the sky above them. The Drake was getting closer. He needed to do something. Though his blades were at his side, the bladesong was alive within him. He wondered if Verona or Sarik had more of the crystal-tipped arrows. No time. The energy still churned within him, waiting to be used, and he drew in more.

Mactar sensed this and shouted, "Enough!" He brought up his hands, sending a beam of dark energy barreling toward him. All semblance of ineptness left, revealing the cold-hearted murderer of nations before him.

Aaron barely brought up the Falcons in time to deflect the beam. He could feel the energy churn through Mactar like an inferno.

Aaron felt the ground slide under his feet, despite the added strength he was pulling into himself.

Not here! This was Shandara. Home to the Alenzar'seth. Aaron pulled more energy from the tree until he was surrounded with a white glow. A lone shaft of sunlight penetrated the curtain of shadow, illuminating the patch of earth upon which he stood. He heaved the gathered energy out from himself, swallowing Mactar's beam, and spread it out to the Elitesmen. The air crackled and pulsated around them.

Aaron pushed outward, and Mactar, along with most of the Elitesmen, was thrust into the air, blown beyond the grove. The ground rumbled under his feet, and the bark of the tree faded to gray and split. The great tree fell with a colossal crash, and Aaron turned in time to hear Jopher cry out as Primus pulled his sword from Sarah's back.

Sarah fell to the ground as if in slow motion, only to be caught by Jopher, who managed to swing his sword, driving her attacker back while catching her. Something broke inside Aaron, and he released the beast within, giving a guttural roar as he attacked Primus faster than the eye could track. The man's head left his shoulders before surprise could even register on his face.

Aaron circled toward Rordan and the remaining Elitesmen with murder in his eyes. An Elitesmen quickly grabbed the prince and pulled him back into the grove, out of sight.

He turned back to Sarah and dropped his Falcons to the ground. A cry from the depths of his soul ripped through the air, and he fell to his knees, pressing his head onto her chest, listening. *Breathe, damn it. Just breathe.* Then he heard it. The barest hint of a raspy breath. She opened her red-rimmed eyes toward him with a gasp.

"Aaron," Sarah whispered.

"I'm here. I'm with you," Aaron said, grasping her hand in his, ignoring the growing patch of blood beneath her shirt. *Not again. I wasn't fast enough.*

"Remember your power." She sighed and lay still.

No... Not her... He rocked back and forth, and a crack of thunder and lightning split the sky.

"*Why!*" His scream echoed throughout the grove. "Haven't I given enough?!"

The medallion flared coolly on his skin, and the bladesong spread like wildfire within him.

Remember your power.

Sarah's sweet voice whispered from the depths of his mind.

"Aaron," Verona said from behind him.

Aaron sprang to his feet, snatching his swords off the ground, and began to wield the Falcons, pouring his own soul into the bladesong. He would do this. Give all that he was so that she might breathe again, even if it meant giving everything he had. Instead of drawing energy into himself, he projected it away and into Sarah's still form. The blade's melody rode along the air, harmonizing around them. A golden light radiated from him, stretching toward Sarah's body and lifting it from the ground. Her long blonde hair hung shimmering like a curtain of light beneath her head. Aaron expanded the energy within her as she had taught him to do within himself. Instead of strengthening his bones and muscles, he urged her body to repair itself using the energy from his own soul. Her body healed, slowly at first and then with the rigorous fervor of that which blazed within all life. When her body was whole, she remained frozen in the air before him.

Breathe.

Aaron urged her body to awaken with a burst of energy, and he felt himself become spent. "Please," he whispered before collapsing, and Sarah's body gently sank to the ground.

The path is blocked, Tarimus's venomous whisper returned, and the air stank of his presence.

Release me, Tarimus beckoned. *Release me, and I will ensure her soul returns to its body. Delay, and she will be lost to you forever.*

Release Tarimus? "How could I release you?" Aaron asked aloud to the stunned silence of those around him. "Answer me, Tarimus! How can I release you?" he asked quickly.

"Aaron, you can't," Vaughn shouted, but his protest fell upon deaf ears.

Tarimus appeared before him, his black eyes appearing hauntingly devoid of life at first, but the raised eyebrows and set features denoted the desperation that lay hidden behind the bitterness. Tarimus untied his dark cloak, allowing it to fall into the nothingness that swallowed the area below his thighs. His appearance was slightly out of phase with reality, but for the first time, Aaron saw the scar that ran down the side of his hairless face. The one that Aaron had given him in the dream realm. A golden chain-link belt glowed around his waist, and Tarimus lifted it as if he were lifting a great weight, then let it fall back into place.

He had given so much. Lost so many people he loved. Would it be selfish of him to allow Tarimus back into the world so he could have Sarah? Tarimus was a monster, despite his talk of second chances with Colind. Whatever Tarimus did if he were to release him would be on Aaron's hands. Tarimus was the gatekeeper between the realms, but it had never occurred to him that Tarimus himself could have been trapped, forced to do the bidding of another. Mactar...

"What will you do if I release you?"

"My will will be my own for the first time in many years, but if you must know, I will hunt Mactar. That should suit you," Tarimus replied. "Hurry, time is short, and my hold on her is slipping."

Silence hung in the air as Aaron regarded Tarimus. "What must I do?" he finally asked, lowering his head.

"You must break the chains that bind me as only you can. The paths of the living and the dead are more intertwined here than anywhere on Safanar. Use your blades to cut through these chains. We have but one chance. Do this, and my final act as gatekeeper will be to allow the soul of this one to return to this realm," Tarimus said.

"How do I know you're telling me the truth?" Aaron asked.

Tarimus's lips curved in a mirthless half smile. "Can you afford not to trust me?"

Aaron clenched his teeth. *No, I can't take the chance,* he thought and nodded to Tarimus. He raised his swords and focused the energy within himself, extending it into the Falcons. The crystals within the pommels glowed with a pearly light. Tarimus heaved the golden chain away from his body, piercing the realm of the living. Aaron heard surprised gasps from those around him, and he immediately shut them out of his mind. He focused his will into the edge of his glowing swords, and with a thunderous swing, his blades shattered the golden chains that bound Tarimus.

Aaron staggered as the energy left him, gasping for breath. Tarimus stepped through with a great thud as his boots hit the ground, and he fell to his knees. Aaron straightened himself and watched warily as Tarimus rose to his feet. He didn't say a word. He didn't have to, as Aaron was ready to pounce upon Tarimus at the slightest hint of betrayal, and they both knew it. The others gathered behind him in silence with their weapons at the ready.

Tarimus surveyed the group and said, "You've become much harder since we last met. That is good." Tarimus turned his gaze to Aaron, and with a fist across his heart, he melted away into a dark mist.

Aaron was about to call out, but at the same moment Sarah coughed, sucking in air with harsh gasps. He knelt at her side. All thoughts of Tarimus were purged from his mind as he held her in his arms, watching as the color returned to her face.

"I heard you calling to me," she said shakily. "I tried to come, but the way was blocked. I saw you, but I couldn't reach you no matter how hard I tried. Then I felt myself being pulled...up."

"Don't worry about that. You're safe now. I promise," Aaron said.

Sarah rose to her feet and looked down at her own blood on her shirt. "What happened?"

"Primus stabbed you from behind, and if Jopher hadn't been nearby, it could have been a lot worse," Aaron said.

Sarah looked at Primus's headless body that lay sprawled a few feet away and closed her eyes for a moment.

"And Rordan?" she asked, and Aaron shook his head. "Another time for him then," she said, finding and sheathing her sword forcefully.

They shared a brief look of understanding, and Aaron looked at the others. "We need to move quickly. Colind doesn't have much time."

"What about Zeus?" Verona asked.

Aaron's face crumpled in grief, and he shook his head, tears brimming his eyes. Before anyone could say anything, he went to retrieve the rune-carved staff that stood planted into the ground where he left it. Sarah came to his side and put her hand upon his shoulder. He reached up and grasped her hand, holding it for second before reaching for the staff. He felt the energy return to him as he carried it. Together, they raced up the path to where Colind's tomb waited. At least he'd managed to save her, but he was still worried about what Tarimus would do now that he was free. He glanced to his side where Sarah was. Worried though he was, he wouldn't change anything.

They only had to run for a few minutes before the path opened to another clearing, where a group of boulders stood stacked upon each other, forming an odd-shaped room.

"We need to spread out and search for a way inside," Aaron said, checking the creases where the boulders met, but all were sealed.

If Colind was awake in there, he would be running out of air anytime now. None of them could find a way inside, and Colind didn't answer their calls. They lined up and tried to move the boulders, but they might as well have tried moving a mountain. The boulders wouldn't budge, even with enhanced strength. The shrieks of the Ryakuls were coming closer.

"There must be a way to move these things," Aaron said in frustration.

"What about the ship?" Verona asked. "I can signal them to come, and perhaps they will have something on board that can help."

"If you send the signal you will give away our position," Vaughn said. "Aaron, can you beat the Elitesmen back as you did before?"

Aaron shook his head. "I used the energy from the tree, and it's gone. The balance of this place is fragile now. I'm afraid I'd only make things worse by drawing too heavily from the energy here." Something skated along the fringe of his thoughts. When Garret was about to speak, he said, "Just give me a minute, please."

He handed the staff to Sarah and knelt facing the boulders. They weren't a natural rock formation. Someone had put them there, and he was willing to wager it was Mactar, but how? Aaron blocked out all the sounds around him so he could listen to the quiet of his mind. The barest hints of crystallized tones echoed from a great distance. He tried to focus on the sound, but it remained elusive. Reaching across the space to a boulder, he felt a distinct vibration emanating from within the rock. He drew his swords, and a few notes from the bladesong reverberated off the boulders, and the vibration increased. He began to wield the blades into a tune that he had never played before. The energy moved through him as before, but it came out through the melody of the bladesong. He focused the energy toward a single boulder. Instead of the notes bouncing away, they were infused into the stone, causing it to vibrate more, and small dust clouds swirled into the air.

"Ferasdiam," Garret gasped.

The boulder lifted a few inches off the ground, groaning as it chafed against its neighbors. Aaron kept the bladesong going and shook his head toward the boulder. Verona gestured for Eric and Braden to follow him, and they all pushed. The boulder moved slowly over the ground. He kept the bladesong focused on the boulder lest it would fall to the ground.

When the boulder moved enough, Sarah slipped inside and emerged with a stooped figure. Garret and Sarik relieved Sarah of Colind's weight and gently laid the old man upon the ground. Aaron released the bladesong, and the boulder dropped down, shaking the ground beneath their feet.

They gathered around Colind, who lay unmoving upon the ground. Aaron leaned his head against his chest and couldn't hear a heartbeat. Aaron brought his fist down twice upon Colind's chest. The old man sucked in air and coughed, and the others sighed in relief. When his breath steadied, he opened his eyes and met Aaron's gaze.

Garret approached from the other side and eased a water skin to Colind's lips, urging him to drink. They watched in silence as Colind slowly drank the water. He looked at his hands, flexing his fingers, then down at his toes, which he wiggled, and then he let out a hearty laugh until he could barely breathe. It was an infectious laugh that soon had most of them joining in.

The clothing he had been buried with had long turned to rags, so Aaron reached into his pack and pulled out his cloak, wrapping it around Colind's shoulders. Colind thanked him and struggled to get to his feet. When Aaron protested, Colind waved him away.

"I've been asleep far too long, my boy," Colind said. He took a few steps and stretched his arms out before him. Colind was tall, approaching his own six-foot-four-inch height.

"I don't suppose any of you brought any food; I haven't eaten in years," Colind said with a twinkle in his eyes. Then he turned to Aaron, reaching out to put a hand on his shoulder. "Thank you for saving this stubborn old fool. I don't know what it must have taken to get you here, but I appreciate all of you coming."

"It was Aaron, my Lord Guardian," Garret said. "He was determined to come here, and the story he told was so compelling that we decided to join him."

"Garret, the last I saw you there was much less gray in your hair," Colind said, seeing him for the first time and reaching out to shake his hand.

"It has been a long while," Garret replied.

"I see you made it to Prince Cyrus's court at Rexel," Colind said, looking back at Aaron.

"Yes," Aaron replied.

"I'm afraid I must apologize to you, Aaron," Colind began. "Reymius forbade me to interfere after our last meeting. He insisted that you find your own way. The way back to your world was closed to me. Unable to be of use, I roamed Shandara and began to doubt that you could ever reach this place. After so many years in my prison, I allowed the darkness and guilt of this place to consume me."

Aaron nodded thoughtfully. "Is he gone then?" he asked quietly.

Colind looked at him for a long moment before answering. "Yes. He held out long enough for you to reach the city and the sacred tree of the Alenzar'seth. And now you know of the trust that has been placed upon your house."

The dark rift flashed before his eyes. "We have to find a way to close it. Whatever is on the other side is trying to get through. Even now it's weakening."

"Close what exactly?" Vaughn asked, but before anyone could answer, a group of Ryakuls streaked into view.

A lone Ryakul perched atop one of the towers still standing, and the Drake unleashed a piercing howl that grated his nerves. The call silenced everything around them. The challenge had been issued, and Aaron knew he had to answer. He took a brief glance at the others, who were all watching the sky, except for Sarah who watched him. Trying to run at this point would be foolish. It was getting harder to deny the ancestral blood. Their yearnings eclipsed his own. Maybe he could buy the others some time.

Aaron sheathed his swords and took the rune-carved staff from Sarah. The dragon tattoo stirred beneath his skin, and the voice of his ancestors' rage roiled to the surface. The Drake was here, searching for him, and perhaps it was time for him to face the beast after all.

"Keep them safe, Verona," Aaron said quietly to his friend.

Keep her safe, he said with his eyes. Aaron squatted down, and the runes flared to life. Drawing energy from the staff, he hurled himself toward a nearby tower to answer the Drake's call.

Sarah began to follow, but Verona grabbed her arm. "We'll be right behind you." Sarah nodded and followed after Aaron as best she could.

Oh, you fool. You stupid...stupid...fool. You're not alone anymore. But it was that same quality that made him do the things that he did that made her love him. She couldn't match his strength or his speed, but please let her be fast enough.

He landed hard upon the top of the tower, jolting even his enhanced muscles and bones. The medallion grew cool against his chest, and the staff glowed, pulsing in rhythm with his beating heart. The dragon tattoo felt alive on his skin as the power from the staff coursed through him. He turned his gaze to the Drake and felt the rage and bitter despair of the ghosts of Shandara feed into him. Shandara had become the broken heart of the Alenzar'seth, from the rubbled remains of this once great city to the dying land beyond.

But he was here. Against all the odds. Reymius had succeeded because he, Aaron Jace, the last scion of the house Alenzar'seth, stood upon this tower in Shandara. It wasn't fair for a child to inherit the problems of his father, or in this case his grandfather, but what other choice could he make? In life, there were no guarantees of fairness.

There are no perfect solutions, not in life, Son, his father's voice resonated through him.

The forces at work here he could never run from, nor would he even if he could. After the visions from the tree, he knew what he must do. The breach between realms was tied to the Alenzar'seth. Should he perish as the last, the invading horde would be released into the world of Safanar. That is what the Alenzar'seth had fought and died to protect. Through Reymius and his grandmother's sacrifice, this world gained a small reprieve from the coming war. The Drake was a sentinel for the horde and an alien being in the truest sense of the word. The Drake was not of this world or even from Earth. That was all he understood, and if fortune were to smile upon him, he would seek the Hythariam, for they were tied to this, of that he was sure.

Aaron reached for the small curved axe at his belt, running his fingers upon its curve. It was his last one. *In case you miss with the first one.* He smiled at the memory. He wasn't going to miss. No, he intended to make his shot count.

The Drake's call echoed throughout the dead city, dripping its acidic challenge, which sowed the deaths of so many before him. Instead of suppressing the ancestral voices within, he gave in to their urgings and was flooded with their command that he face the Drake. He brought the rune-carved staff up and slammed it down upon the stone floor of the tower, sending a thrum of energy away from him. The figure atop the Ryakul snapped its head toward him, and Aaron roared his own challenge.

Like a hound on the hunt, the Drake launched the Ryakul into the air and the beast roared from its gaping saber-tusked maw. Aaron spun and unleashed the axe, using the energy from the staff and the wind to push the axe through the sky. The axe burned through the Ryakul's head, leaving a gory mess, and the dead beast plummeted toward the ground.

The Drake quickly jumped from the beast to land upon the far side of the tower, across from where Aaron stood. It had to be over seven feet tall with yellow eyes that smoldered like liquid steel from within the horned helmet. The dark armor radiated a slight purplish charge that surged throughout its overlapping layers down to the feet, which ended in black claws. It raised a large armored hand, revealing emerald reptilian skin, and a device rose from its forearm, sending a thin red beam toward him. The beam ran the length of Aaron's body and was gone before he could react.

A scanner? Did it just scan me?

The Drake reached behind and pulled out a long metallic rod. The rod extended, doubling its length, and twin blades emerged from either end. The Drake brandished its bladed staff and charged.

Aaron rushed forward with blinding speed to meet the Drake's attack. The staffs met and sparks burst forth. Aaron spun, halting his momentum as the Drake did the same. Each approached the other more slowly, and Aaron lashed out. The Drake countered, and with each bone-jarring blow, Aaron was driven back. He sidestepped and punched, delivering a decisive blow to the beast's chest. As the Drake was knocked back, it grabbed his arm and pulled itself back up. Then it rained down a blow, sending a shockwave through him and pushing him off balance.

He stepped back and regained his footing, gasping from the blow. It hurt, and he could feel blood trickle down the side of his head. This whole fight was out of balance. Being off balance meant death. The ancestral bloodlust flared inside him, but he clamped down upon their urgings. While they had helped him in the past, he couldn't keep a clear head while under their influence. If he didn't take back control, he was going to die. He was his own master. He banished them to the far corners of his mind, but he couldn't erase their yearning entirely.

As Aaron shook his head to clear it, the Drake charged him again. His feet were swept out from under him, and Aaron rolled to the side as twin blades struck the stone floor where he had been a moment before. Aaron spun, planted the butt of the staff into the Drake's chest, and swung around, striking a powerful blow to its head, knocking it back. He snapped a kick to the knee, sending the Drake down.

The Drake reached out to grab his foot, but Aaron jumped away. Frustrated, the creature ripped its dented helmet off and tossed it over the side. Rows upon rows of teeth took up the inside of its mouth, curving in fiendish delight.

Aaron leaped up to the edge of the tower, balancing upon the very edge and ignoring the dizzying depths below. The creature rose to its feet and leveled its staff, aiming the twin blades at him.

Aw, hell.

Aaron leaped off the edge just before a screeching blast demolished the spot where he had been standing. The wind ripped past him as he plummeted down the tower. He used the wind to slow his decent, but he was still falling too fast, so he shifted the wind to push him to the tower wall. The rubble-strewn ground was closing in. His timing needed to be perfect. He drove his feet into the tower wall, launching himself away and into a large building where the wall had partially caved in. A blur of rafters streaked past his vision until he crashed in a heap on the ground.

Aaron rose shakily to his feet. A gun! The Drake had some type of gun. He hadn't anticipated that. Taking a few seconds to study his surroundings, he realized he was in the remnants of some type of church. Most of the wooden pews had been left standing, and on the far side of the room was a statue of a woman standing resolutely with her head lifted high. The statue was the same as the one the dragon led him to all those weeks ago. The fountain below had long since crumbled to dust. She seemed to regard him coolly, almost challengingly.

Fate has chosen you for this.

The dragon's voice whispered in his mind. Aaron stood up straighter, brought his right fist over his heart, and bowed his head in respect. He didn't know if he believed in the Goddess, but he had been through too much for it to be happenstance. It would have to be enough.

I don't know if you're out there, but I could use a little bit of help on this one.

A loud crash drew his eyes skyward. The Drake had followed him somehow. Aaron jumped up to one of the broken windows on the second floor, where he heard several screeching blasts. He gritted his teeth and dashed forward, onto the roof of a nearby building. A glint of metal caught his eyes, and Aaron headed toward it.

His axe!

He kept glancing back over his shoulder as he retrieved the axe, which was in good shape considering. Now all he had to do was get a shot in before the Drake tried to shoot him again.

Aaron could hear the stomps of the Drake's footsteps throughout the church. It wasn't taking any care to hide its position, or maybe it was trying to lure him into a trap. Aaron reached out with his senses, and the rune-carved staff snatched his attention. There was power there. More than there had ever been before, as if the staff had been infused with energy. He could draw upon the staff's energy instead of disrupting the balance of energy in the city—the city reminded him of a battle-weary ship limping along where one rogue wave could sink it forever.

Out of the corner of his eye, a shadow moved along the roof of the church, and Aaron ducked behind the remnants of a stone pillar. *Sarah...that stubborn...* He'd known she would come. They would always come for each other. Her catlike blue eyes challenged him to protest. Not with the Drake so close. He gestured inside the church, and Sarah nodded, pointed inside, then at him and back at herself. Aaron frowned in thought. She wanted to use him as bait. He tapped the roof loudly with his staff, and the noise from within ceased.

Aaron watched the window on the upper level with unwavering focus, waiting for the Drake to emerge. His breath caught in his throat as the Drake suddenly appeared, crouching on the far side of the roof. Its yellow eyes narrowed when it noticed Sarah for the first time.

"Behind you!" he shouted.

Sarah rolled forward and down to the lower roof, out of the creature's line of sight. The Drake quickly trained its weapon on him and fired. Anticipating the shot, Aaron was already jumping out of the way when the blast scorched the spot where he had been a moment before. He turned in the air and sent his axe streaking into the Drake's chest. Purple sparks burst forth from the creature's armor. Aaron landed lightly on the ground and headed toward where the Drake had fallen.

The alien creature was lying on its back with sparks crackling along its chest armor. *Advanced technology?* There was no time to consider further as the armor began repairing itself as the Drake came to its feet. Aaron gritted his teeth and dashed forward. Green blood oozed down the creature's side. The wound did not slow the creature down as it met his attack. The Drake leaped back and howled to the sky. His call was answered by the Ryakuls closing in on their position.

Aaron pressed the attack, but the Drake hooked his staff and twisted it from his grasp. It tossed his staff to the side and swung its weapon savagely with a satisfied sneer across its face as Aaron scrambled out of the way. The Drake raised its staff with the twin blades, ready to strike, but it was knocked to the side as Sarah struck from behind. The creature quickly spun, caught her blade in his armored hands, and grabbed her by the neck, lifting her from the ground. Molten yellow eyes narrowed as it looked from Sarah to Aaron.

Aaron launched himself from the ground, drawing his Falcons at the same time. The Drake swung Sarah between them, freezing him in his tracks. Sarah struggled helplessly. The Drake drew her closer and breathed a noxious green vapor into her face, and Sarah went limp. Aaron rolled to the side and swung with all his might, severing the arm that held Sarah. The Drake cried out in pain, stumbling backward as Sarah landed roughly upon the ground.

Aaron moved between Sarah and the Drake as it clutched the stump of its arm to its chest. The Ryakuls swooped down and landed all around them, hissing and growling. More were circling overhead. Aaron took a step toward the Drake, which almost sent the Ryakuls into a frenzy, so he stopped.

A bright flash of light illuminated the sky overhead, followed by a thunderous crash. The Raven had arrived. Two smaller crafts hovered next to it by no visible means of propulsion. The crafts were the likes of which Aaron had never seen before on any world. They charged ahead, streaking gold, and fired golden bolts, scattering the swarming Ryakuls.

The Drake watched as the crafts weaved through the Ryakuls. Then it collapsed the staff and leaped atop of the nearest dark beast. Aaron heard Sarah stir behind him, and he chanced turning around. Her face was contorted in pain. Her skin paled to the point where she looked like death's mistress.

"Sarah?"

Her eyes were squeezed shut, and she shook her head violently. Aaron tried to approach her, but when she heard him, she lashed out with her sword. Finally, she stopped writhing and stood smoothly to her feet. Sarah opened her eyes, and Aaron stepped back in horror as molten yellow eyes stared back at him through Sarah's beautiful face.

Aaron tried to step forward, but Sarah growled like a rabid beast, shaking her head in confusion. The Drake let out another howl, and Sarah jumped over Aaron to land next to the Ryakul that the Drake rode upon.

No!

Aaron's heart sank to his feet as he watched the woman he loved leap upon the back of the Ryakul, behind the Drake. Too stunned to even move, he stood there as they launched into the air and flew away from him. The remaining Ryakuls pressed in around him, snapping him back to reality. Aaron sheathed his swords and sprinted to the rune-carved staff, dodging tusk and claw. Screaming Sarah's name, he drew energy from the staff and launched into the air. He landed upon the highest building and launched again, moving past the Raven. A passing glance showed him Verona and the others were already on board.

Aaron focused on the Ryakul carrying Sarah, who briefly glanced back at him with those alien yellow eyes. For the briefest of moments, something vaguely like a human expression played upon her features, but it was gone as quickly as it had come. The air was full of Ryakuls snapping with their great tusked jaws, and he narrowly avoided them in his chase. Then a clawed talon ripped the skin along his back like liquid fire.

Aaron plummeted toward the ground, spinning as he fell. Fiery pain blazed down his back, so much that he couldn't draw upon the staff's energy to do anything. Not even to save himself.

A golden craft swooped under, and strong hands grabbed him, pulling him inside. They laid him down upon a cushioned bench. Aaron opened his eyes and jerked in surprise. He was surrounded by people with golden eyes peering back at him.

"It's all right, Shandarian," one said in a smooth voice.

Aaron blinked, trying to stay conscious, but the pain was too much. "He has her," he gasped, feeling blood pool under his back. He heard insistent muttering in a language that he couldn't understand.

"Who are you?" he asked, drawing their attention.

"You would know us as the Hythariam, and we are most pleased to meet the lost scion of Alenzar'seth. I am called Iranus," an older man said, peeking over the shoulder of the one checking his wounds.

Aaron guessed he was older because he was the only one with white hair, but his chiseled facial features were smooth, hardly showing any signs of age. The golden eyes were unsettling. They were too close to those of the Drake. Dark spots crowded the edges of his vision, and Aaron could feel his consciousness slipping away.

"Please," he whispered, "the Drake has one of my friends...captured."

One of the Hythariam whispered to Iranus, who nodded back. "Be still," Iranus said. "We need to tend to your wounds."

Aaron couldn't help closing his eyes. He reached out with his senses, focusing on Sarah from the bond in his heart. He felt her momentary shock and confusion at his touch and the cold bitter refusal as she shut him out. He flinched inwardly at the icy sting of rejection. *You won't be rid of me that easily, love*, he thought, and then the black abyss pulled him away from his thoughts as he passed out.

***

Aaron had been brought on board the Raven and carried to his cabin. They had gathered around his bed, but the haggard expression on his friend's face filled Verona with dread.

"Will he make it?" Verona asked, staring at the unconscious form of his friend before him.

"We got to him in time, I think," Iranus answered. "The claws of the Ryakuls are poisonous, which would kill a normal man within minutes...I think we both will agree that he is anything but normal."

"That's not how Aaron would describe himself," Verona said. "What about Sarah?"

"I'm afraid she is under the influence of the Drake now," Colind answered.

"He'll want to go after her."

"I know, Verona. I know." Colind sighed. "It's how the Drake hunted down the Alenzar'seth. He would turn those that they loved into assassins, forcing them either to die by the hands of a loved one or kill them."

"Is there no way we can help her?" Verona asked.

"I don't know," Colind said after a few moments of staring down at Aaron's unconscious body.

"Aaron will find a way. He won't give up on her," Verona insisted.

"That's what I'm afraid of," Colind whispered.

"Why?" Verona demanded, shushing anyone who dared speak besides Colind.

Colind didn't answer right away. He stood there studying Aaron and then looked up at those who had crowded the small room. More stood in the hallway.

"Because we're the reason the Drake hunt the Alenzar'seth in the first place," Iranus said. "The Hythariam are from the same world as the Drake, and its army is poised to invade your world. Should they succeed, this place will burn as ours did. The Hythariam were once many. A proud people. Aaron, with the power of the bladesong, can control the rift between realms, allowing the horde to ravage this world," Iranus said, his golden eyes haunted and cold.

"Aaron wouldn't let that happen," Verona replied.

"Grief has a way dooming the souls of good men," Iranus answered.

"You don't know him," Verona snapped.

Stillness hung in the air, straining the patience of all.

"Come. We've done all we can. We should let him rest," Colind said, ushering people from the room. "Verona, please," Colind said, but Verona shook his head and instead pulled a chair next to Aaron's bed, waiting silently. Eric and Braden closed the door and stood guard outside after the anxious group left the room.

Verona sat in his chair, and Colind sat across from him, lost in his own thoughts. His faith in his friend was unparalleled to anything else, even in Colind's experience. Both waited silently while Aaron recovered from his wounds. Praying for it to be speedy, for the world of Safanar hung in the balance.

IF YOU ENJOYED *ROAD TO SHANDARA...*

The story continues in Echoes of a Gloried Past - Book Two of the Safanarion Order, which picks up a few days after the end of Book One.

Find out what Aaron, Sarah, Verona, Colind, and many others are up to and learn about the mysterious golden-eyed alien race, the Hythariam and their ties to Shandara and the Alenzar'seth in particular.

To give you a taste of what's to come, here's the first chapter from Book Two of the Safanarion Order - enjoy!

Chapter One

Time passed as Aaron slipped in and out of consciousness, occasionally awakening to the muttering of voices, both familiar and not. The steady rise and fall of the airship as it rode the winds were gone, replaced by a soft bed. He forced his eyes open again, ignoring their determination to remain shut. Sunlight and a gentle breeze oozed their way in through the balcony doors on the far side of the room. The harsh burning on his back where the Ryakul had clawed him faded to a dull ache. Stretching his neck, he slowly turned his head, trying to wake up. Stiff limbs quickly yielded to movement as he sat up in bed, rubbing the sleep from his eyes. He was almost naked except where his wounds had been cleaned and dressed. The skin of his arms and legs was dotted with the remnants of faded bruises. A brown robe hung near a metallic chest across the room. The rune-carved staff rested on the wall near the chest along with his medallion, which sparkled in the sunlight, sending hazy dragon emblems upon the smooth walls. He swung his feet to the floor and bit his lower lip, wincing at the burning pain along his back that flared at his movement. The tiled floor warmed beneath his feet. He took a steadying breath and slowly rose. The more he moved, the less his body seemed to protest.

Aaron crossed the room and pulled the robe on, tying it off at his waist. Its silky fabric felt cool on his skin. His mind still felt muddled as if he were still waking up. He stepped out onto the balcony into the warm sunlight, allowing it to caress his face. He slowly stretched his arms out to either side, feeling the tender skin protest at first and then give way to the slow movements of his arms. Birds chirped nearby, and a few hawks circled high above him. As he glanced to the side, he saw the outlines of white buildings, which appeared more like pods joined together than the grandeur of the architecture of Shandara. He reached out and ran his fingers along the outer wall, and the place where his fingers met the surface turned black. Aaron removed his hand, and the color returned to white. He ran his fingers along the outer door frame, watching as the surface went from white to dark and back again.

More technology, Aaron thought to himself, and with it his thoughts turned to Sarah. She was out there somewhere, under the influence of the Drake. Images of the battle flashed in his mind like lightning. He closed his eyes and tried to draw the energy into himself, but felt as if he were trying to grasp something made of smoke. He couldn't reach out to her. How could the Drake control her so easily? He suppressed a shiver, remembering her baleful yellow eyes looking back at him. With a gasp, he held onto the balcony railing and opened his eyes, filling his vision with the clear skies to keep from seeing her that way, but this last image of Sarah was burned into his mind. He hadn't anticipated the Drake taking a prisoner, foolishly believing that its only aim was to kill him. His pulse quickened while his hands clutched at the railings.

"You're awake!" Verona said, coming into the room through a metallic door that slid silently into the wall. "They said it would be another day." He poured some water and handed the cup to Aaron.

"Thank you," Aaron said, taking a sip of water, "How long have I been out?"

"Three days. It was touch and go there for a while, my friend. The Ryakul's claws are quite poisonous," said Verona.

"Sarah?" Aaron asked, fearing the answer in his friend's eyes.

"I'm sorry, but we haven't seen her or the Drake since Shandara." Verona said.

Aaron nodded slowly, expecting as much. He sipped the water, tasting the faint hints of cinnamon and felt his stomach tighten for a moment.

"It's medicine that will help purge the remaining poison from your body."

Aaron remained standing and allowed the queasiness to pass.

"Where are we?" he asked.

"We're with the Hythariam north of Shandara in a place called Hathenwood," answered Verona.

"Is everyone ... Did everyone else make it?" Aaron asked.

"Yes," Verona smiled. "Some bumps and bruises and a few shallow cuts, but the Hythariam helped with those as well. The repairs to the Raven will be complete in the next day or so, and the Hythariam are installing some extra things that will help against the Ryakuls." Verona said.

Aaron sighed and felt his shoulders slump in relief. He stretched his neck and rolled his shoulders, still feeling the effects of the medicine. He needed a clear head, and the medicine didn't appear to be helping with that. "I'd like to take a walk."

Verona frowned for a second before giving a small nod. "There is clothing in there," he said pointing to the chest. "I'll give you a few minutes to change, and then we should get some food in you."

Verona left the room by placing his hand on a pad near the door, and the door slid silently into the adjoining wall. *More technology,* Aaron thought. He came to the chest, which didn't have any handles. He placed his palm on top of a pad similar to the one on the door, and a drawer extended from the bottom. The clothes were loose fitting and, like the robe, felt good on his skin. He pulled on black boots that molded themselves to the contours of his feet. He stood up and noted how comfortable they felt while being both sturdy yet almost weightless at the same time. They were a clear improvement over the hiking boots he had brought with him from Earth. He hung the medallion around his neck and grabbed the rune-carved staff. It was a good walking stick after all.

Aaron exited the room into a quiet hallway where Verona waited. His stomach rumbled noisily, giving Verona the audible clue he needed to lead the way. As they made their way down the hall, a Hythariam appeared, heading in their direction. His golden eyes flashed briefly in surprise, then with a nod to each of them he turned back the way he had come.

"We've had you on constant watch since we arrived the other day," Verona said. "Eric and Braden had only just left your door earlier at my insistence." After Aaron nodded he continued, "I know you want answers, and you'll get them, but I must tell you that it's really good to see you awake, my friend."

"Was it that bad? The poison I mean," Aaron asked.

"Lethal to most people almost immediately. Even the Hythariam will die if they don't get help in time."

"Colind?" Aaron asked.

"Will be anxious to see you. He's been all but locked in a room with Iranus, Vaughn, and several other Hythariam. I haven't seen much of them since I kept Eric and Braden company."

"Thanks," Aaron said and swallowed a lump down his throat as the image of Sarah's smiling face flashed in his mind. They walked in silence, and the more he moved, the better he felt. Aaron could tell that Verona was holding something back and guessed he didn't want to overburden him. The rune-carved staff proved to be a good walking stick, even on the smooth metallic gray floors. The farther they ventured from his room, the more Hythariam they came across. Most nodded in friendly greeting, but some looked at him with worry in their golden eyes. Those eyes were so similar to the Drake, it was disconcerting.

"Is it much farther?" Aaron asked.

"Not much. We can rest if you need." Verona answered, gesturing toward one of the benches along the wall.

"I'll be fine," Aaron said, waving him on.

The corridors echoed of people walking, and muffled conversations could be heard throughout this place. Wherever they were, was a bustle of activity. They turned down another corridor, and Aaron could smell food, making his mouth water. He just needed to eat, then he wanted answers.

Verona took him to an open courtyard filled with tables and benches, which was a cross between a garden and an outdoor cafeteria. People took plates of food from several buffet stations strategically placed throughout. Aaron selected food by Verona giving either a nod of approval for some or a vigorous shake of his head for things to avoid. He stuck mostly with vegetables and meat, preferring not to experiment with things he couldn't readily identify.

The Hythariam still glanced in their direction, with some whispering to their companions, and others nodding in friendly greeting. Aaron had never seen so many golden eyes and was surprised to see green ones as well. They were very similar to humans except that their eyes were just a bit bigger with an almost feline quality to them. They wore clothing of the same quality as he had been given, which Aaron found quite comfortable. Nothing too colorful, and all could have blended easily in a forest if needed. The occasional cyan-colored scarf adorned some of the women, and similarly colored cords were tied around the arms of some men.

They ate in silence, or more like Verona watched as Aaron devoured his meal. The moment the first bite passed his lips he was filled with an overwhelming need to eat. He was starving. They washed down their meal with water, and Aaron felt his mind clear and more of his strength return.

"You're looking more human now," Verona said.

"Feeling like it, too." Aaron answered.

They were approached by a tall Hythariam with raven hair and green eyes. He had the bearing of a soldier though he was out of uniform. He gave a slight bow to them both and said, "Hello, I am Gavril. Iranus sends his greetings and asks for you to join him and Colind, if you are able."

Aaron shot to his feet, ready to follow Gavril, and Verona rose as well.

"It's not far," Gavril said and led them down a short corridor lined with glass doors. Behind each of the doors appeared to be oval-shaped rooms that hung suspended over tracks heading in different directions. They stepped into one of the rooms, and a panel opened on its far side. Gavril keyed in some of the buttons on the holographic touch screen. "The tram will get us there much faster than on foot." Gavril said, and the door quietly shut behind them.

The tram shot forth, following one of the tracks leading outside. Verona looked delighted, and Aaron reached immediately for something to hold onto before he realized that while they were moving quite fast, he hardly felt as if they were moving at all. Aaron figured the trams must have some type of dampeners to suppress the forces that would put them off balance. Gavril studied their reactions and nodded to himself.

The tram took them outside, and Aaron looked out the window at the complex of buildings from which they left. Some were similar to the style he had seen in Shandara but more modern by comparison. Where Shandara had buildings and gardens complementing each other in their design, the complex of the Hythariam buildings seemed to be more sparse and functional rather than built for appearances. After a few minutes, they approached another set of buildings mostly hidden by the trees, but Aaron could see a few metallic towers strategically placed around a central octagonal dome that peaked over the tree line. The tram entered one of the tunnels near the dome, and Aaron watched the track disappear behind them into darkness. They exited the tram, and Gavril led them away from the platform.

Aaron was growing tired, but refused to give in and straightened up when he felt himself start to stoop. Gavril pressed his palm to a panel, and the metallic door quietly hissed open. Colind and Vaughn turned immediately and came over to greet Aaron.

"You should not be up and about yet," spoke a silky voice behind him. Aaron turned to see a beautiful raven-haired

Hythariam reach inside her pocket and pull out a device. She held the device inches away from his head and slowly scanned down his back.

"Aaron," spoke an older Hythariam, "please forgive my daughter, Roselyn, she is a healer first and person second. Do you remember me? I am Iranus, and I'm most pleased to see you recovering so quickly."

Aaron remembered Iranus with his long white hair contrasted by his golden eyes. He had been among those on the ship that rescued him when he fell. "I do remember you," he replied.

"Since you're here and not resting in your bed where you should be, give me a moment to examine you," Roselyn ordered and ushered the others away.

The others quickly moved to give the healer room to work, save Verona, who stood rooted in place for once and clearly at a loss for words. Roselyn raised the device to Aaron's eyes and slowly scanned downward.

"Can you give us a moment please?" she said to Verona, snapping him out of his reverie.

Verona joined the others across the room, giving them some privacy, but he kept glancing back in Roselyn's direction.

Roselyn focused her attention on Aaron and asked him a few questions about the Ryakul wound on his back.

"You're a remarkably fast healer, Aaron," she said sternly. "You don't realize how close to death you were."

"You'd be surprised." Aaron answered quietly, "but thank you."

"Indeed," she said and then leaned in so only he could hear what she was about to say. "You have friends here, Heir of Shandara, but be careful, as all is not what it seems, and the answers given may not be complete in their truthfulness. Some would see the return of the Alenzar'seth as a very grave threat."

Aaron gave a slight nod, and Roselyn moved away.

"He's recovering well. Do not keep him long," she said looking sternly at Iranus.

"Thank you, my dear. Won't you please join us?" Iranus asked, motioning for them to sit in one of the nearby circles of chairs.

Aaron sat down, and after everyone else was seated all eyes drew toward him. "First, I'd like to thank you for your help and for giving us a place to stay."

Iranus held up his hand, "No thanks are necessary. It was the least we could do."

Aaron nodded. "Second, where is the Drake, and what did it do to Sarah?"

"We don't know where the Drake is now," Iranus said. "As for what it did to your friend, I need to know exactly what you saw."

"What I saw … " Aaron began, and the image of the Drake holding Sarah up by her neck invaded his thoughts. "It blew some kind of green vapor into her face, forcing her to breathe it in. Then she began to writhe in pain, and after only a few moments her eyes began to turn yellow like his. When I called to her, she pulled away as if she didn't recognize me. It was like one moment she knew who I was and the next wanted to kill me. Then the Drake called to her, and she went with it … I could … I could still see …

her, but at the same time she was different." Aaron said. "I know, it doesn't make much sense, but that's what I saw."

"It makes perfect sense," Roselyn said and then turned to her father. "The Drake is using a biological delivery agent to spread itself. We suspected, but no one could confirm before now."

"What is it delivering exactly?" Aaron asked.

"A way to control its victims," Iranus said.

There were a few moments of silence until Colind cleared his throat, "Tell him the rest."

Aaron divided his gaze between Colind and Iranus, expectantly.

"I had hoped to give you more time to recover before burdening you with this," Iranus began. "We have observed your world. Where you were raised."

"Earth," said Aaron. For a second, he thought of his sister, Tara, and how he would have liked for her to meet Sarah someday.

"Yes, I've no doubt you are familiar with machines?" Iranus asked and continued when Aaron nodded. "We've developed machines that are smaller than the finest grain of sand. They can live in our bodies and group together to form larger machines to perform any number of tasks."

"We have something similar. We call it nanotech," Aaron said. "It deals with manipulation on a molecular level." His response drew a frown from Verona, but Colind, he noted, didn't look at all out of sorts.

"Excellent, I suspected you would be familiar with the

concept," Iranus said. "The Drake used a gas to deliver the Nanites into your friend. It was the Nanites and not the gas that caused her to change."

"But what do the Nanites do exactly?" Aaron asked.

"By themselves not too much, but networked together they can perform complex calculations, including probability, and can adapt to a number of situations. They can form tiny power plants to recharge. Within an organic host, they can use the beating heart to convert the movement of the heart muscle into energy. When they were first developed, they were coded with a prime directive to keep the body healthy. They worked with the brain and the body, observing the body's reaction to infection. After some analysis, they would help eliminate infections while allowing the body's natural immune system to still function. This was essential so we didn't lose our natural immunity to diseases. We also equipped them with the ability to communicate with other nanotech so knowledge and methods were shared. This went a long way, ultimately eliminating the visible signs of sickness altogether."

"I think I understand. Like a cold, once you start feeling the effects of the cold you're already sick." Aaron said.

Iranus smiled slightly, "Correct. So, by all outward appearances we 'cured' most diseases entirely, but in truth, the Nanites enabled us to resist them before they were even felt by the body."

"I understand the concept of Nanites, but it doesn't explain what happened to Sarah," Aaron said.

"I'll need to delve a bit into our history to help you understand better," Iranus began. "Particularly how we came from our home world of Hytharia to Safanar. The Nanites' ability to keep the body healthy was only the beginning of their capabilities. We could also use them to manipulate the biological blueprints of a living organism. We learned how to alter the genes for aging, to increase brain function, thus stimulating growth in our ability to calculate, and even increase our bodies durability and strength."

Iranus paused, allowing for what he said to sink in. The gravity of such a momentous advance in technology was not lost upon Aaron.

"The moral implications of those advances must have been profound," Aaron said after a few moments' thought.

"That's putting it mildly," Roselyn said, speaking up for the first time since she had examined him.

"Aging?" Aaron said, "So, you were able to stop aging entirely? Didn't that lead to overpopulation on your world?"

"Much more than that," Iranus said evenly. "When people live too long, they lose perspective. Organisms such as ourselves were not meant to evade death entirely. So yes, we were able to heal ourselves and delay aging, allowing for the possibility of a fuller life. But some wanted to live forever, believing that since we could, in theory, live forever, that we had a right to do so."

"That doesn't sound so bad," Verona said.

Iranus's lips curved in a knowing sort of way, "It sounds wonderful, does it not? But imagine this, if you will, a whole society that doesn't have to fear death or growing old? You would amass a multitude of knowledge, but without wisdom, without the certainty that you were allowed a finite time in this life. People became unmotivated, and their fundamental values changed. Instead of bringing people together into harmony, it drove them apart into chaos. Essentially, we took away the things that made life worth living."

"What did you do?" Aaron asked.

"We decided not to stop aging altogether, but simply slow it down to acceptable levels," Iranus answered.

"How did you decide how long one should live?" Aaron asked.

"We voted on a range and agreed on 200 to 225 years, life-style permitting. To prevent constant lobbying in our courts, an agreement was put into place to revisit the age range every 50 years." Iranus said.

"I can't imagine deciding as a society how long one should live," Aaron replied.

Iranus pursed his lips in thought for a moment, "Is it so foreign a concept to you? If you live a healthy lifestyle, you have a better chance to live longer. People, no matter their origin, have this balance, and ours was the next logical step with the resources at our disposal. We were able to manage the genes for aging so that it still took place, but at a much slower rate."

"Still," Aaron said, "even with a majority vote, conflict or even outright war must have been inevitable."

"Yes," Iranus replied solemnly. "There are those who worked

in secret to thwart the council's efforts to maintain peace. War, as you said, became inevitable. The precious gift stemming from the Nanites became a weapon. You've glimpsed the remnants of Hytharia through the portal. You've seen firsthand the result upon our world."

"Why Safanar?" Aaron asked. "Couldn't you open a gateway to another world instead?"

"I'm sure they tried, but opening a door doesn't mean you're going to like what is on the other side."

"That's not really an answer, now is it?" Aaron replied.

Iranus smiled, "No, it's not. Safanar was the first successful connection to a habitable world we were able to make. But to understand why we came here, I must explain the situation on Hytharia. Our planet was dying," Iranus began addressing everyone in the room. "In developing our technological prowess, we all but exhausted our natural resources. Something happened to our sun that caused it to age faster than we had originally projected. The lifespan of our star should have ranged in the billions of years, but was eventually reduced to thousands and then hundreds of years. Even then, it should have been enough time for us to find a suitable world to colonize. We utilized every means possible in the search. Sending out probes through space as fast as possible, but these things take time.

The search for another home became a cycle of destruction for us. Those in power used the impending crisis as a way to justify reckless decisions that eventually put the stability of Hytharia in jeopardy. Super volcanoes killed millions, and a war for the remaining resources necessary for survival reduced our numbers further. Amid all the death and destruction, we found Safanar. Our beacon of hope. A short distance, relatively speaking, but it still took our probe thirty years to find this place. We could never build ships with enough resources to take a significant number of our people here, so we had to find a different solution, but at least we had a target to reach for. This gave us hope and brought the factions of our society back into harmony ... for a time.

The probe continued to send us information and landed on the surface not far from where we are sitting right now. With all the hope that a new home brings, war all but ceased as efforts were focused on viable solutions to get us here.

The most brilliant scientists of the age were brought together along with a specialized branch of Hytharia's remaining military factions. They acquired the resources we needed and gave us a place to work."

"Us?" Aaron asked. "You mean you were one of the scientists?"

"Yes," Iranus answered, "many of us here, were part of the original group. It wasn't just scientists, though, but our families as well. We focused on opening a portal between our two worlds. At least that was our end goal. All great things have small beginnings, and we were eventually successful. The calculations involved just to open a portal on the same planet were impressive. Imagine trying to hit a moving target across an enormous expanse of space. What we were able to achieve was startling to say the least, but it did come with its fair share of failure and risk. Now, given the discussion I won't go into the details of the intricacies of bending space-time. There is simply not enough time for that. So, I will continue," Iranus paused for a moment. "After our first few successful trips to Safanar, we were happy to report that this world was beyond our wildest expectations. We started to observe the people here and came in contact with one of your ancestors, Aaron, you carry his staff with you here in this very room."

"Daverim," Aaron gasped, his mind flashing back to the abandoned temple he had come to when he first arrived on Safanar. He traced his hands along the rune-carved staff, "But that's … "

"Eighty years ago, yes," Iranus said with a small smile, his eyes growing distant, as he remembered his first meeting with Daverim. "Full of life to say the least," Iranus continued. "He was a good man. We allied with the kingdom of Shandara, because the ideals of that kingdom closely matched our own, before the harshness of survival sapped some of our morality from us. In exchange for their help, we agreed to share our technological advances and knowledge. There was actually quite a bit we learned from one another, and we started bringing our people to this world. Shandara was a buffer for us from the rest of Safanar, but it was always our intent to work with all of the kingdoms here.

When we brought our proposal to our leadership council, a new general was appointed to oversee the whole effort. His name was General Morag Halcylon."

Aaron looked around the room and regarded the cold,

expressionless looks of the other Hythariam as confirmation of the sinking feeling he felt.

"We proposed what was in our mandate, which was to find a way to bring survivors from our dying world to Safanar. To live and interact with the people of this world. But others had a different plan," Iranus said bitterly, "They wanted to conquer and rule what they perceived as lesser people. We didn't realize the extent of the ruthlessness of our leadership and the measures taken to provide the resources we needed. They simply took what was needed from others of our home world. Leaving them exposed and in some cases murdering whole cities. I began researching any information I could find about the new general and cursed my ignorant self. General Halcylon was among the most ruthless of our military who thrived under the guise of survival at the cost of the soul of our people. Most of the council cowered in fear of him, and those that did not were aligned with the means by which he accomplished his goals."

Aaron felt the bile rise to the top of his throat as he tried to imagine what the collapse of a proud civilization like the Hythariam looked like. He realized that like Shandara, nothing in his wildest imaginings would come close to the shadowed horror that lived within the gazes of people who had actually witnessed these events.

"What did you do?" Aaron asked.

"I didn't want to believe it," Iranus began. "We were supposed to be better than this. All of our accomplishments as a people pointed to us being more enlightened than the barbarism being committed. But as great as we were in the good things we did, they were outweighed by the evil done. Evil that was born in the name of desperation under the guise of the good for the many. With my illusions shattered, I alerted others to what was happening and began formulating a plan to get people through the portal to Safanar, people who did not want to bring war to this world."

"Civil war?" Aaron asked.

"Not at first, but yes," Iranus said, his golden eyes becoming steel. "All war is evil, but a war among brothers and sisters is a different kind of evil entirely. We began to resist where we could, bringing people through the portal without notice as best we could. At the same time, we didn't want to alert the Shandarians to what was happening for fear that the doors to Safanar would be closed. Daverim, however, began to suspect that things were deteriorating on Hytharia, and after meeting General Halcylon, he discovered the true intent of the general. He later said that one didn't need to travel so far to know a tyrant when he saw one. After that meeting, Daverim confronted me about the state of Hytharia, and I told him everything. I left nothing out, and he simply listened. Together, we worked on a plan to get as many people as we could off of Hytharia before the portal was to be blocked.

General Halcylon underestimated the people of Safanar, dismissing them as undeveloped, which couldn't be further from the truth. Where we were strong in science to enhance ourselves, they were strong in their connections to the world and its undercurrents of energy. It's something we've never seen. We used inventions like the Nanites to enhance our bodies, while the Shandarians could do similar things by drawing energy into themselves.

The plan was to organize a large wave of our people through the portal then block the passage for those who would ravage this world. We had been bringing people through in small groups and were setting up living space with the help of the Shandarians. Daverim came up with a way to block the portal while keeping it open. My job was to see to it that the likes of General Halcylon couldn't open another portal when this one became blocked. We compiled a list of targets so that our work couldn't be followed after we were gone."

"Did it work?" Aaron asked.

"Yes and no," Iranus replied. "There were many sacrifices, and many good people died so that we few could survive. We brought as many over as we could, but once those in power finally discovered what we were doing, they moved quickly to thwart us. We had some help on the council from like-minded people. Daverim kept the portal under constant watch along with the Guardians of the Safanarion Order," Iranus said, looking to Colind. "When the fighting started to appear on this side as troops came through, Daverim created the barrier."

"How?" Vaughn asked.

"He used the bladesong evoked from the Falcons," Aaron answered. He couldn't help but sympathize with Iranus, who was clearly pained to bring up so many tragic memories, but he needed answers, they all did. The people of Shandara had paid a heavy price in blood to give aid to the Hythariam.

"Yes, that is correct," Iranus said. "Daverim used the bladesong to align the energy from beneath the ground into a barrier that essentially locked the portal open, yet allowed no one through."

"I'm not as well versed on this subject as some," Aaron began, "but my understanding is that what you're describing requires an active connection. How was Daverim able to do this?"

"He was able to connect to the energy deep beneath the ground. That connection is maintained by a living member of the house Alenzar'seth, a secret known only to a few. There is a life energy in this land that is tied to the portal, which forces it to stay open," said Iranus.

"Then how was it maintained when my grandfather and mother left Safanar?" Aaron asked.

"I'm not sure, to be honest," Iranus answered. "Do you know, Colind?"

Colind pursed his lips together in thought, "His soul was able to return to Safanar when he died, so I think it's safe to say that part of him remained connected."

"How does the Drake fit into all this?" Aaron asked.

"The being you know of as the Drake is not of Safanar, but of Hytharia." Iranus said. "We believe that some of Halcylon's people made it through the portal prior to it being locked and were able to send him information."

"How?" Aaron asked.

Iranus looked up to the ceiling, "They couldn't use the portal, but there was nothing stopping them from sending a signal through space. It would take years to reach Hytharia, but it is possible. We didn't find evidence of the Drake until Shandara fell. It appears that those left on Hytharia were able to develop a new weapon to open the portal to this world."

The room was silent for a moment. "You were hoping to wait them out," Aaron said, the pieces fitting into place in his mind. "That was the plan. Block the portal and wait for them to be destroyed with the death of your sun. Except they were able to reach across the stars to get you."

Iranus nodded. "We later figured out that the Drake is a construct of Nanites with a prime directive to open the portal to Hytharia, but these Nanites were different than any we've encountered. Normally, Nanites can be turned off with a kill command, or have their programming rewritten, but not these. They are the perfect sentinels, because they contain all the benefits of normal Nanites, but are able to manipulate the brain on a molecular level, rewriting certain parts, memories for instance, turning love into hate."

Aaron felt his stomach drop out from under him. If what Iranus said were true, Sarah was in more danger than he originally thought. "How long does she have?"

"It's hard to say, but we've seen the process take as little as a few weeks, depending upon how much the subject resists," Iranus answered solemnly. "So, you see she may already be gone."

"I don't believe that," Aaron said, standing up.

"Wait, what do you mean? How is Sarah already gone?" Verona asked.

"The Drake can rewrite your brain so that you are no longer you anymore," Roselyn answered him.

"She'll fight," Aaron said.

"I'm sorry, Aaron, but it is a fight she cannot win," Iranus answered. "Even if you go to her, which is exactly what the Drake wants, what will you do? We've tried to remove the Nanites, but it always resulted in the death of the person we were trying to save. We've tried augmenting our own to seek and remove them, but the results are the same."

"I won't abandon her," Aaron said.

"I know you won't, Aaron, but you must see reason. What if they're right? What if she's gone?" Vaughn asked gently.

"No!" Aaron slammed his fist onto the table. "I refuse to believe that. I know I can reach her. The Drake doesn't control her fully."

"She left you, Aaron," Colind chimed in. "This is what the Drake does. It turns those that you love against you. It's how it hunted down all of the Alenzar'seth. The ones it wasn't strong enough to stand against, it defeated using cunning and strife to weave a perfect web of destruction, using their greatest strength against themselves."

Aaron's body was rigid, and his muscles rippled with the clenching of his teeth. "I'm not them."

"You think to defy what has been proven over and over by sheer will alone? It's not going to be enough. The Alenzar'seth were once many, but those that survived the fall of Shandara weren't able to stand against the Drake." Iranus said. "I say this not to be cruel, but because I want you to live. Playing the Drake's game is the surest path to meeting your demise. Even for you."

Aaron regarded the Hytharium coolly, "Not playing its game will cost me more than I'm willing to pay. Haven't you been hiding long enough? Convinced it was the best course of action? Tell me, did you stand idly by while the Alenzar'seth were hunted down, slaves to a terrible fate because they refused to yield? Even in the face of death, they fought. They didn't hide in the shadows, nor abandon the ones they loved ... neither will I."

Iranus's golden eyes were ablaze with anger. "Do you know how to make war, Aaron?"

"No," Aaron replied, "but I can fight, and it will have to be enough. I will fight for the parts of Sarah that will never submit to the Drake no matter what technology your people have created. However small, it's worth fighting for."

Colind sighed, "Will you at least consider that Sarah may be beyond your reach and that the person you love is gone?"

Aaron shook his head, feeling the stirrings of the bladesong within him. Sarah's beautiful blue eyes looked back at him when he closed his. *I will always come for you.* He looked up, his gaze sweeping across the men in the room. Verona stood up and came to his side. Colind returned his gaze evenly, and Iranus's golden eyes narrowed.

"Colind," Aaron said evenly, "I have considered it, and know this ... I will never abandon Sarah, not for anything. Not for your war," he said dividing his gaze between Colind and Iranus, "and not for this world."

"She wouldn't want you to sacrifice the world for her," Vaughn said.

"I know, Vaughn, and I won't need to," Aaron said. "That army on the other side of the portal is coming no matter what we do. Whether I live or die, that is one thing that you can count on. The barrier between worlds will fall. If you don't believe me, return to Shandara and study it. Things are wildly out of balance. Now, instead of focusing ourselves on keeping things as they've always been, we should be focused on moving forward."

Aaron felt his energy drain and leaned on his staff, beginning to hunch over. "You can't run from the wind," Aaron muttered to himself.

"What?" Colind asked.

Aaron swallowed, and looked up, "My father used to take us sailing when we were younger, and sometimes we'd be caught out on the water when a storm came. As a child, I was so afraid. All the big waves and wind tossing our boat mercilessly. 'You can't run from wind, son.' He would tell me, 'Trim your sails and face what's ahead,' and he was right. A storm is coming, gentleman, whether you want to believe it or not," Aaron said and left the room with the dull thumps of the rune-carved staff trailing in his wake.

Roselyn rose and silently followed.

Colind looked at the door and sighed, "He is right. The barrier was always just a temporary measure. We need to prepare."

"He doesn't understand what will be unleashed if the barrier fails. And to abandon all to pursue the Drake," Iranus said, biting off the last.

Verona cleared his throat, "Without Aaron, none of you would be here. He was lost when I first met him, teetering on the brink of darkness that has claimed many a man's soul. Sarah was the one thing that gave him hope, that brought the light back in his eyes and gave him some semblance of being whole. So, he cannot do as you would want him to, despite the certainty of the science that supports *your* reasons. They are not *his* reasons. Your war has cost him almost everything before he was dragged into it. Are you really surprised that he won't follow the path that you've laid at his feet? Should not a strong leader forge his own path and we as his friends and comrades support him as he would for any of us?" Verona asked, his gaze sweeping the room. "You've had more time than he has been alive to do things your own way. Perhaps it's time for a different approach, because to go against Aaron on this would risk ... much," Verona said, narrowing his gaze. "If you can't help, fine, but don't tell him that what he intends to do is impossible, because my friend has a knack for doing the impossible." Verona glanced pointedly at Colind, then rose and left the room.

***

"Aaron, wait," Roselyn called behind him.

"Is this what you warned me about?" he asked, leaning on the staff heavily.

Roselyn's eyes narrowed as she caught up to him, "You need

rest. It's only been a few days."

"No, Sarah needs me now," he replied stubbornly, and specks of darkness invaded his vision. Aaron sank to the floor, the last of his strength leaving him. *I won't abandon you.*

"She has time," Roselyn said gently.

Verona came up silently behind them, but said nothing.

"Don't charge off like the others," Roselyn said, "I believe you are right. There is a way to stop the Drake. We just need to put our heads together, but first you need rest to recover your strength. You're no good to her like this ... "

Aaron felt himself slipping further away, Roselyn's voice growing distant until he couldn't hear anything at all as the last vestiges of his strength left him.

ACKNOWLEDGEMENTS

As with any big project, the author is only the tip of the iceberg in taking a huge pile of words and transforming them into something worth reading.

First I have to thank my editor, who spent a great deal of time wading through so many iterations of this story while showing enormous patience and helping me find my voice.

Next up is my family, you've all been the cornerstone to my foundation. To my children, who with silent demanding, dared me to be better than I thought could be.

Then there are my "beta readers," Tim and Milosz who helped put the final touches on the book and provide an excellent sanity check for the story as a whole. Thank you so much for you time and support.

Finally, never last or least, my wife. Thank you for your love and support and listening to me talk about this story for years.

ABOUT THE AUTHOR

I've been reading Epic Fantasy and Science Fiction nonstop since the age of eleven. Before long, I started writing my own stories and kept adding to them throughout the years. As a father, I began telling my kids about the stories that became part of the Safanarion Order series. It was their enthusiasm and constant "Tell us more Dad," that lead me back to the keyboard. My main focus is to write books that I would like to read and I hope you enjoy them as well.

Say Hello!

If you have questions or comments about any of Ken's works he would love to hear from you, even if its only to drop by to say hello at KenLozito.com

One Last Thing.

Word-of-mouth is crucial for any author to succeed. If you enjoyed the book, please consider leaving a review at Amazon, even if it's only a line or two; it would make all the difference and would be greatly appreciated.

Discover other books by Ken Lozito

Safanarion Order Series:
Road to Shandara (Book 1)

Echoes of a Gloried Past (Book 2)
Amidst the Rising Shadows (Book 3)

Made in the USA
San Bernardino, CA
02 September 2016